D0015963

FAMOUS ALL OVER TOWN

STORY RIVER BOOKS

Pat Conroy, Editor at Large

FAMOUS ALL OVER TOWN

A Novel

BERNIE SCHEIN

Foreword by Janis Owens

The University of South Carolina Press

Published by the University of South Carolina Press
Columbia, South Carolina 29208

www.sc.edu/uscpress

Manufactured in the United States of America

23 22 21 20 19 18 17 16 15 14 10 9 8 7 6 5 4 3 2 1

Library of Congress Cataloging-in-Publication Data

Schein, Bernie, 1944–
Famous all over town : a novel / Bernie Schein.
pages cm.—(Story River Books)
ISBN 978-1-61117-439-7 (hardbound : alk. paper)—ISBN 978-1-61117-440-3 (ebook)
I. Title.
PS3569.C47928F36 2014
813'.54—dc23 2014007283

This book was printed on a recycled paper with
30 percent postconsumer waste content.

For Martha, always. For Mom and Dad, always, and for all who came before them and after them, always.

CONTENTS

Part II: Summer 1961

FOREWORD

The charming lowcountry port of Beaufort, South Carolina, is one of those sleepy southern hamlets, like Oxford, Mississippi, or Monroeville, Alabama, which has inspired more than its share of modern American novels. The picturesque coastal hamlet's role as literary muse is easy to explain, thanks to its unequivocal beauty, which is found in every corner, from the antebellum mansions to the oak-hung cemeteries; the sunlit tidal marsh, to that old southern scene-stealer, the century oak draped in moss. If you've ever met an artist, in letters or watercolor or charcoal, you'll understand that beauty in all its manifestations it is a great motivator—and that the novel, at its best, is the distillation of a thousand stories from every walk of life and every prism of light.

The truth is that Beaufort, with its long history stretching back to colonial forts and Indian wars, has always entertained a lively dance of human interaction and a fusion of cultures: native and European, Old South, New South, black, white, transplant and tourist. It's a crossroads community where the crew-cut severity of the modern soldier meets the languor and delicate duplicity of the small-town, racially divided Dixie.

Is it any wonder that such a culturally fetid slice of earth has sustained the career of so many writers, the most famous, by far, beloved adopted son Pat Conroy? Pat's love affair with the lowcountry is so thoroughly and dramatically conveyed in his writing that it might be described less as passion and more in the realm of well-aimed obsession. Bernie Schein would know, as he is also a proud son of the exact same slice of the old South, and was in fact a childhood friend of Pat's and of all their shared friends and alliances. The difference is in origin: Bernie did not draw his pedigree from the foothills of north Georgia, or the slaughters at Plymouth Rock, but from a later but equally valiant history: the name-counters at Ellis Island, where his Lithuanian-Jewish ancestors entered the Great American Voice, southern style.

Granted, they came late to the game, but they came in style. They made a mark and came to define what truth and honor were in the New World, though till they last part of the century, they were not as often caught in print as their Scot-Irish compatriots. They more frequently appeared in the fiction in the role of outsides and wingmen; peculiar truth-tellers who encouraged cultural outsiders to bypass the surface of fifties-era emotion and dig deeper to that realm that was actually Freudian in depth and vision.

Yes, I said it: Freudian. Bernie's take on the small coastal town of Somerset, a thinly veiled stand-in for his own Beaufort, isn't the old school Celtic hero's tale, but instead a revealing excavation of the subconscious that is at once poignant and hilarious. Bernie doesn't skim the surface of what the status quo steeple-culture considers right and wrong, he delves into the far less black-and-white realm of the often overlooked (in southern fiction, anyway) truths of reality.

Since Pat and Bernie were childhood friends, Bernie appears in several of Pat's books, both fiction and memoir, so often that he transcends the category of friend and comes close to muse—brilliant, foul-mouthed, clamorous, one-of-a-kind muse. It is but one of the many hats Bernie wears, and like anything he wears—trust me on this one—he wears with aplomb. It is only fitting then, that Pat appears here in Bernie's novel as well, if only as an extended but important cameo amid a town filled with "characters" in every sense of that word.

Varying masterfully from first-person and third-person perspectives in the lives of nearly a dozen representatives of Somerset, Bernie shows us just how symbiotically interconnected seemingly disparate lives can be. In Somerset, as everywhere else, it takes black and white, male and female, faithful and faithless, gay and straight, educated and ignorant, obsessed and repressed, law-breaking and law-abiding, sacred and profane, native and newcomer, empowered and powerless, timid and cocksure, introspective and thoughtless, and countless other traits to make a community ebb and flow like the lowcountry tides.

Famous All Over Town is politically incorrect, raw, bold, honest, and compassionate. It is one man's take on a slice of life, from a perspective not often committed to print, offered from both the inside and outside, from the voices that we've all heard before, plus others that have heretofore only be whispered to us. Bernie's storytelling aesthetic is the fruit of a loving, uproarious, but ultimately jaundiced eye of coastal Southern life, from the Jim Crow era to our present day, of a time and place where beauty and injustice held equal sway. Since Bernie is an unapologetic southern son, his story pulls no punches in documenting life in his fictional small town, where nothing is exactly as it seems until you look a little deeper and consider (Dare I say it?) the psychological landscape of each individual life.

Which is as it should be, as the beloved homeland we southerners call Dixie was not crafted of one story or one race, but of a multitude, all talking at once. Bernie captures that multiplicity and more. I cannot tell you at which part of the novel I had that he-is-telling-my-story reaction that is germinal to the best works of fiction, but it is in there, to be sure. To think that Bernie was able to elicit this deeply personal response from me—a Protestant hard shell insider—well, that is something. It speaks to the universal truths Bernie has found in Beaufort, a story of real people, flawed, complex, loving, obsessed, repressed, candid, comic, but always genuine, always authentic. Read this and laugh. And rejoice. And remember how grateful we should all be, growing up in small-town, real life, real sex, real power, Dixie.

For the ardent fans of all things southern—and especially all things salt marsh and lowcountry—*Famous All Over Town* brings a modern and fresh update, delving both above the Freudian line and well below. You will love it so much you will write a fan letter. You will hate yourself for it, but you'll do it anyway. I did.

Janis Owens
Newberry, Florida
December 2013

ACKNOWLEDGMENTS

Gratitude and love to Jonathan Haupt and his uncanny editorial vision and craft, to Suzanne Axland, Elizabeth Jones, Linda Fogle, and the entire staff of USC Press. Thank you, thank you, thank you.

Gratitude and special love also for my dearest and closest friend, Pat Conroy, editor at large of Story River Books, for his inspiration, his vision, his wisdom, and his doggedly tireless work to make Story River a great series, though he is the most high-maitenance friend imaginable and a royal pain in the ass and not as funny as I am.

Special thanks a million times over to Cassandra King Conroy and Janise Owens for their true friendship, great editorial guidance, and glorious inspiration.

To my wife, Martha, for her overprotectiveness and the acuity of her criticism, my daughter, Maggie, for the relentless honesty and perpectiveness of hers, and to her fiancé, Jonathan Hannah, not only for his glorious eye, but his ear.

Gratitude to my brothers, Aaron and Stanley Schein, for their love, support, and devotion, and most of all, for remaining alive, to Vanessa Joy, and to Lara, Sofie, and Caitlin Williams.

Special thanks to the Lunch Group at Griffen Market: Scott Graber, John Warley, Jonathan Hannah, Aaron Schein, Lynn Seldon, Wilson Macintosh, Laura and Ricardo Bonino, and Pat for footing the bill.

AUTHOR'S NOTE

Famous All Over Town is a work of fiction, the people, places and events fictional, the town of Somerset inspired by Beaufort, South Carolina, which is in fact named after the Duke of Beaufort, Henry Somerset. Lawton Island, Somerset's military base, is inspired by Parris Island, Beaufort's military base. Characters not entirely products of my imagination are based on people I've known, heard, or read about.

The fictional night march of Marine recruits into Oyster Creek in 1960 and the ensuing trial were inspired by the actual night march of recruits on Parris Island in 1956 so accurately detailed in John Stevens' *Incident at Ribbon Creek* and newspaper accounts that John so graciously provided. While I use particulars from those accounts, the time, the dates, the major characters, and most of the details therein are fictionalized as they are in all important events in service to the larger story of *Famous All Over Town*.

Prologue—Fall 1992

Elizabeth Trulove Shakes the Sheriff's World

The sheriff was looking at Elizabeth Trulove now, and in a manner of speaking, shut his mouth for the rest of his life.

"Sheriff, you owe Mama, and one way or another, you gon' pay. You were the sheriff of this town, and you took advantage of her. You found you some little Nigger woman on the island—I'm sayin' it like it was—and you violated her. Don't shake your head at me, What Nigger back in the fifties and early sixties down here in the lowcountry gon' say No to the white sheriff? You conquered her with nothin' but power, old-fashioned racist white power, and guess what, Mr. Sheriff, it gon' be Black power take you down. Come on, you think I don't know what you told your white cronies? How many witnesses you reckon I could subpoena in this town? Comin' over here and leavin' us little ones nickels and quarters, lettin' Driver rub his hands all over your pistol. Shame, Sheriff, shame. Givin' her that brothel to run, the only place a Nigger could find employment downtown, your downtown, Sheriff, lessen' she be a maid or a janitor. What else she gon' do? So you give her the Ritz, the only establishment downtown that white folk entered through the back door. And Mama, my poor Mama. Don't look at her, Sheriff, don't you dare look at her, her back to you now, you hear me? You look at me now. That's right. Me. Yeah, you give her that little whorehouse to run and what's she thinkin'? Why, she thinkin', 'Oh my goodness, money.' At last, money, and for a Nigger she livin' pretty good. Beats teachin' school. Right Mama? Mama, how come you never wanted to teach school? Never wanted to teach school, never. Sho' didn't, did she Sheriff? No, this way she wasn't havin' to give herself to nobody but you, and hell, she already done that a hundred times before. Right, Sheriff? What, you think she like you, wanted you? She survived you. She survived you. And you bein' a white man, a powerful white man, the sheriff of this town, you leave her with the nickels and quarters and pocket the big bucks for yourself. She work the whores, her whores do the workin', and you walk off with some big bucks. That's illegal, Mr. Sheriff, and I'm a lawyer, and if you think I'm gon' be talkin' like this in front of a judge and jury, you got another think comin'. Oh no, this voice for the Island, Sheriff. In town, if you couldn't see me, you'd never know I was Black. If you doubt me, Sheriff, just remember who my daddy was, what he died for. I'm angry, Sheriff, at the way you treated my Mama. And I'm angrier than he ever was at a white man. You gon' pay, Sheriff, unless you pay."

Looking down on him now, facing him, was sophistication, education and money, all grown up.

The smile exchanged with her husband was a threat, a conspiracy, a potential subpoena. Her mother stood at the picture window, her back turned to them, giving away nothing. Her brother Driver just sat there in their mama's overstuffed chair as if he weren't.

"Finally, Sheriff, when you have a chance to really do something good not just for Mama but for every Black person in this town you and every white person in this town stole from, what do you do?"

"Aw come on, Elizabeth, I did what every white man in town would have done."

"Exactly, Sheriff, you betrayed her. After all she'd given you, her body, her money, considering all you made off her work, she finally had enough money to become a legitimate businesswoman, yes, Sheriff, a legitimate businesswoman, to buy her a little shop and some nice shoes to display in the window, that's all she wanted. To buy it with her own money when Mr. Dinnerman, bless his heart, a white man, was dying to sell to her, and what did you do, Sheriff? You betrayed her. You said No, Sheriff, you and Palmer and Liebowitz and all your white fishin' buddies. No, Lila, can't be havin' no Niggers downtown, everyone of 'em would take advantage. Now *we* takin' advantage, Sheriff. Only we takin' what's rightfully ours."

The Sheriff looked imploringly at Lila Trulove, still at the window, her back to them, her gaze neglecting the great oaks drenched with Spanish moss, the overcast day, and the quiet, undulating glaze on the river beyond.

"Lila," he said, "I've got money if you need it. You know that. I always have."

Her days with him, however, had ended long ago. Her back was to him, and he felt he could not approach her. Glancing over at her daughter—the lawyer from Washington—and her handsome young husband from the city in his Brooks Brothers suit, he felt his shirttail needed tucking in.

As he tried to stuff it in his trousers, creating mayhem about his waist, his whole world shook.

It was coming to an end.

Part I

SPRING 1960

| 1 |

Sergeant Jack Mcgowan Marches 71 Recruits Into Oyster Creek

Impossibly beautiful and seductive, the small lowcountry town of Somerset, South Carolina, was nevertheless unknown to the world when on the moonless night of May 3, 1960, Drill Sergeant Jack McGowan rounded up 71 sleep-deprived recruits on Lawton Island and ordered them to Fall In, non-swimmers Take Up The Rear.

"*Ten hut . . . Right shoulder, Arms . . . Forward March . . .*"

Still in his office only a few blocks over base psychologist Captain Bert Levy obsessively worked the dials of his Philco radio, here, there—almost damn it—this way, that way, the other way in what would have appeared to an onlooker, one who was sane anyway, as a caricature of an attempt to catch the Voice of the Celtics Johnny Most calling the action of the Celtics-Knicks game.

"*Your left, your right, your left, right, left . . .*"

On the mainland in downtown Somerset, Lila Trulove locked the day's take in the safe, yelled to Zuleema to lock the door behind her even though she was with a young Marine, and hurried dangerously down the stairs to her car, so worried was she that the kids might not get to bed on time. Drunk from boredom on the Palmer's verandah, Arlanne Palmer was confiding to her father, Bradford Palmer, Mayor Harper Dawes, and the C.O.—all fresh off a golf afternoon—that though the C. O. thought Hell was war and her father that it was bankruptcy and the mayor unemployment, she just couldn't help but see it as an afternoon on the golf course. At their home on Tidal Street Regina Cooley angrily scrubbed and scrubbed and scrubbed away at herself in the shower as Sheriff Cooley pulled out the driveway headed toward Lila's in his Ford pickup with his dog Buddy in the back. A

Chopin nocturne, which in two weeks would raise money for Israel, flew like yellow butterflies from Latta Gold's fingers as her son, the lawyer Murray Gold, sat in an overstuffed chair passing gas after a heavy dinner.

The streetlights across the sound and farther off in downtown Somerset, barely visible from Lawton Island anyway, were as impotent and shrouded in fog as the lights off the rifle range further and further behind McGowan and his platoon as they marched toward Oyster Creek. The moon was black, the night so dark now the young men could see little but the outline of a backpack, an M-1 rifle, and the slow hulking shadow in front of them.

"*Your right, your left, your right, left, right . . . Your right, your left, your right, left, right . . . your left, your right . . .*"

" . . . Cousy . . . ball . . . up the floor . . ." Come on, Johnny, let me hear you, Man. "Russel the rebound . . ." What? Static. " . . . Naulls . . ." Naulls? How'd he get the ball? Did the Celtics not score? " . . . Guerin from the baseline . . ." Static. Did he make it? Who knows? Would the Officer's Club offer him a better connection? What if it didn't? How much of the game would he miss on the way? If he stayed?

"*Your left, your right, your left right left . . .*"

Paralyzed with indecision, Levy pounded on his radio, only to catch a word, a name, an incomplete phrase here and there. At least goddammit give me the score. This was, however, an inside job, a thousand crickets screaming from the wires. Come on, Johnny. Come on, Man. You can do it, Goddammit. Just try.

The night was black, indistinguishable from the sky, as McGowan and his platoon approached the creek, the darkness and the silence intensifying their focus and concentration.

"*Your left, your right, your left, right, left . . . Your left . . .*"

A whippoorwill sounded off in the distance. Tree frogs. A few bird calls. An owl. None of these young recruits were locals, so pluff mud stank in their nostrils like the odor of the old paper mill up the road in Savannah, or sulfuric acid in the science labs of their former lives.

Dr. Levy was in tears, pleading with his radio, cupping it in both hands like he would the face of the baby Jesus himself had he been born a Christian instead of a Jew. Please. He did his damndest to placate the insurrectionists inside. While it was against his principles to negotiate with saboteurs, to bomb the crickets would have destroyed the radio, thus all communication with the Voice of the Celtics. He groveled, the Officer's Club too risky at this point. Leaning in close, knowing they could hear him, he fell back on the first amendment. Doesn't Johnny too, he argued, have the right to be heard?

When they stepped with heavy boots, full gear, and M-1 rifles off the bank into the creek itself, their boots disappeared into the pluff mud, releasing underfoot a frenzy of fiddler crabs, mud minnows and water beetles as the creek water swam up under their armpits. The tiny creatures rode the high tide in dumb obedience to the higher power of an indifferent moon, out beyond the sound and the river north toward the high bluff over which hovered the great oaks and grandiloquent homes and those places of business, both respectable and otherwise, in downtown Somerset, west toward the fishing shacks on the banks of the Broad River, east toward Lady's Island, the bridge to which Sheriff Cooley's pickup was at this very moment crossing on the way to Lila Trulove's.

This is America, goddammit, Shut the fuck up. Johnny calls out the score. "Celtics 77, Knicks . . ." crackling, spitting, sputtering, the screams of a million crickets.

With Boonie asleep in the back bedroom, Regina Cooley checked, rechecked, and checked again every window and every door in the house to be certain they were locked. Turning on every light in her bedroom, she pulled the covers up to her neck, her eyes wide open, terrified of what sleep might bring her.

Despite the awkward sloshing and splashing as well as the surprise of the high tide, Drill Sergeant McGowan led his platoon toward the center of the creek. The three men in back—Riley McGahee, Will Pennebaker, and Patrick O'Hearn—two of them still teenagers, saw only the shadows in front of each of them as up ahead in the middle of the creek Drill Sergeant Jack McGowan made a sharp turn to his right, his platoon snaking behind him, rifles over their heads, chest-high in water.

A marsh hen fluttered and squawked and scolded and splashed about, her beak darting this way and that, hovering, daring the passing soldiers to disturb her universe, picking and fussing her way back through a tiny forest of sawgrass, bulrush, and tall reeds in which her nest of six bone-white eggs, still as tiny moons, floated like the baby Moses in the Nile. Overhead now she spread and extended and drew them under her wings, shielding them from the danger of their own light, enfolding them into the night.

The men followed their fellow recruits blindly; one-by-one led by Sergeant McGowan they disappeared underwater. Later survivors toward the rear reported hearing gasps, cries for help, and screams but they just attributed it to the guys screwing off again, trying to scare each other, which was why there were here in the first place. Too much crapping off: guys late for or out of formation, fighting, jostling each other, and bantering when they thought McGowan couldn't see them, "bouncing," falling asleep during smoking breaks, sloppy shines, sloppy brass, sloppy bunks.

Good kids, McGowan would tell his fellow D. I.'s, but the sloppiest, most unruly bunch he'd ever had. They'd even screwed off at the train station in Yemassee until he'd yelled and screamed at them at the top of his lungs right in their faces and knocked them around a bit, scaring the beJesus out of them. He'd known even then that once the initial shock wore off, they'd get used to being chewed out, even roughed up. It's not that they weren't tough enough, they were just frivolous, unfocused, and immature. He had six weeks, then it was shape up or ship out. A night march into the swamp, if it didn't scare them to death, might just scare them into shape. If the sharks didn't get them, he'd told them, the undertow would.

When Lila Trulove pulled into her driveway across the river and into the trees on Lady's Island, Buddy barked from the rear of the pickup hidden away in the back behind the camellias and pittosporum. Downtown two MP's broke up a fight on the corner of Charles and Main. Over on Lawton Island Johnny Most was still struggling to be heard.

McGahee, Pennebaker, and O'Hearn were as shocked as Sergeant McGowan and the rest of the platoon when they stepped into the drop-off. McGowan should have known it was there, should have checked it out, or so it was deduced during his trial, but he didn't and he hadn't. He was a Marine, a soldier's soldier, a war hero, can-do and straight-on, and he'd made this decision, as he customarily did, as if in the heat of battle, quickly and certainly. Later, some would characterize him as "impulsive," but that would be after the fact.

Already he was diving over and over again into the claws and fangs of mayhem, relentlessly hauling from the underwater chokehold and the pulling of the tide those who couldn't fend for themselves, carrying them one after another, over and over, to the creek bank.

Weighed down by their backpacks filling with water and their heavy boots, those with their wits about them surrendered to the tide pulling them out as they held their breath and swam to the surface. McGahee, Pennebaker, and O'Hearn, however, could not swim, so wit abandoned them as swiftly and surely as had Sergeant McGowan and the United States Marine Corps. Panic precipitated immediate inhalation, and the brackish water set their lungs on fire.

After putting the kids to bed, the beautiful Lila Trulove handed the sheriff a Budweiser, took a long day's drag off a Lucky Strike, and led him to her bedroom, her clothes slipping off her caramel shoulders and dropping away like bread crumbs.

McGahee died as the marksman he was, the faded, yellowed photograph taped to the inside lid of his trunk back in the barracks springing back to life when in the place of his older brother Gary, who had stepped out of it forever to sell appliances in Newark, McGahee began picking off one North Korean sniper after another from the same perch and scrim behind the same third-story window of the Youido Hotel as Company C made their way through the streets of Seoul. Pennebaker had dreamed in secret of becoming a drill sergeant like his idol Jack McGowan, leading his own platoon on a brilliant Sunday afternoon in full dress uniform, Eyes Right passing the Reviewing Stand on the Parade Grounds at Lawton Island, but he died after Lights Out holding a lone flashlight in his lower bunk struggling to decode words, as was his ritual, in an old third grade primer that he'd found on the sidewalk behind the elementary school. O'Hearn, for the first time in his life, had stayed out of trouble and played by the rules, and he died to the applause, pats on the back, smiles and toasts all around in the company of his mom and dad, his grandparents, uncles and aunts, and his otherwise disapproving sister who Spoke in Tongues, Praised the Lord, Fed the Hungry, made straight A's, and was voted Most Likely to Succeed as a senior in high school, all the while looking fabulous as she cheered on the football team off which he'd been kicked during his sophomore year.

Divers the next morning discovered McGahee, Pennebaker, and O'Hearn rigid as sculpture floating face down on the murky water as if straining for the fetal position but failing to approach it, their torsos agonizingly curved, their heads tilting forward, backpacks and helmets a bit askew, their arms slightly bent at the elbows out in front of them as if draped over an invisible cross, their legs slightly bent at the knees, and their hands trying and failing forever to either clench like fists or to reach out.

Studying the photos over and over again, the C. O. deduced that had his men surrendered to the turbulence and tide, McGowan might have spotted them and they might be alive right now. Rigor mortis had contracted and locked them into position, but he couldn't help but imagine them beforehand, the legs of non-swimmers awkwardly scissoring and splaying, their arms the impotent wings of desperate swans, kicking, fighting, flapping, fluttering, propelling themselves upward toward light and air only to sink deeper and deeper into darkness and airlessness.

They had died fighting themselves, but they had died fighting. They were Marines.

Years later, after America destroyed Hue in order to save it, he would apply this same metaphor to the Vietnam War.

The phone rang in the outer office. He had already briefed the Commandant, General Allen.

"Mr. Palmer on line two, sir."

The call he was waiting for, however, was from Dr. Levy who even as he assiduously pored over Drill Sergeant Jack McGowan's file, couldn't help but wonder why the *Somerset Gazette* carried only local box scores.

As Bradford Palmer offered his condolences, careful to place the town of Somerset's resources at the Corp's disposal, the C.O. caught in the bottom left corner of the photo on his desk what he was certain were the three eggs of a marsh hen, refugees caught in the upper reaches of the bulrushes and marsh grass, homeless and motherless.

| 2 |

Dr. Bert Levy Confronts Sergeant McGowan After the Death March

From the view through the keyhole of my office door into my waiting room, a routine procedure in which I try as well as I can to gauge the body language of my patients before they can adjust to my presence, I see no affect in Drill Sergeant Jack McGowan's physical demeanor at all. The two M. P.s are chatting with Lance Corporal McBride as he attempts to repair my bruised and battered radio, clearly having given up on the idea of including McGowan in the conversation. Rigid and upright, McGowan sits on the standard issue sofa as if at full attention, eyes staring directly in front of him at absolutely nothing, as opaque and wide open, it seems to me, as a dead man's. You could give him a slight nudge, it appeared, and he'd topple over. Were I to walk out there and slap him, I wonder at this point if he would even feel it.

Physically, he is classically, iconically American: tall, slender, shallow; with any affect at all a ready fit for every highway billboard, a product of clean healthy living, the grownup version of the blonde, blue-eyed kid named Bill or Tom or Ted, or perhaps more boyishly Chip or Biff I had so envied and admired in the photos of my sixth grade health text when I was a boy. A smile, a bit of light in his eyes, is all it would take to register him as a team man, up and coming, the guy you could count on. He's perfectly proportioned, in tip-top shape; his crewcut standard, almost the length of a flattop. Other than his aquiline nose and high promising forehead he has no real distinguishing features. Take away his severe dissociation, I think, returning to my desk, and he looks pretty much like everyone else, or at least how everyone else, according to the present cultural indicators, is supposed to look.

According to the investigator's report, Drill Sergeant Jack McGowan had been drinking on and off all day—morning, afternoon, and early in the evening—before the march into Oyster Creek. Earlier that evening too he visited a nameless negro lady at Lila Trulove's brothel, a local prostitute he regularly visited at the Ritz Cafe in downtown Somerset, a disreputable rundown joint open only in the evenings, the upstairs of which is reputedly a discreet, back-door house of prostitution frequented often by Marines from the base as well as townsmen, some of them quite prominent.

In the investigator's report McGowan seems to say all the right things, things you might expect from someone in his position, with his background. Not once does he attempt to shift, evade or duck responsibility. He's straight up and straight on. "All the right things," however, in my professional experience, are what a man is taught to feel, not what he truly feels, so under the Rules of Engagement established by my office, all the right things are all the wrong things.

As the base psychologist, my responsibility is to provide a psychological evaluation for the military court: was Sergeant McGowan of sound enough mind to be held responsible for his actions while marching three young men to their deaths, or was there a sinister psychological force so powerful as to render him, at least at the time, out of control of his mental faculties and out of touch with reality?

Assuming that the body doesn't lie, that he cannot feel at this point is problematic. The dissociation could be the result of nothing more than shock. If that's the case, his present state of mind is a natural response to the trauma of the march for which he'll be held responsible. Simple as that.

If that's the case, however, the culprit behind the march is nothing more than mere thoughtlessness, sheer impulse, a dubious proposition in the face of such profound tragedy. McGahee, Pennebaker, O'Hearn, dead because a highly respected drill sergeant entrusted with the care and training of teenagers suddenly went stupid? Why? What caused that?

Such indifference to the potential dangers in that swamp suggest at least at this point severe dissociation, however well it may have been camouflaged, prior to the march. If so, what devil infiltrated his internal fortifications? What terrible God failed to intervene? Who enraged McGowan? Voided him of heart and soul? Of shame and guilt? Not after the march, but before it.

Shame and guilt are the arbiters of conscience, they teach us to think before we act, they are the Gods that say no to the devil, they humanize, they tame the monster, inspiring trust in the handshake, safety and comfort in the embrace, and an openness to heartbreak, to pain.

Where were they? Where are they?

My days here have been spent largely determining the potential of recruits: Will they, or will they not, make it? "There's a war on, Doc," said the C. O. (at the time referring to the Korean War). "No time to fuck around. You judge a Marine recruit," he said "not by the book, but by the cover. What's inside is not only immaterial, but a pain in the ass, an interference with a good day's work now, a potential disruption of the mission later."

Wartime or peacetime, in my estimation the Marine Corps isn't really hospitable to therapy, yet it is only through therapy that I can uncover Sergeant McGowan's motivation, his state of mind at the time of the march. Try as it might in a case such as this, the Corps is impatient with introspection. Self-examination isn't can-do and get-on-with-it. Sergeant McGowan's cover, however, was just that, a cover, and now the Marine Corps, undoubtedly to its profound distaste, is requiring me to read the book and to give them a report on it, on what's inside it. Results, says the C. O., they want results. Yet how can I turn this man inside out and examine his insides without the force of therapy, which is not given to quick answers? I cannot know him profoundly unless he reveals himself profoundly, and without therapy his defenses are as impenetrable as a nuclear facility.

Though it is McGowan's job to break down the defenses of recruits, it is also his responsibility to reconstruct and refortify them the Marine Corps way, just as his drill sergeant did his when he was a recruit. For survival's sake, each Marine is psychologically built as a bridge that must not fall.

Moreover, this is 1960, and the notion of therapy suggests, as it does in the real world, weakness. In the real world, except for unusually sophisticated circles, a visit to one's therapist is as discreet as a love affair. The Marine Corps allows for discretion no more than it allows for weakness, and a weak Marine is an oxymoron.

Yet victory lies in the penetration of McGowan's defenses, well fortified or not, in his surrender, in the falling of his bridge. His victory.

Looking at his file, it's clear Jack McGowan, Irish Catholic, is as he appears, at least superficially: a regular church-goer and family man respected and liked by friends, neighbors and colleagues. His father, Frank McGowan, was a drill sergeant, also a war hero. As a recruit a decade and a half ago Jack McGowan could have been a poster boy for trainees. Eager, daring, all gung-ho and can-do. As platoon sergeant In World War II he received two purple hearts and a bronze star for valor. His men trusted him. He took care of them, they felt. He was tough, but fair. Without question, to a man, they felt, he brought out their best. His men idolized him, revered him, and to the best of their ability, identified with him. He risked his life for them, clearing the way for them to advance by leaping into a machine gun nest, emptying his M-1 on the gunner and spotter then jumping on the loader before he could straighten himself out and get a bead on him, and when the loader opened his mouth to scream, McGowan stabbed him in the throat with such ferocity and murderous intent that his knife went through the back of his neck, pinning his head to the ground with his mouth and his eyes wide open.

Very very interesting.

According to his statement, Sergeant McGowan's purpose in ordering the night march of his platoon into the swamp of the tidal basin off the Somerset River was "to punish the platoon for an infraction of discipline by some recruits (lying on the ground, apparently sleeping-both of which were forbidden—during a smoking break) and for "crapping off" generally, particularly during formation and inspection. The platoon, he said, contained an inordinate number of "foul balls," was unusually "difficult" and "ill-disciplined." Not only his fellow drill instructors, but every member of his surviving platoon agreed with his assessment. They also agreed with his motive for the march, which was to "re-institute discipline" into the platoon. Even "slapping a few of them" and "knocking them around a bit," they reported, hadn't been enough to shape them up. At one point he encouraged three recruits to fight each other; even that, they further reported, had failed to toughen them up.

Survivors reported that even during the march itself, upon initially entering the swamp, before panic set in, there was some "jostling and goofing off, wise-cracks, here and there a sloppiness of formation, a breaking of ranks."

Could the lack of discipline have been attributable to McGowan's leadership style? Absolutely not. From the bottom to the top, all agreed that Sergeant McGowan was an excellent leader, a "Marine's Marine."

He had led the march himself. Whether he had been drinking earlier or not, he was by unanimous testimony in perfect control of himself, no slurring, stumbling or any other signs indicating otherwise. Non-swimmers were at the rear, upon his orders, where it was reasonable to assume there was less risk. Once danger set in, he risked his own life repeatedly diving underwater, hauling men who would have otherwise drowned back to shore, over and over again, rescuing every man he possibly could.

Afterward, upon emerging from the creek onto the bank, he fell to his knees crying, "Oh God, what have I done?" Guilt and remorse were immediate.

Just as immediate, however, according to the records, he "pulled himself together," and to the best of my knowledge he hasn't fallen apart since. Upon his return to the barracks, still soaking wet, he snapped to attention and saluted the investigating officer waiting for him. "I am responsible for the deaths, Sir, of three men," after which he extended his hands to be cuffed. "I expect to suffer the full penalty of the law."

He would rather, he later told the investigating officer, be punished "down here" than "up there," the latter presumably God's domain.

Yeah, yeah, yeah, but what happened to the initial guilt and remorse, so powerful they reduced him to falling on his knees and crying out on the creek bank? Why were they so short-lived, limited to the initial, the "immediate?" Why? Because only in the absence of such strong emotions, which tear a man apart, can he "get himself together," i.e., get control of himself, become soldierly, as McGowan did? Was the Toughest Drill Instructor Of Them All, even such an ardent Catholic as Sergeant McGowan, capable of such swift absolution? Was his immediate and forthright confession a way of absolving himself emotionally if not spiritually, a pre-emptive strike against the full force of the guilt and remorse that he knew, from his experience, upon emerging from Oyster Creek were lying in wait for him? Was "pulling himself together" a defense against his own internal shame? Was martyrdom?

Here was a man, by all appearances and accounts, taking full responsibility for himself and his actions, surrendering as forthrightly to the handcuffs as he would his punishment, a hero who in two wars had dutifully offered up his life—and risked it—for God and country, to say nothing of his men. Was he also a man, however, who caught off-guard by the lethal inhalation of three recruits, been reduced to little more than the wayward child who prefers the whipping to the guilt? The young man who chooses self-flagellation and the hair shirt to lifelong shame? The grown man, as he himself suggested, opting for Hell on earth "down here" with the hope of eternal salvation "up there"?

I couldn't help an encroaching cynicism. This man had marched 71 recruits, his entire platoon, into the swamp. Three drowned. There were 68 witnesses. "I did it," he said, offering up his wrists to the investigating officer, "punish me."

What else could he say? He was guilty. Everyone knew it.

Look at the timing here. Climbing out of the swamp, exhausted, having saved as many of his men as was humanly possible, the man Jack McGowan—devastated, lost, in total despair; shame, guilt, remorse raining on him as if from Heaven—falls to his knees, crying out, "Oh God, what have I done?"

And by the time he has led a soaking wet bedraggled platoon, still in shock, back to the barracks and confronted the investigating officer, the soldier has triumphed over the man. To put it a bit cynically, Duty has trumped Shame and Remorse. As he proffers his wrists to the investigating officer, Shame and Guilt slither back into the muck and mire of the swamp, submerged, out of sight, out of mind.

Harsh punishment can keep them there.

My job is to bring them back, to resurrect the man. That is my responsibility to myself and to him. The court knows what he did. The question they're interested in is, why? What were his true motives? What drove him over the edge? They'll know when I know.

All we truly know at this point is that his professed motive was "to instill discipline," and every drill instructor and member of McGowan's platoon, knowing his character, unquestioningly accepts that as his motive. The recruits themselves say they were undisciplined, fellow drill instructors attest to their "difficulty"; none doubt the sincerity of McGowan's intentions.

McGahee, Pennebaker, O'Hearn . . . would they? I wondered, picking up the phone.

"McBride, get me the C.O."

"Right away, Sir."

The C.O. himself answered on the first ring. "Why'd he do it, Levy?"

"According to the report, Sir, to instill discipline."

"We're not talking here about instilling discipline. We're talking about abusing it. Why'd he abuse it?"

"I don't know, Sir."

"Well, find out, Goddammit. Fast. The quicker this goes away, the better. Without answers, the press will eat us alive. And if 'instilling discipline' is all we have to account for why that son of a bitch did what he did, the question the public's going to ask is not, 'My God, how could this have happened?' but, 'Why in hell's name didn't it happen before, a million times over?' With that horseshit out there, what parent would even consider letting his son volunteer? Levy, we're talkin' confidentially here." To tell you the truth, he seemed a little paranoid, except that he had reason to be. "Is McGowan crazy?"

"At the moment at least, I think we can safely assume he's severely dissociated."

"Speak English, Harvard boy."

"Confidentially?"

"You got it, Bubba."

"Probably, Sir, at least at the time of the incident. Other D. I.'s may have approached the edge disciplining their men but how many go over it? He went 'over the edge'. He didn't just march his men into the creek, he did so uncharacteristically, with such wanton indifference, such reckless disregard."

"Well, if he's nuts you better find out why and how. Because if you don't, it's going to look like we are."

"We, Sir?"

"The Corps, Son. The Corps."

"But Sir, may I ask why you are so worried about this particular incident? The Corps has survived atrocities before."

"Wartime atrocities, son. Not peacetime. Besides, there's urgency here. I'll tell you why. You'll appreciate more how important what you're doing is. It's hard as hell to get military funding in peacetime, yet we need it to prepare for wartime. Right? No news there."

"Right, Sir."

"The Commandant's drawn up the largest budget in history: higher salaries, better housing conditions, more sophisticated equipment, better medical care for the soldiers, including," he added, "better mental health care, particularly for veterans. The budget has to be approved by the House Armed Services Committee. Believe me, they're going to protect themselves before they protect the country, much less me and you. If the press makes this the problem of the Marine Corps instead of one lone solitary D. I. who had to have been out of his fuckin' mind, we could get killed for this. You can forget that budget request. Hell, they could close down this base. The least they'd do is take me down with 'em, along with some mighty fine colleagues."

"Close the base?"

"Well, the mayor of Somerset and the Chairman of the Somerset Board of Education's callin' me three times a day, and it ain't to play golf. Somerset would die without this base. Business, federal money for schools, you name it. Why you think the mayor offered up the courthouse in town for the trial? 'Lease it to you for the duration of the trial for the exorbitant price of one dollar. Sign this, General, and it's Federal property till the trial's over.' He knows the press is going to be swarming around like sand fleas. He knows our courtroom here on Lawton Island is really just the old schoolhouse, way too small to accommodate them. He wants 'em on our side. So: 'What can we do, General? Anything you need? We got to keep you fellas around, you know.' The new parade grounds, who you think owns the company that poured the concrete? The chairman of the Town Council, Bradford Palmer. Who drew up the contracts, took care of the legal business? The Board of

Education chairman, Marty Liebowitz, who just happens to be a lawyer, and who also happens to serve as the conduit for the federal money going to the schools. Lot of people in this town making money off of that money, as they should; it's for a good purpose. Off-base family housing: the government had to buy that property from the town. Guess who owned it? A consortium consisting of Harper Dawes, who just happens to be the mayor; Bradford Palmer; Marty Liebowitz; and your congressman, who chairs the House Armed Services Committee. Reckon they made a small pile once they got that bit of business in the budget? It's about money, Son. And money's about politics. Almost every house rented in Somerset is rented to a Marine. Who owns them? Builds them? Repairs them? Supplies the materials? Draws up the legal documents? Handles the accounts? Figures out the taxes? Some make more than others, but frankly son, everybody makes some."

I hadn't realized any of this, never thought about it, and as so often in my life when blindsided by the Ways of the World, I became humiliatingly aware that the Ways of the World were known and understood by undoubtedly everyone in the world but me. Was this, at least in part, what Eisenhower had meant by the Military-Industrial complex? I didn't even know how to change a flat tire.

"Yours is the world of the psyche, son," he said, apparently picking up on mine quite well. "No one's asking you to enter ours."

"The only thing I know about Somerset, to say nothing of the rest of the world, Sir, is 'Bars, Broads, and Booze.' That's all Somerset means to the soldiers I see."

"Which is as much a part of the system as anything else. So: 'What can we do, General? Anything you need? No problem.' It's either the Marine Corps or McGowan, son, yet crazy as it sounds, only the truth about McGowan will set the Marine Corps free. Fine and dandy if for psychological reasons it helps McGowan . . . Get it out of him, Levy. For coincidental reasons, it serves your purpose, my purpose, the Corp's purpose, perhaps even his own purpose. Find it, son. For whatever reasons, that's your job. I'm telling you all this to let you know I'll give you all the support you need. Anything you ask for. You want him every day, you got him. I'll send word down to the brig. Anything else?"

"Thank you, Sir."

"Keep me posted." "The Corps thanks you, son," he said before hanging up. "It's in your hands."

There was something else. On the day of the march McGowan had slapped a recruit. Again, to encourage discipline. And again, the recruit himself saw nothing unusual in this, agreeing with it, particularly in his own case.

Asked how hard he had slapped the recruit, McGowan, whom I had gleaned from these records was nothing if not forthcoming, had said: "Not really very hard. To tell you the truth, I've slapped my little boy harder than I slapped him."

I slapped my little boy harder than I slapped him.

How old was his little boy?

Three, according to the records. He slapped a three-year-old child harder than a Marine?

Why march them into the tidal basin in the first place? Was that typical procedure? How could he have been totally oblivious to the dropoff, the daily tide changes that resulted in such dangerous currents? The sucking of the marsh?

What was his little boy like?

Sergeant McGowan walked in, snapped to, and saluted smartly. "At ease, Sergeant," I ordered, motioning him to the standard issue sofa. "Remove your boots. Loosen your tie. Lie down. Make yourself as comfortable as possible."

"Sir, yes sir!"

I gave him a few minutes, my eyes on his file.

"Your little boy," I asked him, looking up. "What's he like?"

"He tries hard, Sir, in my opinion," said McGowan. "He means well."

"Tries hard? At what, Sergeant?"

"Sir, he can be 'soft,' Sir, like his mother."

"Go on."

"Needy, Sir. Clingy. Cries too easily, wails, whines. His mama says he's 'sensitive.' That's bad for a boy. Says I'm too hard on him. I say I'm tryin' to make a man out of him, he's too sissified. She says he's scared of me. I say she caters to him."

"Does he prefer his mother to you?"

"Sure, Sir, wouldn't you, in his situation, having somebody at your beck and call? Oh Mommy this, Oh Mommy that? Hey, a slight discoloration or raised welt is like the end of the world, Sir."

"But he tries . . ."

"Sure he tries. If not, he knows what's coming."

"And your father? Did he raise you the same way?"

"Absolutely."

"Made a man out of you . . ."

"You bet, Sir. My old man believed, as he used to put it, 'You gotta beat the girl out of 'em.'"

"Did he?"

"You bet, Sir."

"Can you remember that, Sergeant, 'the girl' inside you, or who was inside you? Where did she go? Is she dead, gone to a far better place, Sergeant? Perhaps merely in retreat, biding her time? Locked away somewhere deep inside you? Does she haunt you? Does she surface periodically, like a guerrilla, driving you crazy, only to retreat afterward to the hills or caves? Every once in awhile can you hear the cries and whimpers which you so despise coming up from a prison cell deep inside you? A tin cup clanging against the cell bars?"

McGowan smiled.

"Is that a smile of recognition, Sergeant, of acknowledgment? A 'knowing' smile, Sergeant, which though patronizing may indicate we're getting somewhere? Or a smile of derision?"

"Permission to speak freely, Sir?"

"Sure, Sergeant, it's a therapy session. I expect you to fight me. Otherwise, we can forget progress here. Though if you have to ask, it means you're not going to."

"Would the captain explain, Sir?"

"Do you think you were *acting* freely when you marched your platoon into a swamp that sucked the lives out of three eighteen year old boys, Sergeant? Or that you're acting freely even when you slap your little boy?"

"I never questioned it, Sir. I was taught never to question it. Not just at home, Sir, but in the Corps. Second-guessing yourself in battle, Sir, also leads to the deaths of young men."

"Admittedly, I wouldn't know."

"I do, Sir."

"And the smile?"

"An involuntary smile of derision, Sir."

"Good. It means you're defensive, which means you're protecting yourself, hiding something, perhaps even someone."

"A 'little girl,' Sir?"

"The one your father beat out of you."

"I meant that as a figure of speech, Sir."

"Representing what, Sergeant, except the qualities of a little girl? In what ways specifically were you like a girl? What are those qualities?"

"I don't remember, Sir. It was a long time ago."

"Were they like your son's?"

"I don't know, Sir."

"You're under orders, Sergeant."

"No doubt they were, Sir."

"Does it bother you that your son prefers your wife to you?"

"I understand it, Sir."

"How does it make you feel?"

"I do not know, Sir."

"Do you know why you don't know, Sergeant? Because your father beat your feelings out of you, just like you're doing to your son. That's how you were able to march those kids into Oyster Creek. But deep down somewhere those feelings are there. They came out briefly upon your emerging from the creek. 'Oh God,' you cried, 'what have I done?'"

His body involuntarily shuddered, then stiffened. He crossed his legs. His eyes suddenly dissociated, totally vague, blank. His left arm lashed out at something only he could see. He grabbed it with his right one, and held it in place.

It was as if rigor mortis had set in.

Kill the body, kill the emotion. He was stiff as a board, hard as a rock. Totally dissociated, just as he'd appeared earlier in the waiting room. Had he been this dissociated the evening of the march? If so, why? In any case, I had gone too fast.

"Look, Sergeant, you're lying on my sofa, my tie's askew, my feet up, I'm here to help you as much as I can, which in my mind means helping you to find the truth about yourself through any underlying emotions you might have of which possibly you're unaware, emotions out of necessity and your own survival you've had to hide even from yourself that might help us get to the bottom of your crossing the line at Oyster Creek. Your conscious motivation was to instill discipline. What, however, was your unconscious motivation? It had to have been powerful to result in such uncharacteristic negligence. The situation we're in must be informal. It has to be for me to be helpful here. I've got to get to know the real you, and paradoxically without knowing me, you've just got to trust me. The Truth can set you free, I promise you, whether you're in the brig or not. My guess is it'll also work in your favor with the court. If you don't mind, while we're in this office, I'd prefer that we speak to each other without regard for rank. Can we drop the formalities, at least for the time being? Call me Bert, I'll call you, Jack, unless that bothers you."

"Permission to speak freely, Sir."

"Absolutely."

"Your title is Captain, Sir, mine is Sergeant. According to the Uniform Code of Military Conduct we are to address each other as befits our rank.

There is a reason for this, Sir. It suggests that proper respect for rank, Sir, is essential to the proper functioning of the Corps. Further, it suggests, Sir, that you, Sir, are of a higher status than I, and accordingly possess greater authority, an authority, Sir, that extends over me. The Marine Corps has designated me a lesser Marine than you, Sir. 'Ours is not to question why, Sir; ours is to do or die.' You may frequent the Officer's Club, while I may frequent the non-commissioned officer's club. You have earned your rank, Sir, as have I. You are in charge here, Sir. I am here to follow your orders and instructions, to do as I'm told, Sir, which as I understand it is to answer all questions honestly and to volunteer information in a forthcoming manner, Sir, and to do so in a manner befitting your rank, Sir. I intend to do just that, Sir, because you are my superior, Sir. To trivialize the Uniform Code of Military Conduct would, in my humble estimation, Sir, trivialize your authority over me, suggesting further Sir, that I have as much authority to demand that you lie on the sofa and subordinate yourself to my authority as you do of me. Sir, such a breakdown in authority inevitably results in a breakdown of discipline. The Code, Sir, in my humble opinion, Sir, exists to prevent such a breakdown. Sir, such a blatant, conscious contravention of the Uniform Code of Military Conduct would require, according to the Code itself, a disclosure to the proper authorities. Consequently Sir, as required by the Uniform Code of Military Conduct, I respectfully request of the Captain that we address each other formally as befitting our respective titles and ranks, Sir."

"Request denied, Sergeant, on the basis that three men under your responsibility are dead, because they followed your orders, Sergeant, as required by the Uniform Code of Military Conduct."

"That is true, Sir. However, it was I who showed neglect, irresponsibility, and terrible judgment that, as such, was an egregious insult to the Code. Therefore it is I, not the Code itself, who should suffer the consequences."

"But if they had disobeyed your orders . . ."

"They couldn't have, Sir, they were trained to obey orders—"

"They would be alive now."

"Affirmative, Sir."

"Then the hell with the Code, the hell with following orders, the hell with formality."

"It is all we have, Sir. I pray that my abuse of it does not lessen respect for it. Democracy and consensus, Sir, are as ineffective in the heat of battle as prayer. Independent thinking, Sir, is an invitation to rebellion, subversion, and treason. American lives are lost when the chain of command is subverted."

"As your superior, I am giving you an order," I said, instinctively, curiously. How far could he go with this? "Call me 'Bert.'"

"Sir, I could no more address you as 'Bert' than my recruits could have refused to enter the swamp, Sir."

"Because of your training, because of theirs?"

"Yes sir, but the training derives from the Code, Sir, as the Captain is aware. If I may repeat myself, Sir, a breakdown in the Code leads to a breakdown in discipline, which defeats the purpose of the Code and consequently the Corps and the recruit training program."

"I think I know now where this is heading, but I'll ask anyway. The 'purpose' being?"

"Yes sir. To instill discipline, Sir."

The C.O. called, within seconds of the Sergeant's leaving.

"What you got for me, Bubba?"

I liked it when he called me 'Bubba.' Made me feel like I was a real Southerner, one of the boys.

"Not much, Sir. Maybe a chink in the armor, a dent. He's tough, and he shuts down instinctively at a moment's notice, which probably means we're getting somewhere. We're on the porch, knocking on the front door. Automatically, however, the alarm goes off, and the entire house shuts down. He's never been permitted to question any authority, has indeed been taught not to, and he's been subconsciously briefed—brainwashed, really—on just how much to give away to the enemy, the interrogator; maybe he just doesn't realize yet that I'm on his side, and in a way he's right to be suspicious. Which side of him am I on? The interrogator, to him, probably means a representative of his government-in-exile—his repressed feelings, perhaps even submerged personalities—planning an internal coup and I am behind that coup. I don't know, maybe he's just calculating as hell, thinking that the only way out is to stick to his guns. Maybe in his own mind he's simply following orders, continuing his role as the good soldier, shallow but eager and willing. Maybe he's humoring me, or thinks he is. Maybe he's honest, an ideologue, a true believer, a man fighting with himself."

"You mean he's either your typical patient—strike that; his crime makes him atypical—a shark, or a fanatic?"

"Probably. Otherwise, he'd have to be just a simple guy with a shallow integrity."

"A Marine."

"Maybe, deep down does such a guy really exist?"

"Let's hope not, son, because if all he is, is a Marine, and the world knows it, the rest of us are out of a job."

"Tell me, Sir, do you know of a Lila Trulove, the prostitute mentioned in the report?"

"Yeah, I know Lila. Negro lady. The sheriff's whore. Hell, she's famous all over town. Somerset's small, Doc. Everybody's famous."

3

Bert Consults With Lila at Her Brothel for a Second Opinion

In military jargon, she'd been "briefed."

It's odd: walking up the musty, dimly lit back staircase to the second floor, the one above the Ritz Cafe, I regressed momentarily to the teenager I was at 17, sneaking out of Macy's with a shoplifted alligator belt under my trench coat vowing to myself that if the cops didn't catch me I'd never show off for my buddies again. I hadn't been to a house of ill repute since college, and I'd been so drunk at the time I could scarcely remember it. Only the odor of mildew, however, summer humidity's rotten leftover that you could never completely get rid of in the coastal lowcountry, trailed me as I made my way up to the second floor landing. There the sunset over the Somerset River appeared as muted klieg lights through thin white curtains covering the windows, translucently veiled, hinting at itself, teasing, threatening fire—a violent display of reds and purples and oranges and blues—in the Western sky.

At my knock a young Negro woman in white bra, white panties and white-painted nails opened the door, turned away, and yelled "Lila, he's here," jerking her head toward the back. Several scantily clad women, also Negroes—most of them showing middle age—lounged around on sofas and armchairs in negligees, assorted undergarments, one in her housecoat and slippers.

The door to Lila Trulove's office, through which I could see her in lamplight leaning over her desk adding up the day's deposits, was ajar, and without looking up she said, "Come on in, Baby, I know who you are. You one of them Yankee boys talk fast." She managed a quick wink, but she didn't miss a beat adding up her money, which she'd arranged in stacks according to the size of the bills, recording the day's earnings on the deposit slip at the top of which read THE SOMERSET BANK. "Give me just a minute and I'll be right with you."

Behind her the shades, over the windows facing Main Street, were drawn. Lamplight brought out their whiteness in contrast to the rich, darkly furnished room, the somber twilight afterglow on the walls, the dusky black and white photograph of a Negro teacher with a pointer peering over the shoulder of a child reading at Penn Community Center. It illuminated a lovely cursive on her deposit slip, pooling around the ledger that lay closed next to it, lighting up an inkwell, hovering about the desk, settling comfortably in her empty chair, rising like a sun tide over Lila Trulove herself.

She was striking: tall, languid, feline. A stunning split-second lick of her index finger, and she was checking one after another the number on the topmost corner of each bill—tens, twenties, fifties, a modest stack of hundreds—recording her sums with the delicacy required of a fountain pen on THE SOMERSET BANK deposit slip, her fingers dancing with the grace and harmony of ritual to the next stack, a split-second lick of her finger. She was perhaps the handsomest woman I had ever seen, thoughtful and feminine, with just the right amount of cynicism affording her toughness and intelligence. She was not a bully. Charming, she was a thinker.

Lila had the caramel coloring of a mulatto, with features more Indian, perhaps European, than African. Her nose was straight, her cheekbones high and pronounced, queenly (with a suggestion of haughtiness) reigning over a triangular face humanized with barely perceptible freckles. Above a clear, open brow and expressive green eyes (hinting of calculation and perhaps mischief), her hair, the color of rust, appeared resigned to a stubborn unruly curliness, giving her strong, intelligent presence a coy twist. Her red dress, somewhat muted, hung on her casually, almost carelessly, like a shrug.

The safe in the corner was open. She placed the money, the deposit slip and the ledger inside, closed and locked it.

Her feet were bare: her toenails pink, her soles dirty.

"Sit down, Honey," she said, and she lowered herself into the antique chair behind her desk, with me directly across from her. "You are Dr. Levy . . ."

"Yes," I said. "I am."

"You don't need to say no mo', you got plenty of billin'. Yo' man talk to the sheriff, the sheriff talked to me. They want to know if Ol' Jack crazy. Boy, ain' nobody come here an't crazy Between me and you ain't nobody in this town *don't* come here that ain't crazy. Now what do you boys want?

What the hell y'all mean by 'crazy?'"

"I don't want to know if he's crazy. I'll determine that from his therapy. But I do need help, whether he is or isn't. You can tell a lot, as I'm sure you know, from a man's sex life. Let me give you an example—"

"You gon' explain to me what you can tell about a man from his sex life?"

I was caught, handcuffed and shackled by nothing more than my own officiousness. I couldn't help but smile. "I'm sorry. My God, that was patronizing."

She chuckled. "He don't come here for sex."

"Excuse me?"

She reached into a desk drawer and pulled out a quart of Jack Daniels and a glass. Behind her, on a shelf, was an ice bucket, beside which on a clean white cloth napkin lay an ice-scooper, a bottle-opener, and several bottles of club soda and Coca Cola. "Neat?" she asked me, glancing at the Jack Daniels. "On the rocks? Straight up? Little Co-Cola with it?"

I was so disarmed, confused and though I didn't fully realize it at the time, so taken with her—her unpretentiousness, her effortless beauty and sensuality, her clarity and simplicity—that momentarily I lost sight of the difference: Straight up? Neat? On the rocks? The latter, however, was obvious enough. "Ice," I managed. "On the rocks, please."

She poured a glass of the dark amber liquid over ice and handed it to me across her desk. Her hand, for a second, was all I could see; it was lovely, at eye-level, her fingers long and fine, suggestive of a delicate touch, a gentle caress, easy languor, a touch so casual as to drive a man crazy.

I was, I realized, intimidated by the ease and clarity of her presence.

Acting solely on their own, my fingers slightly (and probably suggestively), brushed hers as I accepted the drink from her hand. Her fingers were cool. Their touch made her real, dangerous, promising. Instinctively, I pulled back, almost spilling my drink, as if her fingers, cool and slender as clear mountain streams, were a hot stove, property perhaps on which I was afraid to trespass. She smiled, as if she were used to it.

"Won't you have one?" I asked.

"Don't need one. I ain't the one nervous. You pretty cute. Want me to find you a girl? Helena'll be free, the one in white bra and panties who greeted you at the door . . . ?"

"No no no. Another time maybe. That's not why I'm here."

"So you ain't interested in havin' sex with one of the girls while you here."

Jesus. "No. No. That's not my purpose, that's not at all what I'm here for."

"Well," she said, as if the conversation might as well close on that note. "That ain't what Jack come for neither."

"Right."

"And he just as nice and polite as you. Not one ounce of trouble."

"So if you don't mind my asking, purely for professional reasons, I assure you . . ."

"Why does he come?"

"Exactly."

"Speakin' purely professionally, Baby, are you askin' me for personal information on one of my clients?"

"It's hopefully to help him."

"And has he authorized you to seek out this information? Is he aware . . . ?"

"No."

"And if I asked you for personal information on one your Marine patients or clients who might visit here regularly—to help him, mind you, to improve his sex life, which as you know, is very important for the self-regard of these young men—would you give it to me?"

"Of course not."

"Then I'm sure you understand. But you come back anytime for a drink now, you hear?"

Walking down the stairs, all I could think was one thing: Sheriff Cooley was a lucky man.

Once in the car, driving back to the base, however, all I could wonder was, what is she hiding?

| 4 |

The C.O. Reads the Yankee Newspapers

There are no stories, as yet, in the *Somerset Weekly*, concluded the C.O. after his newly ritualized morning scan. Three days, and the average Somersetonian has no knowledge of Sergeant McGowan and the deaths of the young men at Oyster Creek. Not that it really matters, the C.O. realized, the average Somersetonian knows who butters his bread. The *New York Times* has reported it, as have several other prominent newspapers, among them the *Washington Post*, but those stories are pretty much confined to the Pentagon's press releases, which are standard: acknowledgement of the incident, the tragic loss of life, and compassion for the victims' families; since an investigation is under way, there can be no further comments until it is completed, rest assured that no stone will be left unturned.

At least locally, for now, we're protected. Somersetonians wouldn't be caught dead reading the *Times*, thank the Lord, or the *Post*. "Yankee" newspapers. The *Times*, in fact, is already banned in the Somerset schools, the journalistic equivalent of a communist, integrationist, atheist, or unwed mother.

Nationally, however, the press needs more, figured the C. O. Circling the wagons is an invitation for the press to attack. If the Commandant of the Marine Corps really wants to control this story, he's going to have to do a hell of a lot better than this.

He filed away the *Post* and the *Times* in a desk drawer, which he immediately locked, as he had begun doing every morning since the incident at Oyster Creek was first reported.

5

The Sheriff Diddles, Jesus Gets in the Way, and Elizabeth Burns

Hoke Cooley parked his Chevy Pickup behind Lila's house, wedging it into an orgy of multi-colored camellias just off the back steps, where it couldn't be seen either from the road or the river. A forty-year-old pittisporum, clearly the hostess of the garden all decked out in elegant white lace, perfumed the air like a long-awaited sigh. Enough, Lila once commented to Hoke, to make a man drunk with love, which is why, he'd figured, in springtime she left the windows up in her bedroom where they made love.

He was actually wrong about that, she'd told him. Pittisporum perfumed every back yard in the neighborhood, and like anyone else, she just enjoyed the intoxication of the scent on the fresh breeze. After all, she'd pointed out, driving him insane, Ida Perch left her windows up for the same reason. Now that she thought about it, Lila told him, "Sarah Washington leave her windows open, and she close to ninety years old. She sho ain't makin' love to nobody. Then there's Bertha Bell down the street. Her windows open, and she once told me she so ugly she refuse to make love with herself, much less anybody else. And how about Edna White, her windows open, yet her man long gone. Willa Bee, everybody know that well dried up long time ago . . . But now on the other hand, Billie Longtree, she make love with her windows DOWN. Yep, closed. As a matter of fact, so do Velma Turner and Gracie Mossback. You know Gracie . . . now that I think about it . . ."

Hoke conceded he thought he was getting the picture.

What she really liked, she'd told him, was the cool, elegant scent of pittisporum intermingling on the breeze with the fecund, pungent odor of marsh gas coming off the river, the intertwining of the elegant and the earthy.

"You and me," he'd offered.

"Hoke, shut up."

"Yes, ma'am."

Goddamn, he thought, getting out of the truck, the mosquitoes are worse here than in Somerset. He pulled out his pistol, waving it at them, swatting them away. Go on, get out of here.

"God damn it," he said, as one got him on the arm.

Reminded him of Jesus gettin' in the way when he was trying to drive. Regina'd hung Jesus from the rear view mirror inside the pickup and Jesus'd wait till it was raining cats and dogs and you could hardly see anyway and you had to make a sharp turn at the intersection with a thousand pissed off cars and pick-ups behind you or come to an abrupt stop because of the car in front of you and Jesus'd start swinging, back and forth, back and forth right in front of your eyes like a hypnotist with his pocket watch while you were trying to make out the road in front of you. Then when naturally you'd lean forward, straining to see better, Jesus's alabaster toe would get you right in the eye, every time. But Regina wanted the Son of God watching over Hoke, keeping him safe. "Driving while distracted," she'd told him, "is the Devil's way of doing his work. You're the sheriff, and if the Good Lord put you on this earth to protect Somerset County, then for the Good Lord's sake let Jesus protect you."

Yes, ma'am, he'd told her.

Elizabeth could see him through the parted curtains of her bedroom window. The backyard outside light was on. She'd cut it off when Mama told her he was comin' by, but Mama cut it back on again. Every time Elizabeth would cut it off, Mamma'd cut it back on. She didn't get on her like she did Driver, probably 'cause she did everything right, like she was supposed to, but Mama did let her know that if she touched that "damn" light switch one more time she was goin' to get her first lickin.'

The way he was standin' there arguin' with a bunch of mosquitoes . . . was he a stupid white man or what? Did he think he was gon' shoot 'em?

Spanish moss from a low-hanging branch of a water oak caught and draped over his pistol, waving about like the melancholy timeworn banner of a lost cause as he shooed away mosquitoes. Would he walk into the house before holstering his gun? She clenched her fists and prayed. "Jesus, please make him forget. Please make him forget. Please . . ." But she knew he wasn't that stupid. Her mama would "raise the roof." And he knew it.

Every time she saw him she saw her own father's blood splattered all over the living room walls, his head lolling in her mama's lap, his eyes wide open, sightless, staring straight at her. The sight of the sheriff's pistol always numbed her, and she would imagine herself sleepwalking, picking it up off her mama's dresser, unholstering it herself, and shooting him in his sleep.

She'd fire and fire and fire, just as she imagined now the mosquitoes, grown fat as blimps off the meat of his body, sailing away satisfied as buzzards, like him driving off after leaving her Mama's bed.

A tiny residue of bones, blood and tattered clothing all that remain in the driveway.

A mosquito flying off with his pistol between its teeth, dropping it way, way off in the middle of the ocean.

Until from behind the parted curtains of her bedroom she saw Driver all excited, running across the back porch to greet him. She could see the screen door burst open and slam shut as he raced down the back steps. Mama had waved her finger in his face and told him a million times not to slam it, but to close it gently. She had even made him walk through, practicing, which he performed dutifully, as if it were the most important thing in the world to him. Something wrong with that child. He dumb. Unfortunately, Mama couldn't hear it slam either. She was in the kitchen fixing supper.

"Hey, Mr. Cooley."

"Why, hey there, Burrhead," said Mr. Cooley, picking him up, carrying him onto the porch, disappearing into the living room. Elizabeth closed the curtains.

"Not till the kids are asleep," whispered Lila to Hoke in the darkness of the hallway. "You know that. You may be the sheriff of this town, Honey, but you ain't by any stretch of the imagination the sheriff of this house. Come on," she said, leading him toward the kitchen, "I'll fix you somethin' to eat. And don't think I'm gon' be screamin' and yellin' like some teenager in some parked car. It ain't gon' happen. As long as the kids are in this house you go on puttin' yo' hand over my mouth." She smiled over at him, forking the roast on the stove to see if it was ready. "Kind of turns me on anyway, if you want to know the truth."

She handed him a Jack Daniels straight up and sat across the kitchen table from him, her fingers playing over the toy car he'd bought for Driver, stealthily teasing it across the table towards him. "Do you?" she asked him. She knew Regina had already fed him. She knew he'd act like he was starvin' and eat a whole 'nother meal if he thought it'd please her.

"Do I what, Lila?"

"Want to know the truth?"

"Why sure," he said, "why wouldn't I?"

She quickly checked the kids' bedrooms to make sure they were asleep. Upon returning to the kitchen, she reached for his hand. "It's this way," she said, leading him to her bedroom.

"The truth?"

Her dress casually fell away, forming a criminally red puddle on the bedroom floor. She slipped under the cool white sheet, holding it up like an invitation.

"The truth," she said, and her easy, effortless beauty caused him to trip over his pants legs as he stumbled greedily into bed beside her.

Afterwards, while they were smoking, she said, "You heard anything more about that business on Lawton Island I told you about a few days ago, what that psychologist asked about? He too nice to be pokin' and sniffin around cathouses, I tell you that."

"The whole mess is bad for business, bad for Somerset, bad for the country. The C.O., Dawes, Palmer, we can't anticipate what the fallout's going to be."

"That McGowan man's as nice as any of your big shot buddies come in there. You ain't told them boys what I told you, trying to act like some big shot."

"Course not, Lila."

"I don't want my girl in court, bad business or not."

"Whatever I've done, have I ever lied to you?"

She rose up on one elbow, facing him, the sheet falling away from her caramel shoulders. "No," she said gently, her Kent cigarette held away from him. "But you lie to her."

She nodded, gesturing over the river toward the mainland, toward Somerset itself, toward his wife Regina in their modest brick home at 179 Broome Lane with a charcoal grill on the back patio and a chainlink, fenced-in backyard for Buddy their Boston Bull who, at that very moment, was whining like a banshee in the rear of Hoke's pickup in Lila's backyard. Why he had to bring Buddy every time he came was beyond Lila. They went through this every time. Buddy couldn't stand to be without Hoke. Hoke even took him to work with him, where Buddy apparently had the run of the place. Riding through town, observed Ledbetter Greene, one of Hoke's young deputies, Buddy stood in the rear of that pickup like he was on the prow of a ship or the lead float in a parade. Ledbetter dubbed Hoke's pickup "The King's Carriage." Buddy'd settle down, both Lila and Hoke knew from experience. At least, thought Lila, they didn't need to get up and go out there and say anything. Still, she couldn't help but wonder, why persist in bringing the dog when he could just as easily leave him at home? Why? She knew hers was a lost cause long ago when after her protests Hoke kept showing up with him anyway and, in the face of her screaming and yelling, apologizing up, down, all around, north, south, east, west, every which way seventeen times over swearing EACH TIME that he must be losing his mind "or somethin'" because he couldn't even remember the subject having ever been brought up, much less discussed. Did she think, he'd wonder aloud, maybe something had gone wrong with his mind? Could be. He was kind of like Buddy, he'd point out, never had been all that bright. Tonight was no different than any other night. They waited him out, as they had learned to do. Hoke was right. Buddy was downright dumb, just like Hoke was. Without instant gratification, Buddy'd forget he was even whining, much less who for, spend a minute or so trying to sniff it out again, then failing that, curl up in the rear of the pickup and slumber off into dog-dreamland.

"No, Lila, I don't. And whether I did or didn't, she'd just turn the other cheek."

"Like she do when you touch her?"

"Regina's a good Christian woman, Lila. Doesn't believe in all that stuff. Her daddy's hard, all that fire and brimstone. Made her cold, I suppose. But she gives. All that charity work, helpin' the poor, she works. Does the Lord's work, I'll tell you that."

The nightmares, he couldn't help but wonder about them. Screaming bloody murder, enough to wake up the neighbors; shakin' so hard it looked like her body parts was threatenin' to fly off. The more he tried to soothe and calm her, the more hysterical she became. *Don't touch me. Don't touch me.*

At first he'd wondered if there was something wrong with him, but then he began realizing that while she was good to Boonie and took care of him, in some ways probably overprotective, he couldn't remember the last time she'd loved on Boonie and cuddled and hugged him like most mothers did their little boys. Too busy, she used to say. Idleness is the Devil's workshop.

Maybe that's why Boonie liked comin' over with him to Lila's on Saturday mornings. She'd love him and hug on him and all, he loved Lila. 'Course he got to play with Driver too.

He looked over at Lila, sleeping now, nestled in the crook of his arm. Maybe he'd take 'em fishin' Saturday. He got a kick out of watchin' Driver fish. He was so damn uncoordinated. You'd never know where in hell his line was goin' to wind up. Besides, he'd talk so much he'd talk the fish out of takin' the bait. Even as young as he was, Boonie was patient, quiet. He could sit there out there on the river all day, just waitin'.

Pittisporum touched now with the scent of white jasmine and sweet yellow roses drifted through the open window on the river breeze. Across the river Somerset was lit like candles. Gently, without waking her, he slipped his arm from around her, crawled out of bed, rummaged around in the dark for his clothes, and slipped out the back door.

Finally, Elizabeth thought, and fell asleep.

6

The *New York Times* Stumbles into Action at Last

"What have you got for me, Rob?" asked Max Rubinoff, Rob's editor at the *New York Times.* "Sit down. Close the door."

"The Commandant's statement, Max. General Allen's, from the pentagon. That's about it."

"So: The Commandant of the U.S. Marine Corps is 'taking responsibility' for it, he's 'investigating' it, he's 'not limiting the investigation in any way, shape or form.' And on top of those juicy little nuggets, which he's given us before, 'The entire Marine Corps is on trial here.'"

"You read the same paper I did."

"Can you tell me what that means? Other than that he's taking responsibility for nothing? That there'll be no more info coming out until the investigation is concluded—which means he's waiting us out, counting on our moronic attention span and an influx of newsworthy disasters to swamp and bury this story?"

Settled in comfortably—pleasantly arranged, he felt, for the long haul—in the leather armchair across from Max's desk, Rob Vicker, although coincidentally in agreement with his boss, nodded quietly, earnestly, out of sheer habit as much as anything else. Max, however, was standing at the window gazing out over the Manhattan skyline, his back to him.

"Are you still here, Rob?"

"No, Sir."

"Where are you, Rob?"

"I'm in Shreveport, Louisiana; Harrison, West Virginia; and Addison, New Jersey."

"You're interviewing the families, the friends of these poor kids, their teachers, former scoutmasters, you're digging, Rob, you're pressing. But who is it you're really pressing, Rob? Is it these locals? Of course not. We're just having 'em talk, human interest stuff, right? But if their stories can put pressure on Allen . . ."

"Anything to keep the story alive."

"Shut up, Rob."

"Right."

"They're the only voices at present the victims have. Find out what they've got to say about 'em. Make 'em live again. Remember, it's Allen we're pressing. This story's going to be knocking on his office door until he's ready to come out with something to say. While you're down there, head over to South Carolina. Who knows? Maybe somebody down there's dyin' to talk. Goddammit, Vicker, what the hell are you still doing here?"

7

The *Times* Covers the Story, the C.O. Covers His Ass

Excerpts from the *New York Times,* May 7, 1960

" . . . Eighteen year old Riley Francis McGahee joined the Marine Corps March 25, a week after completing a course in radio mechanics at Shreveport Vocational High School in his home town of Shreveport, Louisiana. In a recent letter to his parents he wrote proudly of his accomplishments on the rifle range, where he scored 227 out of 250 points. Drill Sergeant McGowan, he wrote, had 'almost smiled.' McGahee wrote that he was 'very happy' to be a Marine . . ."

" . . . In Harrison, West Virginia, Mrs. Anna Leigh Pennebaker was in deep mourning for the death of her son, seventeen year old Woodrow ('Woody')

Edward Pennebaker, who had left Harrison High School a year early, pleading to join the Marines, he had told Mrs. Pennebaker, 'because I don't want to get in trouble like the other boys around here.'"

" . . . At over six feet tall and 200 pounds, he joined the Marines because the Army and Navy, he had insisted, would be 'too easy.'"

" . . . According to his fifteen year old brother Danny, Private James Patrick O'Hearn had tried two or three times to join the Marines. 'He kept taking tests, and he finally got in. It was the only thing he wanted to do, be a Marine.'"

"His mother and father, Mr. and Mrs. Daniel Timothy O'Hearn, remain unavailable for comment."

"Sad," thought the C.O., perusing the article. He knew these families. He had talked with each of them. Families destroyed, psychologically wiped out. For what? Why? For no reason.

A sad day for families. A sad day for the Marine Corps.

And it wasn't because it was bad P.R. for the Corps. On the face of it, it wasn't.

Though it could turn out that way, if Allen insisted on putting the Marine Corps, instead of Jack McGowan, on trial. Did he really think he could co-opt the press' investigation with the simple announcement that the Corps would investigate itself? That he would "take responsibility?" That by publicly calling into question the "entire Corps" the press would back off of their own explorations? And if they didn't, what would they find? Hazing? Physical punishment? Sure, that happens here and there. Hardly, however, a death march. He was making it look like there was more there than was there, on the one hand, and like he was covering his ass on the other. Either way he was throwing out shark bait. Though it also looked like the *Times* might not let him get away with it, at least not this Vicker fellow. Looks to me like he's saying to Allen here that if he thinks he's got a patent on this story, he's got another thing coming.

I'm a Marine, thought the C.O. Don't you drag me and my boys down into the muck and mire of that swamp with you, McGowan. One of us is crazy, you sad son of a bitch, and neither me nor my boys are the ones turnin' into a fruitcake every week at Lila's.

What do you do there?

What the hell were you doin' out there in that swamp?

How'd you fake it for so long? The highest rated drill instructor on the base. War hero. A man who risked his life to save his platoon. An unblemished record. An unblemished reputation.

Who were you out there, leading that death march?

Who are you?

Jesus, I feel bad for you, Jack. After all, for better or worse, you're one of my boys too.

Get to the fuckin' Truth, Levy. Help him.

That's all you gotta do.

| 8 |

Bert Continues to Treat Jack and Discovers They are Not Alone

May 8

Sergeant McGowan marched into my office, snapped to, and saluted smartly.

" . . . Stand at ease, Sergeant."

"Sir, Yes, Sir!"

"Have a seat."

"Sir, Yes, Sir!"

"Lie down."

"Sir, Yes, Sir!"

Stiff as a corpse, from the moment he walked in: snapping to, sitting, lying down, Sir, Yes Sir—Sir, Yes Sir—Sir, Yes Sir, all by the numbers. "Loosen up. Relax. Take your time."

McGowan allowed himself to exhale, loosening up his body a bit.

"Let your body go limp."

As soon as he began to relax, his body involuntarily jerked and shuddered, after which he lay at attention, once again stiff.

"Take a deep breath, Sergeant. Exhale slowly. Close your eyes."

Once again: the involuntary jerking, then shuddering, after which a repeat of the stiffness.

"One more time, Sergeant. You must be totally relaxed for feelings to emerge. Your body aches to feel, but as soon as it begins to do so, there's an automatic switch inside you that cuts it off. It stiffens you, deadens you. You think it keeps you in control, but in fact it shuts off all control, in the same way rigor mortis does. Don't feel badly if you can't do this right away. It's not as easy as it seems. This time, as you exhale and begin to relax, once again your body will react involuntarily, jerking and shuddering in the same way it just did. You're familiar with that now. You've twice experienced it. Let's go just a baby step farther."

McGowan nodded, stiffly, like a child in the doctor's office readying himself for the inevitable shot. He seemed much more malleable today. Despite the obvious pressure from the C.O.—he had given me free reign to schedule McGowan's sessions and interviews as I saw fit. At this point in his life, without me he was utterly alone, himself in his cell in the brig his only company. I couldn't help but think that a little time between sessions might disarm him a bit; that the enormity of his crime and the inevitability of his guilt and shame—"Oh God, what have I done?"—instead of playing brief calls on his affect, might pressure to move in, squatting, threatening to upend the lid on Pandora's box. Perhaps the pressure was so great that, at least for now, standing and fighting was not an option. Was retreat, in his mind now, falling into the hands of the enemy, or the arms of a friend? That uncertainty was enough to make him vulnerable.

"You'll close your eyes, exhale deeply, and let your body go limp. Afterwards, your body will once again convulse or shudder. This time, however, don't stiffen up and stop it. Let it continue, surrender to it, let it follow its own natural course. It's trying to tell us something. The stiffening is a retreat, a sign of fear. Do you understand?"

McGowan nodded. He did.

"It takes courage to listen to what may be frightening to hear. However, it will provide answers to your uncharacteristic negligence at Oyster Creek, and it will make you happier, in the long run, and give you a chance to put your life back together again. In short, you'll be able to live with yourself without fear."

"I never knew I was afraid, Sir."

"Were you? Are you?"

"I think so, Sir."

"Are you willing to try to listen to what you may be afraid of?"

He looked hesitant, for the first time, uncertain.

"Only for one minute," I suggested, "to start with. How's that?"

He nodded.

"Do you have a blanket, Sir?" he asked.

"You're cold?"

"Yes, Sir." He was almost stuttering. "I believe I am, Sir."

"Sure." I retrieved an army blanket I used for afternoon naps from the closet, though I certainly wouldn't need one this time of year. Outside the window men passed back and forth in short sleeves. It couldn't have been below 85 degrees.

By the time I laid it over him, his teeth were almost chattering. No fever. He was beginning.

"Close your eyes . . . totally relax, surrender your body and mind, give up all control . . . breathe deeply, exhale . . ."

His arm involuntarily lashed out, flailing, at some invisible threat, he shuddered, jerked . . .

"Stay with it now, I'm timing you, let's see what happens . . . one . . . two . . . three . . . four . . . that's it, breathe deeply, relax . . . I'm counting slowly . . . your body's surrendering . . . five . . . six . . ."

Was he falling asleep? I wasn't sure.

"No no noooo . . . please, please . . . I'm sorry, please . . . I'm so cold . . . please stop, please . . ." I could barely hear him. His voice was small, like a child's.

He was freezing. I piled on several blankets, arranging and pulling them close about him.

Was this a regression? The freezing a defense, albeit a weaker one than the prior stiffness?

Eventually he warmed up and, smiling with relief and gratitude, he wet his pants.

May 11

"Sir! Sergeant McGowan reporting as ordered, Sir!"

"At ease, Sergeant."

"Sir! Yes, Sir!"

"Lie down, Sergeant."

"Sir! Yes, Sir!"

"Will you need a blanket today, Sergeant? I'll be happy to get you one."

"Sir! No, Sir!"

"But you remember why you might need one . . ."

"Sir! No, Sir!"

He lay flat on his back, perfectly aligned, his eyes staring at the ceiling, his hands cupped at his sides, his feet turned out. Though prostrate, he was once again at full attention.

"Sergeant, I told you to be at ease."

"Sir! Yes, Sir! Begging the Captain's pardon, Sir!"

"Well?"

"Sir! Yes, Sir!"

"At ease, goddammit."

"Sir! I'm trying, Sir!"

"Trying, Sergeant? Trying? You're disobeying an order, Sergeant."

"Sir! Yes, Sir!"

"Do you know what happens to men who disobey orders, Sergeant, to men who aren't up to snuff, Sergeant, who can't suck it up, Sergeant?"

"Sir! Yes, Sir!"

"Do you know what such men are called, Sergeant?"

"Sir! Yes, Sir!"

"What are they called, Sergeant?"

"Scumbags, Sir! Worthless scumbags, Sir! Sissies! Pansies! Queers! Mama's Boys! Losers! Slobs! Incompetents! Do-nothings! Sons of bitches! Assholes! Crybabies! Crybabies! Crybabies! Crybabies! Crybabies! Crybabies—"

"And are you a crybaby, Sergeant?"

"Yes—No—Yes—No—Yes—No—No No No! Please, Captain don't make me do this Please . . . please . . . please . . . Sir! Yes Sir! Sir! No Sir! No Sir! Sir! Sir! Yes Sir! Sir! No! No! No! There. There. There. I'm all right Sir. I'm all right."

"That's right, Sergeant, you're doing fine. Who calmed you down?"

"Who. Who? Not me, not me. Oh no. Him, Him! That's not me. That's him. That's him. Okay, Sir? That's him, Oh yeah. Little fairy. Little worthless . . . aw, does the little pussy need a good cry? Do you, little pussy? Don't look at Mommy! Goddammit, turn your head. Look at me, son! What does Mommy think, Huh. Get the fuck away from him, you bitch, before I tear you in two. Move it, Bitch! Yeah, that's right. Move it! Now. . . . Now . . . now. What's the little pussy gonna do now, huh, now that little pussy's mommy ain't here to spoil him. Well, goddammit. What? What's the little pussy plannin' to do now? Huh? Tell me, you fuckin' thumb-suckin' little ass-kisser. Huh? What's the plan, mama's boy. Come here, you little . . ."

"NoNoNo . . . please . . . please . . . Now no Mommy . . . no Mommy . . . Mommy Nobody . . ."

"Cry it out, Sergeant. Cry it out. First time?"

"Him, Sir. He cries."

"Who? Who is 'him,' Sergeant?

Once again his arm lashed out, thrashing about wildly, uncontrollably. He looked around, frightened, terrified. "Sir, who am I?" He grabbed my sleeve. "Please don't leave me, Sir. Where am I?"

"You're with me, Sergeant, Captain Levy, in my office, where it's safe. He can't get you here. I'll protect you."

Slowly, very slowly, McGowan registered his surroundings, but the arm that had been lashing and thrashing about so wildly earlier would not let go of my sleeve.

May 15

"Sergeant, do you remember marching your platoon into Oyster Creek? In the report, it says you do."

"He remembers."

"Who is 'He?'"

"I don't know, Sir."

"Tell me who is 'he.'"

His arm again lashed out uncontrollably. He shook his head violently, warding off an invisible demon. He sat up, turned around on the sofa, and on his knees facing the wall; he began banging his head against it.

I placed my hand there, my palm cushioning the contact, where finally he let his head rest.

"It's okay, Sergeant. Tell me what you remember."

"Saving my mother. Trying to, over and over again, until I was exhausted. Back and forth, back and forth . . . I tried my best, Sir."

"Swimming, diving underwater, hauling her back and forth?"

His head shook involuntarily, like a dog that's been in the water shaking itself dry, suddenly alert.

"'Failed again. You worthless scum. Ha. You ain't worth shit, Boy.'"

"You're his dad? The drill sergeant?"

"I'm also a fuckin' war hero, you Jewish prick, and don't forget it."

"Well, hello. How are you?"

"He got no balls. Never has. I'll say it for him, Shrinko. It's killed or be killed. Shape up or go home to mommy. You got to do whatever it takes to make men out of boys. My son's too soft. I stepped in and did what was necessary for him. Too bad, but if you're training men to kill, it's split second: kill or be killed. Any distraction, and your buddy's going to get it in the gut. And believe me, Shrinko, that platoon was full of distractions. Those boys: collateral damage. The remainder'll be ready. In the long run, lives will be saved."

"And the one who saved as many as possible that night . . ."

"That was him. Do-gooder. I only step in when necessary. Just savin' him from his Momma. Always have."

"And the machine gunner, the loader, back in the war . . ."

"That was actually him too. He did pretty good there. Was proud of the little pussy. If his mamma had had her way, the boy would be somewhere writin' poetry or arrangin' bouquets. I made him a man."

"But how could a 'little pussy' have killed so brazenly?"

"You know what war heroes are made of, Shrinko?"

"What's that?"

"Hatred. All he had to do was picture his old man."

May 20

" . . . Okay, Sergeant, Let's go slowly here, safely . . . okay?"

McGowan nodded, stiffly but courageously; the motivation was there.

"Relax, I'll count slowly, just like we did before. Remember? Time-travel, go back as early as you can, as young as you can . . . see what images, feelings, memories come . . . one . . . two . . . that's it, close your eyes . . . three . . ."

His body was loosening up, again as if he were going to sleep, the most relaxed I'd seen him.

" . . . 4 . . . 5 . . . 6 . . . 7 . . ."

Suddenly the body, again as before, convulsed and shook violently, uncontrollably, the arm lashed out, again and again, his eyes flashed dangerously.

" . . . You gotta be shittin' me, Shrinko. You're worse than the kid's mama. You'll hurt him. You soften 'em up, they get hurt."

"Do you have a name?"

"Frank, Sir. Frank McGowan. I'm a killer, Sir. That's what I do. I serve my country and protect mama's boys like you. You are a mama's boy, aren't you? I know you, son. I know who you are. You're a smart boy. All brain, no brawn. Jew boy. Jew boys don't fight."

Ah, the old 'lambs to the slaughter' stereotype, never failed to rile me up. It's why I became a Marine in the first place, to punch the hell out of assholes like him. Yet it was not the bully but the coward inside him that compelled my attention, which is why I suppose I became a psychologist. "Given my druthers," I told him, "I'd rather talk."

"Ah, you're just a softie, like he is—"

"Jack?"

McGowan nodded. "You gotta fight it, toughen up. Hell, like anything else you gotta work at it. Overcome it."

"But how? I mean, especially when you're younger. What if you're just born that way?"

"Every fear can be overcome. You scared of rats? Eat 'em? Heights? Jump. Getting hit? Get hit. Hitting? Hit first. Water? Jump in."

"Is that what you did?"

"That's what the old man made me do, son. And if he hadn't I'd have ended up like you."

"He made you eat rats? Come on . . ."

"Served 'em up raw, son. Made me pick 'em up, put 'em on the plate, cut 'em up, and eat 'em till I could do it without pukin."

"But could you do it without puking?"

"Oh no, Oh no. I see what you're doin' here now. I ain't goin' there. Oh no, oh no, oh no."

"Let him out for one minute."

"Oh no."

May 25

"Hello, Sergeant, a blanket today?"

"I may need one, Sir. I'm fine now."

"You're Sergeant McGowan, Jack, who tried to save the men in your platoon from drowning at Oyster Creek?"

"I tried, Sir, but I failed."

"And who else did you try to save, Sergeant?"

"He is a cruel man, Sir. He should never have marched those boys into that creek in the first place. He knew what he was doing . . . No, no, no . . . No! Get away from me, you son of a bitch. Captain, please, help me out here. He's a killer. He killed my mother! I'm going to kill you, you son of a bitch, I'm going to kill you, Frank . . ."

He was lashing out again, thrashing wildly on the sofa. He banged his head on the wall, dangerously hard before I could get to him, wailing No, no, no . . . then he stopped, looked at what only he could see, reached out and strangled him, only to get confused, his hands going back to his own throat. Back and forth, back and forth, reaching out, strangling an invisible opponent, only to fall back, grabbing himself by the throat, choking himself, fighting off hands only he could see.

Two adults were fighting each other, and they were one and the same man, Frank and Jack McGowan. They were off the sofa now, on the floor, all over the room. They were even talking to each other. "You son of a bitch . . ." "Come and get me, Mama's boy." "I'll kill you . . ." " . . . You think pounding your head against the wall can get rid of me? You're so stupid, just like your Mama, you don't even know I'm in control here. You idiot, I've got you by the neck. It's me banging your head against the wall, you pussy, It's me killing you, yeah, just like I did Mama—"

Jack kicked Frank off him, screaming at the top of his lungs, and choked him until exhaustion, but when he rose and dusted himself off, returning to the sofa, the smile on his face was Frank's.

| 9 |

Bert Requests Emergency Procedures, Jack's Graffiti Reveals a Clue

To accelerate emergency procedures, I phoned the C.O., requesting him to order the staff officer at the brig to place Sergeant McGowan immediately upon his return under suicide watch in a padded cell.

"Will army mattresses do?" asked the C.O.

"As long as he's being watched carefully, and as long as he can't remove or somehow detach them from the wall."

"No problem. We've done this before. Why the sudden change?"

"He's making progress. To get better, you get worse. That's the nature of the psychological process."

"Speak English, Levy. Goddammit, if he kills himself, the Marine Corps will get blamed for that too."

"He's been running for a long time, Sir. Now he has to turn around and confront the enemy. That's terrifying, Sir, as you know, but even more so when the enemy is himself. Pogo's wisdom—'We have met the enemy, and he is us'—is at work in McGowan's psyche. At this point, Sir, the enemy is attacking, peace is not an option, not yet. Yet if he kills the enemy, he kills himself."

"At least the mattresses will cover all that graffiti on the walls."

"What graffiti?"

"McGowan's. 'Let me out. Let me out . . .' all over the walls. I'll tell you this. Your man's a fuckin' sociopath."

"What do you mean?"

"He says with a perfectly straight face it wasn't him who wrote it. Well, it had to be him. He's the only one who's been in the cell. And he's the only one with the motivation. Who else wants to get out of his cell if he's the only one in it? Casper the Friendly Ghost? Besides, what does he think: all you gotta do is ask? Hey, you know something strange? I mean, the guy has an education."

"Go on, Sir."

"The staff officer over there told me that it was written in a small child's hand, a kid in pre-school or kindergarten. He said he could barely distinguish it from his four-year-old's. Not only that, but 'out' was spelled 'uot.' And a few times the sentence is incomplete, as if he got distracted, just 'Let me,' or as if he got gagged in the middle, 'Let out.'"

| 10 |

The Boys Fish as Elizabeth Asks a Damn Good Question

"Now you look here. We downtown now, so stop all that yellin' and screamin' at each other."

"He keeps reachin' back and pinchin' me, Mama. It hurts."

"Stop it, Driver."

"She kickin' my seat. Her foot stickin' up my butt."

"Driver, look at me now."

Driver was sulking. "You always take her side."

"That's 'cause she a girl," piped up Elizabeth's friend Annie, in the back seat with her. "And girls is always right. Ain't that right, Mrs. Trulove?"

Lila parked her new Chevy station wagon in front of The Somerset Bank. She had enough money now where she could afford a new one every year. Not to be showy, she figured, but respect came in two ways: blatant honesty—there was power in that; it frightened people (the right ones, she hoped)—and money, or the appearance of it—for example, a new car every year. One she had, the other was sho' comin' her way.

Once she'd paid off Hoke, she'd headed straight to the bank, just as she always did, to make her deposit. She didn't want to lose a day's worth of interest.

Damn, she thought, emerging from her car, it's hot.

The windows were down, but she knew she'd better hurry 'fore the kids killed each other.

Sure enough, she made her deposit, then stood talking a minute with Mrs. Eileen Hunter, the principal of the black elementary school, on the front steps just to give the kids enough time to catch a glimpse of her and straighten themselves out before she returned to the car.

"Funny thing," said Mrs. Hunter to her, "when you stop to think about it."

"What's that, Eileen?" asked Lila, watching her kids killing each other out of the corner of her eye.

"White homes and restaurants, we enter through the back door. The bank, also owned by whites, we enter like they do, through the front door."

"Money talks."

"'The great equalizer', if you ask me, though Jefferson applied that particular phrase to the courts."

"How my kids doin'? They learnin'?"

Mrs. Hunter looked over at the fighting heap in Lila's car.

"Better than they doin' right now," she said.

When she dropped Driver off at the boat landing, which was right over the bridge near her house, Hoke and Boonie were waiting for him so they could go fishing.

"Now you be careful in that boat, Driver. Don't get all worked up and excited and start running around in that thing, you hear me."

But Driver was already out the door, running toward Boonie, who was helping his dad uncouple the boat from the trailer and slide it into the water. "Yes, ma'am," he yelled over his shoulder.

Driver'd been fishin' with them a hundred times, but he still didn't know what to do, so he urged them on while they did all the work, making suggestions here and there that Hoke did his best to take seriously and that Boonie mercifully rarely heard, so intent was he on helping his dad, organizing everything in the boat, checking the cooler, baiting hooks. Boonie had a knack for fishing, for all practical physical activity. Driver didn't. What he liked to do was read, talk, and run around all over the place doing nothing, going nowhere. Elizabeth pretty much summed it up when she said to no one in particular, "Don't know why he'd get all worked up and excited. He ain't never caught a fish in his life."

"It's like Mr. Cooley said," Lila answered, "Driver's in it for the social experience."

"Ain't supposed to talk while you fishin'," said Elizabeth. "Everybody knows that."

"Elizabeth," Lila said, waving at Hoke and Boonie as she drove off, "shut up."

But Elizabeth couldn't shut up. She tried, but the very sight of Hoke Cooley caused her to smolder with resentment.

Annie looked her way, then gazed out the window daydreaming. She didn't want to get in no trouble.

Back at Lila's house, Elizabeth and Annie ran back to Elizabeth's bedroom to play with her dolls. In her most tired voice, her patience clearly "tried," resigned to the inevitability of lifelong resentment, Elizabeth kept telling her doll Janie to shut up. "Shut up, shut up, shut up. You hear me, girl? Don't want to hear no mo'," after which it occurred to her that though her momma had heard enough from her for right now, that didn't mean she'd heard enough from Annie. Meanwhile, Annie dressed and primped the rest of the dolls, combing the knots out of their hair, readying them for school.

Lila stood in her living room and switched on the 12 o'clock news. John Kennedy and Fritz Hollings, the senator from South Carolina, were standing together on the steps of the Capital in Columbia smiling and waving at an enormous crowd. Them is two good-lookin' white men, she thought to herself. KENNEDY FOR PRESIDENT banners waving above the crowd made the two handsome young men now only partially visible.

"Mama?" said Elizabeth in the doorway. "Annie wants to know somethin'."

"I hear you, Honey."

"Is they eatin' dinner over here tonight?"

"They catchin' it right now," she said, cutting off the television. "So I reckon they are, which is why I'm headin' to the kitchen. Got to have somethin' to go with it."

"Is we gon' clean the fish?"

"Who else you think gon' do it?"

Elizabeth crossed her arms. "Mama?"

"Yeah, Honey," she said, tying her apron around her, looking for something she needed in the kitchen cabinet above the sink, tiptoeing.

"Annie want to know how come the men get to catch the fish, which is fun, and we got to clean 'em, which is nasty."

"Come here, Sweetie," she said, kneeling down, tousling her hair. "Give Mommy a kiss."

Elizabeth smiled, falling into her mother's arms.

"You go back and tell Annie that that's a damn good question."

"Hey Annie," Elizabeth yelled, running off happily to the bedroom, in which Annie was disciplining her dolls for fighting with each other.

"You do not," said Annie, pointing her finger at them, "hit each other."

"And don't say 'damn,'" Elizabeth heard her mama yell behind her.

"Guess what Mama said?"

"What?" asked Annie, looking up from her dolls.

"She said that was a d— good question."

Annie giggled, her hand over her mouth. "She said 'd—?"

"Yep," said Elizabeth, "she sho' did. She said it was a d—good question."

Annie was momentarily pensive. "What question?" she asked, puzzled.

That night they had a feast: fresh okra and tomatoes, corn, green beans, all right out of Lila's vegetable garden. The trout, Hoke said, was "exquisite." Surprised at his terminology, Lila asked him where he'd learned such a highfalutin' word.

"Yeah," giggled Driver, "where'd you learn such a highfountain word, Mr. Cooley?"

"Yeah Daddy," chorused Boonie, "Where'd you learn . . . What'd you call it?" he asked Driver. He couldn't help too but lapse into giggles, he and Driver falling all over each other. "Some butler on a television show," said the sheriff. "Sillytime is bedtime for you two boys. Don't you reckon, Lila?"

"All right, you boys got exactly five minutes to run around in the back catching fireflies, then it's bedtime. Elizabeth, you and Annie can watch one television show."

Alone at the table, Lila and Hoke both noticed that every morsel on every plate had been eaten, except for Elizabeth's. On her otherwise empty plate, between them, lay a lone trout.

| 11 |

Bert Escalates the War Between Jack and His Father

May 27

"I am going to try to help you let out the child inside you, Jack—the one pleading to get out, who needs his Mama, the one who Frank hurt so much you've spent your life locking him away—imprisoning him, if you will, inside you. We're not getting rid of Jack or Frank, but we want also to let out the child. There may be more than one. He's going to drive you crazy until you at least let him out in the prison yard. Say, for three minutes, after which I'll lock him back up myself. Fair enough? Then we won't have to go through the fighting, like we did last time, and the head banging. This little fellow wants to have his say, to come out. You don't want him out because of the pain he brings with him. When he starts climbing over the prison wall, Frank comes in to frighten him away. You want no part of

Frank either. He's also a reminder of your pain. That's when the fighting with him begins."

"Am I crazy, Doc?"

"Who are you now? Who's asking that question."

"I don't know." McGowan glanced about, terrified. "Who am I, Doc?"

He sat up.

"Who do you see?" I asked him.

He grabbed my hand, holding on tight, as if for dear life, squeezing so hard I thought my hand might break, but I didn't want to stop him. He was coming out now, the child inside him, the little boy shattered and broken by his father, Frank McGowan, the same Frank McGowan whose name was right in front of me on the first page of Jack's files, beside which it read "deceased."

The drums of the U.S. Marine Band beat quietly in a steady cadence from the far end of the island, faintly upbeat, determined, on the march. The drill team practiced almost directly outside my window. "Eyes right . . . Halt . . . Lower arms . . . Parade . . . rest! Hup, two, three, four . . . Hup, two, three, four . . . I don't know but I been told . . ."

"I don't know but I been told . . ."

Through the window sunlight bathed the island, the architecture of which was otherwise entirely noncommittal, all browns and grays, drab, nondescript. Bird shit crashed against the window screen. Horseflies were enormous. Mosquitoes in the early summer humidity strafed the bare necks of the drill team with impunity. Against a blue sky a formation of sea gulls swept over the island. Ibises occupied a small cluster of trees on the lagoon beyond the parade grounds. And always the odor of the marsh gas. To Somerset natives it was perfume, to me acrid and poisonous, the foul, vaporous breath of a monstrous rabid undertow.

It was as if Sergeant McGowan himself now had been caught up in some monster's grip or deadly undertow. He held on to my hand tight now, as if being pulled away, pulled under, by a terrifying force.

"What do you see? Can you tell me? Is it him?"

He whispered, "You won't tell?"

"Let him go!" I screamed at Frank McGowan. "I know you're in there. Come out and let's talk."

Again, a torturous writhing, jerking and convulsing of the body, almost throwing him off the sofa, after which an involuntary shudder. Then: a big wide-eyed grin: "I will if you will, Shrinko."

"When you let go, you'll disappear."

"That's right, Shrinko, but so will you. Then it's mano a mano."

"Let him out all the way, without holding on. Let him go."

"I don't know who you're talking about, Doc . . . Let's talk about something else."

"You're frightened, like a little girl. If you let him out, you're afraid you'll disappear. The big killer's afraid of pain."

The arm lashed out.

"Can I see Jack?"

"Let's talk cowardice first. Bravery. I could tear your ass in two. Go away, goddammit it. Go away." Again, the arm lashed out. "There."

"Who was that?"

"Nobody."

"Tell me who it was. I'll make sure you don't disappear."

"Sorry. Can't do that."

"Totally relax, Frank. You're under orders. Just relax. Surely you can handle that. I just want to see who's there, then I'll call you right back. Just tell me this: is it the child?"

"No, Sir."

"Ah, I hear a little more respect . . ."

"Okay, goddammit. No. No. Fuck you, Jack. You fuckin' . . ."

His facial muscles relaxed. He looked exhausted.

"Hey, Jack, how you feeling?"

"Like I've been whipsawed by a tornado."

"Keep going."

"There's a heaviness in my chest. My head's killing me. Something's happening inside me, Sir."

"Do you have the courage to let that happen? If not, Sergeant, Frank McGowan, given the opportunity, will kill again. Trust me, Sergeant, I want you to totally relax now. I'm counting slowly . . . one . . . two . . . three . . . you're totally relaxed now, open, free . . ."

He looked about, suddenly wide-eyed and terrified, grabbing my hand, as if to keep from falling.

"Sir, will I come back. Sir?"

"Absolutely, Sergeant, absolutely, anytime you want. Let him out, Sergeant. He's you, as a child. It's not right to keep him down. What's happening?"

"I'm falling . . . falling . . . falling . . . spinning . . . what's happening to me, Sir?"

"Go with it, Sergeant, stay with it, give up. Surrender, Sergeant. Do you understand? Surrender."

Stricken with terror, McGowan managed a nod.

He covered his eyes. "No . . . please . . . No Daddy . . . Mommy, please help me, Mommy . . . OH GOD."

"Tell me what's happening, I'm right here . . ."

His voice now was small, quiet, almost a whisper. "No, no, no, Daddy . . . please . . . I can't breathe . . . I'm afraid I'm going to die . . ."

"That's okay. Let yourself, it's okay . . . it's the only way you can resurrect yourself . . ."

"He's choking me. No No No." Once again, he was fighting off hands at his throat, barely able to breathe.

"I'll choke those goddamn mama's boy tears out of your pansy ass if that's what it takes. Tell me, is that what it'll take to dry 'em up. Men suck it up, Son. Act like a man. Goddammit, stop your fuckin' mewlin." And then the hiss of a reptile: "You hear me, Boy?"

Jack sat up straight, like a soldier at attention. Perfectly stoic, totally expressionless. "Sir! Yes, Sir! Sir, I do, Sir!"

12

Bert Contemplates the Photo of Jack's Wife Mary Beth

Two days later, on the afternoon of May 29th, McBride walked in and handed Captain Levy a Xeroxed copy of a photograph from the May 29th *New York Daily News*. A memo from the C.O.'s office, also dated May 29th, was attached to it with a paper clip.

The world, Bert concluded, was apparently closing in on McGowan. A photographer with a telescopic lens had gotten a picture of his wife through the window of her classroom, where she taught Business courses, at Tifton Community College in New Jersey. Clearly from the evidence of the photo she had had no awareness of it being taken. The photo was black and white. In it she appeared to be teaching with genuine verve, purpose, and passion. A business course? And her students, at least those visible on the front rows, appeared to be just as taken with her, or at least with whatever was in the air among them. She seemed to be leading a discussion rather than lecturing from behind a lectern, which stood behind her naked and unattended, an unnecessary appendage.

What, wondered Bert, was she saying? What questions might she be asking? What were her students saying?

By all appearances professional and conventional, slim, attractive, a model of propriety and decorum, her eyes, and those of her students, their air of thoughtfulness, their body language, betrayed something bolder and unconventional, something perhaps at least to them novel and daring, perhaps a surprising truth.

This Professor of Business Administration at a community college, married to a drill instructor, a non-commissioned officer in the Marine Corps . . . how had she aroused such clear interest, such curiosity? Bert felt this urgency to enter the photograph just to find out what the class was talking about.

Would her husband have been as interested?

Clearly, she was a catch: bright, pretty, committed.

Devoted too. She phoned and talked to Jack every night.

According to the C.O.'s memo, she insisted that jack *not* be informed of the photo. Any involvement on her part whether intentional or not would upset him unduly and she surmised, retard his progress. In any case, she asked that her wishes be respected.

Your call, said the C.O.'s memo.

An easy one, concluded Bert.

| 13 |

Bert Frees the Children and Exposes the Saboteur

May 30

"We're going to try to go back earlier today, Sergeant. I think it'll be less painful for you. Okay? I've got the blanket here if you need it. You might. We want to go back to before your dad began choking you, to as little and young as possible."

I began counting as he slowly, slowly began falling, spinning, once again, traveling back through time. "Go straight to the bottom, as young as possible. Skip everything that happens later, including the choking incidents."

He lay there quietly for a few minutes, his eyes closed. "Falling," he whispered. " . . . falling . . ."

"Yes. That's right. You're doing great, I'm right here."

"I'm at the bottom of a well . . . wait, there are two of me . . . it's hard to see . . . there's a lid on the well . . . it's very dark, but it's safe . . . the water tastes salty, this is where we hide her tears . . . we hold each other . . . please can we come out and play now . . . she yells 'Mommy' . . . I'm too scared to . . ."

"And does Mommy come?"

"Yes . . ." he nods.

"Go on."

"I'm in the bathtub. I'm playing with my boats. Mommy's playing with me. I'm splashing. Mommy lets me splash, but this time Daddy comes in and he starts screaming and yelling about the water all over the floor. 'Cleanliness is next to Godliness, you whore.' He shoves her out the way. 'Please, Frank, don't,' she says, but he slaps her and she falls against the toilet. Her eyes are closed. I think she's unconscious. I worry that she's dead. But she's not dead . . . she's not . . . He picks me up and I begin crying and that's when he chokes the tears out of me and then goes into the bedroom and throws away my dolls. That's when I left her."

"Left her?"

"Jacqueline. She played with dolls and cried tears when she hurt. We hid them in the well. That's why the water tasted salty."

"And you? What's your name?"

"My name is Jackie."

June 3

It was time, or almost time—I wasn't sure—to put Humpty Dumpty back together again, though he would remain vulnerable to fragmenting and falling apart. To survive a brutal father he had instinctively and involuntarily—subconsciously—compartmentalized his psyche, abandoning his open heart and childlike instincts—his capacity for joy and pain and tenderness—at the bottom of a well in the forms of Jackie and Jacqueline, only to emerge as Jack, hard as a rock, immune to pain and joy, a gung-ho Dudley-Do-Right living his life by the numbers. The compartmentalization of his personalities was evident also in his memory lapses, which psychologists call, in his case, blackouts. As the drill instructor, the man in charge, he could cover those lapses simply with the posture, which no subordinate dared question, that he was changing his orders. Or he could pin the blame on his men: "Maggot, that is not what I instructed. Are you questioning me, Maggot? If you are, Maggot, I have a latrine that needs cleaning. Are we clear, Maggot? Maggot!"

Frank McGowan, marching "Jack's" men to their deaths in the swamp at Oyster Creek, was finally who exposed him. Subconsciously, was that the result of a death wish, Frank McGowan's own, or was it a coup plotted—or at least exploited—from someone else on the inside?

If the latter, somebody else on the inside knew. And if that person knew, it was logical that he (or she) would remember everything about the death march into the swamp at Oyster Creek.

Of McGowan's various personalities, which one knew, if any, other than Frank, that a lethal drop-off and vicious current lay waiting to siphon off every last breath from three men who couldn't swim? Was it Jack, who hated Frank, who wanted finally to have him stopped at any cost? Did he simply watch and wait—doing nothing—as Frank finally crossed the line into blatant madness and crime? Perhaps Jack tolerated unusually flaccid discipline in his platoon to lure Frank over the edge, to bait him into insane action that would expose him, rendering him harmless forever. Jack said he didn't remember. Selective amnesia nevertheless did provide him a way out, psychologically if not legally. At this point, however, there was simply no evidence of guile in Jack's personality. His defensive fortifications didn't seem to allow for it.

Was it Jackie or Jacqueline, surfacing secretly from the well, exploiting an opportunity to rid themselves of Frank altogether?

Or was Humpty Dumpty still missing a part? Was there another personality? Was the real murderer, or the one who set it up, or at least one with prior knowledge who saw it coming and could have prevented it, still in hiding? Who had the motivation, the will, the deviousness? Always, I knew from experience, that Truth lay in that which was omitted, not in what was said but unsaid, in the mystery of the unexpressed, of the unanswered question, of the thread left hanging.

"Tell me, " I asked him, "about your mother."

"No," she said. It had to have been her, his mother. The voice, though feminine, was pitched low and quiet. She had sat up, and seemed to be knitting with an invisible needle and yarn. At one point she moved about the room, as if tidying and straightening things up. "No more. Frank's gone now, thank God. Jack's innocent. So are the children. I'll tell you about myself," she said, looking directly at me.

She had so quietly, so swiftly, so unobtrusively emerged, from nothing but Jack's warm, easy smile, a smile admittedly I had never seen before, one, which I imagined now, included a bit of Jackie and Jacqueline.

"You're a nice man, a gentle man. Neither the children nor Jack have ever known that."

"Thank you."

"I am the guilty party, the match which set off Frank McGowan. Always he had accused me of it. This time I really did it. I finished him off. He was right, you know. I did bring out the tenderness, the sensitivity; I suppose you'd call it, in the boy. A natural mother's instinct, I think. Perhaps Frank was right. Perhaps I overdid it. I certainly wasn't going to get it from Frank. He was too afraid."

"Afraid?"

"A fear, as he told you, beaten into him by his own father. I never knowingly tapped that fear—I myself was too afraid of him—until Jack got his new platoon."

"Why then?"

"Jack was starting to forget himself, to lose himself. Jack and Jackie had always been there, but with this platoon becoming more and more unruly, a naturally rambunctious bunch, Frank couldn't help but step in and reassert himself more and more. Jack was forgetting who he really was. His memory lapses were becoming, I was afraid, embarrassingly frequent. If people begin noticing . . . plus he hated being Frank, Frank wasn't really him, or who he wanted to be. Jack just wanted to do everything right. If I fought Frank directly and openly, he would win, as he always had. I became devious. It was easy. I hated the man. I was hardly even afraid of him anymore. In my heart he was dead long before he died. My son kept my heart alive. And I kept his alive, the only way I knew how, surreptitiously, secretively.

"I sent him to the prostitute, though for a woman's reasons, not a man's. I visited him in his dreams with fresh milk from my breasts. I stroked him tenderly. He so needed this; often he would immediately go into a swoon. In his dreams I told him stories, love stories, always love stories. I sang him gentle songs and as I softened him up, as his father would say, naturally he became softer with his new platoon until his father could stand it no more, stepping in over and over again with his brutal ways. My boy was not only his—but my—surrogate fighter. Unaware of his father's interference, pushed out of sight, he grew with my persistence even softer, more tender, more tolerant until his father, as I knew he would, exploded in flames, the shards and glass killing those poor boys unable to withstand them. Dr. Levy, I watched as my husband marched those boys into Oyster Creek. I drove him there through the softness, the sensitivity and the tenderness I gave to my son. I knew they couldn't swim. I knew my boy Jack would do his best to try and save them. In the end, I sacrificed those boys with mothers of their own for my son. Like Frank, I deserve to die. In all of his brutality Frank thought, as I did, that he was only protecting his son, he protected Jack from the world, I protected Jack from him."

"Will you testify in court?"

"Naturally, for the protection and freedom of my son. Dr. Levy, Jackie and Jacqueline are ready to grow up now. And Jack is ready to accept them."

June 15

Jack knew what to do now. He walked in, greeted me with a shy, polite smile, situated himself on the sofa, lying down, and relaxed on his own, his eyes closing. I didn't even need to count or give him instructions.

For now, he seemed comfortable with himself, anticipating what might come.

" . . . Where's Jacqueline, Jackie?"

He nodded agreeably, as if already awaiting their presence.

In what seemed almost like no time at all, I heard Jackie's voice. "She's right here."

"Is she separate from you, or a part of you?"

"She's inside me, but she can leave whenever she wants, like if I get frightened, or if I have to be a little man."

"She can leave you, or you can leave her?"

He thought for a minute. "I can leave her if Frank comes back."

"Like before?"

"That's right. He won't hit me as much."

"How does it make Jacqueline feel when you leave her?"

"She goes off and plays with her dolls."

"And how do you feel about that?"

"That's okay."

"And Jacqueline? How does she feel when you leave her? Can we ask her?"

"Just a minute," he said. Already in an altered state he seemed to relax even more. When his eyes opened, he was Jacqueline.

"Hi," she said.

"Jackie and I have been talking."

"I know."

"You heard?"

She nodded. "I was there."

"So how do you feel when Jackie leaves?"

"Okay."

"Okay?"

"As long as I know he's coming back."

"Will he?"

"Frank's gone."

"Does Jackie fully realize that, for now, Frank's gone?"

"He does, but he's still a little afraid."

"How do you feel about that?"

"Okay."

"Do you think it might be a good idea if you let him know it's okay to be afraid."

Her eyes closed. I waited, not privy to their conversation.

She opened her eyes, smiling, looking up at me. "He wants to come back now."

"Let him, and vice-versa. Jackie, if you agree with her, let her in all the way, or let her let you in, either way. As fully as you can this time: since Frank's gone, there's no more reason to be afraid. Is that right?"

"Frank's gone . . ."

"Again, the process is unpredictable. In one way or another, let your two personalities come together, get together, like you did in our last session, as one. Remember? That doesn't mean you'll never separate again; still, you'll be more 'together' . . ."

When people say, Get yourself together (I couldn't help but muse), Little do they know . . .

Clearly something was happening. "Ah . . ." he said. His eyes gradually opened. He smiled at me. "I'm Jackie Lynn," he said. "Jackie Lynn McGowan."

June 20

" . . . Jack, Jackie Lynn will move up in time and join you, becoming integral with you, making you more connected, if you will, less compartmentalized, or you may find yourself going back in time, getting younger, joining with Jackie Lynn, then getting older once again. First, is he inside you? Can you feel him?"

"They're inside me. They can talk to me, and I can talk to them. I can't let go though."

"Relax, totally, let's see what that is. Is it Frank? Has he returned? There are more memories to go through . . ."

"It's Mommy. She won't let go."

"She won't let go of you? Or you won't let go of her? She's no longer necessary now that Jacqueline is present as part of Jackie. Right?"

"I can't . . ."

"Totally relax now, keep your eyes closed. I'm going to hold your hand, replacing your mother's with mine. Take your time. And when you're ready, knowing that you have her inside you in Jacqueline, try to let your mother go. She's no longer needed, and she knows that. Ask her, if you like . . ."

He nodded. "Yes, I know. She knows. I'm holding on . . . I'm frightened . . . he might return . . ."

"Yes, but now a fully mature grownup will be ready for him. Okay? As I squeeze your hand, try to let her go. I won't let go myself until you tell me you're ready. Okay? Do you trust me?"

Jack began to cry.

"That's good, Jack. A man is crying now. Bleed the wound. Cry it all out. Don't stop . . . keep going . . . you have her inside you, that's why you can cry, she'll always be there, her legacy is the girl inside you your father forced you to abandon, you don't need Mommy now, you're ready to grow up . . ."

Slowly, very slowly, his weeping subsided, and he begin to let go of my hand. He was embracing himself now, breathing deeply, exhaling . . . breathing in . . . seemingly expanding . . .

"I'm holding Jackie Lynn."

"Does he like that?"

"Yes."

"And you? Do you like that?"

He began crying again, only this time happily.

"Let him grow inside you now until he fills you up. Or you inhabit him and grow older that way, as him."

After a few minutes, he opened his eyes. "I'm me," he said.

"Where's Jackie Lynn?"

"Inside me. He's me. I'm him."

"How old do you feel?"

"Jack's age. I'm Jack, but it's a different Jack . . ."

"More connected?"

"I'm one person, it feels like."

"How do you feel about Frank?"

"I can handle him."

"Good," I said. "Now we're ready to begin. Let him in. Accept him as a part of you. Be totally vulnerable to him. He is the murderer, the savage inside you—the murderer, in fact in all of us. Fully accepting and absorbing him, feeling his feelings, is the only way they'll subside, let you alone, leave you in peace. Good feelings—joy, for example—don't last because we feel and experience them, if we trust them, because they feel good. Painful feelings—fear, guilt, shame, rage—relentlessly stalk us, in one way or another, to the degree we spurn them. You've got to accept and feel those feelings now, your feelings, what you have been calling his feelings. It's the only way to appease them, the only way to tame him, to make peace with him, to make peace with yourself. You are his legacy as much as you are your mother's. Fighting him, denying him, frightens him, makes him have to prove himself; desperate, he becomes stronger, more and more out of control. You're strong enough now, Jack. You can do this. You can recognize and acknowledge his legacy in yourself. Otherwise he'll never leave you alone, not entirely. Already he's much weaker. Can you feel that?"

"I can handle him."

"Can you accept him?"

"I have to."

"Only then will you be able to let him go."

"It's going to hurt. I'm frightened. You won't leave?"

"No, I won't. But you're aware you'll have to go through it all again. The memories, the most gruesome ones, will haunt you until you go through them and accept them. If not, they'll keep you apart from yourself, certainly from Jackie Lynn. You cried tears of pain today, but also tears of joy. Are you ready? Let's begin . . ."

"Hold my hand."

"I've got you, Jack, and I'm not letting go."

"Bert?" he said.

"Yes?"

"Thank you."

"You're welcome, Jack. Now totally relax. You'll feel these memories physically as well as emotionally. If it helps, describe them as you feel them. Once again, you're a little boy now, before Jack and Jacqueline split off, when you were one child . . . one . . . two . . . three . . ."

His father stormed into his heart, over and over and over again, session after session after session, oblivious to the flora and fauna wilting in the dog days of summer, the September tans of young and pretty Marine wives, Fall's yellow cassia and exploding Japanese maples. Drunken blows, wild rages, broken bones, bruises covered over the next day with makeup and the right clothes. Scumbag, mama's boy, pansy, worthless piece of shit, fuckin' little girl, crybaby . . . the lies to his teachers at school, the cover-ups . . . wave after wave after wave of pain and brutality.

About the time Christmas lights began flashing gaudily and happily across the bay in downtown Somerset, the mattresses were taken off the walls of McGowan's cell. Where each of his therapy sessions had almost always consumed several hours (the inevitably tedious details and lengthy sustained silences, some profitable, some not, of which I have tried to spare you), they were now reduced to the conventional fifty minute slots once or twice weekly, mostly when a residual painful memory caused him to re-dissociate (as would probably happen on and off for the rest of his life).

Though the pain of his childhood memories would lessen, his guilt and shame over the deaths of the three young men in his charge—Riley Francis McGahee, Woodward "Woody" Edward Pennebaker, James Patrick O'Hearn—would at least for a time intensify, inspiring within him not homicidal but suicidal tendencies. McGahee, Pennebaker, and O'Hearn, boys really, deprived of manhood: McGahee a marksmen who had almost made him smile, Pennebaker who told his mom he joined the Marines to stay out of trouble, O'Hearn who had already fulfilled his ambition just by becoming a Marine—they would reach out to him time after time from the same swirling hellhole into which over and over again they would disappear, from which would emerge in a fiery tableaux writhing in the black flames of a living Hell, Mrs. Kathryn Robertson McGahee, Mrs. Anna Leigh Pennebaker, and Mrs. Eleanor Turner O'Hearn, reaching out not to Drill Sergeant Jack McGowan but to an invisible God cold and pitiless in His absence.

The pain of fathers, at this point, was naturally beyond Jack McGowan's imagination.

"The C.O., Sir, on line 2."

"Good morning, Sir. Merry Christmas."

"You're to meet with the lawyer Murray Gold at his office in Somerset first thing in the morning. The boys over in Somerset say he's the sharpest knife in the lowcountry. Young fellow, like you."

"A civilian?"

"Not unusual in a high-profile case like this one's sure to be."

"Yes sir. Absolutely. But Sir—"

"Tomorrow's Christmas?"

"Yes Sir."

"His name's 'Gold,' Son, just like yours is 'Levy.' You'll make yourself totally available to him for the next six months, then throughout the trial. Am I clear?"

Part II

SUMMER 1961

14

Driver Worries About Everything from Alligators to Communists

'Cause his daddy was at the court house and Mama was workin', me and Boonie spent most of the first day of the trial of Sergeant McGowan runnin' around outside on the courthouse lawn and swimmin' off the dock across the street in the Somerset River. I'd be Huck Finn and he'd be Tom Sawyer in that book Mama was reading to us and the dock was our raft, only it wouldn't go nowhere less we pretended, which could only carry you far as boredom. Boredom's where we'd dive off and leave the raft behind, though not too far. We was too scared. We told each other we was scared because we knew if we did venture too far out my momma would burn my backside and Boonie's daddy would tan his hide, which was true, but truth be told we was scared anyway. What if you swam way, way out, and couldn't get back? Wadn't no pretend raft gonna bring you back what I told Boonie. And he said "yeah, and no shark gonna swallow you whole then spit you back up the same way on the riverbank neither," which made me hug that raft like she was my momma for longer'n I care admitting.

During a break in the trial his daddy and Mr. Marty Liebowitz, the chairman of the Board of Education, was standin' on the seawall gettin' cool under the shade of a great oak on the riverbank, waitin' for us to come out of the water so we could get fifteen cents to go to the store and get a Coca-Cola and some peanuts. Boonie's mama wouldn't let him get no candy so I knew I wouldn't either, even though Boonie had told me I could 'cause it was his daddy give us the money. Mama had told me the polite way to do things, particular around white folks. Well anyway, me and Tom, we beach the raft, jump off onto the riverbank, and by the time we run up drippin' wet to his daddy I be Driver and he be Boonie again, Boonie holdin' out his hand for the money. His daddy give us each fifteen cents, a dime and a nickel, then he rub my head, chucklin' a bit, and said, "Burrhead, wouldn't it be a bit more appropriate if you was Nigger Jim?"

He winked over at Boonie, who was forcin' a smile for his daddy, but who looked underneath it like he really didn't know the proper thing to do with his face, and at Mr. Liebowitz, who said to me, "Well, Burrhead, Nigger Jim was one smart Colored boy, I'll tell you that. Nothin' wrong with aspirin' to that."

I didn't want to be Nigger Jim, that's why I was Huck Finn, but Mama had told me never to argue with white folks. If they white, she say, they right. That's just the way it is.

Besides, I wanted to know what "aspirin'" meant, so I asked Mr. Liebowitz, and then ran off to catch up with Boonie.

The trial of Sergeant McGowan, Boonie's daddy had told him, was a military trial which had been transferred from the Lawton Island Military Base to the Somerset County courthouse to accommodate all of the out-of-towners: reporters all the way from New York City—the largest city in the world, Mama had told me—curiosity-seekers, Marine observers, parents from as far away as up North whose sons had drowned that night in Oyster Creek over a year ago. Even the Somerset County courthouse wasn't big enough to fit everybody in, Boonie's daddy had told him. Mama said she didn't know nothin' about it and didn't want to know nothin' about it, that Boonie's dad didn't know that much about it either, he was just down there to act like a big shot and keep order.

Well, he acted like he knew what was goin' on. He and the C.O. of the Base and the chairman of the Town Council and Mayor Harper Dawes and the editor of the *Somerset Weekly*, they all acted like they knew what was goin' on, like they owned the place, like it was their trial and they were just lettin' these uniformed officers with their briefcases run it for them.

Were they?

Strange men in suits—men never before seen in Somerset—their hat brims shadowing their foreheads, milled about seriously on the courthouse steps, all business. One checked his watch, then glanced over and perused another's note pad.

"Reckon they're Communists?" Boonie whispered in my ear.

Me and Boonie, we was scared to death of Communists too—we was scared to death of just about everything, now that I think about it, least I was—like they was sex perverts or somethin' that would jump out of the shrubbery and do who-knows-what to you. We were scareder of Communists than Indians or outlaws or even ghosts.

One time I was Roy Rogers and he was Gene Autrey and we was ridin' around the back yard on Trigger and Thunder, which Mama had given us after the broom thistles had outlived their resilience, when we decided it was time to settle in for a spell, maybe stop in at the saloon or head back to the campsite and hustle us up some grub, wash up in the creek, and refill the canteens. It was gettin' late. Already we'd saved the wagon train. Since the only good Injun was a dead Injun—so said every cowboy in every Saturday afternoon Western we'd ever seen—Indian corpses lay strewn all over the yard. One was moving, clearly wounded, but with just enough left to reach for his tomahawk on the ground next to him. Gene was out of bullets. I knew I had one left. The Savage rose up on his knees, aimed the tomahawk at Gene, when I pugged him right between the eyes.

"Owe you one," said Gene.

" . . . would've done the same for me were it the other way around."

After that, for some reason, we shot and killed each other about ten times, even though we were out of bullets.

Finally, we reined in, holstered our cap pistols, pushed our cowboy hats back on our heads, and I asked Boonie whether he'd rather be captured by a communist or eaten by a shark and he said he'd rather be eaten by a shark 'cause his daddy had told him nothin' was as bad as Communism, that it was "Godless," and if you had anything to do with them, anything at all, any 'sociation whatsoever, you would not only be tortured to death in life but burn in Hell forever after.

"Forever after?"

"Yep," said Boonie. "Forever after."

"Even after you dead?" The need for absolute certainty here stalked me like the Devil hisself.

"Least after you get eaten by a shark you can go to Heaven for your just reward."

Just reward . . . burn in Hell . . . forever after, I knew, had come straight from the mouth of the preacher, into his daddy's, then out of Boonie's.

Me, wadn't nobody to give it all to. I had to swallow it. Wadn't no raft in the backyard to hang onto for dear life. Wadn't no air raid whistle tellin' us to hide under our desks because we wadn't at school.

I eyed the river: Was that a buoy far out? Or was it the periscope of a submarine?

Boonie eyed the shrubbery, but he looked like it was the shrubbery eyeing him.

"You thinkin' what I'm thinkin'?" he asked.

"You bet I am," I said, and so was Trigger, jumping and neighing and straining at the bit.

"Vamoose," he yelled.

"Let's ride!"

Darned if we didn't hightail it right out of there.

Boonie didn't say much, but when he did he always had the right word—in this case vamoose— for the occasion.

Anyway, that's what his mama had told him.

We weren't about to be sitting ducks so whenever we did happen on any communists, we were pretty stealthy, the way Boonie's dad had to be, he'd told us, going after bootleggers. We'd hide behind shrubbery—azaleas, cameilas, legustrum, we weren't particular—and spy on 'em, like J. Edgar Hoover in *The F.B.I. Story,* by J. Edgar Hoover.

We knew what Communists looked like 'cause we'd seen pictures of 'em in *The F.B.I. Story*, no doubt put there by J. Edgar Hoover himself so ordinary people like us could identify and shoot 'em on sight. Any unfamiliar face in a business suit could be one. They looked just like Americans. After all, they were spies. They were supposed to.

J. Edgar Hoover was Boonie's dad's hero, Boonie had said. His dad had read two books, Boonie had said proudly, tryin' to sound just like him, *The F.B.I. Story* by J. Edgar Hoover and the King James version of the Bible.

Boonie's dad had told him once that when he was in Dr. Cohen's office with his sleeve rolled up, watchin' Doc load up a syringe, Dr. Cohen had informed him that when he was reading the Christian Bible it so happened that he was also reading the Jewish Bible, since the Old Testament came from the Jews.

What'd you say to that? Boonie had asked his dad, thinkin' to himself naturally that were he in his dad's shoes his regard for Doc's people would have risen proportionately with the length of that needle.

Nothin' wrong with Jews, his dad had told Boonie. God's chosen, even if they can be a little tight . . . good family people, shrewd businessmen, he admired that. Still, he'd said, then come up short, like you do when you're caught up in the middle of the intersection on Ribaut Road and Boundary Street and suddenly you forget whether you're supposed to turn right or left. Happened with his momma all the time, Boonie'd explained. Anyway, that's what it had seemed like to him. His dad, however, as Boonie would momentarily realize, was seeing himself more as the little league umpire, or as Boonie saw it, "empire," over at the Basil Green Baseball Field with a Saturday afternoon storm threatening. Though in Boonie's mind still stalled at the intersection, his dad in his own mind has called timeout, taken off his mask, and is staring up at the dark clouds gathering in the sky, contemplating not what he did say to Doc Cohen but what he might have said were truth to have prevailed over tact. Finally, with Boonie silently urging him on through the force of sheer concentration—turn left, turn right, who cares? Answer the question—after what Boonie had felt was head-scratching deliberation his dad, in his own words, was ready. Ready for what? Ready to answer the question. Ready to "call the game, lock up the equipment, head on home," at which point naturally Boonie, still stuck at the intersection, had to jump out of the car to join his father at the ball field so he could hear him Call It As He Saw It.

And this is how he saw it: The only difference, he confided to Boonie, between a Jew and a white person is religion.

"Game over," Boonie'd said.

"Everybody went home?"

Boonie'd looked a little puzzled for a minute or so, like maybe he'd found himself stuck at the intersection again. But before I could say, "Jump out the car" he was up and running.

"Ate supper," he'd said, "cut off the lights, and went to bed."

The reporter Rob Vicker from a paper called the *New York Times* was a Communist. Boonie and me knew that because if he was a reporter for the *New York Times*, then that meant he lived in New York, just like the reporters for the *Somerset Weekly* lived in Somerset. And Boonie's dad had told him that everybody who lived in New York was Communist.

New York, said Boonie, was Communist country.

Boonie and I were wondering the same thing. I know because he told me.

The strangers on the courthouse steps . . . were they from New York?

15

Murray Recalls Showing Bert the Town

Murray Gold, attorney for Drill Sergeant Jack McGowan, arrived in court early, as always, shaking hands, greeting people, chatting with the cops and the clerk, allowing himself time at the defense table to review his questions, his case, and to sit alone with his thoughts. Justice for Jack McGowan depended solely on the testimony of Dr. Bert Levy.

He had gotten to know Levy, even taken him to the synagogue.

Officers, particularly Northerners like Levy, often ignore Somerset as if it's some decrepit little halitosis-ridden, rube-run Southern backwater, the general run of the denizens of whom chew with their gums, shoot Negroes in their spare time, and stew Canebrake rattlers for supper.

The Jews of Somerset, however, elude the stereotype. Most Yankees don't even know we're here, Murray realized. Who are we? Levy was curious.

Hell, Murray'd told him, his granddaddy, dodging the draft in Russia, hailed from the same village as the Jewish writer Issac Babel. He was on embarrassingly familiar terms with the Jewish mafia Babel wrote about. The Jewish mafia in Odessa actually did his granddaddy the favor of cutting off what we call in America his "trigger finger" to keep him out of the army. That was the standard practice among the Jews of Russia since the Russian army at the time routinely took pleasure in choking Jewish soldiers on pork or throwing them in the Dnieper River and watching them drown for Sunday afternoon sport. Though Murray had gleaned this latter information from the great Russian writer Gogol in undergraduate school, his granddaddy had confirmed it. His great-uncle Herman Gold, he'd said, in deference to his finger as well as his life had fled the Pale of Settlement in 1897, which he also told Levy. Why? To further bestow upon the Jews of Somerset a tribal relevance that in Levy's mind they might not otherwise have had.

It was difficult, Murray could tell, for Levy to reconcile a Jew with segregated water fountains, segregated bathrooms and a Southern accent. Murray tried to explain to him, somewhat defensively, he realized, that being Southern made them no less Jewish. You have an organ in your synagogue, Levy pointed out, not without a certain glee (or was it utter fascination?). Well, that's because the Episcopalians do, Murray responded, and immediately recognized what Levy must have thought about that. Murray couldn't stop himself. It's a matter of geography, he explained. At the turn of the century, upon arriving at Ellis Island, the Jews checked out the east side of New York. No room there. Too many Jews already. The place was teeming. So they headed down the East coast until they could find a spot, literally, to peddle their wares, to later make enough to open their own places of business. By the time his granddaddy got down this way, both Charleston and Savannah had no more room for Jewish peddlers. The logical spot between them: Somerset. Hell, did Levy realize two of the oldest synagogues in America were Charleston's and Savannah's, one just up the road, one just down it? Why no, Levy said, he had had no idea.

But the truth, Murray soon realized, was that Levy probably didn't much give a damn who in the hell they were. Like Murray himself, like just about everyone who lived here or visited, Levy seemed infatuated with Somerset itself, the thousand-year-old great oaks heralded and garlanded with Spanish moss, sages graced with natural impartiality, inhuman objectivity and eternal silence, gods of unsurpassable strength and beauty presiding over their own shaded, sun-dappled kingdoms, over the luxuriantly green, sun-swathed gold of the riverbank, Eden rambunctious with yellow daisies, purple wildflowers, wild white margaritas, red ginger, miniature fanlike palms, Eden festooned with azaleas green, sunlit, and game but for whom clearly the seasonal party was over. Fragrant verandahs, fronting antebellum homes, reigning over plantation lawns, overlooking all: the magisterial oaks and the Spanish moss; the sunwashed-green, Glory-to-God birthday colors of the riverbank, Jubilation in bloom, an explosion of fireworks; virgin-white sails, a settled barge, a shrimp boat heading out, a great blue heron locals referred to as Lord of the Sandbar, the subtle, mesmerizing shifts in the time-changing, mood-altering hues and colors of the marsh grass and the river, the Somerset River Bridge and the barrier islands to the east, and the twilight promise of a Western sunset so intoxicating and hallucinatory as to cause fainting spells, it was said, among the gentler of our ladies, whoever they might have been; a characterization, Murray told Levy, as perhaps apocryphal as the promise of such a sunset itself. If you looked closely at the exterior of the antebellum homes, at the molding and cornices of the verandahs, in the eaves and gables of the upper stories, you could see sporadically dry tongues of paint peeling, miniature hangovers from the relentless summer humidity. Gardenia and honeysuckle and residual wisteria scented the river breeze, mixing with the stink of pluff mud and the salt air from the ocean just beyond the barrier islands, giving it just the right amount of bite. Levy couldn't seem to get enough of it.

Murray never could, he confided to Levy. When he breathed it in, he felt like he was breathing in the whole world, his world. He never wanted to be anywhere else, only here. That was what interested him, inspired him, called out to him and sang to him. Not fishing, not hunting, but the waters themselves in which the Gentiles fished, the woods where they hunted, sunlight and blue sky, grandiloquent homes, modest neighborhoods, tarpaper shacks. Somerset itself, the place in which he lived: his home. Yes, his home. And while he knew not only the names but the character and temperament of every single person in town, all the families, black, white, and Jewish, where they lived and worked and played, he was surprised to find out that when his Aunt Rosie, visiting from Atlanta, asked him for street directions he didn't know their names. Like every other local, he'd never had to learn them.

Lanny's Crab Shack? Turn right a few blocks past Bobby's Esso. You know where that is . . . take a left at the light, just a few blocks down, can't miss it. Only half a block or so from LaVerne and Tommy's place. You want the short way or the long way? Long way might be easier. In that case . . .

Lucy's Spit and Polish? Just head downtown. Two blocks off main street, you'll see Ray's truck out front, always hangin' around there in the back.

Later, once they'd gotten to know each other, Bert would confess that this inevitably drove him crazy. He knew every street name in Manhattan. Yet here in tiny Somerset he had to know where Bobby's Esso and LaVerne and Tommy's place was was in order to find Lanny's Crab Shack? What truck Ray drove in order to find Lucy's Spit and Polish?

Walking through Somerset after lunch downtown in the early afternoons, pointing out on the one hand the Old Slave Quarters (now rented out by the rooms for $55 a month) and on the other the divinely-inspired (yet legally-segregated) St. Helena Episcopal Church, observing the light filtering through the leaves of the great oaks and Spanish moss onto the cool shaded cemeteries, registering the cobblestone streets, Murray began, as always in these situations, seeing it anew himself. Sunlight browsed among the palm fronds on the Bay and on side streets and in interior gardens turned Cherry poplars into blossoming gold. Even the tiny white churches in the Negro slums stood out like clean, well-scrubbed children. Evinrudes gleamed in driveways. Station wagons waited for the kids to pile in. Kids played baseball in the streets, only to stand politely aside if a car hummed through. Harper Dawes' '57 two-toned, fin-tailed Plymouth, which everybody knew he'd rarely drive since he walked to the office every day, looked as if it had outgrown his garage, the tailfins sticking out so far the garage door wouldn't close.

Some things were constant: the 12 o'clock whistle, lunch the big meal of the day, leftovers for supper; Dacus the drunken taxicab driver, the only one in town, careening and maneuvering his banged-up taxi about town as if it were a bumper car. People pretty much knew to stay out of the way. It was quite a spectacle. The kids would place bets on what he was likely to hit next. Gave 'em something to do, Murray supposed. At low tide you could see the rear end of his previous cab jutting out from the marsh. At high tide the kids would dive down there looking for treasure as if it were a sunken ship.

You knew too that right around 2:00 p.m. Mrs. Overbeck would head down North Street, take a left on Ribaut Road only to drive as slowly as humanly possible, lowering her windows regardless of the weather, joined now by housewives, grandmothers, and elderly spinsters as they drifted out as if in a neighborhood trance onto their verandahs and front porches with iced tea, Chopin nocturnes pouring and swirling like bright yellow butterflies from Murray's mother's open windows and billowing curtains, after which Mrs. Overbeck would circle back down Bay Street to do to her grocery shopping at the A&P as the last butterfly drifted away and his mother, who did not own a television, would rise from her piano stool as the neighborhood women rose from their wicker chairs, returning to their chores as she did to hers, their letter-writing, or their soap operas. No one asked Murray's mother for monetary donations to local charities, but everybody asked her to raise money with her playing. Should he mention to Bert that she raises money annually for Israel? The United Jewish Appeal? The Jewish Community Center in Charleston?

The beer guy and the bread man were constants, as were their easy, boisterous jokes, their trucks making their rounds from one grocery store to another, summertime kids hanging off fenders screaming at the top of their lungs and waving like crazy and lording it over passersby, most of whom happened to be their buddies standing enviously on the sidelines; next stop, a new set of kids, and on and on from one neighborhood to the next. And in summertime, the ice cream man would bring the peal of children's laughter with the ringing of his bell.

No one walked by without saying "hello" or "how are you?" or "tell the family hello" or "when you coming to see us?" Amazing, Bert had said, grinning. He had even joined in: "Hi, how are you?" "Hello." "Good afternoon." Murray didn't mention his mother's fund-raising concerts for Jewish causes. On one hand, incomprehensible as it might seem, he wasn't any longer at all certain Bert was interested in Jewish causes. On the other, Levy being a New Yorker and all—you know, used to bigger stuff, what they call around here big-time, the New York Philharmonic, things like that—he might find such events, for want of a better phrase, small-time. Murray did prattle on pompously a bit about "local concerted efforts" to raise money for Jewish causes, keeping it general and safe, but hell, that would have bored anybody. It even bored him, now that he thought about it. Besides, Levy seemed infinitely more infatuated with Somerset than with Somerset Jews. And him a Jew!

Why do I somehow feel less Jewish, Murray wondered, not quite up to Jewish snuff, when I hear a Jew with a Northern accent? Always have, he supposed, even at Camp Sabra when he was a boy. He wasn't about to admit to Levy, who whatever he might have been was nevertheless a "real Jew," a "New York Jew," the nervousness of the Jewish community here about his taking this case. They preferred a low profile, a preference, in Murray's own Jewish opinion, against their nature. Hell, the C.O. wanted a civilian lawyer. Though military lawyers were reputedly less competent than their civilian counterparts, the C.O. knew that in a high-profile case such as this one, the Pentagon would send in only its best prosecution team, and its best, the C.O. also realized, was top-flight. It was in the Marine Corps' best interest, he felt, and so told the mayor, that McGowan have a smart lawyer. So the mayor and Hoke showed up on Murray's doorstep on a Sunday morning and asked him.

For smarts, Murray's mother used to say, they always go to the Jews.

For smarts, Murray scoffed once he became a lawyer, prepare.

"All rise," ordered the Sergeant-at-Arms as the judges entered the courtroom.

| 16 |

Bert Takes the Stand

"Dr. Bertram Levy to the stand."

"Raise your right hand, Sir, place your left on the Bible. Do you swear to tell the truth, the whole truth, and nothing but the truth under penalty of perjury so help you God?"

"I do, Sir."

"Witness may be seated."

Murray Gold knew what Levy was going to say. Like any good lawyer, he had already interviewed him privately; Murray didn't want to be put in the position of asking Levy a question, once he was on the stand, that he didn't already know the answer to. How to make his psychological smorgasbord of a defense of Jack McGowan palatable to a general public? This might be a three-judge military tribunal, but it was a political trial. If unpalatable to the public, it would be unpalatable to the court. Besides, Murray Gold was a Somerset lawyer, and this trial mattered to Somerset.

Murray had rehearsed Levy carefully. No jargon, Murray had stressed. Stay simple. Tell a story a man on the street can understand. If we can't make the case that McGowan was at least temporarily insane, then the Corps will need to set an example, assuring the public that what he did that night in Oyster Creek was nevertheless aberrant, so alien to standard disciplinary procedures and practices, so shocking and unacceptable to the Corps itself as to be criminal, assuring them of the seriousness with which it was taking this so that it could never happen again.

"Dr. Levy, you are the Chief Psychological Officer at Lawton Island?"

"Yes, Sir."

"You are the consulting psychologist for the defendant in the case in question?"

"I am."

"You have treated him and diagnosed his condition?"

"I have, Sir."

"And what is your diagnosis?"

"Sergeant McGowan suffers from a multiple personality disorder, the result of extreme dissociation caused by childhood trauma."

"Could you explain the diagnosis and the relevance of the diagnosis to the case in question?"

Already light bulbs from cameras were flashing. Reporters from all over the country stood in the back, note pads at the ready, milling around the three pay phones. Fans hummed overhead, and a floor fan was turned toward the jury, but the air circulating through the open windows off the river was hot and heavy, drenched in humidity. McGowan had testified that he had ordered his platoon into the swamp aware that the three men who drowned couldn't swim. He was guilty, he readily confessed, and ready for whatever penalty the court ordered. However, he couldn't remember doing it. He remembered diving in and out of the swamp in desperate attempts to save the men. He remembered afterwards crying out on the bank of the creek, "Oh God, what have I done?" He couldn't remember, however, doing it. How in the hell, wondered the reporters, was his psychologist going to explain that? How would the explanation, Murray knew they were wondering, affect the case? Would it even matter, they further wondered, since all the surviving members of the platoon, all of whom liked, respected and admired McGowan, remembered him giving the order and marching them into the swamp with rifles and full gear in shoulder-deep water. His men even believed his expressed motive, to "instill discipline," was sincere. Was McGowan lying? In denial? How could he remember everything else down to the last detail, take responsibility for the death march, and not remember ordering it and leading his men further and further out into the creek?

Was McGowan crazy? They wondered. He didn't look like he was crazy.

Murray'd never seen so many people packed into the Somerset County courthouse at one time. Hoke had had his boys bring extra chairs from the high school lunchroom.

"Sergeant McGowan suffered from what are called blackouts," Levy explained, "which are memory lapses. In treating him I've identified two child personalities, Jackie and Jacqueline, and three adult personalities, a woman who represents his mother, a man who represents his father, whose name is Frank McGowan, and Jack McGowan himself. Frank McGowan marched the boys into the creek, in full gear, with the knowledge that three couldn't swim. Jack McGowan would never have done such a thing and had no knowledge of what Frank McGowan was doing at the time. Frank McGowan has little, if any, remorse. The lives lost were "collateral damage," in his mind, sacrifices for the instillation of "discipline," the inevitable price paid for teaching Marines 'to kill or be killed.'"

"Did Frank McGowan himself tell you this?"

Murray knew that behind him the prosecuting attorneys were smirking. That was to be expected. However, it was clear the judges—especially the chief judge—were beginning to wonder if either Bert or Murray himself were crazy.

No objections from the prosecution. They were counting on Murray hanging myself. Clearly they wanted him to keep going.

"Yes, Sir."

"And you believed Frank McGowan?"

"Yes, Sir, I did."

"Still?"

"Yes, Sir."

"Would you tell the court why?"

"Frank McGowan has nothing to gain from his story. He did it, he says, he had justifiable reason for doing it, consequences be damned. He felt Jack McGowan was too soft to discipline such an unruly bunch, so he stepped in to cover for him. If for no other reason, psychologically it makes sense."

"Go on."

"The platoon was, by all testimony, unusually lacking in discipline. The men knew it, as they testified, as did Jack's fellow drill instructors, as they also testified. The men in his platoon also testified that Jack McGowan took pains to be fair, to do the job right, and that his motives regarding the incident in question were sincere and even honorable. Not one of his men testified against him in any negative way whatever. They liked him, and they admired him. Discipline, however, did not improve, as the testimony shows. Why not? Why couldn't a war hero, a man who had killed men in battle, a man with an outstanding record of disciplining his troops fail to do so in a situation in which the recruits were "abnormally unruly," a characterization used over and over again in previous testimony?

"He was afraid, terrified of an atrociously abusive father who lived inside him, who bequeathed him his same anger and penchant for violence. Jack wanted to have nothing to do with that man. He was terrified of him, and he hated him, for the simple reason that he was a bad man. Above all, he banished him from his psyche, his personality, or thought he did. How? By maintaining control. By doing everything 'right,' by the numbers, by the book. By being 'good' at all costs, even sadly at the cost of truth.

"This is why his record is so honorable, why still his men love and admire him. He was scrupulously fair, obsessively good. Obsessives, men of such dogged determination, however, often are in denial. They can lack the flexibility, the mental dexterity, abnormal and unusual dilemmas require. Jack McGowan couldn't afford real anger, real feelings, certainly not Frank McGowan's, a murderer, a man who repeatedly choked the breath out of him and beat him unmercifully when he was a boy, a man who tried to beat the 'girl' out of him, reminding him over and over that he was a sissy, crybaby, worthless scumbag, mama's boy, 'shit' . . . pardon my language. I could go on and on with the labels he pinned to the child's psyche. However, I'll leave that to the imagination of the court. A murderous man had imposed himself on the psyche of Jack McGowan, and Jack's entire life was spent denying him a voice. He was too dangerous to be let out into the world.

"Unbeknownst to Jack, however, Frank McGowan had him in a cage, tied to structure and inflexibility. Frank could roam freely, coming out whenever he wanted, whenever he felt he was needed. Remember, like all evil men, like Hitler, Frank McGowan was certain he was doing the right thing: raising the child Jack in the right way, that he was simply doing what was necessary to counter his mother's 'softness,' to 'make a man out of him.' Such men view tentativeness and open-mindedness as weakness. Self-doubt has been perfunctorily dismissed from their psychological repertoire, a feminine luxury, they perceive, they cannot afford. Toughness, Frank determined, would serve Jack in the real world. When Jack was 'soft,' at least in Frank's eye, Frank stepped in, even when Jack was a child. Frank McGowan stepped in to protect his son Jack from the failure to discipline his platoon when he marched them into Oyster Creek. And Jack did as he had done as a child, dissociated, in the same way one can pass out from fear or torture or too much pain. Jack was horrified when he realized what had been done. 'Oh God,' he cried afterwards. 'What have I done?'

"Sir, he didn't know, because he hadn't done it. It was however, as might be expected, Jack McGowan who finally surfaced, saving as many men as was humanly possible, just as it was Jack McGowan who saved his platoon in the last war.

"It was Frank McGowan who slapped Jack's son, just as he slapped Jack. Jack doesn't remember doing that either.

"Denial, unfortunately, feeds the monster, making him even bigger. Frank McGowan, totally unbeknownst to Jack McGowan, sacrificed men in Jack's platoon, he felt, in order to save it. He provided the discipline that was necessary, in his mind, for the platoon to be successful—to remain alive—once in battle. Thus, the deaths of three young recruits he views, as I've said, as 'collateral damage' while Jack, as I've also testified, upon realizing what has happened, is horrified, aghast, and falls on his knees crying out for penance: 'Oh God, what have I done?'"

The chief judge checked his watch and ordered the court to recess for lunch, after which, he announced, Dr. Levy's testimony would continue.

On the way to Schein's Grocery—right down the street from the courthouse—for a snack, Bert and Murray passed by Hoke's kid Boonie and Driver Trulove shooting marbles over a bare spot of dirt on the courthouse lawn. Murray's foot slipped on a Cat's Eye that had gotten away from Driver, but before back-somersaulting halfway across the lawn Murray managed, with a bit of help from Bert, to right himself.

"'Scuse me, Mr. Gold!" said Driver.

"Yeah," repeated Boonie. "'Scuse me, Mr. Gold!"

They were proud of themselves for being so polite.

"Perfectly okay, Boys. Who's winnin'?"

"I am!" they both chorused.

"Well," said Bert, though he didn't know them. "Congratulations to you both."

"Thank you, Mr . . ." their voices simultaneously trailed off, and they looked at each other puzzled.

"Dr. Levy," Murray told them.

"But not the kind who gives shots," Bert reassured them.

"Thank you, Dr. Levy!" said Driver.

"Yeah, thank you, Dr. Levy!" said Boonie.

By this time Bert was on one knee, marveling over their novel storage units: a Coke bottle in front of each of them, each filled with gaily-colored marbles in which sunlight appeared to be jitterbugging. "Like stained glass," he said.

"What do you know about stained glass?" Murray asked him, as they tousled the boys' heads and walked on across the lawn. "You're a Jew. You know what was in those bottles before they turned them into stained-glass storage units?"

"Something other than Coca-Cola?"

"Something in addition to it."

"What?"

"Peanuts."

"Peanuts? In Coca-Cola?"

"You pour 'em in right from the bag, just a 10 cent bag of Lay's peanuts, shake it all up a bit till they float on the surface, then swallow the entire concoction. Essentially, Bert, you're chasin' peanuts with Coca-Cola."

Bert appeared to gag.

"Goes down every time. Tasty."

Murray waved at Hoke, Boonie's dad, and Marty Liebowitz chatting across the street under the shade of a great oak on the riverbank; Murray hadn't seen them in the courtroom since the mid-morning break, so they must have at the very least missed Bert's testimony. Can't say that I blame them, figured Murray. Had I my druthers, I'd have preferred chattin' it up in the cool of the shade myself. Sunlight showered the river, turning it from a sad dawn-breaking gray to a dazzling blue that seemed all lit up with the world. Sailboats tilted with the river breeze. The fragrance of summer phlox and strawberry lilies from Mrs. Overbeck's front yard across the street made the summer heat a bit more tolerable, made you pause a bit, breathing in all you could of that hot neck before banging into the cool shade of Schein's Grocery.

"MoonPies I understand, but peanuts in Cokes? That's disgusting."

"Best-tasting snack in the world," Murray told him, popping the top off a cold bottle of Coke from the refrigerator in the back, handing it to him. "'Cept maybe for pig's feet. Though I have to admit, I also favor Bull's balls."

"You're full of shit."

"That too."

They both downed their Cokes in no time. It had been hot in the courtroom, but at least the fans were humming. Outside it had been even hotter.

Going out, Murray yelled to Morris behind the counter. "Owe you twenty cents, Morris. Two Cokes. Pick it up next time, ain't got change."

"No problem, Murray. No problem. You leavin' the bottles?"

"Yeah, right by the refrigerator."

"Okay, see you fellows later."

On the courthouse steps Arlanne Palmer handed Rob Vicker, the reporter from the *Times*, what looked like a sheaf of papers loosely held together in several folders. So that's why she's following the trial so closely, Murray realized, buggin' me with questions, flatterin' and flirting' a decibel or so above the usual. He'd heard she and Vicker were gettin' it on over at Peeple's Motel, but he hadn't realized she was working with him, getting him information. She had the inside track: her father was a powerful man in this town; plus, she knew everybody, and if she wasn't spreadin' gossip she was creating it.

She was an old friend, a good friend, but like every other man in town Murray was putty in her hands, and he knew it. Her hair, flirtatiously wild and black, accentuated her porcelain complexion, which suggested, as did her subtly revealing cleavage, skin the sun had not yet touched.

As Bert and Murray approached she stepped back, bumping into Bert. Papers flew, scattering across the steps.

"Oh, excuse me!" she said to him. "I'm so clumsy." She touched his arm. "Are you all right? I'm so embarrassed. Hey, Murray," she said, but her eyes remained on Bert even as they both knelt down to pick up the scattered papers.

"Wow," he said once they'd sat down at the defense table. "When all this is over . . ."

"Tell the court, Dr. Levy, a bit more about the term 'dissociate.' How could Jack be so unaware of what Frank was doing?"

"When Jack was very small, like many boys his age he played with dolls. He was affectionate, loved Mom and Dad, showed tenderness as well as strength and independence. He adored his mother, and often climbed into her lap to suck his thumb. Like any healthy little boy, he laughed with joy, and when hurt he cried.

"When he climbed into his father's lap, however, his father pushed him away and called him a little 'girl.' When he caught him playing with dolls, he tore them apart and beat little Jack unmercifully. He'd tear him from his mother's lap and simply throw him onto the floor, saying 'that's what happens when little boys act like little pussies.' Often he choked him. Any show of sensitivity or weakness Frank McGowan choked or beat out of him. Crying out in pain—any show of tears—only incited his father to greater violence. 'Cry?' he'd say, 'I'll show you cry,' and he'd hit him again until he stopped crying or passed out. The more uncontrollable the crying, the more uncontrollable his father's violence. If he told anyone, his father told him, he would kill him. Tension and anxiety caused Jack to wet the bed, for example, until he was 15 years old, each time inciting in his father further and greater violence. When his mother attempted to intervene, he beat her. Often he was drunk.

"The one thing Jack learned was obedience. Survival, if indeed he could survive, depended on perfection. He did as he was told, both at home and at school, and he strove every minute of his day to do it perfectly.

"A perfect boy, however, does not wet the bed. Nor when he is little, as well as later, does he cry or suck his thumb or play with dolls. The perfect drill instructor does not instill discipline at the cost of risking the lives of his men; paradoxically, however, he does not tolerate discipline problems among them. The perfect boy needs no one. Affection is for sissies."

"So who wet the bed, sucked his thumb, played with dolls, surreptitiously sought affection from his mother and wept in her lap? Who remained in control: the perfect son, the perfect man, the perfect drill instructor? And finally, who led his men into Oyster Creek, three to their deaths, through indifference and negligence, both sacrifices to the God of discipline, obedience and manhood?

"The sensitive part of him, the 'girl' his father beat out of him, Jack had to discard. Her existence sent his father into uncontrollable violence and rages. Hospital visits and cover-ups were a ritual of his childhood. He left that part of him, abandoned the 'girl', if you will—that part of every man who can be tender, sensitive and loving, even if only to his own children—extricated himself from all tendencies toward warmth and affection. Psychologists call this kind of dissociation 'splitting off.' This particular personality—these particular feelings and traits—are housed separately from the little boy—metastasized from him—in the form of a personality called Jacqueline, who remained in hiding from her father, Frank McGowan. She only showed up in places where he could not possibly find her. Here she could suck her thumb, climb in her mother's lap if her father wasn't around, and play with her dolls. Here she could weep.

"From whom, however, did she separate? Not Jack the man. It had to have been Jack the boy. Is Jack the boy, Jack the man? Not on your life. Jack the boy is a real boy. It's okay for boys to be angry and fight back. His name is Jackie. He's also the one who wets the bed, who takes the beatings, who has had his bones broken by his father.

"There's Jack, the dominant personality who holds it—himself—all together. Does everything by the book. No excuses. No complaints. No mistakes. He's the consummate drill instructor, respected and admired by his men. At home he's in church every Sunday, a respectable family man except in those instances when Frank steps in to slap Jack's three-year-old son when, in Frank's eyes, the little fellow whines, cries, openly hurts, openly needs affection, or otherwise steps out of line. Jack's the war hero. Jackie's in him, so he's angry. Jack loathes Frank: his cruelty, his violence, his meanness. When his wife hints at his cruelty toward their son, Jack is truly puzzled, and finally dismissive. He has no memory or awareness of it. He wants no part of his father, refuses to accept that part of himself. Hates it. His life is arranged to keep Frank at bay, locked away. So he is obsessed with playing by the rules, living by the book, doing it by the numbers. Perfectly. He knows that if he slips and falls, Frank McGowan, in all his cruelty and violence and rage, will rise up in his place. Ironically, to save his platoon in the last war, to do the right thing, all Jack McGowan had to do was see the cruel face of Frank McGowan in the faces of the enemy. There was little personal satisfaction in it though, because the more savage he became with the enemy, the more he could hear the cackle and applause of Frank McGowan, i.e., the devil.

"Needless to say, on the night of the incident in question at Oyster Creek, Frank McGowan stormed the fortifications of Jack McGowan. Once inside, Frank broke out. Why now? Because for the first time in his career, Jack McGowan was at a loss as to what to do with his platoon, as to how to instill in them the discipline they so sorely needed. Jack's mother, another personality inside him, refused to step in: she saw a desperation in Frank's takeover that she felt certain would lead to his demise and her son's liberation. I must tell you, she did anticipate the possibility of those three young men drowning. She was close enough to Jack beforehand to have the same knowledge he did. And she was willing to endure their sacrifice for her son. A tragic failure of such terrifying gravity would precipitate public exposure, and sunlight, she felt, and only sunlight, would finally destroy Frank McGowan. And he would not be able to blame her, so she was unafraid. In Jack McGowan, however, was a growing fear of failure—the failure to instill discipline in his platoon—he could not face. His fear and his denial brought in Frank McGowan.

"And afterwards an even greater fear, the fear of losing his men in the swamp, his penchant for survival, his fear of losing himself, his need to be good and right, brought in Jack McGowan to clean up the mess and salvage who he could. He had done it all his life."

"But why can't he remember creating the mess," asked Murray, "ordering the march, leading his men deeper and deeper into dangerously precipitous waters?"

"Because he wasn't there then, just as Frank wasn't there when Jacqueline wept. Had Jack been there, he would have stopped it."

"Dr. Levy," the prosecutor began, "As the consulting and treating psychologist in this case you are aware that a just verdict in this trial hinges on establishing whether or not Sergeant McGowan was or was not in control of his mental faculties and whether he was or was not aware of his actions regarding the incident in question?"

"I am, Sir."

"And that the degree to which he was or was not in control of his mental faculties and was or was not aware of his actions will determine the degree to which he was or was not responsible for the crime committed at Oyster Creek on the night in question?"

"Yes, Sir."

"A responsibility that the court naturally assumes you take with the utmost seriousness. Would you agree with that too, Dr. Levy?"

Levy smiled. The condescension had aroused his curiosity, Murray could tell. "I would," Levy responded.

"You testified too, Dr. Levy, that his father called him names, slapped and beat him, to make a man out of him . . ."

"I did, Sir."

"And was his father, Frank McGowan, also not in control of his mental faculties while visiting such violence upon his son Jack?"

"Objection. Speculative."

"Overruled."

"Dr. Levy, isn't your testimony that Jack McGowan was at least temporarily insane—that is to say, unaware and out of control of his faculties—also speculative? Based only, in one way or another, on what he has told you?"

"It's my professional diagnosis."

"Based on what he has told you, verbally or non-verbally, directly or indirectly?"

"I suppose you could put it that way, yes."

"A man, according to you, himself given to bouts of insanity, of being unaware, out of control."

"That is correct, Sir."

"Would you agree then, Dr. Levy, that such a man's word might invite skepticism?"

"Objection, Your Honor. Trivializing the testimony, leading, beyond the latitude granted even for cross-examination."

"Withdrawn. Still, how convenient for him. Perhaps he is more aware than you have given him credit for. In your career as a psychologist, Dr. Levy, have you ever been—let me resort to the vernacular here—'played' by a patient.'"

"Of course."

"Outsmarted by a patient?"

"Naturally."

"Fooled by a patient?"

"Yes, as all psychologists have. Otherwise, ours would be a perfect profession."

"By a patient, perhaps, in search of a lenient verdict? Here is a man whose *behavior*—not his words, Dr. Levy, but his *actions*—reveal nothing more than a man with a callous disregard for human life, indifferent to risks, a man rather than unaware and out of control so aware and in control of his faculties as to lead an entire platoon into dangerous waters and three of his young charges to their deaths. That is all we *know,* Dr. Levy, is it not? This is a court of law, Dr. Levy, not a theoretical discussion.

We deal only in facts. Would you agree that those are all the *facts* we have?"

"Objection. The prosecution's again trivializing complex testimony, drawing conclusions."

"Overruled."

"And that the rest, Dr. Levy, is 'speculation?'"

"Objection. Dr. Levy is an expert witness. Leading."

"Sustained."

"Dr. Levy, You testified that Sergeant Jack McGowan himself has slapped his own boy when he has 'stepped out of line . . .'"

"No, Sir," he said. "Again, it was Frank McGowan, a personality separate from Jack McGowan's, who slapped Jack McGowan's son."

"Ah, I see. Again the father of Jack McGowan? A busy man."

"A stand-in for the father of Jack McGowan, a part of Jack McGowan, yes, but a different and separate personality—so frightening and detestable to Jack he could not even recognize him."

"So not Jack's real father, but someone somehow inside him, the same Frank McGowan responsible for the death march at Oyster Creek?"

"That would be accurate, Sir. Again, someone so distasteful and frightening to Jack McGowan he cannot accept him."

"Objection, Your Honor, where is this going?"

"Your Honor, The question for the court here is this: was Sergeant McGowan, whatever his real name—"

"Your Honor, again, trivializing the testimony is hardly evidence."

"—aware and in control of his actions on the night in question at Oyster Creek? If so, he was responsible, culpable, and guilty as charged."

"Overruled." But to the prosecution: "Drop the sarcasm. The witness is not on trial here."

"So, Dr. Levy, let me try to get this straight. The guilty party here is not Jack McGowan, but Frank McGowan?"

"I'm not a lawyer, Sir, but Frank McGowan had taken complete control, at the time of the incident, of Jack McGowan's mental faculties, so much so that Jack McGowan, again at the time of the incident, was unaware of Frank McGowan's actions."

Good, Bert, thought Murray, but the prosecutor's playing to the press.

"Ah, let me rephrase it, if I may. In your professional opinion, it was not Jack McGowan but Frank McGowan who was responsible for the deaths of three young men at Oyster Creek on the night in question?"

"Yes, Sir. That is correct Sir."

"Would you agree then that the wrong man is on trial here? And that if the guilty party is Frank McGowan, he is the one who should be on trial here?"

"I—"

"How, Dr. Levy? How?"

17

The Headlines Speak for Themselves

The *New York Times*
MCGOWAN PLEADS TEMPORARY INSANITY

The *Washington Post*
PROSECUTION CHALLENGES MCGOWAN INSANITY DEFENSE

The *Charleston News and Courier*
SOMERSET LAWYER GAINING NATIONAL PROMINENCE

The *Evangelist*
WAR HERO A HERMAPHRODITE

The *Somerset Weekly*
TIDAL WAVE 9, COUGARS 3!!!

18

Elizabeth Concludes That Being a Good Girl Is a Lot of Work

"Who my daddy, Mama?" asked Driver.

"A very important man. Now go on out and play and quit botherin' me. I got vegetables to heat up and fish to fry."

"'Important?'"

Following the voices, pausing just outside the kitchen doorway, Elizabeth knew it anyway, but overhearing her mother actually put it in words, saying it to Driver . . .

" . . . Yo' daddy the sheriff."

No, Elizabeth insisted to herself. No, no, no.

"And you go runnin' your mouth about it and Sister Mae gon' be stickin' pins in your likeness."

That's when she began stirring the food about her plate, making her mama coax her into eating.

She knew she wasn't supposed to do what she was about to do, but she couldn't help it.

Before she asked Driver, however, she lured him onto the tire swing in their back yard, where he couldn't get away. He loved for her to push him on the swing, higher and higher. Usually she agreed to only if her Mama was around, reinforcing her image as the good girl happily martyring herself for Little Snot-Nose. Now, however, on this particular morning her Mama had left for the grocery store, and Elizabeth's motive was similar to what it was when in her Mama's previous such absences she used to pinch his arm until he cried like a baby so she could call him one. Yet as much as she disliked Driver, she disliked the sheriff even more. And as much as she disliked her brother and hated the sheriff, what she really hated was that her mama, for some reason, seemed to take to both of 'em. Each in his own way had taken her mother from her as surely as if he'd hog-tied her, gagged her, thrown her in the trunk of a getaway car and driven off with her, her return predicated on her serving up her main courses of time and attention to each of them on her best china while shoveling under the dining room table the nasty, half-eaten, gnawed-up leftovers on paper plates that the dogs actually got to before Elizabeth did. And Elizabeth was compelled, without knowing why really, to rid her mother of both Driver and the sheriff, especially the sheriff. All she knew was that it was in her mother's best interest to be with her, and that's all she wanted to know. She hated Sheriff Cooley. He wasn't her father, and she didn't want him around, and she didn't want him to be Driver's father either. He wasn't part of their family. She wished they'd both die, Driver and the sheriff. She and Mama would do fine. Besides, she was tired of surrendering the front seat to Driver and actin' like it was perfectly fine just so Mama would love her more than him.

Bein' a good girl, she concluded, was a lot of work.

He was as high now as she could push him, squealing with delight, his little toes reaching for the sky, shattering the atmosphere, just like Casper the Friendly Ghost traversing walls, his hands preceding him on the other side. Peals of laughter—Driver's joy and happiness, in short—was all it took.

"If the sheriff yo' daddy, then how come you call him Mr. Cooley?"

| 19 |

Mary Beth's Visit Excites Bert and Murray

Despite Jack's pleas to the contrary, early Saturday morning just after glimpsing the latest headlines and reading the *New York Times* account of Dr. Levy's testimony, Mary Beth McGowan dropped off little Jamie Mac at her mother's, hopped on a plane to Savannah, Georgia, rented a Chevy Chevelle, and headed straight to Somerset. She got pulled for speeding on Highway 170, didn't even bother to flirt her way out of it, professed guilt immediately, asked 'where do I sign?' and showed up in the reception room outside Murray Gold's office just as Dr. Levy was leaving. She recognized Dr. Levy from newspaper photographs, introduced herself to him, and thanked him. She was a refreshingly pretty blonde, her eyes an alert lively green, a perpetually surprised (if not startled) look about them. She was dressed conservatively in a tailored camel-color suit with the slit rising just above her right knee, the camel-color pleasantly setting off her blonde curls. She was at once sensual, demure, and professional.

She placed a delicate hand on Bert's forearm, which precipitated in him an involuntary tremor. "I realize it would be professionally unethical for you to disclose details to me, Dr. Levy, but I do want to thank you. I've read the papers and talked to Jack. You're absolutely right. As long as I've known him, he's never been himself. When he's violent I'm convinced he doesn't even remember it. Whether or not he goes to prison, you've saved his life. The Jack I know now, so kind, thoughtful, gentle, and loving, that's the Jack I always knew was there but rarely reached. I thought I could save him, but I couldn't. I suppose that makes me about as crazy as he is. Thank you, Dr. Levy, from the bottom of my heart. When all this is over, and it's professionally ethical, I'd like to see you myself. Is that possible? I really don't know how to handle all of this. And Jamie Mac, I'm so worried . . ."

She wanted him to embrace her, and he almost did, just as Murray stepped into the outer office. "Mrs. McGowan," Murray said, "Nice to see you. Sorry, my secretary doesn't come in on Saturdays. You've met Dr. Levy. Good. Won't you come in?"

She looked at Bert one final time. "If there's anything I can do . . . anything . . . he's a good man, and you've found that goodness in him."

"We'll do our best, Mrs. McGowan. He's fortunate to have you behind him. You're very understanding."

She looked from Murray to Bert. "Those poor boys . . ."

She smiled sadly, fatalistically. "You know what's ironical?" she asked them, referring to the account of Bert's testimony in the *New York Times*. "His father did do it."

Murray too couldn't help but notice how lovely she was. Briefly, he wondered what it would be like to clamor about underneath that tailored suit. One leg was crossed, idly swinging a shoe, over the other. Suggesting wonders known perhaps only to Sergeant McGowan was a bit of thigh exposed just above her right knee.

"What can I do for you, Mrs. McGowan?"

"What can I do for my husband, Mr. Gold? To support him, to stand up for him?"

"Were this a civilian trial, Mrs. McGowan, I'd have you sittin' right behind him, your presence alone a show of support. Unfortunately, it's a military trial. No jury to impress, just a trio of judges who wouldn't be swayed by that kind of personal support in the slightest. Fact is, at most they'd be irritated by it. They'd feel the defense was condescending to them. And they might even see it as exploitive. Plus, Jack won't allow it. 'Keep my family out of it. They'll have enough trouble without being involved in all the publicity. I did it, they didn't.' I suppose he wants to protect you as much as you want to protect him."

"What can I do? Just go on teaching my classes and worrying about Jamie Mac?"

"Just do what you're already doing. Phone him. Support him. Let him know you understand, and where you don't, Dr. Levy suggests you ask him to explain himself to you. According to Dr. Levy, that'll be good for Jack, and for you too, for your relationship."

"Is that what he told you to tell me? Just now, while you two were meeting?"

"He cares, Mrs. McGowan, and so do I."

"I know," she said. "You do."

"He feels your long-distance relationship with Jack may be, up until now at least, closer, more intimate, than when you were physically together. I'm not a psychologist. Does that sound possible to you?"

"It does," she said thoughtfully. "It does. It's a safer way to begin, or I guess I should say, begin again. Those poor boys, their parents . . . a march of shame . . ."

"Yes, ma'am. It was. And while the families suffer the loss, no one feels the shame more than your husband."

"He hurts. Do you know what's odd?"

"What's that?"

"I do love him more." She smiled, rising to leave. "You know what else is odd?"

"What's that?" he asked, standing.

"I just might end up loving you two fellows a lot more too."

"Well," said Murray, blushing.

"I just might," she said, turning towards the door. And just before closing it quietly behind her she added, "You two better watch out."

20

Arlanne Discovers the Love of Her Life

The rumors were awry, thought Arlanne, as she opened the door to Rob Vicker's hotel room. She hadn't been fucking Rob Vicker, the reporter for the *Times*, at Peeple's motel on the outskirts of town, but right here at the Gold Eagle, an elegant downtown hotel overlooking the Somerset River, that had during the Civil War, she had informed him, housed Union Soldiers. Not that a cheap motel on the outskirts of town didn't hold a smidgen of back-street sexual sway over her; on the contrary, it excited her. You can't fuck a room, however, regardless the seedy, sweaty, beer-swilling, banging air-conditioner, down and dirty lowlife, alley-cat, take-it-all-in and give-it-all-away, everything-be-damned, blow-it-sky-high seductiveness of it. No, fortunately or unfortunately, fucking required a man. And the man, at the time at her disposal, was a man in a hotel, an elegant man in an elegant hotel. Romance required elegance, stateliness, high-status cocktails, and a panoramic view from the verandah. Lust, on the other hand, which was all she was interested in, was a challenge, a throwing down of the gauntlet: it required dirt under the fingernails, stale beer, flies, the smell of urine in the hallway, and a view through the window, over which mildewed shades hiked up at an irritating slant, of rebel flags, gun racks, and dangling Jesus' on the pickup trucks in the parking lot; what could really get her going more even than the rusted appliances or coiled bedsprings spilling out of the truck beds was a barbecue pit. That barbecue pit . . . that would do it every time. Still, the stateliness of the Gold Eagle was less than bothersome, she'd told Vicker, since she'd always wanted to fuck a writer, a real writer.

Lying next to him in bed in the aftermath of their first coupling, however, sighing and blowing smoke rings like the world had just passed her by, she also told him how disappointed she was, that it was just like fucking anybody else. No difference whatsoever.

"Writers are human," Rob had replied. "I apologize."

"Not the ones I like," she'd said. "They're omniscient."

Tonight he was waiting for her, though still at his desk poring over some of the notes she'd given him. "Jesus, Arlanne, do you have any idea how well you write? These are terrific little sketches, stories really. God, I wish I could steal them, use them. This stuff is so rich, much more than just background."

"Really?" She sat across from him, her pocketbook slipping off her shoulder, onto her lap. She tensed with excitement, anticipation, an odd stirring inside. It made her want to retouch her lipstick. "How about that?"

Yet he wasn't even looking at her, so focused was he on her writing. "Listen to this."

Was she getting turned on? Did praise turn her on? Not really. So what is this, she wondered? It wasn't Rob himself, she knew that: she liked Rob, but lust had somehow made a detour around them. And his staring at her over his bifocals like a math teacher going over a test paper was clearly not in the slightest an invitation to return to the main route. It was too much like a man on the sidewalk in front of the downtown Marina in those checkered Bermuda shorts with black socks up to his calves, scrutinizing a map. No, this was the thrill of the Beginning, the dangerously giddy anticipation of First Love, perhaps even the First Time. Could it really be, she wondered, the prospect of hearing her own writing read aloud to her?

"Hoke Cooley epitomized the aged athlete, as at home in his black flattop and his great lumbering body as the moneyed aristocracy were in their pompadours and great mansions overlooking the river. In his eyes, however, as in theirs, something was missing. Perhaps excess flab at once hid and protected them from

the good little boys they once were, their lost innocence. If nothing else, racism will do that to a man. And if the great Egyptian pyramids were built on the backs of God's Chosen People, God's country right here in Somerset was built on the backs of black men and their children, God's Neglected here in the Bible Belt . . ."

"That's good, Arlanne, whether or not you realize it."

"You wanted stuff on the leading men of the town gathered outside the courthouse."

"They gathered about with the ease and confidence you might expect from successful businessmen, breathing in the air of easy wisdom, casual and self-assured as gamblers, checking their pocket watches now and then, as if on a railway platform waiting for a dignitary, or a big haul, whatever it might be, flattering themselves through association, through their mere presence together. Friendly and polite to all who walked by, they socialized only with each other. On the high school breezeway at recess, they'd be the popular kids, and the most popular of them all was my old man, Bradford Palmer, the town patriarch, the wealthiest and consequently the most self-assured of them all . . .

"They stood about as though they owned the town. They did. And though they had absolutely nothing to do with the trial of Drill Sergeant Jack McGowan, they were there to be sure no dog peed on their tree."

It's true, she thought.

"Dangerous," he said.

An outright affront, she realized, to the town patriarchs, pompous old fools, shrewd though. "Dangerous?"

He nodded. "I'm a Southerner too, you know, small-town Tennessee. You're not exactly toeing the party line here. References to the racism, the snobbism, fairly subversive stuff," he said, again looking at her over his bifocals.

She wished he wouldn't do that. In fact, she was wondering if she'd be better served by a recording. He was turning into the tourist again with the map in front of the Marina in the checkered Bermudas and the black socks. Does he really need those bifocals . . . staring up over them like an accountant? The defining image, it seemed to her, of asexual, without which she could be surrendering, at least in her own mind, to the thrill of her new favorite word, "dangerous," lighting up every nerve in her body.

Involuntarily, to her surprise, she shuddered. For a minute there she thought her entire body might leap out of the chair and take off, though she didn't know where, without her.

"Marty Liebowitz would have his nose fixed if he thought it would get him into the Country Club."

"That's funny," said Rob.

That was true, too. Marty's wife Cessalie would tell you that. She'd tell you anything. She was Jewish. My Lord, could those women talk. Actually, the men too, now that she thought about it. Maybe she should include that in her sketches. The Tribe with the Runaway Tongues. Murray'd love that.

He was so cute. And that Dr. Levy . . .

"The mayor of the town stood about like a used car."

Rob winced with pleasure.

"Hurts, doesn't it?"

He nodded ruefully, this way and that, looking back over the line, offering a tentative shrug. Finally, he laid the page on the desk, looked over at her, and smiled, as if to himself, "Yeah. It does."

"But you're smiling."

"To keep from crying."

"You know people like that."

"My father," he said. "Editor of the *Loris Weekly*. Prints what the town's privileged says is fit to print."

"Which is why you got out?"

"Sure," he said. "If you're going to be told what to print, why not be told by the nation's privileged?"

"Cry," she said. "And you'll feel better."

And, she concluded privately, you'd be a hell of a lot better in bed.

He looked at her thoughtfully. "If I could," he told her, "I might well be the writer you are."

"Rob! Thank you."

"I mean it," he said. "Not that that doesn't hurt too, but it's true."

"That's very generous," she said, but he then resumed looking at her over his bifocals.

"Discovering a writer like you, to tell you the truth, makes me want to run a magazine or newspaper rather than write for one."

"So you, instead of the nation's privileged, could tell writers like me what to write?"

"Honey," he said, scrutinizing another passage, "if I could tell writers like you what to write, I would be one of the nation's privileged."

"The local policemen, used to waiting, stood about like chauffeurs. Ledbetter Greene, however, less reserved and dignified, to say nothing of infinitely more fun, mingled a bit, surprisingly comfortable, with the college kids from the University Extension, scratching his balls. He was always scratching his balls, whether he was standing around bored at shortstop during the men's night softball games, lounging around the pool hall, having a beer with the neighbors. I told him once that he'd probably spend his wedding night scratchin' his balls.

That he either had a perpetual rash or was deathly afraid of losin' 'em. Well now, pretty girl, maybe you ought to offer the old boy here some relief and scratch 'em for me, he said to me. No thank you, I told him, but thanks for tellin' me I'm pretty. And you know what he said? Arlanne, Baby, that's an easy one. Such a gentleman. Off duty, he'd go out and get drunk with the town boys. On duty, late weekend nights, he'd warn 'em good-naturedly and give 'em a free pass. Ledbetter always went hunting with the Country Club boys. They loved him: he drove, gathered up the equipment, packed the truck bed, supplied the liquor. And, I once heard my daddy say, the jokes.

"I like the voice," she said.

He brightened. "Oh, thank you," he said.

I meant mine, she wanted to scream, but so infatuated was she with her own that she sat on it, offering up instead her most encouraging smile. "You read so well," she said, reaching over and touching his arm.

"Thank you again," he said.

"You really do, Rob."

Yet it was the sure knowledge that it wasn't his voice but her own (her own!) that so swept her off her feet, electrifying her. She glowed. Her womb stirred, arousing and opening her every pore. This was her first kiss. No other counted. And it empowered her in a way she could never have imagined. Such was the miracle of her art. And it was inside her, inspiration powered solely by pen and paper. Indeed, the Truth did liberate, though she'd had no idea. Her antennae quivered with anticipation, every pore open to the world, though not necessarily to Rob, the flower of her sexuality blooming madly, wildly, though again apparently not for Rob, tilting toward the sun, taking on a life of its own. The pocketbook in her lap she held hard and fast to her in a discreet attempt to keep the flood waters at bay. Alas, for every action there is an opposite and equal reaction. "Wow," she said, wiping her forehead.

"That good?" said Rob absent-mindedly, totally and quietly absorbed, thank God, in a particular passage further along in her notes. "Come on. Let's not overdo it, Arlanne."

"That good," she said, about to faint. "In fact, great. Great."

"Must be the heat," he ventured, upon looking up, but he did so only out of politeness, and again over his bifocals, only to immediately return to his love affair with whatever passage was presently consuming him. It was as if, it seemed to her, her presence was unnecessary. But then, in a sense, it seemed to her, as if his was too. "Ah, yes," he said. "Yes, yes, yes." And though clearly now all set for the dive before once again plunging headlong into her prose, he allowed himself a brief, mild distraction: "It occurs to me that no one's ever complimented me before on my reading aloud." He smiled, not without modesty. "I think I know why."

And it occurred to her right then that he had forsaken all interest in her for her prose.

"The military, ah yes, the military was money in the pockets of Somersetonians, especially those whose pockets were already filled with it, a great deal of money, in fact, flowing in from across the creek as regularly as the tide."

Apparently, so was she, the incoming tide of her prose an elixir of anticipation washing over her, filling her bloodstream, through which she floated helplessly, threatening once again to burst.

"So naturally, above all, Somerset was an intensely patriotic community. The C.O. played golf with Daddy and the boys. And to him they showed a special deference. After all, he was a general. Short and potbellied, he actually looked much more like the stereotype of the Southern sheriff than Hoke did. And, as he waved his fat cigar about telling story after story, the smoke unfurling as if from Toscanini's wand, the orchestra—Daddy and the Boys—followed his every move, his every gesture, chiming in at just the right time, never missing a beat. Even Ledbetter ambled over with a lopsided grin on his face, checking out the music."

"Rob," she said, standing.

He looked up to see her standing before him, as if she'd just come in out of a heavy rain, dressed as she was, shaking her hair as if to dry it.

But as she looked down at him, there he was again, looking up at her over those goddamn bifocals.

"Get rid of them," she said. "Now."

Afterwards, they both lay in bed, she blowing smoke rings, he staring up at the ceiling, absent, thank God, his bifocals.

Still, their minds were elsewhere.

"More tomorrow?" he asked.

But what, she wondered, did she need him for, except to give her a job writing this stuff so she could get paid for it? Otherwise, who was she? How was she any different than the downtown patriarchs, other than that they had sold their souls for riches while she, dumbbell that she was, had GIVEN away not only her soul, but her body, to the thrill of her own voice.

Downtown, right outside her window, curved quietly along the river.

Every one of them, she understood with a freshly-minted clarity and finality, every single one of them, from her father Bradford Palmer to the used car Harper Dawes to even the lackeys like poor Ledbetter Greene, every single one of them: prostitutes along the river, up and down, up and down.

She rose, slipping her feet into her sandals and her summer sheath over her head, throwing her hair back and slipping her pocketbook over her shoulder, all, it seemed to Rob, in one motion. Then she looked down at him.

"More what?" she challenged.

He looked truly puzzled, as if the answer was obvious to both of them. He even put on his bifocals so he could see her more clearly, which made her want to slam the door in his face forever.

"More notes," he said. "More notes, more sketches. Gold, the lawyer . . . that psychologist, you know him?"

"Oh," she said. "Sketches? Notes?"

"What else?" he asked.

| 21 |

Bert Desperately Turns to Lila for Help Once Again

Clearly my testimony had been unconvincing. "Insufficient, Bert," Murray had informed me over drinks at Harry's Bar. He was blunt. "Still standing between Jack and a life sentence in prison is proof—specific evidence from a credible source—of his multiple personality disorder."

He don't come here for sex.

I walked up the same flight of stairs I'd traversed a year or so ago, and couldn't help but notice through the window on the upstairs landing how the moonless night was so dark it was hard to tell the river from the sky. Lights on the waterfront twinkled like bodiless candles. Near the marina you could barely make out a white sail that seemed to be suspended in darkness. Otherwise, darkness, blinding, blurred all distinctions, and before I knew it, I was once again in her office, doing my best to be as clear and direct as I possibly could.

"If Jack McGowan did not come here for sex," I asked her, "What did he come for?"

22

Boonie Walks Out of Driver's Childhood Forever

Regina Cooley had never said a disapproving word about Boonie and Driver playing together; after all, regardless of segregation, black and white kids often played together until they began school. However, right before both kids started first grade, Boonie noticed within her stern Anglican features a new unmistakable look of reproach whenever he'd ask if he could play with Driver. She didn't say, as she usually did, "Ask your daddy if he'll run you over there." Until he pressed her, frustrated, she wouldn't answer him at all. Finally, resigned to the inevitable, she'd relent.

As sweet-natured as Boonie was, he was confused, and his anger at his mother made him feel guilty and ashamed, which made him even madder, since he didn't know what guilt and shame were, only that he didn't like being in such close proximity to the storm clouds darkening, gathering in his soul.

He was mad, so Saturday morning while they were playing hide-and-seek in Lila's backyard, instead of hiding as he usually did when Driver closed his eyes and counted to ten, Boonie strapped on his gunbelt and pinned the sheriff's badge on his shirt himself and before he knew it he was Johnny Mack Brown, sheriff of Copper Gulch, sneakin' up not behind Driver, who had just yelled "6!" trying to somehow sense where Boonie might be hiding, but instead behind Mad Wayne Morgan, the most feared gunfighter in these parts, given to snarling and waving his bottle of bourbon like it was the devil's banner and shootin' up the town and yellin' "Dance, Hombre" at Ol Doc Evans jitterbuggin' as bullets tore up the earth around him. Johnny Mac calmly tapped the gunslinger on the shoulder, just like he'd done the Saturday before in the Western both Boonie and Driver had seen, Driver from the theatre balcony, Boonie from the floor below. When the gunslinger turned around, surprised, Johnny Mack caught him with his fist square on his nose.

Driver lay on the ground, his nose bleeding, counting the cumulus clouds instead of counting to "10," while Boonie walked around to the front of Lila's house, up the driveway to wait for his dad to come pick him up, out of Driver's childhood forever.

Lila knew this day would come, as did Hoke. Both thought it had happened, as it would have had to at that time in the Deep South, because Boonie was white and Driver was black, and that it was inevitable.

That wasn't, however, the reason. Without realizing it, Boonie had chosen his own mother over Driver's.

Later Driver would regret that he hadn't bitten Boonie's hand off, that he hadn't ripped off an ear, that he hadn't gotten up off the ground and whipped Boonie's butt. But at the time, he simply never thought about doing such a thing. Why hadn't he? Isn't that what boys do? Fight? You're not a man if you don't fight back. Isn't that what he'd always heard? Men back up their words with their fists. "You're not the type," his mother told him.

That made him feel even worse. What type was he?

He did what came naturally. He refashioned the story to make himself that type. He had a knack for making things up. By the time he'd re-shaped and re-fashioned it to his own liking, not only his buddies on the Island but he himself was convinced that it was Boonie lying on the ground with a bloody nose as Driver, without having broken a sweat, walked off without even a glance over his shoulder, leaving him "for the buzzards."

Besides, he told them. He was gettin' too old for hide-and-seek. Hide-and-seek was for "babies."

"You my baby," his mama told him, salting the meat.

He grinned, but this time he looked about to make sure nobody saw him, even though nobody could have, since they were in the kitchen and nobody else was there.

23

Bert Watches With Fascination as Lila Takes the Stand

"How are you this morning, Mrs. Trulove?"

"Fine, Mr. Gold. Let's get on with it. I've got a business to run. And if I hear any giggles from this group I might just feel put upon to disclose who my customers are."

For some reason, Bert thought to himself, observing from the front row, I am in awe of this woman; for the same reason, I think, that Murray is. She has nothing to lose, having lost it already.

"Mrs. Trulove," Murray asked her, "are you familiar with the name Jack McGowan?"

"I am."

"Is he in this courtroom?"

"Yes, he is."

"Can you point him out to the court?"

"Right over there. Been sittin' right next to you. You didn't know it? I thought you was supposed to be his lawyer."

Good for her, figured Bert. She was getting everyone's attention. Even the chief judge smiled. Reporters were pulling out their pads.

"Well, I suppose I am, Mrs. Trulove, but I thank you for pointing him out. Now Mrs. Trulove, could you tell me where you've seen the defendant before?"

"My place of business, where I regularly see half the men in this courtroom."

During the course of the trial, that was the only time Bert had seen Jack smile, and he knew what was coming. Murray and Bert had prepared him.

"And that place of business is above the Ritz Cafe, is it not?"

"It is. Thank you for the free advertising. We welcome one and all. If things get tense around the house or at work, come on over, relax, and have a drink."

Bert thought in that moment that she must have more power, just because of who she knew and the way she knew them, than anybody else in town. For her, power truly was knowledge, and she knew just how to play it. The legality of her work wasn't an issue; besides, any investigation would expose her customers. She was freer, in some ways, than the prominent Whites she serviced. She had their names, and it didn't much matter to her if they had hers. Everybody, including Lila herself, already knew who she was. She had nothing to hide. The wisdom of the Chief Judge issued in his chambers, Murray had confided to Bert, prevented if not for legal reasons then for the sake of propriety the explicit naming of her profession. Such a disclosure, the Judge had concluded, was not "evidentiary," and therefore "irrelevant" to the particular matter at hand. When the Judge emphasized, according to Murray, that this was a military trial and therefore there was no reason to "involve" the town beyond the use of the courthouse, "in itself," he'd pointed out, "a gracious and generous offer," it was clear to everyone in the room that particular signal had come from on high, just like the all-too-easy granting of the request not to have Big Momma herself testify. "Clearly," said the judge after hearing Lila's testimony in his chambers, "Mrs. Trulove has first hand knowledge of her entire business, not the least of which is the employee in question's relationship with the defendant. Besides, sounds to me Mrs. Trulove's place is as much a bar as anything else," the judge had offered vaguely, keeping his head above water, "maybe a bit of a honky-tonk, a place to relax, entertainment, masseuses. After all," he concluded—in Murray's words, treading nebulously—"my understanding, naturally never having frequented the establishment, is that liquor is offered, music played, attractive women serving you . . . Leave whatever's left to prior knowledge and imagination."

"And what is the purpose of Sergeant McGowan's visits, Mrs. Trulove?"

"He comes to visit one of my girls there."

"And can you tell the court what takes place during these visits?"

"The girl takes him to her room where she often entertains."

"Can you describe the girl?"

"She not really a girl, she a woman, a real woman. She older than the rest of 'em, been there since I started. Big fat woman. They call her Mammy, Big mama. Big old woman. She take care of everybody, all the girls there too, she like everybody's mama."

"And does she take care of Sergeant McGowan."

"She sho' do."

"And how does she do that?"

"She let him be a little boy. She the only one he'll see. She take care of him just the way he likes it."

"Be specific, please."

"She draw him a nice warm bath, and he plays with his little toy boats in it, probably like he do as a little child, I don't know. She say he splashes all about. Oh, she say, he have a good time. Just playin."

"Go on."

"Then she dry him off, just like his mama used to do, and he puts on a pair of pajamas. Then she just hold and rock him for a few minutes while he suck his thumb. I guess his mama let him do that too. My boy did. Why, he sucked his thumb till he was five years old. Still sits in his mama's lap. Then Sergeant McGowan he gets up and pulls the dolls out his briefcase, where he keep his boats and pajamas, and he plays with the dolls for awhile. She hugs him. He puts back on his uniform, picks up his briefcase, and leaves. First she wondered, him playin' with dolls and suckin' his thumb and all, but she say he the nicest man of all of 'em. No trouble at all. She want him to know that she don't believe none of this stuff the papers is printin' and to come see her and she'll make him feel better. Honestly, I think she miss him a little bit."

"Thank you, Mrs. Trulove."

The prosecution, for once, had no questions.

After the defense rested, the judges rendered a verdict in less than two hours.

They concluded that Jack McGowan was not in control of his faculties or his actions on the evening of the Death March into the swamp at Oyster Creek; that his prison time be limited to time served; that consistent with the testimony of the base psychologist, he be housed in the Psychology Ward at Lawton Island Military Hospital for as long as the base psychologist deemed necessary; that he be transferred to a different Company on Lawton Island; that he be demoted to private with no opportunity for future advancement; that he surrender his Smokie (the hat worn only by drill instructors) and his duty belt.

On the courthouse steps a woman who he had condemned to a living hell for the rest of her life and whose son he had condemned to death, approached Jack McGowan. Mrs. Pennebaker, who had been seated at the rear of the courtroom for the duration of the trial with the parents of Riley Francis McGahee and Patrick O'Hearn, waited as the military policeman, at Bert's signal, moved aside, and she handed McGowan a note. At the touch of her hand on his—a tenderness of which, McGowan would later confide to Bert, he naturally felt he was totally undeserving—he appeared stricken, totally unnerved. "Please," he said. "Forgive me." She carefully folded her hand over his, closing it over her note.

What he meant to say, he later confided, was "Please, forgive me my sentence," the lack of severity for which he also felt he was undeserving. The outstretched arms of boys reaching out to him, the pull of the undertow, that's what he deserved.

But the note he was slowly opening would cast doubt, in his mind, on the lack of severity even of that sentence.

Pulling himself together, he opened it.

"'Only God judges,'" he whispered just loud enough for Bert to hear.

He folded it and placed it carefully in his pocket. Across the courthouse lawn a Military Police Car waited for him, but his eyes were pulled and compelled by the river beyond it, he would further confide, to the outstretched arms of three innocent boys disappearing underwater, from which rose a fiery tableau, immovable and irretrievable, of three women innocent as their boys aflame in a living Hell.

"And has He?" Bert asked him.

"He's condemned me to live."

24

Murray Smells Trouble, Then Serves the Noble Cause of Love

Murray slept late the next morning, and by the time he arrived at his office, his long-time secretary Angie White, who drove him crazy, greeted him in the outer office with two sets of messages on her desk for him: two or three in a small pile, and next to that a fairly large stack of congratulatory messages, almost all of them telegrams, including one from Attorney General Robert Kennedy.

"Open it," said Angie, handing it to him.

"Goddammit, Angie, I've told you to quit reading my mail."

"Honestly, Murray, looks to me like it's sealed," she sang, focusing her attention on something inside her desk drawer.

"Resealed," said Murray without even a glance at it. "As always."

"Now, Murray," she said, touching his arm, "false accusations will get you nowhere. Flattery, however—"

"Angie! Fine. I'm wrong. You didn't read it."

"Would you like me to tell you what it says?"

"No. Nor anyone else, if you don't mind."

"But, Murray, I'm honestly and frantically about to burst." She put on her eyeglasses, purely "ornamental," she had confided to Murray, so which normally hung modestly and stereotypically from a silver chain around her neck. "Ah, the better to see you with," she told him now, for no reason at all, as far as he could tell. "To see into your eyes, Murray," which she scanned like an MRI.

"Ah, I see," he said, but suddenly he was stricken: Had he left his keys in his car?

"No," she said. "You don't. I do."

He fumbled about in his pockets.

"That's why I wear the glasses in this office. You wear the pants, Murray, but I, Angie White, I wear the glasses. Never forget that. Other pocket, please."

"Ah," he said, "here they are," holding them up as if for a photo opportunity.

She allowed him his moment of triumph. They went through this every morning. Panic would catch him off guard before he even got to his desk, and he'd reach for his car keys, which would always be where he'd put them. Dr. Levy had once told her it was a Jewish trait, panic the ancestral legacy of persecution, but she upped and told Dr. Levy, she sure did, that she didn't see anything Hebrew about it at all, with or without her glasses, which seemed to nudge him off-center a bit.

"Would you like to know what your eyes tell me?"

"No," he said, patting his wallet to make sure it hadn't somehow jumped ship.

"They say, 'Tell him, Angie. Tell him.'"

"Tell him that you have, once again, illegally opened his mail?"

"'Tell him,'" she said, once again checking into his eyes, "what I have psychically discerned."

Her pencil, exquisitely sharpened and perpetually tucked behind her ear, also "ornamental," was nevertheless pointing disconcertingly toward him, an over-the-shoulder missile in a cradled-in-the-ear delivery system, he observed, directly in his line of sight, suddenly angling downward, aimed directly at the cup of Maxwell House on her desk that she now held up to him like an offering, the missile once again aimed straight for his eyeballs: "My cup," she said, "threatens to runneth over."

She dressed conservatively, as was appropriate for secretaries—conventional skirt, white blouse—but why, he wondered, did he have to have the only secretary in town who wore red sneakers?

"If the dam is to burst, shouldn't the flood be confined to the area—the square footage, if you will—of this office, instead of spilling over into the community?"

Murray sniffed the air, puzzled, sniffed again, wrinkling his nose in disgust.

"What is that smell?"

She stood, her eyes on her shoes, her hands demurely intertwined like a little girl's over her stomach, the coffee cup back in its saucer. "Horace, I fear."

"Horace?! I told you to keep that damn dog out of here, Angie. It happens every time. He stinks up the place."

"Horace has a confession to make." Maintaining her posture, she glanced, just barely, under the desk. "Horace?"

Horace the hound poked his apologetic face from under the desk, looked at Murray pathetically, and whined.

Murray leaned over to pet him.

He barked, baring his teeth. Murray jumped back.

"Never, Never," said Angie, shaking her finger at Murray as if he'd been naughty, "pet a dog during Confession."

"Confession."

"You're catching on, Murray. In dog language, which needless to say is not offered in the Somerset Schools, he was admitting to you that he farted. Dogs, however, are loyal creatures, man's best friend, so I know what you're asking yourself right now. Is he guilty, or is he covering up for his best friend, Yours Truly? I assure you . . ."

"What's in the other stack there, the short one?"

"Phone messages: one from Arlanne, the other from Mary Beth McGowan. Both want you to call them."

He grabbed the telegram and headed into his office.

"Murray," she said, peeking in. "I think he wants you to work for him, for the Justice Department."

Integration, Murray thought, heading Somerset's way.

"Arlanne, how you doin', pretty girl?"

"Aw, Murray, you're so sweet."

"Ah, you want a favor, and I'll bet I know what it is."

"Do you now?"

"I saw that look you gave Bert Levy after you accidentally on purpose bumped into him on the courthouse steps. I was besotted with jealousy. I thought you and Vicker were gettin' it on. He headed back to New York?"

"Actually, Murray, I learned something from that relationship. It wasn't Rob I wanted to screw."

"Who was it?"

"Me."

"Well, Baby Doll, can't blame you for that. I'd like to screw you too."

"Murray, I don't deserve you. Can you set me up, Baby?"

"Sure, I'll call him this afternoon."

"Then you'll call me?"

"What should I call you?"

"Jesus, Murray, you've got the downright lamest sense of humor . . ."

"Sorry, Sweetheart, I'll call you tonight, I promise."

"Bye bye, Dahlin'."

"Hey, Mary Beth, how are you?"

"Murray Gold! Congratulations. You're famous. Your picture's everywhere. Unfortunately, so is mine."

"Not in Somerset, Mary Beth. Not down here."

"You don't say?"

"Nobody'll even mention it within a week, soon as everybody's left town."

"I don't understand. They sure aren't going to forget about it up here, and they aren't going to let me forget about it."

"You might want to re-locate. Oddly enough, the best place to do that is probably right down here. You'll be with Jack. The boy can get to know him again, as the gentle man he can be, which would be good for him, I'd imagine, and believe me, you'll hear no talk. Somerset's too patriotic for that. Plus, it'd be impolite. Whatever's said, you won't hear it, and neither will Jamie Mac. And again, odd as it might sound, anything said negatively about the military down here, whether publicly or privately, is considered bad taste, and talking about the trial is talking about the military. It's like talkin' bad about your family. What goes on behind closed doors, people feel, should stay there. What goes on at Lawton Island, people feel, should stay there. 'Treatin' a war hero like that. War will make you crazy.' Rightly or wrongly, that's the way people around here'll feel. The last newspaper in America to even mention the incident at Oyster Creek was the *Somerset Weekly*, and if it hadn't been for the outside pressure and the trial taking place in the town courthouse, it might never have mentioned it. Somerset feels like it hosts Lawton Island, and you don't hang out your guests' dirty laundry in the front yard."

"Bad business. I know. I teach it."

"You could probably teach it down here, over at the University Extension."

"You know anybody over there?"

"Honey, everybody knows everybody here."

Part III

FALL 1966

25

Elizabeth Integrates the Somerset County Schools

Thirteen-year-old Elizabeth Trulove, the best student in Somerset Junior High School—later the valedictorian of Somerset High—integrated the Somerset County Schools all by herself.

In the beginning, particularly the first day of school, September 1, 1966, the silence was overwhelming. Menace was in the air. The residual summer heat, heavy and simmering, swam along the breezeway, down the corridors, and into the classrooms. Perspiration stained September-tanned faces, the armpits of Gant shirts, and the waistbands of panty girdles. With the Devil breathing hellishly in the cold, calculated silence, Somerset Junior high School turned its back on Elizabeth. No one looked at her or even glanced in her direction. No teacher called on her. No one sat in desks in front of her, behind her, or on either side of her. No one sat at the same table with her in the cafeteria.

The instructions from white parents to their children had been made explicitly clear.

Marty Liebowitz, the chairman of the Board of Education, had announced in the *Somerset Weekly* that he didn't want his kids sitting next to no "picaninny." He could say it without fear of retribution, he told Hoke Cooley, since he never went to Lila's whorehouse. Anybody who did sit next to a picaninny, he said privately, was a nigger lover.

"A fairly safe limb to crawl out on," Murray told him on the steps of the synagogue after Friday night services, "right here in the Deep South with segregation pretty much the order of the day. Take a real stand, Marty, then see if you fall off."

Everybody else had gone home. It was September-humid, and Murray loosened his tie, contemplating the stars.

"I'll leave that to you civil rights fellows," Marty responded with a collegial pat on the back.

"The limb's gettin' shaky," Murray warned him. "Be careful what you hold on to."

"Murray, now you know as well as I do where all this is leadin'."

"Equality? A fair shake for everybody?"

"That don't bother me. I'm for freedom of choice. Separate but equal. You know that. Ran for the Board on that platform, ain't backed away from it. But I told you, you give a nigger an inch . . ."

"For every inch you don't give us, Marty, we're going to take a mile. It's 1966. The law is on our side. You respect the law, don't you, Marty?"

"I respect the law, but I can't say I respect busin'. Kids need to go to school in their own neighborhoods."

"Marty, you been busin' white kids past black schools to avoid integration for as far back as I can remember."

"Separate but equal was the law of the land. You respect the law now, don't you, Murray? 'Course you do."

"And if the law changes, Marty, as it has, and it renounces freedom of choice as a viable option, which it has, you respect the law now, don't you?"

"Murray, I'm as liberal as the next man, but you gon' make us look bad here, I'm tellin' you. This race-mixing . . ."

"I know, leads to intermarriage?"

"'Course it will."

"Well, that would legitimize half the sexual relationships in this county. But I'm a bit surprised here, Marty. I didn't realize black women were so compulsively attractive to you. If you got to hate 'em not to love 'em, Marty, well, go ahead, resist. Resist, Man. Exert all the will power at your disposal."

Marty chuckled. "I'll do my best, Murray. You take care, hear?"

"Take care, Marty."

None of the Jews had gone to Lila's whorehouse. They were too family-oriented. Marty's guns and fishing rods were one thing, but whoring, that was another . . . Murray Gold suggested privately to Bert Levy that he thought Jewish men were probably scared of whores. And if they weren't scared of whores, they were certainly scared of their wives. Jewish women didn't believe in turning the other cheek, he said, and most could beat up their husbands in a fistfight. Fistfighting too was an activity foreign to Jewish men, he added. We prefer talking our enemies to death.

"Am I your enemy?" asked Bert.

"Of course not," said Murray.

"Then shut up."

Murray placed a tender hand on Bert's shoulder. "You're right," he said," we Jews should be looking out for each other, not killing each other."

"Jesus . . ." said Bert.

"Exactly," said Murray.

"A myth," Bert said dismissively. "We had nothing to do with that."

"Just for the record, in case anyone asks, I wasn't around then."

"Perfect alibi."

They were in Harry's, late on a weeknight. Just a few people there: Kick Haygood, the Director of Maintenance for the Somerset Schools who long ago coached Murray in Little League, and his buddy Al Hummer who worked for the Somerset Recreation Department and did "odd jobs" around town which meant he also coached Little League baseball and did just about nothing else, except maybe drive the fire truck if Wade Ellis was drunk. Everybody liked these guys, Murray had told Bert. They were fun. Tough too. And they really enjoyed kids.

Bert looked over at them from across the bar. They were over there having fun, telling jokes, teasing and yelling at Millie behind the bar, who was giving it right back to them without even breaking stride.

"They *are* kids," Bert said.

"You sound envious."

"They look to me like the healthiest men in town."

"You're speaking professionally? Psychologically? Bert, they barely have a pot to piss in."

"Look at them. They truly enjoy themselves."

"Well, sure," said Murray, "They're not us, all fearful and panicky."

"Speak for yourself. I'm a real man. Hey, look at me."

"I am," said Murray.

Lila Trulove announced in the *Somerset Weekly* that unlike Marty Liebowitz she was a nigger lover, and as a result, she was planning to run for a seat on the Board of Education, and if Marty Liebowitz was so averse to sitting next to a "picaninny" then he might as well resign his position as Chairman now and save the county a lot of time and trouble, because she was planning to win. She added that while normally she didn't mind sitting next to white people, Marty Liebowitz was another story: Wasn't no nigger she knew wanted to sit next to him. And it wasn't, she couldn't help but add, just because his attitude was so ugly but because he was. Black, white, Jewish, no problem. But butt-ugly, ain't nobody she knew wantin' to sit next to that.

After which Arlanne Palmer wondered in a letter to the editor if that's why so few people, white or black, attended school board meetings.

Murray Gold announced in the *Somerset Weekly* that if the school board remained all-white, with no black members, Somerset could lose federal funds for its schools. When you took into account both the federal funds traditionally provided for the schools enrolling children from military families, which included every school in the town of Somerset, and the funds provided by the Civil Rights Act passed two years earlier, which included funds for every school in Somerset *County*, you were talking, Murray contended, about a lot of money. Subtract only the military funds, and the schools would have to close, Murray told the *Weekly*, which would result in no kids, black or white, going to school; which is why, he told Bert, the *Weekly* decided to print Lila's announcement. When money talks, he said, even rednecks listen.

After taking the Somerset County Schools to court and legally forcing Elizabeth's admission to the all-white junior high school, for which he had gained national attention, Murray was appointed civil rights attorney and legal liaison to the Department of Health, Education, and Welfare, the arm of the government empowered by the Civil Rights Act of 1964 to desegregate the schools. Bert marveled aloud at the absence locally of social repercussions. "I'm a native," Murray explained. "Natives can get away with anything."

Though Elizabeth's grades were perfect, after awhile she began to disappear.

No girls would use the girls' restroom now that Elizabeth was at the school. If they had to go, they went next door to Velma Pritchard's house where, according to Velma, they were very respectful of "the facilities." Cheerleaders now changed into their uniforms for after-school practice at Velma's.

Alone in the girls' bathroom, when Elizabeth looked in the mirror she could no longer see herself.

"You ain't there to admire yourself," said Lila, "and you ain't there to make friends. You there to make somethin' of yourself. And your little brother Driver, he gon' be right behind you."

Murray Gold, Lila's attorney since he had won for Elizabeth the right to attend Somerset Junior High, was concerned about Elizabeth. He phoned and asked Bert Levy if he'd see her. "Lila'll agree. She trusts you. And behind that tough facade, she's worried as hell. She keeps saying Elizabeth's 'different,' that she used to be happy and curious and excited about things and pick on Driver and all . . . you know what she said that really worries me: 'Elizabeth doesn't seem to have any feelings anymore.'"

"If that's the case, she's been traumatized."

"Ride out there and talk to Lila. Just let her know this time it ain't just social. I think she must've convinced herself, deep down, that if she turned respectable, everything'd go all right for her kids."

"She did give up the business."

"That was no more her business than she was the town whore, not that she didn't make a nice wad off it, enough to buy two liquor stores and a little colored restaurant on the island."

"Damn! She's got a monopoly on liquor stores in Somerset now."

"Nobody said Lila was a fool. She's pissed off as hell though. She wanted to buy respectable, one of the shops downtown. Freddie Dinnerman was selling, wanted to retire early. Still is."

"So. Why didn't she?"

"Are you kiddin' me. Right now black people only come to town on Saturdays. That's their shoppin' day. The only other time they're here is to clean, mop, and stock the shelves. You think the white community ain't raisin' hell at the idea. The Jewish community's about to go crazy."

"What does Freddie say?"

"What any good businessman would say: 'She's the one with the money.' That's what scared half the Jews in this town to death. You should've heard Herschel Linowitz at the B'nai B'rith meeting last month. 'These are People of the Book here in Somerset: they like us, respect us, see us as God-fearing family men—God's favorites, in fact—with good heads for business. Why upset the apple cart?' Freddie said he did have a good head for business, that that's why he wanted to sell to Lila. But then Hymie Shindel said, 'Blessed be the Negro, for he is to America as the Jew is to Europe," after which the entire congregation (it sounded like) chorused: 'Amen, better him than us.' Then Avery Latta said, 'If it weren't him, it'd be us.' Then Freddie said, 'Look, Gentleman, this is business.' Well, believe me, everyone in that group, as you can guess, understood that and nodded gravely. The pendulum was about to swing Freddie's way, until Marty Liebowitz piped up and said, 'You're right, Freddie. It is business. Our business.' Believe me, everyone there knew what he meant. We do business with coloreds, whites won't do business with us. And guess who's got all the capital? Except of course for Lila."

"You said the whorehouse wasn't her business, that she herself wasn't a prostitute . . ."

"Not unless you want to call her Hoke Cooley's prostitute. Other than that she was untouchable. She was really his mistress. Anyway, that was his business; he owned the building. He set her up in it. She ran it."

"The sheriff?"

"That's why she's so pissed off. She was his little 'nigger gal', people said. And she was. Hoke's wife's more or less a natural Christian martyr. Turns the other cheek. Looks the other way. Most people in town don't know about this anyway. Hoke's circle pretty tight. I found it out from Marty Liebowitz. They fish together."

"Fish?"

"Marty does everything the Gentiles do. He's even got a moose head on his den wall and a collection of rifles. Hell, he sails. His older boy, Lance—hardly a Jewish name, need I point out—can tell you all about four-barrel carbs, drag pipes, and frog-gigging."

"What's frog-gigging?"

"How the hell do I know? Last year Lance got suspended from school for a few days for fighting; Marty put him to work that week but you could tell, deep down, he was proud. The kid's a good athlete, holds his liquor well, likes to have a good time, so naturally he's popular, fits right in. That's really all it takes around here. Those Civil War reenactments they have annually over at the old armory? Marty's as avid a participant as John C. Calhoun's grandson. Knows everything down to the last detail about the Civil War. Hell, I'm more interested in East European history, that's where my folks hail from. His did too, though you'd think after talkin' to him they rode with Robert E. Lee. Anyway, after Lila turned respectable and made both she and Hoke a ton of money, naturally she expects Hoke to help her find a nice little shop on Main Street. Hoke couldn't do it. There's no question: Hoke thinks the world of Lila, but he's the biggest racist redneck in town. That's the only qualification you got to have to be sheriff here. And of course he lives in fear she's going to run her mouth about everything. Last time he was at her house over on the Island, parking behind the shrubbery so the truck couldn't be seen like he always did, she had a few of her boys let the air out of the tires. He's standin' there in the middle of the night with nobody to call. Marty says she told Hoke to get his white ass out of there any way he damn well could and that if he ever came back she'd have her boys shoot him. He got the message. Hell, the car could still be there for all I know."

"Jesus . . ."

"We both know he ain't much help. As for the little girl, Lila's lookin' to you instead. And Bert, talkin' to her and all, it ain't officially 'therapy.' It ain't like she's crazy. If rumor gets out that she's 'crazy' it'll create even more problems for her. Kids would have even more reason to stay away from her. With his nose up white Somerset's ass, Marty'd probably even try to take us back to court. Speaking of which, how's Jack?"

"He's holding up. Bought him a little place out on Scataway Island, brought down the wife and kid. Now that I think about it, the kid must be about Driver's age."

"Wish he was black and three years older. Elizabeth would have company."

"She talk white now, Bert. Pure white. You want sugar in that coffee? Here, that enough? Lord, that girl catch on quick. White kids snub her. Black kids say 'cause she talk white and go to white school she too good for 'em. Even their parents say, Whatsa' matter, Elizabeth, we ain't good enough for you? I feel bad for her. I do. Makes me wonder if I did the right thing. She even talk white at home, like she forget herself, who she be."

"She does? At home?"

"My fault too, I guess. I insisted: when you with white, I told her, you talk white. Otherwise, they think you stupid. A damn lot of good that did. But you know what, when she walk across that stage at graduation as the class valedictorian, the one with the highest grades in the entire class, I'm gon' be a proud mama. And don't think that ain't gon' encourage a lot of other black folk too. Education. That's the key."

"To what, exactly?"

"To freedom, boy. The freedom to buy and sell white folk just like they buy and sell us."

Elizabeth had started losing weight, Lila told Bert, and her smile had gone. "She stir her food around a bit on her plate then she go off and study. Spend all her time studying. Can't get her to eat."

"Sounds like for her everything's about achievement now, Lila. I hate to tell you this, but she sounds lonely and depressed, like she's martyring herself."

"That's 'cause white people is crucifying her."

"Are they, Lila? Or are you?"

26

Bert Finds It Difficult to Look and Not Touch

Mary Beth McGowan was a looker, thought Bert the first time he met her, during Jack's trial years ago. He hadn't seen her since, but he realized now as she sat on his sofa, smoothing her skirt under her, arranging herself, that whether she knew it or not, she was arranging herself for one purpose: to look as pretty as possible. No, as sexy as possible, sacrificing neither a whit of poise nor showing an iota of intent. The nipples of her small breasts penetrated her bra, if she was wearing one. Her breasts, when she fidgeted, frolicked a bit among themselves, suggesting themselves in a minor key. Her toenails, he knew without knowing, matched her perfectly manicured fingernails. Back in New Jersey she'd taught business administration at the local community college. She's the kind, thought Dr. Levy, who inevitably engendered sexual—if not rape—fantasies in her students. She was genuine, down to earth. The child of hardcore Christian missionaries, she'd been brought up in Africa. She had given up God long ago, she told Dr. Levy, didn't give a "dime's worth of drivel" about him, but with her blonde hair, blue eyes, and pretty legs—her mini-skirt fashionably short—she looked like a junior leaguer. Jack had started drinking again, she told Dr. Levy.

"He doesn't know I know, but I do."

"Why doesn't he know?" Dr. Levy asked her.

"That I know?"

"Right." He was smiling with all the charm at his disposal while simultaneously studiously avoiding glancing at her legs. Glancing at Mary Beth McGowan's legs, he realized, was like a man prone to suicide climbing the stairs alone to the top of the lighthouse at Lady's Island.

"Should I say something? He's not going to like it."

"So?"

"Well, do you want us to be one of those couples that fight all the time? Haven't we had enough problems?"

"Maybe I'm just stupid, Mary Beth, but I was laboring under the illusion that alcohol was a 'problem.'"

"Oh, I don't know. Let's talk about something else. Do you drink?"

"Sure. Some. I enjoy drinking."

"So there! What's the problem?"

"I'm not an alcoholic."

"So it's safe. Heck, it's safe with me too. I'm not an alcoholic either, but I do enjoy taking a drink. Want to go have one?"

"What?"

"Hey, I'm not here because I'm worried about Jack's drinking. I'm just looking for somebody to drink with who isn't prone to alcoholism."

"Jews generally are afflicted with neuroses other than alcoholism."

"So let's get the heck out of here, go have some fun. You know, I've always wanted to be Jewish. It's a fantasy for me."

"That comes from having an unhappy Irish-Catholic childhood. Believe me, once you got to know us, you'd realize you're simply trading in one neurosis for another."

"Oh," she said, "you're crazy."

"Of course I am. I'm a psychologist."

"Hey, you got married too. Jack told me. Sorry I couldn't make it to the wedding. Jack said it was a pretty fancy affair. Three. Four years ago? Local girl, wasn't it?"

"That's when I moved into town. Still, I'm only a five minute drive from the base."

"Well, married people are allowed to have fun, so you promise me we'll have that drink some time. How much I owe you?"

"Free. The Marine Corps pays me. You know that."

"For how long? You might need some extra money, from what I hear?"

"You've been talking to Jack."

"How do you do it?"

"Do what?"

"Counsel soldiers to fight a war you think's crazy?"

"Honestly Mary Beth, I don't know. But I'll tell you this much: it was from the soldiers who've been over there that I learned it was crazy, whether they thought so or not."

"If you asked this little girl, I'd tell you you're counseling the wrong people."

"And who should I be counseling, Miss Know-It-All?"

"Are you flirting with me, Dr. Levy?"

"I might be. You're downright dangerous."

"I like that. I'll be back. After all, if I'm telling you Jack's got a problem, then I'm saying he hasn't got a problem, I guess that means I might be part of the problem. That's what you're thinking?"

"It's called 'enabling.' We have to find out what you're getting out of minimizing it, out of not fully facing it, out of avoiding a good old-fashioned fight with your husband. What you're afraid of, in other words. It's probably the same reason you're so seductive with me. Hell, probably to some degree Jack drinks for the same reason."

"Gosh, I've got to leave on that cute little remark?"

"That's my point, Mary Beth. That's probably what you're afraid of."

"I don't get it. Afraid of what?"

"Of leaving. Of being left. Of feeling too much. Same thing."

"Off of me, onto you. Don't you want to know who this little girl thinks you should be counseling?"

"Yeah, I'm curious."

"McNamara, you idiot shrink. It's his war."

She embraced him as she left. Too long, he berated himself. Too tenderly.

When he got home that evening he was extra affectionate with his wife. Plus he talked too much, too enthusiastically, about absolutely nothing. For all this, and for guilty thoughts too about potentially betraying Jack, he further berated himself.

But he also entertained himself with fabulous sexual fantasies.

As much as he loved his wife Arlanne—yes, the girl he'd met on the courthouse steps five years earlier—as pretty as she still seemed to him, as much as he trusted her and as intimate a couple as they were, their sexual life, which for the first couple of years had been nothing short of a thundering crescendo, had quieted down. Well, at least had slowed down, that's for sure. Still, had interest waned? At times she still excited him, no question, but had she become more his best friend than his lover? Was simple tenderness, while before orchestrating, accompanying and finally harmonizing with lust now supplanting it, overwhelming it as the major theme, diminishing it to a barely audible pianissimo? Was simple tenderness now not only the underlying, but the dominant, overarching melody of their relationship? Not enough back-alley challenge there, insufficient grit. It's what happens, figured Bert, when romance, fleeting anyway, bids bon voyage, blowing a kiss, to the relationship. Yet even after he was married, immediately after, he had never lost his appetite for sexual fantasies.

Look, but don't touch, Arlanne had admonished him. What that means, she told him after he looked, is neither look nor touch.

But times have changed, he now thought, this is the age of the sexual revolution!

Until he thought about her taking part in it.

| 27 |

Lila Shows Bert What 'The Cause' Really Is

Bert always looked forward to Saturdays: the day off, the weather great, sleeping late, not a damn thing to do, no decisions to make. Edward Albee's play *Who's Afraid of Virginia Woolf?* had been made into a movie, and it was playing tonight at the Breeze Theater with Elizabeth Taylor, Richard Burton, George Segal, and who was that whiney little actress, what was her name . . . He'd never liked her; she always looked and sounded as if she had a sinus condition, all stuffy, as if her nose was threatening to run. What was her name? Sandy Dennis! Anyway, he wanted to see it, and he knew Arlanne would. Maybe that evening . . . Meanwhile, he took his time reading the Sports section of the *Charleston News and Courier,* looking for whatever football game might be on television that afternoon. Looked like Green Bay vs. Cleveland. Jim Brown's brawn running up against Lombardi's brain. Could be good. Arlanne had bought the new Beatles album. It was the next album in the stack on the Hi-Fi, so he'd switched it on earlier. Now he hummed their latest hit *Michelle* along with them as he looked to see if Florida might be playing. He liked Steve Spurrier. Great quarterback. Ah, playing Tennessee. He also wanted to begin reading Bernard Malamud's new book *The Fixer.* He'd loved *The Assistant.* Arlanne had told him that what he'd actually loved was the depression it had left him with. It had given him, she had said, an excuse to brood and sit on his ass. Looking back on it, he figured, she was probably right.

He was growing restless now, fidgety. Could he do all he wanted to do in one day? The game took hours. Which one should he watch? If he watched either, he'd never get to *The Fixer,* and vice-versa. Plus, he wanted to jog. He needed to call his parents; he hadn't in over a week. What about just settling down with *Newsweek* or *Time* or *Sports Illustrated?* He should catch up on the newspaper editorials, but that felt like work. In fact, like most Saturdays around this time, no matter how much he looked forward to them beforehand, this one was beginning to feel like work. Should he have lunch with Murray? Jesus, why was he so tired all of a sudden?

Every Saturday. Same fucking thing. He found himself bored, restless, fidgety, unable to decide what to do. Plus, Arlanne had deserted him for the day, spending it with her dumb parents. He mimicked them. *"Hey, how y'all doin'?"* Her dad's manly pat on the back, her mother's *"We just love it so much when y'all drop by."* Fuckin' racists. And they thought they were somehow superior to him? You've got to be kidding me.

Ah yes, a time to nurse old grudges. God, he was depressed. No wonder he'd liked *The Assistant.* At least Morris Bober had something to do every Saturday, even if it was work.

And like every Saturday about this time, he sat there, doing nothing, waiting for something to happen, going out of his mind. Anything. A phone call. A friend inviting him for lunch or a softball game. A pickup basketball game. A work-related problem. Anything!

Though a crisis of some major kind was preferable.

Either that, or some form of adventure. Something he'd never done, like a visit to the South Sea Islands. Anything, as long as he didn't have to decide what it was.

Sometimes somebody phoned. This time it was Lila.

"Look here, Bert, meet me in back of Harry's Tavern, in the parking lot. One O'clock. Tell Arlanne I'm gon' borrow you for a while. We goin' on a picnic. You'll be the only one eatin'. Elizabeth got me so upset I can't hold down a glass of water. It's Saturday. You ain't got nothin' to do, and dammit, I need your help. You can take some fried chicken and all back to Arlanne. Tell her she don't need to cook tonight."

When Bert drove into the parking lot behind Harry's, he saw the kind of thing he had seen so many times before in Somerset but that never failed to surprise him, to confuse him, and to make him guilty, complicit and resentful. What could he do about it? Unlike Murray, he wasn't a native. Besides he was already flagellating himself over the hundreds of men who after his counseling went off to a strange little country they knew nothing about to murder people they knew nothing about. Already he was probably in trouble. Fighting racism in Somerset, the Corps had been informed, was the job of Somersetonians. And fighting Communism in Vietnam? Is that not the job of the Vietnamese? He was embarrassed. He pretended not to see Lila hand money to the white teenage girl in the tiny take-out window at the back of Harry's facing the parking lot, after which the girl passed Lila through the tiny window paper bags of whatever lunch she'd bought for their "picnic." He even heard, though barely, the girl say "Thank you, Lila." Not Mrs. Trulove, as she would've a white woman. But "Lila," as if Lila had just served the teenager her lunch in her home.

"You welcome, Darlene. You stay pretty now, you hear?"

"I'll try. Thank you, Lila."

Lila hadn't thought a thing about it, or so it appeared. If she'd been insulted, concluded Bert, she didn't show it.

What would've transpired had he suggested they forego the picnic and have lunch inside?

"You'd have been transferred to a faraway place," Murray Gold later told him, "and you'd never have been given the real reason. Somerset needs the Corps, but the Corps also needs Somerset."

Lila stuck her head through the passenger window of Bert's Satellite Plymouth, as simultaneously regal, casual, and feminine as ever, her sunglasses up on her forehead. Her feet, he couldn't help but notice as she had walked over, born to sandals. "New car?" she asked, giving it a once over.

"Nice." Hell, Bert had forgotten about the fact that it was new. He could care less about cars, new or old. He wasn't that goddamn assimilated. "Follow me," she told him. "I'm parked right over here."

The bridge over to the Island was closed. In his Plymouth behind Lila's Buick, he waved self-consciously. He wasn't quite sure what to do, with nothing to do. Lila didn't notice; he could see her through her rear-view mirror directly in front of him, looking at the car directly in front of her, grim with thought. A large sailboat passed like a snail under the bridge. Reopening, the bridge spit them onto the island, past the fruit and vegetable and boiled peanut stands, past Penn Community Center, where Martin Luther King had planned his March on Washington, past the lone service-station grocery store—Hudson's—past the shrimp boats and the landings and the water lapping up against the tiny bridge the farther and deeper they drove into the far corners and reaches of the island where he saw milling about in dirt yards in front of tarpaper shacks with collapsing porches the distended bellies of the most malnourished children he had ever even imagined, much less seen. Pictures maybe . . . kids in undeveloped African countries maybe, in times of great famine . . . but here? In America?

Following Lila's lead, he pulled over to the side of the dirt road in front of one of the shacks. From a wooden porch precariously supported by two concrete blocks at each corner a little boy of about three pulled his thumb from his mouth and studied them. A horse fly alighted on the railing. A little girl, probably a year or two older, sheltered from the harsh sunlight by a downpour of oak leaves and Spanish moss, jumped off the tire swing yelling "Mama, she here!" and banging the front door open, she ran into the house. When the screen door opened, however briefly, Bert caught a glimpse of a television on which a man was handing a drink to a woman, a photograph of Jesus on the wall, and faded linoleum turned up at the corners on the floor.

When Lila unlocked her trunk and it flew up, Bert saw it was loaded with food—cardboard boxes stuffed with sacks of corn meal and flour, sugar and salt, paper bags filled with potatoes and onions and carrots and green beans and black-eyed peas, milk and butter, bathroom supplies, cleaning supplies, soap, and detergent—from the Somerset Piggly Wiggly.

"How you think Piggly Wiggly gets away with stayin' open on Sundays, when it's against the law in South Carolina? They donate all their surplus stock to the Colored out here, every week, and Hoke just look in the other direction every Sunday. That his deal with 'em. Weren't for Hoke Cooley, these niggers be dead by now. Almost is anyway. Look at 'em, poor chillun'."

"I wondered about that, with the blue laws and all. Can he really get away with it?"

"He's the sheriff. He can get away with anything."

In a surprisingly short time, Fritz Hollings, the junior senator from South Carolina, would visit the island with a camera and television crew and the very kids they were looking at today would appear in photographs in major newspapers across the country, prompting the pilot for the first Food Stamp Program in America here on St. Helena's Island. Hoke would have something to do with that too, though the Yankee publicity would infuriate him.

"Murray told me Hoke was the biggest racist in Somerset," Bert said.

"He is. He do it all without fanfare. He love me, I tell you that. Probably still do. And he a lot nicer to my Driver than he have to be. Though Elizabeth, she wouldn't give him the time of day, act all sulky around him. Piss Hoke off. He ain't like that. Uppity little nigger, that's what he'd call her. Why? I tell him. 'Cause she don't kiss your white ass? He a racist, but he sho' took care of me. Course I took care of him too, and old Mary Magdalene, that wife of his, sho' wasn't goin' to. Ain't nobody put her on the cross but herself. Yeah, Hoke a racist, think he better than niggers, that nigger got littler brains and all, no doubt about it. But not this nigger, I'll tell you that. He love me, and he sho' respect me, and he know I a hell of a lot smarter than he is, even now."

"Loves the individual, hates the race?"

"You got it. But I gotta tell you, he do more to feed the hungry, get the poor to the doctor, all that stuff, than anybody in this county, and he do it without anybody knowin' and talkin' about it."

As they began carting cardboard boxes of goods to the front porch, setting them there, a tall, angular black woman in a print dress with the matching cloth belt unbuckled, hanging loosely at her waist, appeared at the front door, barefooted. Her hand visor-like over her eyes, she swatted away mosquitoes and peered into the sunlight.

"Hey, Rowena," Lila called out. "How you doin'? Them younguns' lookin' mighty cute. Might have to take 'em home with me. How 'bout send me that big load of a husband of yours to help us with these boxes."

"He on his way. Get on out here, baby. Thank you, Miss Lila. I got these. We just set 'em right here on the porch and I'll run 'em on in. We mighty grateful, Miss Lila."

"Somebody gotta' eat it."

"Thank you, ma'am. I got that now, just set it right there. Thank you, ma'am. Baby, you go out and bring in the stuff from the car. I got all this."

"You just sit back and point," her husband told Lila, after she introduced him to Bert. "Then I'll just set it all down here by the car and take it in myself after you all leave. You done too much already, bringin' all this out here to us folks. We grateful. You folks doin' all right now?"

And on they went, to the next house—"Hey, Willa, how you doin', Honey?" "Hey, Lila, how them little ones, that Driver keepin' you straight?" "Got some foodstuff out here, Angie, yo' old man home?" "Efram, where yo' mama, run in and tell her got some stuff she been waitin' for." "Johnnie Mae, lend me one of them big strong boys of yours, got somethin' for you, Honey." "Why thank you, Lila. Jamal! Get yo' ass out here right now. Don't you be duckin' out like you busy. Get on out here 'fore I come after you with a stick . . ."

After making her weekly rounds, she and Bert "picnicked" at her kitchen table, looking out the kitchen window across a greensward out over the bluff at the twilight curtain in deepening shades of lavender and violet falling silently, spreading gently, over the Somerset River, over the town of Somerset itself. She made the sweetest ice tea. Always did. Bert waited for silverware.

"Not with fried chicken," she said. "Not with this nigger."

Her fingers picked at her chicken naively, delicately, erotically.

"If it ain't all over you by the time you finish," she told him, "it means that if I were to ask Arlanne if you were good in bed, she'd say 'No.'"

Bert ate like a savage.

"No wonder she stickin' with you," said Lila.

"Well, you must be feeling a little better. You're eating."

"I need hope for my little girl, Bert. They's somethin' I can't figure out, somethin' she ain't tellin' me. Maybe somethin' she don't even realize herself. I tell you one thing: Old Murray scared to death she goin' back to the colored school. Says it'll set 'the cause' back a decade or more. He right too. It all come with integration."

"I'm a psychologist, Lila. I work with individuals, not groups. I see individuals, not groups. I hear more concern in your voice about Elizabeth than 'the cause.'"

"That's why we talkin'."

"But those little children, their scars and white patches and ringworms, their distended bellies . . . you could see the docility in their eyes, some of them. How can they keep up in school?"

"Who you think 'the cause' is, Yankee boy? Why you think I drove you out there this afternoon? Jesus, you a mess. Here, you need a napkin."

| 28 |

Arlanne's World Goes 'Round and 'Round

"You know what, Bert?"

"What?" he said. His eyes, however, attended only to Havlicek and Russel and West and Baylor racing about with their tall Black and white buddies in short pants all over the color television screen. What does Bert get out of this? Why watch other people having fun when you could be doing it yourself? To me, the idea of other folks merely enjoying their lives, much less having a blast, is enough to send me to bed for the day with a Valium. Look at those goddamn cheerleaders, jigglin' their playful young titties and twitchin' their cute little asses . . . goddamn exhibitionists. Flaunt 'em, Baby. Still, too in-your-face-happy and wholesome to be truly sexy. Sexy is subtle, suggestive, alluring. By this time, however, Bert probably thinks about as much of my titties and my cute little ass as he does the living room furniture.

"Russel the rebound, K.C. walks it up the floor . . ."

"Why should they have all the fun?" I asked him.

He nodded, but with way too much vigor, an obviously compensatory gesture, a pretense, a poor substitite for a genuinely-engaging response to your wife, even if she was, after five years of marriage, less than novel. Had those silly little cheerleaders frisky as puppies ripped off their skimpy little halters might his eyes have at least momentarily vacated the bouncing ball for the bouncing breasts?

"I've got breast cancer."

His eyes widen, like two enormous orbs; he's nodding now with so much vigor his head's about to fall off. And this time it's authentic. But that's because the Celtics scored on Havlicek's jumper.

"Hazzard charges down the court, looks one way, passes another, and West sweeps in for a layup. Lakers by seven."

"Bert?"

"Uh huh . . . " *"Baily Howell's hook shot clangs off the back rim."* "Shit," says Bert. "Goddammit."

"Yeah, I know what you mean. It's pretty sad. They're going to remove both breasts this afternoon."

"Baylor the rebound. Outlet to Hazzard, Hazzard to Goodrich in the lane. Goodrich hits the short jumper." "Goddammit," says Bert.

You can't say I wasn't sympathetic. "I know," I said. "I'm being selfish. Breast cancer in both breasts is one thing, but the Celtics losing . . . that's a whole other ball of wax."

"Don Nelson misses on the baseline. Hazzard corrals the rebound, he's taking it in himself, stutter-steps—freezing K.C.—at the foul line, spins around Nelson, fakes a pass to Baylor, and puts it up himself." Still, Bert manages a nod, however feeble, a pretense once again at not only hearing but understanding my words, his eyes nevertheless still entranced by the boys in short pants running up and down the court with their ball. The vigor, however, has left the nod; his head continues to bob up and down, but absent-mindedly, thoughtlessly, as if whoever was manning the switch simply walked out and left it on. Fascinating. His shoulders droop, those shoulders on which the weight of the game—his Sunday afternoon world—rests. The light, indeed hope, drains from his eyes. *"Lakers, 78, Celtics 65. Seven minutes, 37 seconds left. The Celtics have only one time-out remaining."* Still, his head keeps bobbing mechanically up, down, up, down, as though I'm still rambling on . . . even though I've said absolutely nothing for several minutes.

I stand in front of the television.

"Goddammit, Arlanne. Move! You always do this."

"Do what?"

"Arlanne. Would you please move?"

"News flash! 'PSYCHOLOGIST UNABLE TO CONTROL HIS EMOTIONS.' Are you angry yet?"

"Goddammit Arlanne," he says rising, threatening.

"Good," I say, "because anger turns me on."

And it does.

Apparently it turns him on too.

Afterwards, he's attentive. But boy, what I have to do to get him there.

"Is Elizabeth going crazy?" I asked him. "I can tell you Lila is. She's so worried. We talked when she called about the biracial council meeting."

Bert sat up in bed. Shafts of late-afternoon sunlight sprawled horizontally, cresting and waving over our bare ankles at the foot of the bed. The light autumn breeze off the river surfed and segued through the open windows, drying and dancing an incongruous tango with the after-sex sweat on our bodies. It was sensual, earthy, and refreshing, like cool fertile soil, black as night, sifting through your fingers. Outside the window the ginkgo tree exploded in yellow. In a few weeks the leaves would turn into a golden waterfall, curtsying about as they fell, golden boats in miniature floating beneath naked limbs on the surface of the earth, as pure in color and form as the bright-red fire trucks of our youth.

I hated Autumn leaves when they turned brown and brittle, curling up at the edges like linoleum in poor peoples' houses. They were ugly and sensually abrasive. I hated them even more because I was the one who ended up raking them. Since the old Civil Rights days, black people rarely sought that particular kind of work anymore. What was it Daddy used to say? Can't get nobody to mow the lawn nowadays, "nobody" naturally a pseudonym for "nigger." As if the problem with the Civil Rights Movement and integration was it'd left him havin' to mow his own lawn.

White people are lazy as hell. Always have been. If we got to do the work ourselves, you can forget it; we're headed for the hammock.

Which is exactly why I hate rakin' the damn things. Bert won't do it. He's too busy playing the Jewish card. Says Jews have been ghettoized for centuries, that they're "at two" with nature. Says they've had their noses stuck in books for so long mustiness is the only smell they know. Says fresh air, country air, is anathema to them, and can further enhance their propensity for gastro-intestinal diseases. The head, he says pointing to it, is all the Jews had to work with for centuries. The hands, he shrugs, mere appendages. You don't just shake off all this in a few generations. Raking leaves, he concludes, is a purely Gentile phenomenon. Jews don't even see them. Pretending otherwise is an unnecessary compromise with the majority. Encouraging it a barbarous act of anti-Semitism.

"I'd love a drink," he said. "Wouldn't you?"

"Sure, Honey, why don't you get us one?"

"Come on, Arlanne. It'll just take you a second."

"Ah, and it'll just take you a second."

He was going to pout. Did he think I gave a rat's ass? Still, I wanted to talk to him about Elizabeth. God, was he spoiled. I could already tell: He was going to wait me out. Fine. I didn't need a drink. He did.

"I can fix us drinks," he said, "or I can think about what you asked me about Elizabeth. Which do you want me to do?"

"So, so, so pathetic. I want you to fix us a drink."

"Okay, fine," he said, making a gesture—an empty one, I might add—toward getting up. "But that's it. I'm not fixing the drinks and talking about Elizabeth. It's too much. I do that kind of thing all week."

"Poor, poor boy. Come here and let little ol' Arlanne rub her little sweetie."

"Jesus Arlanne, I'm not a baby."

"You're not?"

"Okay, that's it. I'll get the drinks. But I'm not talking about Elizabeth right now. Of course," he said (starting to make a move again), "You know how you get off walking around naked in front of open windows . . ."

It's true. I did.

So did he.

It was time now, I figured, to make my move. "If I get you a drink, will you listen for five minutes?"

He settled back against the pillows. "Is it really five minutes? I mean, really, five minutes? All I do during the week is listen, or pretend to, which is just as much work."

"That's such a load of shit. If you weren't a psychologist, you still wouldn't listen, not to anything reasonable. You're incapable of it."

"Listening is boring. If you have to work at it, it's patronizing anyway. Talking's a lot easier, particularly if you're not really saying anything. If you are, well then, admittedly, it's back to work again, back to the old grind, yes sir, putting the old shoulder to the wheel, trying to say what you mean and mean what you say, as likely to happen, I hasten to add, as lightening striking. Which is why Jews never listen, why we argue so freely and happily, waving our hands about with such joy, slapping our foreheads and going "oy vey," having the time of our lives screaming and shouting and tearing out our hair over absolutely nothing at all. We're not really saying anything, and here in The Promised Land of cathartic laughter and meaningless tears, we're free to say it! See? There's nothing to listen to. Isn't that beautiful? And if everybody's like us, their ears cocked to the meaningless chatter of their own endlessly wagging tongues, we're all lost in the bliss of saying nothing at all."

"Utopia is everybody singing in the shower at the same time."

"Exactly. Rational discourse is so tedious: if we're all basically full of shit, why not relax and enjoy it? Were Jews to contemplate the idea that there was somebody out there truly, seriously, listening, considering, perhaps even judging, what we might be saying, why honey, I honestly believe that would shut us up for the rest of our lives."

"Sweetheart, let me get this straight: would that be a bad thing, or a good thing?"

"It—"

"—'it' being Listening?"

"Jesus, Arlanne. Listen. Am I talking to myself here? Yes. Listening. Listening is essentially a socially acceptable form of eavesdropping; it's social wiretapping; voyeuristically intrusive. The temptation may be there, at least for you Gentiles, but Dammit, Arlanne, resist it. Fight it. This, Arlanne, this is worth fighting over. Besides, if someone were to suddenly find themselves really listening, captive, caught in the trap, ensnared in the net, do you have any idea what that would mean? That somebody was actually saying something real, something honest, something true. Who wants to hear that crap?"

"That latter point is probably true."

"You heard it?"

I looked at him sheepishly. And it wasn't because I was naked.

"Sorry," I said.

"It's okay. Promise you'll never do it again?"

"I promise."

Leaning over me, he looked at me indulgently, patiently, with the understanding one has for the infant in his high chair who keeps throwing his baby food on the floor.

"You just did," he said.

"Oh, for God's sake, shut up. This is so ridiculous. I can't believe I let you get away with this stupid stuff. Listen—"

"'Listen?'"

"Yes Goddammit. If it's against your fuckin' religion, then Goddammit, convert. And quit being stupid for a minute. I'm serious."

"Arlanne, you're asking me for too much here. I'm a psychologist, and as a psychologist I can tell you: listening is psychological abuse."

"Are you done? Are you ready? You're nuts, a fruitcake."

"And you just did it."

"Good—"

"Ah, and you did it again. I cannot, in good principle, allow this to continue."

"Shut up."

"Listening, Arlanne, is a violation of the constitution of the United States. It's an invasion of privacy, a threat to free speech everywhere. The constitution doesn't guarantee the 'right to listen.' And you know why? Because it guarantees 'freedom of speech,' the 'right to talk.'

"Five minutes."

"Did you hear what I just said?"

"Absolutely not."

"Oh Honey, you're learning!"

"I'm also gritting my teeth. Can you hear them grinding against each other?"

Waving his finger in my face, he sang, "You listened again. Naughty, naughty."

"Five minutes."

"Johnny Walker on the rocks?"

"You're such a bastard."

"And when you walk in front of me naked, you have to do it slowly, as I take in and digest the marvelous contours of your bod."

I checked myself in the mirror. "It's holding up pretty good, isn't it?"

"I'd say so."

"Not like those sexy young cheerleaders on television though."

"I've never been a fan of glamor. It's neither sexy nor beautiful to me. You know that."

"That's the only reason I can think of to justify my marrying you."

"That, and my large penis. Jesus, look at this thing. A Canadian tent! An entire battalion could camp out under here."

"Here's your drink."

"Thanks."

"It's not for free."

"Elizabeth's certainly not crazy. That's for sure. Dangerously unhappy, yes. Dangerously confused, yes. Crazy, no."

"So what exactly is the problem?"

"The world is."

The world is crazy, I thought later, watching him sleep, but so is Bert. I think I love him most when he is asleep, when he's quiet and I can study him absent all his neurotic obsessions, which drive me as crazy as they drive him. Or when he's talking about Elizabeth. Why? Because Elizabeth he can help. I can tell by the way he talks about her, so clearly and comfortably.

Uncertainty, however, the prospect of irresolution, unhinges him, spiraling him into an uncontrollable orbit of rumination, repetitiveness, circular logic, 'round and 'round and 'round. Trying compulsively, poor man, to make everything right. Why? Because he can't.

Which is why I asked him about Elizabeth. With her, he can and will make things right. Not that the question wasn't an honest one. I love Lila's whole family. I journal about her constantly. The former matron of a whorehouse who happens to be the bravest, most honest woman in town? She's downright heroic.

But the soldiers, the soldiers, those kids on their way to Vietnam. I can't ask him about his work there. Why? Because he can't make that right. He can't.

Over and over he explains how he's trying. At his alma mater they're hiring counselors to keep kids from the war. And he's getting them mentally fit to go to war.

But am I? He asks over and over. Just by getting them healthy, declaring them fit?

Should I leave them unfit, sick? How do you even do that? Lie? Declare them unfit when they're not?

Is that the choice? Lying, or sending them off to war?

One's as immoral as the other.

But he knows all this. Yet rather than face it honestly and make a decision and take action one way or another, my husband the psychologist persists in trying to make me his psychologist, his therapist, going 'round and 'round, on and on, tying himself in knot after impenetrable knot expecting me, of all people, to unravel him.

And of all people, accusing me of not listening to him.

After all, he says with a sly smile, desperately manipulative, his mother always did.

She would do anything for him, he says.

She didn't have to stop a war, I told him, grabbing up my pajamas and heading off to the guest room, at the time, forever.

Not only, I told him, do you lack the balls to act. You, Mr. Self-Professed-Truth-Seeker, don't even have the balls to face it.

Fear, he said, makes me go 'round and 'round.

If you could truly accept that, you'd shut up.

Will you sleep with me if I do?

Yes, but if I do, tonight, I'll resent it.

That's okay, he says, I don't mind.

See why I love him while he's sleeping, or at least when he's not making his world, of which I am a part, go 'round and 'round?

| 29 |

Bert's First Therapy Session With Elizabeth Is an Education for Both

Sept. 17

"I don't want to talk to nobody, Dr. Levy. Excuse me: 'anybody.' I don't care nothin' about all this racial stuff. What that got to do with me? I don't care 'bout no 'cause.' Everybody lookin' at me, nobody see me. Can I go now, call my mama to pick me up?"

"Why, Elizabeth, you don't like my plush office, the wonders of Lawton Island, all the joyous and happy faces? A kid's paradise!"

I almost got a bit of a smile out of her.

"Guys marching around with guns, bang bang, all that—"

For a split second, fragility cracked her otherwise stubborn demeanor.

"What's happening, Elizabeth?"

"Nothin'," she said, reorienting herself, her features coming back into full focus.

"What was happening?"

She smiled, coy and mischievous. "Wadn't nothin' happenin'." She looked at me, shaking her head as though I was crazy. Then she started laughing at me. "Ain't nothin' happenin'. What you talkin' about? You imaginin' things, Dr. Levy. Quit botherin' me with yo' crazy self."

"Sorry. I lost my head."

"You a funny man. No doctor I ever went to was funny."

"If you don't tell me what was happening, I'll give you a shot."

"You ain't that kind of doctor. You don't think I know what kind of doctor you are? You need one like you more than I do."

"Whoa! That girl gettin' sassy."

A dubious smile showed through her frown. "You tryin' to talk nigger talk," she said. "Man, you sound stupid."

"That's because I'm a white guy who's about to give you a shot."

"You ain't. I know you ain't. Is you?"

"Not if you tell me why you're talking black all of a sudden and your mother hasn't heard it from you in months. She's afraid you'd forgotten how."

"She the one want me to forget how."

"She's just preparing you for a white world, saving you from embarrassment."

Her smile became so bitter I wondered if it was a taste she would ever get rid of.

Gunfire began faintly echoing off the rifle range a few blocks over. She flinched, looking about, for an instant it seemed to me, once again frightened, disturbed.

It couldn't have been just the noise. It wasn't that loud and her reaction was beyond annoyed. Almost like battle-traumatized soldiers—several back from Vietnam I was presently seeing.

"Elizabeth?"

She looked at me as if there were no combination in the world clever enough to open that safe.

"Guys," I repeated, returning to her earlier discomfort, looking for what she might be hiding. "Guns . . . guys marching around with guns."

Something, it seemed to me, was happening. Resistance, in her mind, giving way.

"Gunshots?" I said, gently.

Vulnerable and hurt now, she looked as if she were looking for someone but afraid of finding him.

"Who is that, Elizabeth? Tell me, please, so I can help you. Who are you looking for, thinking about?"

I could barely hear her. "My daddy," she whispered, looking down.

Then she refocused, once again, looking directly at me, by all appearances once again free, for the moment, of whatever was bothering her; her sadness—and perhaps her father as well—adrift, far far from the shores of her consciousness. Finally she said, matter-of-factly, as if daring me to contradict her, "Ain't nothin' wrong with me."

| 30 |

Bert Tells Lila What 'Elizabeth's Cause' Really Is

As soon as his last patient left, Bert phoned Lila. He knew she'd be anxious. She picked up on the first ring.

"Lila," Bert began, "Elizabeth also has a 'cause.' It's her father."

"Oh my Law, I was afraid of this. I knew it was all balled up inside her, somethin' more, you know. He ain't comin' back. No chance. I done told her over and over and over."

"She misses him."

"He ain't never been here. He was all involved in the Movement, up there with Huey Newton, that group. Never had no time for us. No money neither. Wouldn't have even if he did. Rather serve breakfast with Black Panthers than feed his own."

"Well, she feels his absence, maybe that he'll come back if she stays at the white school, sets the right example for her 'people,' beats 'the white man' at his own game, I don't know. What I am sure of is that there's trauma there. It worries me."

"That child. Too much religion. Don't know who she got it from. After he dead and gone every time somethin' bad happen, every time somethin' bad looked like it might happen that little girl'd get on her knees, 'What would Jesus do, Mommy? What would Jesus say?' One day I looked at her and said, 'Honey, I ain't got no idea, but I tell you this, I ain't heard him say much yet.' She look at me just right then like all hope had gone out of the world, just like it did for her daddy, poor thing, nothin' I could do to comfort her after that. That man dead. Shot himself. Died right there in front of both of us. How she figure he comin' back? She think he Jesus Christ, gon' come back from the dead? After she starve herself to death? Or she want to join him?"

"He killed himself?"

"Yeah, he did. She was five years old, saw the whole thing."

"Maybe she's trying to join him. Martyring herself for him. She didn't tell me he was dead, much less that he killed himself."

"She talk to him at night, 'bout the only one she talk to now, I hear her, she don't know I hear her, breaks my heart, Bert. But yeah, he shoot himself, took me days to get the blood off the walls, blood everywhere. Guilt wiped the blood off those walls. Guilt and anger. All of it right here in these hands. Poor man. Eaten up with hate. Used to blame myself, you know. If I'd have done this, if I'd done that . . . there wadn't nothin' I could've done. His own daddy tellin' him he worthless, the white man tellin' him he worthless . . . He was either gon' shoot him or shoot himself . . ."

"'Him' being the white man or his daddy?"

"For him, wadn't no difference. Might not be for her neither. She never give Hoke the time of day. Wouldn't have a damn thing to do with him. Driver loved Hoke comin' over. They got along, Hoke teaching him to fish and all that. He'd give Driver a quarter and ol' Driver'd head straight for the store. Not Elizabeth, wouldn't even touch it. Drove him crazy. 'You too good for my money, little girl?' Wouldn't even look at him. 'Course he wasn't her daddy."

"But did Driver know, back then?"

"Oh, I think Driver sensed it long before I told him. Elizabeth too . . . Driver had a sense of it anyway 'cause he and Hoke, they did have a relationship, whatever he called him or however he thought of him they had a relationship."

"And Elizabeth didn't, not with a man."

"You know, now that I look back on it, I think I got rid of Hoke 'cause of Elizabeth, I thought maybe she'd start feelin' better about things, you know . . . I know I told him it was 'cause of business and him not lettin' me buy into downtown, and it was, but deep down, I know now it was 'cause of Elizabeth, the way she felt and all."

"But Driver . . ."

"Driver loved him. And you know what, much as a white man can love a black child, Hoke love that little boy, no doubt about it. He showed him too. He just didn't show anybody else. He couldn't. He couldn't."

"Well, that's something."

"It's something. Still . . ."

"I know, its something, but still it's sad, isn't it?"

"It is. You gon' see her again, right?"

"I'm going to see her till we get her right, Lila. How's that?"

"Thank you, Bert," she said, and as she hung up the phone Bert could hear her heart breaking.

| 31 |

Bert Tries to Get Elizabeth to Be Wherever She Is

Sept. 21

" . . . white people killed my daddy. He ain't dead. They dead, don't even see 'em, just like they don't see me. I see my daddy. See him everyday. Talk to him. And he see me."

"Why aren't you eating, Elizabeth?"

"Ain't hungry."

"How do you feel?"

"Ain't got no feelin's. Can't afford 'em, got no time for 'em, got to work, show the world what a black child can do, pave the way for Driver, for my people, for . . . for . . . for . . ."

"For who, Elizabeth? For what? Deep down."

"I don't know, Dr. Levy," she said helplessly. "I don't know."

"It's too much, isn't it?"

She nodded.

"What is it exactly that's too much, Elizabeth?"

"Raisin' the dead."

Sept. 25

"Was he really ever alive for you, Elizabeth?"

"Yes, of course he was. My daddy loved me."

"Would you like to go back to that time, to re-experience what happened back then?"

Sadly, she shook her head, her hand playing across the texture of the sofa.

"However you experience it, I promise you you'll feel better afterwards. It's a promise, Elizabeth. No shots."

She smiled, doubtful.

"Okay?"

"I guess."

"Lie down now, relax."

"Can't I just do it sittin' up, like we talkin'?"

"No, Sweetheart, lying down makes you more vulnerable to feeling, more open to it. Relax your body, your muscles. That's it. Take a deep breath. There you go. Was that so hard?"

She lay there, frowning, reluctantly resigned to the process.

"Now close your eyes . . ."

"Why?"

"Afraid of what you might see?"

She closed them.

"That's it. Now I'm going to count slowly. You're going to time-travel back to when you were as small as you can remember. That's it. Once you get there, tell me where you are and what you're doing. Okay? One . . . two . . . three . . ."

She was already regressing. "This weird," she mumbled, her face wrinkling in anticipation, as if she wanted to first just get a peek at her inner life before deciding whether to enter it. Intensity shut her eyes tighter. Concentration tightened her facial muscles.

"Try to remember as far back as you can, as young as possible. Okay? Three . . . four . . . five . . ."

She nodded, submerging into her past, her smile now relaxed, thoughtful.

After a minute or so, her eyes closed as if she were asleep, she said, "I'm on the playground over at the school. It's Saturday, 'cause it's just me and Annie Mae, nobody else there. We like to play school. She sit on the swing, 'cause she the pupil, and I stand there and explain everything to her 'cause I'm the teacher. She say, 'What make the sun shine, Teacher? Why the wind blow? Is rocks alive? Can they breathe?' 'Law,' I say, 'Chile, you got too many questions.' 'Aw please,' she whines, 'please answer my questions, Teacher.' She looking at me all doe-eyed. 'Okay,' I say, 'but one at a time now.' Now I'm answerin' 'em, one at a time. Annie Mae, she like that."

"How old do you feel?"

"Three, maybe four . . ."

"And you're happy playing with Annie Mae?"

"Yeah, but she leave me when I go to white school. Said she wouldn't, but she did."

"That's bad."

"Yeah."

"But that hasn't happened yet. Stay the age you are."

"I am."

"What's happening now?"

"She want you to tell her what to do next."

"Annie Mae?"

"No, not Annie Mae."

"You mean 'you' when you were little? That's who you mean by 'she?'"

She nodded, her eyes shut.

"But she's too smart for me to tell her what to do! Too pretty too!"

She's grinning, squirming, like she knows it, just like a three year old.

"She like that?" I asked her.

"Yeah," she said. "She like that."

"She likes it when I tell her how pretty she is. Because she is! The prettiest litte girl in the whole wide world. Smartest too."

"'Okay,' she say, 'you can go on now.'"

"She says that, or you say that?"

"She say that."

"You sure? Check with her."

"That was me."

"Ask her if she likes it when you speak for her instead of letting her speak for herself."

"She don't like it. It make her go back into her books where she can't come out. She say I close the book on her. 'Boom!' she say. Slam it shut, right in her face, right when she open her mouth. Don't let her speak."

"Ask her when was the first time that happened."

"After Mama come home with Driver from the hospital, after he born, she say. She don't like him then, though he all right now."

"She didn't like him?"

"That me again. She okay with him."

"How does she feel about you?"

"All right."

"That's it?"

"She don't like it when I close the book on her. But she understand why I do it."

"How do you feel about her?"

"She want to play with me. She miss me."

"Does she want you to hold her?"

Elizabeth nodded.

"Can you?"

She shook her head, "No."

"Do you know why you can't?"

"I don't think so."

"Ask her. She'll tell you, I think."

"She say I'm not ready, I'm scared. She say I will when I'm ready. She say it'll happen naturally."

"Is knowing that a good thing or a bad thing?"

"Good. It a good thing."

"Comforting?"

"Yeah."

"And what are you scared of?"

"My mama leavin'."

Sept. 31

" . . . Mama love Driver more than me. Used to love me. Read me stories, sing me songs, put me to bed every night, now she always with him."

"Singing him your songs? Reading him your stories? Tucking him in?"

She opened her eyes. "How you know that?"

"Well, an awful lot of people who've been on that sofa have little brothers . . . Close your eyes."

"They closed."

"That's it. And guess what? Everyone single one of them wanted him dead, or at least thought they did, so they could get their mamas back."

She nodded sagely; she knew what I meant by that.

"If you've been to church you know that. Cain and Abel. You know something else? They all wonder, 'Is there something wrong with me? How could she possibly prefer that little wrinkled old thing to me? I'm interesting and fun. She likes lying down with me. Or liked to before he came along. Now all she does is make woo-woo over him. I'm not the cutest anymore. And all he does is cry, burp and poop.'"

"That how I felt. Same thing. Like something wrong with me."

"Like maybe you didn't clean up right or pick up your toys or whined too much or were ugly or stupid or something? The older sibling's always trying to make up for it, always. But she's mad too. But she won't show her mama, too scared. I'll tell you what a lot of them do."

Her head turned just a bit toward me, her eyes still shut.

"When Mama's around they pretend to be all lovey-dovey and careful about holding him right and all that. You know what I mean?"

She nodded. She knew, all right.

"But when she's not looking or not around they'll push at the soft spot, where you're not supposed to touch—you know where I'm talking about? The soft spot on his head?"

She smiled.

"You did that too?"

"Yeah," she said sheepishly.

"Everybody does, then they think, 'I'm this awful person, I'm the only one in the whole world who does this!'"

"'Cause your mama and the Bible and all tells us we supposed to love our brother."

"Tells us we're supposed to love everybody. I don't. Do you?"

"I sho' didn't love him. 'What the Lord giveth, the Lord taketh away.' I used to get on my knees every night and pray to Jesus. 'Jesus, dear Jesus, please take the baby. Please take the baby. Please take the baby.'"

"And every morning you'd wake up and he'd still be there, whining and pooping and crying and burping, no personality whatever. And Jesus, he never took him."

"No. He took my daddy instead."

Oct. 3

" . . . There's a lot of guilt there, Elizabeth, probably the kind that makes you the kind of kid who does everything right, so mom won't leave completely? Are you back to the little girl you were yet?"

"She say that what made me study so hard in school."

"To make yourself worthy of Mama? Keep your eyes closed."

"Somethin' else . . ."

"Yeah?"

"Them other people you talk to, when they mamas do try to do things with 'em, you know, later on, after their brothers get older, what they do then?"

"Oh, they don't give an inch then. Too mad. Too resentful. 'She didn't want me before, she can't have me now.' You know? Something like that."

"Yeah. Me too. Some of the time. But if I keep studying and do what's right, then she still stay."

"That way you keep her without having to be afraid of her leaving again."

"Yeah. That stupid. Ain't it?"

"Yeah."

"That what they did?"

"Yeah."

"Then they stupid too."

"Yeah, if she were going somewhere, she'd have already done it. I mean, you know she loves you, right?"

"She say that right."

"The little girl?"

"Yeah."

"What do you say?"

"Same thing, but . . ."

"Yeah?"

"Makin' good grades and all, workin' hard . . . it make me feel important too . . ."

"Sure."

"But, I don't know . . ."

"Physically, in your body, you can feel something, or the absence of something, sometimes . . . close your eyes . . ."

She placed her hands over her heart, delicately, barely touching it.

"My heart empty," she said. "All that hard work, it don't fill it up. I still empty."

That's when she started crying.

"That's a girl," I told her, holding her hand. "Get it all out, then eventually it will fill up."

Oct. 7

" . . . Okay, something, or somebody, is missing. You know who it is . . . right?"

She sighed, closing her eyes, relaxing.

"You're three or four years old, happier now. Right?"

She nodded.

"Now let yourself get older until something stops you. Okay?"

"She make him do it."

"Who?"

"Mama. That why I so mad at her now. That why I turn away when she try to love on me, just study instead."

"So she can't leave . . ."

"Yeah . . . that right."

"How'd she do it?"

"She bring Driver home. The Lord punish me for prayin' for Driver to die. That why he take my daddy. Right in front of me so I could see it was His work."

"And if your Mama hadn't brought Driver home, you wouldn't have prayed for his death . . ."

"She kill my Daddy."

Oct. 11

"Close your eyes, Elizabeth, relax, let your body go limp now . . . tell me what happened . . . you're how old . . . five?"

"I can tell you without going back. I remember every last thing about it."

"It'll be without emotion though. Right?"

"Yeah, that what bein' smart do for you."

"You can know it without feeling it."

"Yeah."

"Without feeling, Elizabeth, your heart remains empty. The 'head,' if you will, sees to it. The head's a tricky customer, and in your case, you've outsmarted yourself. It's placed a 'Closed for Business' sign over your heart."

She nodded, ruefully. "Okay," she said. "Wait a minute, I'm going back."

"Tell me when you're there."

"It's before I started school. I think I'm about five, almost five anyway. He busy in the living room. I'm afraid of botherin' him, so I stand in the hallway, out of the light, partially behind the door to the living room. I hear Driver crying for his Mama in the next room. I look back toward his bedroom to see if Mama comin' since he just woke up from his nap. I almost shout to her, Mama, Driver woke up just so she hears him and then I hear an explosion. I don't know what it is. I can't move. All I see in the living room now is blood everywhere, coverin' the walls, on the doorknob in front of me, my mama comin' in screamin' and yellin' and cryin.' Oh God Nathan what you do what you do. Oh somebody please help me and she holdin' him and she got blood all over her too—her face, her yellow dress—it all stuck in her hair . . . I remember thinkin' it look like fingerpaint on the picture window . . .

"Then she see me standin' in doorway and she scream NoNoNo Go on Not in front of her NoNoNo Go on sweetheart, don't look at this Go on get out of here GoGoGo . . .

"But I can't. I can't move . . ."

"That's it, Sweetie, let yourself cry. That's a girl. Feel all that feeling coming in, filling up your heart."

After a few minutes of good hard crying, she opened her eyes and said, "Dr. Levy . . ."

"Yes, Sweetie . . ."

"I been there ever since."

"Who studies, works hard in school?"

"That ain't me. That her, the one who died that day. I'm her heart. I'm her heart."

Oct. 17

"I'm ready now," said Elizabeth. "I can hold her. Can I?"

"Absolutely. She's waiting for you."

She submerges deeply into her emotions, into her heart and soul, her imagination, her eyes closed. She seems peaceful, confident, in a place all her own. She begins cradling and swaying in her arms the child she once was, a bit awkwardly at first, then in a steady rhythm, to and fro, to and fro, like her mother once did her, and quietly, almost imperceptibly, I could hear in her own voice what at one time must have been her mother's singing to her: "Summertime, and the livin' is easy . . . so hush, little baby . . . hush little baby . . . don't you cry . . . no, no, no, don't you cry . . ."

By the time she finishes, I'm almost crying. I am a Jew, but without question, in my mind I am looking at the Madonna and Child, at suffering and purity beyond reason, beyond scientific explanation. Whenever this happens, every single time, I'm not only humbled, but a bit envious. To become who you truly are, to be the child you were, who will lead us . . . Isaiah's prophecy. Amazing. Exciting. Inspiring. Always. Every single time. Yet I don't really know why. That too, I suppose, beyond explanation. Is that what keeps me interested?

"Hold her tight now, until your heart fills up, until you're one and the same . . ."

Her entire being twitches, shudders, as though she's being tickled. She giggles.

Then quietly, peacefully, naturally she places her hands comfortably over her heart.

"You there yet?"

She glances down at her heart, patting it. "She right here."

Oct. 21

" . . . You're together, right?"

"Sho' am." Her hand over her heart, her eyes closing. "I'm here."

"Let yourself get older now, until something stops you. Okay?"

She knew just what to do. Kids were much better at this than adults. Less fortification built up.

"That's why I'm at the white school. She not with me now. I leave her again. Empty again. I don't want to do this no more. Don't do me no good. This whole thing stupid."

"Absolutely. Accept that completely. Feel that all the way, then you'll know for sure."

After a few minutes, she opens her eyes, thinking, staring ahead of her at nothing in particular, contemplating something inside of her. Outside the window it's gray, sadly overcast. Faintly, in the distance, from the drill field, a drill sergeant and his men sing of a new war in an old cadence as compulsively inviting and mesmerizing as the Pied Piper.

"The Hippies say America's wrong . . ."
"The Hippies say America's wrong . . ."
"Whadda' we say Whadda' we say . . ."
"Kill the Cong Kill the Cong . . ."
"Whadda' we say Sound off . . ."
"Whadda' we say One two . . ."
"Whadda' we say . . ."
"Sound off. One two three four."
"THREE FOUR!"

Tomorrow morning, Cunningham. His file, he'd said in his letter, most of it done up by his superiors, was pure propaganda. If I'm not careful, he's going to get us both either in the brig or dishonorably discharged. He has to be a nut to do what he did. Crazy. Did the war bring it out of him? Would it eventually have come out anyway? Or is it just the war that's crazy? Is he really going to go public with all this? Should I report it? Am I liable if I don't? How can I not support him without being nuts myself? Worse, without being an accomplice to murder? And Arlanne wonders why I'm so preoccupied, so obsessive. She's scared, protective, but it's undermining, makes me yell and scream. Her family didn't do that. They just remained suicidal their whole lives. In our house whoever was the loudest won the argument. Volume equals truth: the Jewish equation. In Somerset almost everybody's like Arlanne's family. Arguing, rather than a way of life, a cultural imperative, seems impolite and tiring here. It's hard to think in this place. The beauty and languor here work on the mind like an aphrodisiac. The crazier I get over this war, the more I start to argue with Arlanne over every little thing that comes up. She thinks I'm crazy, which I am. All Jews are. If by and large Irish Catholics are drunken brutes and WASPs cold and undemonstrative, Jews are fanatically obsessive-compulsive. We're all at war with ourselves. Is that why we're in Vietnam? Better them than us? Thank God for the Negro here, the Asian there?

"Something's happening, Elizabeth?"

She nods, taking a deep breath as she closes her eyes, preparing for and surrendering, it appears to me, to the inevitable. I wait a few minutes, as I generally do with patients, before once again cranking up my obsessions. Sometimes, when a patient's in an altered state and the drawbridge is down and the truth appears on the other side, sleep can send it into the moat. I haven't had that happen much, but you have to watch for it.

You don't listen, Arlanne tells me. You don't say anything, I respond. Hell, listening's not an obligation, I say. Make it worth my while. But you want me to listen to your obsessions, she counters, which are agonizing, to say nothing of endless. You're saying I'm crazy? I ask her. You weren't when I married you, she responds, in fact I married you because I thought you were a good listener, sensitive. Yeah, I faked that really well, I know. Naive me, she says, I thought all psychologists were good listeners, that you had to pass a 'listening test' or something. Bullshit, Arlanne, makes me inattentive. Well then, she says, grabbing her pillow from the bedroom on her way to the guest room, to which naturally I follow her, it's obvious the great psychologist doesn't want to sleep with bullshit. Fifty-thousand men are being drafted every month, Arlanne, at least according to Rob Vicker here in the *Times*. I'm supposed to decide whether they're Vietnam potential, but they'd be insane to want to go there. They'd be like McGowan—Frank—when he marched those kids into the swamp, like Charles Whitman. Why go to Vietnam to kill? I ask myself. Just climb a tower in Texas and fire away. The dissociation required to kill in a situation like this must be the psychological equivalent of nuts, which is what Cunningham is going to tell me, and if I support him, I'll lose my job, among other things. "Well, if you're willing to kill for it, Bert, that's your prerogative." "My prerogative?" "Yes, your preregotative." "I'm not killing anyone, Arlanne." "No, but if you're aiding and abetting murder by deciding who and who isn't fit to kill . . ." "Who says I'm doing that? Am I doing that? Look, here's what I've told the guys I've counseled. I'll tell you and you tell me whether that's aiding and abetting murder or not." "You already have, over and over." "Okay, okay, can I tell you what I plan to tell Cunningham?" "Stop, Bert. Stop. I can't do this anymore." "You mean you're not going to 'listen,' Arlanne? How incredibly hypocritical." Then after awhile get I down on all fours: I salivate, I grovel, I crawl. I know I'm subjecting her to misery because I can't face who I am now, who I've become, who I might become, who I might be becoming.

"You hate me," I say to her, "and I can't blame you." "Oh stop it," she says. "Self-pity doesn't become you. You're trying too hard. Besides, I don't hate you. It's worse than that, which is why I feel ashamed. You're preoccupied, Bert. You're not really here, present. You're only present for yourself, at least when you're home, all caught up in a perpetual psychological bout with yourself. It's so excessively rational: round and round and round, in circles, going nowhere. Maybe you do that to yourself to keep from going somewhere, from getting anywhere." "You mean I'm a coward?" "If you have to ask the question . . ." she says cheerfully, making up the daybed in the guest room. "Isn't that what you always say, Dr. Levy? 'If you have to ask the question, you either already know the answer, or you don't want to hear it . . .'"

"I'm disappearing, Dr. Levy. Doing just what my daddy did."

"By not eating?"

"I'm killing myself. That why she not here. Why my friends gone, why Annie Mae gone."

"Close your eyes, relax, and slowly, very slowly, let yourself disappear, let yourself die."

She looked at me, annoyed, to say nothing of incredulous.

"It's the only way to come back to life. As you do, they will. Emotionally, you're dead now, empty of feeling, of life. For example, did your friends leave you, or did you leave them? Could you have at least prevented them from leaving, the ones you really cared about, like Annie Mae? You said she never phoned you after you changed schools. Have you phoned her? Have you somehow given her the message you didn't want her to phone you?"

"She's smiling."

"The little you?"

"She say 'I told you so.'"

"Ask her why you're not eating."

"To protect her. I not want her to get hurt again, so I leave everybody."

"Her too?"

She nods, her eyes closing.

"Is that 'protecting' her?"

"No, no, she say I protectin' myself, not her."

"Keep going."

"Ah, that why I couldn't hold her before. I too scared of her hurt."

"Of feeling it, of being swallowed up by it . . ."

"That right. I be ashamed of her, want nothin' to do with her."

"How does she feel about that?"

"She say she understand."

"She does?"

"How does that make you feel?"

"Bad and good."

"Bad that you left her, but good that she understands?"

" . . . she say if I had her, wouldn't need nobody else. She just miss me."

"And you miss her?"

She nodded.

"Tell her. Then ask her to wait and tell her you'll be back in a few minutes."

"What good this do again?"

"As you feel your feelings, they subside. They'll return, but not so powerfully each time. You'll understand them better. For example, do you still feel responsible for your father's death, like you caused it . . ."

"Not like before."

"That's because you felt a lot of that guilt. As you feel it, it goes away. The only thing wrong with joy and happiness, as you know, is that they're temporary. You feel and experience them—a good grade, a home run—and they leave. We like those feelings. We welcome them, because they feel good. Negative feelings, like guilt and shame and fear, we don't like those so we keep them inside until we're ready, capable of feeling them. Sometimes a lot of time has to pass. But as we feel them, they too subside. Usually we find they're not nearly as scary as we thought."

"How'd you learn all this?"

"When I was really little, when I was hurt, maybe because I didn't get my way or my feelings were hurt for some reason, after crying I felt better. I wasn't really conscious of this as a child but in my training as a psychologist I went through the same thing in many ways as what you're going through with me. And as I looked back over my childhood it occurred to me that it was hard for me to cry—I didn't want to since I was a boy—but that afterwards I did always felt better, and I started asking myself, why? Why did crying make me feel better? My analyst was pretty impressed. Pretty neat?"

"Yeah, it is. Simple too."

"Ready?"

She closed her eyes.

"One . . . two . . . three . . . let yourself die now, slowly, slowly let yourself disappear . . ."

Finally she said, "I'm in a book. No, I am a book. It's closing on me. I don't like this, Dr. Levy."

"Let it close."

"It's dark. There's a blank page. It's white. Nothing on it. Now it's a wall. It's a page that's a wall. It's huge, like the side of a tall building. I'm small compared to it, in the dark, looking up at it. A white page blocking the whole world."

"Can you see or get around it? Under it? Over it?"

"No, but pages are peeling off of it. I'm in it now. I'm really little. Mama readin' to me, singin' to me. My daddy here, he play with me, but then he on a different page. When he leave I go with him, but I ain't really there. I'm here, on the same page. Little. Now me and Annie Mae, we playing, gettin' older, the page turnin' again, Driver's on it. He cute at first but I don't like him now. Mama read and play with him. I'm alone, so I go to different page, but that ain't really me neither. It's like when my Daddy leave and I go to different page . . . when I leave to go to different page I ain't really in the book. I out of it. Oh, I readin' it. But the real me, I in it still, and I see Mama all tired out now. She tryin' to play with me and give me attention too, but she too tired really from dealin' with Driver. Law, he a handful. Make me tired just watchin' her. I helpin' her now, 'stead of going to a different page and leavin'."

"Which means being in the book instead of reading it."

"More like being the book. Like I am the book, like the book me, like I it. Like I am the book, but my photograph also in it, standin' out from it at same time. Oh, I know, the book me, but I also the book at the same time. This strange. The book and me, it's like we both in charge. It do what I want. I do what it want. I don't understand."

"The you that isn't you. Where is she? The one who leaves."

"Gone. She reads the book, but she ain't in it. When she leaves, she reads. She flyin' off on the blank page, like she on a magic carpet made of white. I feel sad. She say I don't need her no more. No, that me sayin' that to her. Bye-bye. I wave to her, she flyin' away, her magic carpet ripplin', fluffin' up underneath her, turnin' into a cumulus cloud. Sunlight pourin' through it. She gone. She dead. In Heaven. I alive."

Her eyes slowly opened. She looked around, as if she'd just awakened from a dream. "My heart open," she said. "I here now."

"The book?"

"I come out of it."

"And the white school?"

"I be wherever I am."

32

Arlanne Gets Caught but Her Heart Beats for Bert

"I hear his car in the driveway, Murray. I'll call you back later. Okay? Why didn't you ask me to marry you, Murray?"

"Chicken shit, Arlanne. Pure fright."

"Yeah, right."

"It's true, sweetheart, you were always too pretty and too popular for me. I was lookin' at you though."

"Oh, you're a sweetie. Wish I had known. Call you later, okay?"

Bert walked in, throwing his briefcase on the kitchen counter as he always did (though I'd asked him a thousand times not to) just as I hung up the phone. Mama had warned me since I was a teenager to exercise discretion in my phone conversations: Ella Maples, the town operator, was known to repeat private conversations verbatim around town. I'd never even given it a thought until now, when I suffered a momentary vision of Ella phoning back and telling Bert about the conversation I'd just had with Murray. Well, what would be wrong with that? I didn't say anything wrong. Neither did Murray. He's Bert's best friend, right?

"Who was that?" he asked looking in the refrigerator, probably for nothing. That's what he did every evening he came home. Throw the briefcase on the kitchen counter, open the refrigerator door, and come out with nothing. "What're you lookin' for?" I'd ask him. "Oh nothin," he'd say. Well, what the hell was he doin' in there every evenin'? Takin' inventory?

"Why do you do that?" I asked.

"What?" he said, looking at me.

"Look in the refrigerator every night when you come home, first thing; close it, and come out with nothing. When we were first married, I'd try to figure out what you might be looking for and put it in there. You'd close the door as if you didn't even see it."

"I don't know," he said, thinking about it. "I never thought about it."

"Well, it's strange."

"Who called?"

"That was Murray. Just chatting. Wanted to know how we were doing. Thought we all might do something this weekend."

"Did you talk about me?"

"Bert, don't be silly."

"Did you? About my obsessiveness? My craziness?"

"Please, don't start. You're starting."

"It's fine if you did. Just tell me the truth."

"Why? If it's fine?"

"Aha, you did tell him."

"What?"

"If it's fine or not fine, whichever, you told him something, or it couldn't be fine. Or not fine, for that matter. Jesus, Arlanne."

"I'm leaving this room. I'm going into the guest room. Do not follow me."

Of course he does follow me. He can't help it. At this point I'm apprehensive. I quickly slip into the guest room and lock the door. He threatens to break it down. He's banging on it. Should I call the police?

Wait. He's right. We were talking about him.

"Yes," I said through the door. "We were talking about you."

"Thank you," he said. I could tell he was crying. I felt awful.

I opened the door and sat huddled with him in the hallway, my back against the wall, holding him. "Tell me," I asked him. "What is it?" Just as quickly, however, with both of us collapsing into giggles, I said, "No. Don't. Please don't."

He knew exactly what I meant. It may do most people, including his clients, a lot of good to talk about their problems, but for some reason, it just makes his worse. It's like the more he talks about them, the more obsessive and confused he becomes—maybe my husband is a psychologist incapable of talking about his own problems.

"What did you mean by 'Thank you?'" I asked him. "Not that I'm not afraid to ask."

"Since you were talking to him about me, it means I'm not entirely crazy, paranoid."

"Oh, I see."

"You were, weren't you?"

"Yes."

"Talking to him? About me?"

"Yes. Would I say I were if I wasn't?"

"Maybe to make me feel better."

I took his face in my hands: "I was talking to him about you, Bert. You're not crazy. Okay?" His five o'clock shadow was a little rougher than usual. I let my hand rest on his chest, whether to calm him or myself, I wasn't sure. It was a nervous hand still, with a life of its own. Perhaps it wanted to reach up and choke him to death. Who knew? He glanced at it, then looked up at me again.

"I'm not?"

"No."

"Then why are your fingers crossed?"

I looked down, taken aback, puzzled, irate. My hand lay across his chest, his tie askew, off to one side. The index finger casually (but clearly) overlapping, intertwining with the middle finger as if in the initial stage of macramé.

Was I crazy?

The body, Bert always said (quoting some choreographer only a New Yorker or fancy officer's wife might know about), doesn't lie.

I was hopelessly, helplessly caught. Crossed fingers had snitched on me.

I was infuriated, and there in the hallway, my back to the wall, my husband's head in my lap, I looked upwards, and with clearly no help available I screamed at the top of my lungs.

I had never in my entire life screamed like that before. My family was averse to loud noises.

And as I realized, slowly, that I was going out of my mind, Bert, my husband, looked up at me and asked, "What'd you say?"

"What?"

"What'd you tell him? On the phone? About me?"

I began to cry.

"Whatever you said, I promise I won't mind, I promise I won't get all, you know, crazy, obsessive."

Right, I thought to myself. Right. Fat chance. How much of this, I wondered, could I take? Life with Bert was becoming a vicious cycle. He liked it that way. Or suffered it that way. I couldn't. And here he was, about to start it up again.

"Well, what'd you say?" he asked, looking up at me, lying in my arms in the hallway, as if this were the kind of conversation couples normally had in the evening after hubby returned from work, over cocktails say, sunset-gazing on the patio while dinner simmered on the stove inside waiting as patiently as propriety, convention and decorum to be politely devoured, as I was being devoured, eaten, it felt, alive.

Or was he eating himself alive, in front of me?

Either way, I was beginning to prefer my family's silence, the WASP way of life. Shhhh . . . be very quiet . . . tiptoe . . . leave well enough alone, turn the other cheek, let bygones be bygones . . .

"Please tell me, and I won't bother you the rest of the evening, I promise."

"Why?"

"I just want to know. The truth."

"No you don't," I told him. "No, Honey, that's not what you want to know." I pulled him to me as if he were a child, rocking him slightly back and forth, his ear against my heart, and I asked him if he could hear it beating.

He nodded, smiling, his eyes closing.

"It beats for you," I whispered to him. "Always, my heart beats for you."

We fell asleep in each other's arms, on the floor in the hallway. The carpet was thin, and the next morning my butt hurt, which made me irritable.

| 33 |

Bert Counsels a War Criminal

Captain Royal Cunningham had at once the looks and the arrogance of a matinee idol and the personality and the humility of an apologist. He had plenty to apologize for, and he was apologizing all over the base, scaring the hell out of the top brass. They'd trotted him out as a decorated war hero only to discover, to their horror, that the only thing he could really talk about was, as he put it, his "crimes against humanity" which he'd talk about with anybody and everybody and which, if made public, would fuel the fire of the anti-war activists, who were growing in number daily.

"It's all I can talk about, Doc. It's all I can't stop talking about."

He was doing to anybody and everybody what I was doing to Arlanne. "Which suggests you're not really talking about it, right?"

"That's why I'm here."

"Not really re-experiencing it, with feeling."

"Only in my nightmares."

"What about flashbacks otherwise?"

"Talking about them keeps them at bay."

"Oh, I see. Interesting. So if you shut up—"

"I'd be dangerous."

Well, at least I wasn't that.

"I am dangerous."

He was ready. He wanted help for what he was unable at this point to do for himself. He lay on the couch, I counted slowly . . . 1 . . . 2 . . . 3 . . . 4 . . . 5 . . . as he fell into an altered state, into the experience itself.

". . . 100 degrees Fahrenheit, wet, always wet, everything, hadn't showered in weeks, haven't slept in days. Dampness a second skin. Coming out of the jungle now, approaching the village, can smell the buffalo meat cooking. A bamboo viper two-step, more lethal than Cong, Smitty freezes, pisses in his pants, but with the stink and the wet no one can tell . . ."

"You could?"

"I was in front, looking back just to check over the men, I saw the shame on his face."

"I see."

"The intelligence reported that the village housed Viet Cong moles—that's what the two interpreters, two boys who lived in the village, had told us, but how could you tell? A flash of light, an explosion, Richards flying through the air, plastered against the cement wall of the village well. My ears ringing. Another landmine, booby trap, see it, do I hear it? Sniper fire! From where? Over from the rice paddies, the trees? The smoke, the smell, can't see. The huts themselves? From the drainage ditch? It's a setup, Goddammit! Another landmine. Fire, fog, mayhem, the air on fire. Can't breathe. From there! The trees! The woods? No. No. Nobody there! A grenade . . . from the hut? The villagers hauled out of their huts, one by one, family by family. Where were the young men? More fire. This time from inside a hut. Sheffield down. Medic! Turner screaming in pain, his flak jacket in shreds. Goddammit, Medic! Delano on his back, wide-eyed, blood trickling out the corner of his mouth. Oh my God, you sons of bitches, please not Vagnetti. Please, whispering right before his eyes closed forever kill anything yellow. Rampage now, kill anything yellow. Goddammit! Kill everything, kill yellow. Goddamn you sons of bitches. Waste 'em. Die, you fucking gooks. Firing and firing and firing totally out of control the Wild Wild West yippee yi yaa fury in the shells of bullets. Die you mother fuckers. Die and when it's all over and it's hard to tell who's who even after the air cover even who they hit and who they didn't. Goddamn. Goddammit! Kill 'em all. Disappear the whole goddamn thing. Wipe out everybody, goddammit. Fuck 'em. Waste 'em. That's it . . . Go on . . . Waste 'em. All of 'em. The ghosts of all of it, the ghosts of all of it, and when after the young father he shot his own conscience out of the village elder's eyes, and when Corporal Buchanan fondled the fifteen year old and he aimed for the corporal and he saw the fear and horror in his eyes, the rifle shifted to the fifteen year old. She's dead. It's over for her too she won't remember either."

"'He,' Captain? 'He' killed that family? The 'rifle' shifted?"

"I did, Doc. I did."

| 34 |

Jack and Royal Confide on Scataway Island

Dr. Levy had advised both Jack McGowan and Captain Cunningham in their respective therapy sessions to seek each other out and talk: both had been war heroes, and both were guilty of atrocities. That one had occurred in peacetime and one in wartime was irrelevant, he suggested: their feelings were the same.

And they were, they realized, on Royal's first visit to Scataway Island. They had taken a walk in the nearby woods, and were sitting, partially shaded, under a palmetto tree. Sunlight shot through the thick fronds, exploding in the ferns surrounding them. Horseheads of Spanish moss dripped so low from oak branches they appeared to be feeding off the rich fertile trough of the forest floor. Wildflowers splashed about the clearing in front of them, camouflaging the remnants of a campfire in which were fragments of collapsed beer cans, and a dented canteen, nakedly open, the cap on a tiny chain lying next to it. A black snake crawled from under a rotten log. The odor was of the river and the marsh, hovering in the humidity over the clearing, intermingling with that of the naturally mulched soil.

"Our 'feelings' are the same," Royal said operatically, mimicking Bert's emphasis.

Jack smiled. Royal felt rewarded. He felt it must have been the first time Jack had smiled in a long, long time, and as his heart broke for Jack, it broke for himself.

"Feelings," he repeated, but his previous gusto deserted him. "Feelings," he repeated again, pensively. The word brought up the emotion, and the emotion caused tears, for which he felt gratitude, to form in his eyes. He looked over at Jack, his eyes unashamedly wet. "Feelings."

"Enough to drive a man to drink," Jack offered.

"To drink, to kill, to murder . . ."

"I did it," said Jack.

Cunningham nodded.

"I killed those boys. My father didn't do it, I did it. He was part of me, he's still part of me, inside me. "

"He's inside of me too," said Cunningham.

| 35 |

Driver Advocates a Nonviolent Response to His Report Card

Mama washin' dishes. Percy Sledge singin' "When a Man Loves a Woman" on WAPE radio from Jacksonville. She cut it off right in the middle though and cut up the little television on the kitchen counter so Walter Cronkite can tell us the way it is. And the way it is now ain't lookin' too good at all. Some white boys done shot and killed Medgar Evers while he marchin' from Memphis to Jackson. Medgar a Mississippi boy. That what my mama say. She tell me that before. His brother Charles sayin' somethin' now in front of a bunch of microphones, but before I can figure out what he sayin', he through.

"What'd he say, Mama?"

"He say for you to shut up so I can hear."

Stokely Carmichael, he the new head of S.N.C.C., the Student Non-Violent Coordinating Committee, his man H. Rap Brown right there beside him. Stokely, he talkin' now. He black, but he don't really look like coloreds I know, and from what I get watchin' him now, he ain't exactly preachin' non-violence. Man, he scary. He talkin' about doin' to white folks what they did to Medgar, about black folk armin' theyselves in self-defense.

What I'm hopin' for now is when Mama see my report card that she follow Dr. King's message of nonviolence, though I'm afraid she partial to Stokely and Rap. I like their names. I'm waitin' for Dr. King to come on with his message, so's Mama more tolerant when she see my report card.

Without avertin' her eyes from Eric Sevaried, who always come on, Mama says, to punctuate the show—I ain't never understood nothin' he said—Mama holds out her hand for my report card, which I place in her palm, prayin' for nonviolence, knowin' just what Martin mean.

Evidently liberty and equality for black folk ain't near as important to Mama as my report card. She look that thing up and down, and she forget all about Stokely and Rap and Eric talkin' about Medgar and she look hard at me—her eyes as cold as the glaciers in my fourth grade science book. All Christianity gone right out of her. Forgiveness out the back door, which she told me to walk out of into the back yard and get her a switch and bring it to her before she decides to double the lickin'.

Well, I come back in. I startin' to cry so she'll take pity on me and go a bit easier, but she ain't havin' none of that. I ain't never seen her so mad. But then she turn away and bite her lip and I start to feel guilty.

She tappin' that leg of hers with that switch on the one hand and bitin' her lip on the other. She say, "What happened, Boy? You ain't never had a report card like this in your life. C's? This the first time you ever gotten' below an A." That switch makin' evil music against her leg, she just lookin' at me, waitin'.

I look over at Elizabeth. She grinnin' at me when Mama ain't lookin'.

"She the reason," I tell Mama. "I don't want to go to no white school."

"Aw, honey," she say, "come here." And she place the switch on the table. I know, 'cause even though I cryin', I can see out the corner of my eye. Mama hold me and I grin back at Elizabeth where Mama can't see me.

Then Elizabeth, she point at me and say, "He fakin', Mama, he over there grinnin' at me like a Chessee cat."

The funny thing was: I was tellin' the truth.

| 36 |

Bert Obsesses Over Mary Beth, Then Screams into a Towel

The odd thing about an obsessive-compulsive disorder is that rather than affecting your work negatively, often it affects it positively. Not that I wouldn't trade it in for a smoother, safer, more comfortable psychological model, one more easily adaptable to the shocks and strains of the psyche's more precarious highways and thoroughfares; it does nonetheless make me a helluva therapist. Perfectionism, purely for its own sake, is not all bad, particularly if your work is fundamentally a search for truth, which mine is. Obsessiveness requires thoroughness, the exploration of every viable option, that no stone be left unturned. Work, in fact, often quite naturally "re-orders" the obsessive-compulsive disorder, making it "orderly," making the psychological trains, if you will, run on time; that is, except my work with Cunningham, who can't help but get my wires crossed. It's embarrassing, if not shameful. At least I know how I feel, which is a lot more than I can say about some other people I know, if you know who I mean. Or have I made that clear yet? In any case, the equation goes like this: Lie = wrong. diagnosis = wrong treatment. So a compulsion to find the truth = accurate diagnosis = correct treatment. Pretty neat?

I'm going out of my mind. But that's beside the point.

The point is that directly across from me on my sofa in my office are the emerald, come-hither eyes of Mary Beth McGowan telepathically (without even the arch of an eyebrow or a suggestive glance) giving me the green light to just bang on through the intersection. Come on, man, you're holding up traffic. Drive. Hard. Fast. Inside me. Read my mind. Act. Do. Don't stop. Keep going. There are no more red lights. All are green. Go. Go. Go. Come. Come. Come. All this, with neither word nor gesture; her sea-green eyes, the Gulf of Mexico, waiting for you to fall in; her mere presence, like Odysseus' sirens, sufficiently seductive, clearly invitational. It was as if she had gracefully dove from her outlying rock into the Aegean, swam upward through the twentieth century, surfaced in modern attire on the streets of Somerset, South Carolina, oblivious to the automobile crashes and collisions all about her—stopping traffic, to employ modern parlance here—only to perch finally, fashionably, and eternally seductive on my sofa.

Ah, she is a festival: gloriously blonde truffles and curls flower about a tiny forest-green hat like spring flowers around fresh grass; those emerald-green eyes illuminating her soul, or at least her passion and sensuality; a see-through blouse a playground for frolicking breasts; a matching green pocketbook; and a dangerously brief, matching-green mini-skirt revealing dangerously demure, perfectly-tapered, sun-kissed thighs. Ah, lust. Such a simple, uncomplicated need. Accept it, Bert, as truth. Don't obfuscate it with obsessiveness, with overthought.

And what is the truth? The truth is I want to fuck her.

There is just no getting around that. And the truth is she wants to fuck me.

She speaks, she gesticulates, she gestures. She makes a point. About what? I have no idea. All I can think about is placing a hand between her thighs, where I know she's so wet her panties could wash my face. I want her panties now, to take home with me so I can hide them where nobody but me can ever enjoy them, in a little corner of a tiny closet where they'll never dry.

As she gestures to make a point—a different one? Who knows? Who cares—her small breasts, young and coltish under her thin blouse, tussle and wrestle and jump about, begging me to squeeze them until they hurt.

She is, in psychological terms, a "caretaker," I tell her. She tells me something about her father, about taking care of him, about his being an alcoholic or something like that. She embraces me tenderly upon leaving, planting a soft, sensual kiss on my neck, smiling at me shyly, suggestively, telling me that she has a need to take care of people, that for her it's fulfilling and satisfying, that that's why she "enables" Jack to drink, even if only on the sly.

Oh, let's you and me be on the sly, Mary Beth.

Take care of me.

Relieve me of my uncontrollable desire, my involuntary erection.

When she leaves, I go into the bathroom, stuff my face in a towel, and scream my lungs out.

All in all, a profitable session, at least for me. I realize now I'm truly going out of my mind.

Or am I?

Good question?

If I were, how would I know?

| 37 |

Arlanne Displays Revolutionary Zeal, but Bert Still Yearns for Mary Beth

The Palmers are an old Somerset family. Arlanne's ancestors go back to the Revolutionary War; her great grandfather rode with Robert E. Lee in the Civil War, surrendering with him at Appomattox. If you look closely at the sepia photograph in the family album you can see him in the background, gaunt, wily, and undistinguished, in dramatic contrast to the statesmanlike foreground in which Lee, martyred and ennobled in defeat, is surrendering his sword to Grant.

The family store, Palmer's Department Store, so "sophisticated," marveled the locals, that it advertised in Esquire Magazine, was over 150 years old, the family home built in 1743. The store was lucrative, as were the Palmer's numerous holdings, including the Somerset Concrete Block

Company, the materials from which were (and would be) used by the city to build everything from sidewalks to roads to a Waterfront Street. Such projects were often proposed by Mr. Bradford Palmer himself, who coincidentally just happened to be on the town council, as well as a business partner of the mayor, Harper Dawes.

Bradford Palmer was her daddy, and in her own way she loved and admired him, even if she did disagree with his politics and loathe his racism. He loved her too; she knew that, but he was an Episcopalian and reluctant as she was to contribute to Bert's penchant for stereotyping, she'd told him, her father was physically undemonstrative, distant and aloof, which is why she married Bert. Jews, at least the ones she knew, were physically and emotionally demonstrative. She married him, she told him, because she wanted to be "touched." Though popular and beautiful as a youth, she was also dangerously promiscuous. Pregnant at 17, she was sent to an unwed mother's home somewhere up in Virginia where she was to have the baby and then give it up, after which she'd return to Somerset from a "trip abroad" (according to her mother's fiction) and finish high school. Her "trip abroad," however, was cut short when after six weeks at the home she miscarried. If her father remained oblivious, or at least appeared to be so, and her mother's relief palpable, she felt briefly an immobilizing loss, a stunning emptiness, a tiny chamber of her heart empty now of soft blankies, baby toys, picture books, a rattle, fresh paint, and a crib. The tiny soulless chamber in her imagination became nothing more than an empty tomb, echoing and opening onto the larger one long ago vacated by her father.

Bert, however, was overwhelming, to say nothing of self-absorbed. His emotion at least lately since he'd begin seeing Vietnam veterans, particularly those suffering from Post-Traumatic Stress Disorder, seemed more like hysteria and self-flagellation than anything else. His self-flagellation made her wonder if Catholicism hadn't somehow lurked secretly and subversively somewhere in his family background, like a dwarf perhaps, or a sword-swallower, or a hermaphrodite.

And if he wasn't hysterical or beating himself up, he was obsessive, replaying his sessions with Royal Cunningham over and over, futilely reassuring himself that he was handling him the right way. Was he? Who knew? She certainly didn't, since each scenario was played out in such obsessive detail she lost the essence of it. Even when normal, or under normal circumstances, Bert was the worst listener she'd ever been around, too much in his own world, which early on she was jealous of. The only thing that would bring him out of it was something "personal," as he put it, something "risky" (which was no doubt why he was such a good psychologist), exactly what she'd been taught all her life not to bring up.

She was just sitting there in one of those irritating little desks in a second grade classroom at the Lady's Island Elementary School waiting for the Somerset Biracial Commission to meet. She was early, the first person there, in fact. Still, she knew the meeting would start late, as it always did, because the black members would be late. Maybe that's why they came in friendlier than the whites, like it was all cakes and cookies and fried chicken and goodwill, a bountiful church bazaar, instead of a concentrated effort aimed at figuring out how to seriously take power and money from white people like herself and her family. Friendliness diffuses confrontation. It's difficult to jump someone's ass while they're glad-handing you, asking about your family, and giving you a good ol' hearty slap on the back. Makes anger seem somehow downright charmless, futile, unnecessary. Maybe they feel guilty. Guilt makes Jews friendlier. She had seen that. Guilt could make Murray, who hadn't arrived yet either, a walking talking bear hug, even more expansive and solicitous, even more sentimental than usual. Still, she couldn't help but wonder, Why are black people always late?

She asked Bert that one time. He shrugged. Maybe they're being passive-aggressive, he'd said. That's often the only recourse for people who've been victimized, who are essentially powerless. Then he said, How the hell should I know? As if he were somehow wondering if he *should* know. Her poor haunted husband, the favorite, you could tell, of his mom. Do you feel guilty about that, about being her favorite, she asked him? No, he said. It's in the genes. Then hopelessly, helplessly, he just couldn't put the skids on it: Why? Should I?

Should you what?

Feel guilty?

How the hell should I know?

That response, he informed her, was itself vengeful and passive-aggressive. All she had to do, however, was wait. He was so insecure, so unsure of himself, so frustrated by ambiguity and irresolution. Sure enough, in less than a minute, he couldn't help it: Well, do you?

Do I what?

Know whether I should feel guilty about it. I don't think I do, but maybe I do and just don't know it.

Maybe you do and I don't know it.

And 'round and 'round they went until she was drawn into one of his obsessive spirals, a spiral admittedly of her own making.

All she wanted to do was to have a Goddamn argument inspired, for once, by her, one of those yellin' and screamin' throw-the-kitchen-sink-at-him arguments like you see in the movies, followed up with some ferocious lovemaking—a genuine rip-your-clothes-off rape—not some therapeutic disaster in which having pushed the right button, a disorder pops out, driving them both nuts. They had those yellers and screamers, especially when they were first married, but she wasn't ready for them then, and he was too good at them. Now that she was, he was no longer interested, because he's gone crazy.

Perhaps her parents had it right after all. Perhaps the wisest relationship is a distant one. Perhaps familiarity does breed contempt. Certainly at this point she was contemptuous of Bert. And certainly he was resentful of her. He'd have to be. She was giving very little right now.

Perhaps it's not a matter of choice, of "getting it right," of following a philosophy. Perhaps relationships create distance: the closer people get, the farther away they become. The more they know about each other, the more there is to hate. Or at least the more they infuriate each other. She wished she'd been more apprehensive early in their relationship. Maybe she'd have married Murray. He's so easy.

Mrs. Eileen Hunter, the Lady's Island Elementary School principal and the Chair of the Somerset Biracial Commission has already called the meeting to order. Pardon me, thinks Arlanne, I was self-absorbed. Shoot me. But she'd only been faintly aware of everyone coming in. She could wave and nod and say, "hey Eileen" or send a smile Murray's way but she's back in her own world in a millisecond. Bert never even bothers to leave his own world to say "Hi"; he's too lost in it. Here's the conundrum. She couldn't help it: she was dying to check her watch. Were they starting the meeting on black People's Time or White People's Time? This was risky in a group like this. She knew that. If she were to be seen, she'd be seen as a racist. But she was compulsively curious about the oddest things. She wanted to know. She acted with all deliberate speed. 8:17 PM. . . . seventeen minutes late. Hell, she thought, for this group that was early. No one had noticed, not even Murray. She could tell by the way he smiled at her. Does he notice anything? Bert only notices what he's not supposed to notice. What a contrast. Clearly all Jews, stereotypes notwithstanding, are not all alike. Neither are they like Gentiles, however, who are.

Obviously the discussion has been going for awhile. However, according to Bert's Law of Human Interaction, nothing of import has been said, or it would have caught her attention.

Bob Cousy is the greatest passer of all time on the greatest basketball team of all time coached by the greatest coach of all time, Red Auerbach, a Jew like me, an athletic Jew, Bert says. You know what Auerbach tells Cousy?

Yes, she answers.

If a teammate misses one of his passes, says Bert, it's the Cooz's fault. If I don't "catch" what you're saying, he explains, if I somehow "miss" it . . .

I've thrown a bad pass? she asks, incredulous.

Exactly, he says.

Nor is anything of import, at least according to Bert's way of thinking, being said right now, or she wouldn't be at this very moment contemplating his Law of Human Interaction in action. Let's take it off the court, back into the home:

Are you listening to me, Bert?

Are you saying anything, Arlanne?

Yes, I am!

No, you're not, or I would have been listening.

Perhaps she should offer that up here in this meeting if she's caught daydreaming:

Are you with us, Arlanne?

Why no, I'm not, because you're boring.

That's funny. And when she imagines Bert appreciating it, she grows sincerely fond of him again. That is, until she actually sees him again.

" . . . People got to see us," said Eileen. "We got to block traffic. It's got to be on Main Street. The most lucrative business on Main Street is Palmer's Department Store. I know that's your daddy, Arlanne, but if we gon' tell it like it is, that's the symbol. He's rich, and he's powerful. If he ain't hirin' colored folk—excuse me, Stokely, wherever you are, 'black' folk—nobody else will. Simple as that. We got to use him to scare them. Right now downtown controlled solely by white people. Black people hired only for custodial positions, and only then if they keep their mouths shut. On Saturdays when us Negroes come to town, the only day really when we welcome, who all ready to sell to us? Who stocks our clothes, our food, our hardware? The same whites that won't hire us."

"We talkin' boycott," said Lila Trulove.

She looked at Arlanne. "You with us, or you against us?"

A S.N.C.C. organizer, some punk from somewhere up North all dolled up in an afro and a dashiki, down here 'facilitatin' the Movement, said: "Ain't no middle ground here, white girl. You with black folk, you got to have a revolutionary zeal."

"Let me ask you something, black boy," said Arlanne. "Where you from?"

Without a word, with a barely perceptible smile and an even less perceptible gesture, he completely dismissed her.

"I just want to know in what pompous, self-important, language-forsaken place a person learns to talk like that. 'Revolutionary zeal?' Prove yourself. That's my daddy's place you talkin' about, you son of a bitch. In your 'revolutionary zeal,' what the hell do you have to lose? Where you from, black boy?"

"He's from Boston," said Eileen. "Grew up in Roxbury."

"Then what the hell you doin' down here?"

He didn't even look at her, had no time for her—he didn't have to; he was a black man in a biracial, i.e. "black," forum—so suave, so confident, so self-assured. Clearly, suggested his manner, he knew things she didn't, had had experiences, as a black man, far beyond her understanding as a mere white woman, even though he was only 23.

Which really pissed her off.

She started to ask him if his mama let him date yet.

Instead, however, she glanced around the room, taking everybody in. Unlike our 'revolutionary,' she had time for everybody, and she was taking it. Members of the commission seemed to diminish in stature in direct proportion to the authority of her gaze. Even Ol' Murray was staring at his new wingtips. He'd been so proud of them, new and all, stylish. She looked at the young black man now as though she knew him, as though she knew just who he was.

"You get your know-it-all little ass back up to that ghetto, where you live, and round up all 'yo' boys' and gather up the signs and placards and reporters and T.V. cameras and protest the drug dealer on the corner, I want to see his and his source's mug on the Evening News. Right beside it, your mama's absentee slumlord, knowing he can evict her on nothing but two weeks notice. Organize a boycott of the white man's pawnshop, since that's where the boys get money for drugs and guns. Or is it your daddy's or your uncle's shop? What are you gonna' do then, hot shot? Maybe 'yo' daddy's' an Uncle Tom black school principal. Organize the teachers, the parents, the children! Boycott! He can still teach. Anybody can. Get somebody in there who'll fight. Risk lives. Risk livelihoods, like yo' 'brothers and sisters' are doin' down here. Boycott yo' daddy until there's a change. Then you can have braggin' rights to a 'revolutionary zeal.' Meanwhile, this little 'white girl' will let you know about hers after she leads a boycott of her daddy's store. Her daddy, you condescending son of a bitch. The man who brought her into this world, who took care of her, who loved her the best way he knew how, a man I love with all my heart."

And she burst into tears.

"That', Lila said, "is what you call a 'revolutionary zeal.'"

And Lila knows, thought Murray. Of everyone here, Lila knows.

That night, when Arlanne got home, Bert listened.

Afterwards, as he held her, she said, "Why can't you be like this all the time?"

To which he responded: "Why can't you be like this all the time?"

In bed as he studied his wife sleeping peacefully, even with the glare of his flashlight on her face, Bert realized that Christian courage, natural courage, courage which doesn't question or argue with itself, is a pure liberating thing.

He enjoyed watching her sleep, knowing that she was always her prettiest, her cheeks blooming, when she woke in the mornings. Why was he using a flashlight? Why, the better to see her with, naturally. Normally he'd switch on the lamplight, but it'd wake her, and she'd yell at him. Are you crazy? Cut off the light, you inconsiderate bastard. NOW.

Okay, the lamplight, though it did produce a relatively soft glow, bothered her. So, to show his consideration, in case she awoke, he thought he'd try a flashlight. He couldn't help but note the halo surrounding her face, and deduced immediately that it meant nothing. That the glare of the flashlight was infinitely more severe than that of the lamplight also apparently meant nothing. At least to him. You figure out the logic, except that if she did wake up he could claim that she'd complained about lamplight, not flashlight, and now that he understood she meant flashlight too, why, he'd happily, without compunction and with all deliberate speed, cut it off. Why? Because, he'd explain, that's the kind of person he was, caring, considerate, magnanimous, always careful to place the other person's needs above his own, which would naturally piss her off even more.

In a way, he wanted her to wake up so they could argue.

But she was sleeping so peacefully now, so serenely, nothing could have awakened her, except maybe a nuclear bomb. He kissed her lightly on the cheek. She purred, still sleeping.

As a fiercely neurotic Jew, he marveled at his wife's courage, a courage she would express through action, through her visible public behavior, hiding from no one. Compared to such courage, words were easy. She didn't worry about what to do. Totally aware of the tragic consequences, she did it anyway, much like Lila had when she sent Elizabeth to Somerset Junior High where, thank God, she was now eating.

Thanking Arlanne in his heart, he knew what he had to do, and he was ready to do it.

He just couldn't help but worry about ruining his life, his career, and anything else he could find to worry about. Would she ruin her life? Could she stand the potential estrangement from her parents? He couldn't, not from his. Of course, they could care less what he did, as long as he was happy. And in his case if he weren't, he could pretend to be, for their sake.

She, however, was much too honest and real for that kind of fakery. Obsessiveness obscures, honesty simplifies. Did she know what she was doing?

At this moment as much as any other, he realized in a more mature way than he ever had that Arlanne was his true love.

That, however, was at this moment.

In later moments—in fact, in countless later moments—he still wanted to fuck Jack McGowan's wife.

Part IV

WINTER 1966

38

Royal Surrenders, but to Whom?

Royal Cunningham was a Man, thought Murray, as Cunningham approached the lectern, in the same way that Arlanne and Lila were Women: If the hard road was in front of them, and the hard road was the right road, they never considered a detour. If it hurt, they suffered, but without anxiety, without complaining, and without second-guessing themselves. Undeterred by debate or discussion, they just did what had to be done. Like Bert, Murray concluded that such quiet heroism was distinctly non-Jewish, even if you were a Southern Jew, as he was. Jews could talk themselves into anything, but also they could talk themselves out of anything. Mostly, they just talked, just as, mostly, Gentiles remained silent.

Murray remembered the NAACP meeting a few days ago at Penn Community Center, just across the bridge on St. Helena Island. Formerly the first Industrial School for Blacks in the nation, Penn was now a Community Resources Center as well as the leading conference center for people in the Movement. At this particular meeting Andy Young, one of Dr. King's most promising young lieutenants, spoke about Dr. King's recently expanded vision of publicly conjoining the Civil Rights Movement with the antiwar Movement. Cunningham, thought Murray at the time, were he to expand his passion, could be influential as one of the 'conjoining' spirits. He mentioned it to Arlanne who mentioned it to Bert, who reported back to Murray that Cunningham was indeed magnificently and tragically inspired, but by only one compulsion, one which filled his heart to the breaking point, leaving room for no other, regardless how worthy: Stop the killing in Vietnam.

"My name is Royal Cunningham. I am a captain in the United States Marine Corps. I am trained to kill," he announced to the small crowd in the town parking lot on the waterfront. "To kill the enemies of the United

States of America solely in order to protect it. That is my duty, and I have done it. However, I have gone far beyond that: I have killed for no reason at all, which is to say for the relief, the pleasure, the pure catharsis of it, and like the ancient King Herod, I am responsible for the Massacre of Innocents." The twelve o'clock whistle sounded. Pigeons fluttered. A lone sea gull circled overhead. A motorboat revved up over at the dock. The whistle stopped on the minute. If the crowd heard it, they certainly didn't show it. "I am a murderer."

No scraggly veteran or unkempt student-protestor here, he presented himself to the crowd as Captain Royal Cunningham in full dress uniform, two purple hearts and a bronze star parading magnificently across his chest. He had nothing to hide, he felt, nothing to lose. Already he had hidden it, already he had lost it. According to his therapist Bert Levy, standing off in the corner by the crowd, it was time to come out with it. The only way, Cunningham figured, to return to sanity and humanity. Stop it. Save lives. Rebalance the world as he rebalanced himself, or at least make the attempt, however futile it might be.

Bert was nervous. Murray knew that. Bert thought it was because he was Jewish. Hell, Bert thought, everything was because he was Jewish. That wasn't the reason. That was a way out. Bert was frightened because unlike Royal Cunningham, he had everything to lose, in particular his career, a career to which he was devoted, at which he was superb. An antiwar counselor in the Marine Corps? To the Corps, that's treasonous, aiding and abetting the enemy, grounds for a court martial. Defending that would make even a native unpopular, the thought of which began making Murray nervous.

It's not like Bert and I aren't Men, he figured, it's just that we're nervous men. Fear makes us that way. But what's courage without fear?

Courage without fear is Captain Royal Cunningham. What a commanding presence. A war hero, his chest ablaze with medals and honors. The American flag furling and unfurling, powerfully, proclaiming a moral authority naturally refreshing, if not sadly naive, in the river breeze. Though it was chilly—windbreaker and sweater weather—sunlight glorified the birth of the afternoon, a rousing hallelujah laying hands on the blue of the river behind him, on the green slope of the riverbank, on the leaves of the great oaks towering over it, and out into the river on the marsh grass, turning it a wheat-golden hue. The marsh breathing, the river pulsating, the stink and the fish-smell visceral and reassuring. Off the town parking lot where Cunningham was speaking was the tiny police station, a block over the Ritz cafe, the upstairs of which was Lila's former place of business, directly across the street from which was Palmer's Department Store. Since Saturday was the day the Negroes came to town, the only white people around were those running and managing the stores and shops and those here in the parking lot listening to Cunningham speak. As many Negroes had avoided the parking lot today as whites every Saturday avoided downtown. If you listened closely, you could hear the river lapping against the tabby wall of the parking lot, the wall eventually curbing around and forming the seawall protecting the riverbank. In the far distance, across the river, barely visible even on a sunlit day, was Lawton Island.

Jesus, Murray realized, that's Jack McGowan down there, in uniform, albeit a private now stripped of his sergeant's stripes. He's directly off to the side of the podium, attentive, looking up at Royal from an angle, so close as to be part of his entourage, as if the two of them have some kind of private, personal connection. Do they? What's he doing here? Surely he's not against the war. And across the lot, over there with the students, talking with Arlanne, isn't that that guy from the *Times*? What's his name? He was the one she had that fling with, who did real good work, Murray remembered, on the McGowan trial. Vicker? Wicker? Tom Wicker? Rob. Rob Vicker? A Tennessee boy, originally.

Jesus, this story's going to get some play. No wonder Bert's so nervous. The more play it gets, the more crap he'll get.

How did the *Times* get this story?

Who called them?

Couldn't have been Arlanne. She just doesn't have that kind of clout. Besides, she knew how he felt. She would have confided in him. Bert would've known, and Bert would have confided in him.

Had to have been somebody pretty damn powerful, somebody up in the ranks. A veteran, one of those retired generals coming out against the war? But how would he have known about this little affair? This was local. Only the *Somerset Weekly* and the local radio station had been informed, and neither was even here. Had to have been someone from the inside, someone who somehow got wind of this little protest, somebody in on it? Secretly in support of it? Who knew Vicker, or even a higher-up at the *Times?*

" . . . to kill in defense of our country is the mission of the Marine. The Vietnam war is an abuse of that mission. As a soldier in that war, I have abused that mission. Only if the soul of my country is cleansed might mine be purified. And if there is blood on our country's hands, blood that my men and I have spilled—not just of enemy soldiers, but of innocent wives and children, of innocent fathers and aging grandparents—there is blood on your hands. We are your representatives in Vietnam. We serve, for better or worse, our nation. Our nation is comprised of its citizens. You are its citizens. The blood on my hands is on yours. The responsibility, as Americans, is yours. I call on you today to help stop the madness.

"And this war is mad. It has turned soldiers into killers, lusting after prey, human prey. In my platoon alone men collected and made necklaces of Viet Cong ears. I hold up this necklace now for you to witness, not as a necklace of pride, but a necklace of shame. It is my shame. It is the shame of my men. It is also your shame if you continue to support the madness or to close your eyes to it. After today, this small group of Americans gathered here today can no longer say, 'we didn't know.' My purpose here today is to inform you honestly. To spare you is to to be complicit in greater mayhem and murder."

What an oddly human scene, thought Murray: disgust, turning away, a bit of rubbernecking, particularly from the younger ones from the University Extension; self-consciousness; confusion; a studied neutrality. Is it somehow traitorous to the cause to wonder why the necklace must be blatantly displayed? Is what is perhaps necessary for his psyche, necessary for ours? Yes, I'm asking myself the same question that inevitably frustrates me coming from conservatives: Is this really necessary? Or should I be questioning myself, which is what I ask them to do. If I really look at this necklace, what morally am I compelled to do about it? Throw away my life to save theirs? My career? Go to Canada? Fight for the Viet Cong? Publicly rail against the war? Protest Lawton Island? Take the town to court for accepting money from a government conducting an illegal war under false pretenses, i.e., the Gulf of Tonkin resolution? Charge the President of the United States with crimes against humanity? His generals? His cabinet? All soldiers not in compliance with the Geneva Convention? Captain Cunningham?

What is the shame of turning away from the necklace of human ears? Is there shame upon looking at it? Upon displaying it? Is the reward of doing good—my social activism included—being good, and therefore feeling good? Or is taking the moral high road simply a way of looking down on the malnourished souls chugging aimlessly and sightlessly along the low road? Is Cunningham rubbing his necklace in our face, and if so, is it because it is necessary to show us the truth, or is it a sadistic psychological variation on the physical atrocities he committed in Vietnam, a refusal, in other words, on his own part to completely surrender to the truth of his sins, a perverted way to strengthen his own psychological hand, to retain power, to reclaim, in short, the moral superiority of the higher ground? Knowledge, especially the kind of knowledge to which he lays claim, is power.

Is cynicism—if cynical I am—a defense mechanism, the easy dismissal of bad news? In this case, Cunningham's?

"Elderly grandparents, loving fathers, young daughters, gentle mothers—good, quiet, peaceful people—are being slaughtered all over the Vietnam countryside by platoons just like mine, with soldiers just like mine, with platoon leaders just like me, soldiers who in the absence of reason have succumbed to the lust of killing for the sake of killing. Evil flowers in Vietnam, engulfing and engorging innocent civilians, to say nothing of the souls of our soldiers.

"The Devil's work has been ours. I beg you to look directly in his face. Let him cower in the presence of God, knowing God is watching and judging. To see, hear, and speak of evil, I tell you from my own experience in Vietnam, is to wrench evil from our souls. I judge myself. I find myself guilty. Of the murder of an aging grandparent, a young girl, and her father in the village of Luc Tho on the afternoon of August 27, 1965, in the country of South Vietnam. Let us judge ourselves now as a nation. Let us find ourselves if not guilty, responsible. Let us assume the responsibility for stopping the madness . . .

"I surrender," he shouted, and the light from Vicker's cameraman flashed as he raised his hands to the heavens, to a United States Government ironically in hiding from him.

Cunningham's photograph was on the front page of the next day's *New York Times*, underneath which the caption read: "In South Carolina Decorated Veteran Speaks Out Against the War."

When it got to the C.O.'s desk, he saw the picture and immediately smiled, then hurried through the accompanying article to make sure his name wasn't mentioned.

Neither, he noted, was Cunningham's specific confession of his killing of the village elder, the young girl, and her father.

Unlike Cunningham's, the *Time's* surrender, like his own, was conditional.

"So much for the *Times* stereotyping the South," Murray said, showing the article on Cunningham's speech to Arlanne over a late lunch at the No View restaurant. "Had to drive all the way over to Savannah to get it."

A late lunch was an excuse for drinks, since both had already had lunch. Manny Hartwell had called his restaurant the No View, he liked to say, for the sake of honesty. Since it was the only one downtown with no view of the river, on a side street surrounded by a Piggly Wiggly, Davis Furniture Store, Hardy's Appliances, and Bumpy's Army Surplus, it really had no view to speak of. In the Somerset telephone directory's yellow pages, Manny tried to turn that to his advantage. One year it was: "Dine without Distraction:

No view at the No View." Another year, an apparently desperate variation on the same theme: "Need a glimpse of dry land? Come to the No View." Finally he decided to just keep it simple, he had explained to Murray, to just hit 'em head on with the truth: "Sick of the view? Recuperate at the No View."

"Yeah," said Arlanne, her eyes on the caption under the *Times* photo. "Looks like we're a veritable state full of liberals because a man from Minnesota stationed on Lawton Island makes an anti-war speech to a handful of people in South Carolina, a speech so threatening to the locals the police don't even show up for it."

"And a self-professed war criminal can't even get himself arrested. Still, it's a start," said Murray.

"Those kids from the University. 'L.B.J. lied, Thousands died . . . L.B.J. lied, Thousands died . . .' About three chants, all excited and enthusiastic? Did you her them? You were on the other side. Probably no more than three or four kids, tryin' to get the crowd goin'. You'd have thought it was a God-damn pep rally or somethin'. But nobody, not one person, picked up on it. On the contrary, all the people standing around 'em looked at 'em like they were three monkeys goin' at it in the zoo."

"Their professor probably let 'em out of class for the Protest. Probably write a paper on it."

"They're going to have to use a lot of imagination. Thanks, Mayetta," she said as Mayetta slapped a scotch and soda on the rocks in front of Bert and a Rebel Yell straight up in front of Arlanne so hard, as was her way, Arlanne thought they might slap her back. "How these drinks don't spill, sweetheart, is beyond me."

"Trick of the trade, honey. Anything else? Manny'll probably be able to hustle you up some leftovers less he's already stuffed himself with 'em. That man's stomach is downright bottomless, you ask me."

"And you know," said Arlanne, "he never gains weight."

"Metabolism," said Mayetta. "Metabolism. That's the secret. Anything else for you folks?" she asked.

"We're fine, Mayetta," said Murray. "Already had lunch."

"Can't blame you for that," she said, pocketing her ticket in her apron, scoping the restaurant, drifting toward the cash register. "Yell if you need me."

"What made you so liberal, Arlanne, so feisty about it all?"

"At first I think I was just rebelling against Daddy, but then, as time passed, I began to truly believe what I was reading and hearing. What about you?"

"A sociology course I took at the University. It was all about prejudice, the nature of it, race relations, but it included the Holocaust. I knew the statistics, but that was about it. My parents never really mentioned it. Why would they? All my friends were Gentiles, maybe they thought it'd make me paranoid. The images, the photographs . . . after graduating I spent the summer slumming about in Europe and visited Dachau. Afterwards, thinking about all those malnourished kids on the island, the separate water fountains and bathrooms and schools right here in town. Negroes stepping off the sidewalk downtown to make way for a white man, I think it all just brought out the Jew in me. He wasn't that far away anyway. Dad voted for L.B.J. Lifelong democrat, like most Jews. He nor Mom would've ever dreamed of using the N-word, which was the case in most Jewish homes."

"Using the N-word was taboo in our house too, but that's because we were snobs and it was considered 'common.' It was everywhere, the racism —we knew nothing else. However, like you've said before, a native is allowed room to change. That's because everybody already knows who he is. He can even be a liberal as long as he's a native. People are afraid of what they don't know more than what they do know, and let's face it, they're much more afraid of who they don't know than what they don't know. My Friend, right or wrong? It's like defending your child even if you know he ought to be in jail. And you're not even a criminal, Murray, just a small-town Southern Jew, one of God's Chosen, gracing us down here in the Bible Belt: 'A bit liberal? Hell, he's young. He'll grow out of it.'"

"And not too Jewish . . . All this had to have been harder for you, Arlanne, coming from such a prominent family."

"Bullshit," she said, downing her bourbon straight up, looking about for Mayetta.

"I'm not having to boycott my daddy."

"And not havin' to get drunk to do it? Oh hell, Murray, have another drink. Just for this afternoon, forget you're Jewish and act like an Episcopalian."

"Probably not a bad idea," he said, finding Mayetta and signaling her over.

"That way we can play around," she said, toying with the stirrer in her glass, "and you won't have to feel guilty about Bert."

"Jesus . . ." he said.

He looked around, his smile agonizing, as if the whole world was his small town and his small town had perked up its ears. "There's nobody in here," she said, laughing, "'cept Hoke and Marty, and they're over in the corner, plannin' their own mischief."

"So they are," managed Murray, opting for something approaching a cavalier chuckle. "So they are."

At which point Arlanne just couldn't help herself. Raising her napkin from her lap, coyly, exquisitely dabbing at her lipstick, she revealed, for Murray's eyes only, thighs so pure, so virginal-white, so perfectly-sculptured as to invite worship as much as touch.

He worshipped them, and touched them with his eyes, and when for some reason he thought about his mother's homemade whipped cream and bent over to devour them, paranoia jerked him back to reality. "Hey, Boys!" he said, turning toward them. "Didn't see you over there. How y'all doin'."

Lost in their own conversation, the two men looked up, turning toward the voice. "Why, hey there Murray. How you folks doin'?" said Hoke.

"Got the whole restaurant to ourselves today," offered Marty Liebowitz. "Course, you come late, you get the leftovers. Right, Mayetta?" he said just loud enough for her to hear, winking conspiratorially at Arlanne and Murray.

"I hear you, Marty."

"Come on out from behind that counter and talk to us."

"Too busy workin' up them leftovers you hollerin' about."

"Enjoy your meal," said Marty to their table. "Y'all hangin' in there, Arlanne? Daddy and Momma doin' all right? Saw Mama uptown this morning. Looked like a million dollars."

"Hell," said Hoke, "she is a million dollars. Ain't that right, little lady?"

"Hoke Cooley," said Arlanne, "go out there and arrest somebody!"

"Now you know I'm teasin' you, Arlanne. Been teasin' you since you were knee-high to a grasshopper. How the world treatin' you, honey? Doin' all right, Murray?"

"Yeah, but we got a Yankee husband waitin' on us for a golf game over at the Club," he said, getting up. "You fellows playin' today?"

On the way out to the car, Arlanne was laughing so hard she couldn't stop.

"Goddammit, Arlanne, what the hell are you laughin' at?"

"That was the dumbest, most idiotic excuse for a cover story I've ever heard in my life! The only way you and Bert could play golf at the Club—not that I could ever imagine either one of you playin' golf anywhere, much less there—would be as my guests, actually as my family's guests! The Club doesn't accept Jews as members, Murray. Marty goes as a guest every Sunday."

"Maybe it was harder for me than you," said Murray, fumbling around for his keys, which as Arlanne pointed out, were already in his hand. "Maybe I was just too dumb to know it."

"You were," said Arlanne. "That's why you ain't married. You need to do like your mama's been tellin' you for ages. Find you a nice Jewish girl to marry. You know how you used to wonder why you always ended up gettin' the shaft instead of givin' it?"

"Yeah. Never could figure that out."

"The rule about Jewish boys was clear as candlelight: 'You can date 'em, but you can't marry 'em. Nice boys, good people . . . 'But what will the children be?' This is the Bible Belt, honey."

"You married a Jew, a real one."

"New Yorkers are so xenophobic. I was a rebel. I married worse than a Jew. I married a Yankee. And you know what? My daddy was such a gentleman that just like you Bert never even knew he had a problem. 'Til I told him, of course."

"Of course."

"That was fun. You know why? Because for once in his life, Daddy couldn't do anything about it. You know why he couldn't do anything about it? Because Bert didn't give a shit. I just loved him for that, I did. I do. I always will. All that aristocracy crap didn't mean a goddamn thing to him. Who gave a rat's ass about John C. Calhoun and John Hancock and 'that crowd,' as he referred to them, when he'd descended from Freud, Einstein, and Marx. Who did Daddy think, Bert asked him, gave the world the Ten Commandments? Then for good measure he threw in he also descended from Jesus' 'line.' The question, he told Daddy, was not whether he was good enough for me, but whether I was good enough for him. Daddy thought that was the funniest thing he'd ever heard."

"What about Bert's parents?"

"His daddy was a union organizer and his mother a schoolteacher. They were both communists. They could've cared less whether Bert married a non-Jew. They were just worried sick though about him marrying money."

"Was Bert rebelling too?"

"Naw. There wasn't nothin' to rebel against. Hell, you know that. It's like Bert says: Jewish kids don't worry about pleasing their parents; rather, their parents do their best to please them. Gentile kids whine for more attention from their parents. Jewish kids scream for their parents to leave 'em alone."

Murray turned onto Main Street. "Where we headin', boss lady?" he asked, glancing in her direction. That was a mistake. As he was, in that moment no longer consumed with anxiety or compelled by conversation, her legs, flaring from her mini skirt, once again surprised him. Studiously, he kept his eye on the road in front of him.

"To the beach. Nobody'll be there this time of year. But pull up at the ABC store when you get over the bridge."

"Bert won't be worried?"

"He'll be worried about himself. He's meeting with the C.O. this afternoon."

39

Bert is Ordered to the C.O.'s Office

"Hey, Bert, how's it going?" asked the C.O. "At ease, son. Pull up a chair. Need anything? How's that pretty wife of yours. Palmer's kid, isn't she? Good family. Good family."

"Fine, Sir. Everything's just fine." *Though I wonder why I've been called to the Principal's office. No clue. Phone call from his aide late yesterday afternoon, only a few hours after Cunningham's speech. Is it about my presence there? 'The C.O. wants to see you immediately after lunch tomorrow at . . .' Did he not think I might lose a night's sleep over this? Of course not. That's silly. Unless he's bugged my therapy sessions. Have some of my clients, having bared their poor agonizing souls over their participation in this war, gone into denial, turned on me, and complained? Am I going to be dishonorably discharged? Court martialed? Tried for treason? Who'll take care of Arlanne?*

The C.O. drummed his fingers on his desk calendar. He stared out the window, following with total disinterest a platoon marching by, eyes left, looking directly and expressionless into his window. The afternoon had turned gray, overcast. As the platoon passed, blooming cassia unfurled like a flag of subdued gold across the street. Gunfire sounded faintly from the rifle range. For at least a minute, the C.O. just stared out the window, as if by looking away from me he could avoid what he had to tell me. Terrified, I had this momentary urge to help him, to somehow make it easier for him, as if that might somehow make it easier on me. Clearly, he liked me.

"Cigar?" he offered.

Was this tantamount to the proverbial 'last cigarette?' Why not? I loved a good cigar. Why not go down smoking. But if he's going to run me out of the Corps, why wouldn't he be angry with me? He's not. Maybe he's going to, but the nice guy in him—and perhaps even in me, the nice guy he knows and likes—is making it difficult for him.

"Thank you, Sir," I said, reaching into the proffered box. "I think I will."

He lit mine, reaching over the desk, then opened and lit one for himself, despite the fact that his clearly unfinished one, not even half-smoked, awaited him aglow in his ash tray.

Again, he turned towards the window, clearly preoccupied, apparently lost in thought, the ash at the tip of his new cigar steadily devouring the rest of it, working its way back to the beginning; finally, having exhausted itself, it just dropped off, settling harmlessly on his desk calendar, turning November 27th into, ironically enough, ash Wednesday. He turned away from the window towards me, facing me directly, his left elbow squatting comfortably now on Ash Wednesday.

"Levy," he said, after apparently settling on a tact, "how's it going over there in psychology? Okay, eh? Pretty damn good, considering the state we're in and so forth?"

I must have appeared a little uncertain, because before I could say anything, he said, "Is that a nod, Levy? It looks like a nod, Levy."

"Why, yes Sir, I think . . ."

"Now, Levy, I'm interpreting that as an affirmative nod. Would that be a correct interpretation?" he asked, with what I 'interpreted' to be an encouraging nod on his part.

"Why, yes Sir, I think—"

"You think, Captain?" he asked, looking at me dubiously. "You think?"

"I know, Sir. Absolutely. I know."

"Going pretty damn good, eh, Levy. Encouraging those boys to do the right thing."

"Absolutely, Sir," I said, and by this time I was nodding so vigorously I thought my head might fall off. "Absolutely. Affirmative, Sir. Affirmative."

"People naturally get upset in therapy. A non-com comin' complainin' to some of the officers, you know how it is."

"Naturally, Sir."

"Officers reported he'd said somethin' about an anti-war influence or somethin' like that. I said if that boy was finding himself doubting our mission over there, he needed to face up to that himself, not to blame the therapist. This therapist has seen hundreds of soldiers. Never once have I heard such a thing, I told 'em. Hell, to tell you the truth, I was offended about the complaint, and they knew it. If the boy had doubts, I told them, Levy's office was the place to deal with them. But don't act like a goddamn baby and blame 'em on him. Blaming the therapist, I imagine, is a common defense mechanism documented, I'm sure, by the standard research."

"Absolutely, Sir."

"And of course they mentioned Cunningham. I almost laughed out loud at that. I asked 'em if they thought Cunningham was the type of man susceptible to any type of brainwashing, much less propaganda, and did they think any man, therapist or otherwise, could influence a man of his strength and courage more than his own experiences actually over there? Am I right about that, Levy?"

"Without question, Sir. A silly assumption on their parts. And surprisingly gullible with the non-com, if I may say so, Sir. Frankly, Sir, I myself am offended and am considering, as we sit here, lodging a complaint against the officers. That kind of talk could undermine my work with the men, Sir."

He hurriedly dismissed that idea with a wave of his cigar, the smoke unfurling like a flag. "No need, son. I'll take care of it."

"Thank you, Sir."

"The important thing is that you're not guilty of encouraging the men in the wrong way."

"Right, Sir."

"I know that. You know that. And I'll take care of the rest."

"Sir, if I may point out to the general, Sir, it's not the job of the psychologist to 'encourage' anything. My job is to listen. If I do that well, Sir, they'll make up their own minds to do the right thing."

"To do the right thing . . ."

Surprisingly pleased, he quickly grabbed up a pen and wrote that down, repeating the last phrase aloud as he wrote " . . . to do the right thing."

Please, I thought to myself. Please don't ask me what 'the right thing' is.

He stood up. I too stood, and saluted. He came around the desk, however, and offered his hand. "Keep up the good work, Levy."

His grip was remarkably firm, firmer than usual, I deduced, to show commitment. On the phone that evening, however, my father's take was a little different: he felt it was to show "comradeship."

"I mean it," said the general, ushering me to the door. "Keep up the good work."

| 40 |

Arlanne Learns That Bad Girls Can Go to Heaven Too

Now before I get into what happened between me and Murray at the beach, let me explain a few things: first, never in my life had I fucked a "friend"; I mean a real friend, a close friend, and I'd been buddies in one way or another with Murray since high school. People change. Admittedly, I knew he kind of liked me in high school, and I liked him, but really as a source of comfort, "like a brother," though, goddamn, in retrospect that sounds insulting as hell. I didn't fully appreciate nice boys then. I trusted them but to be honest with you, it was the bad boys—them rednecks with the shivs and Rebel Yell, the ones that sweated it all out on the football field, flunked out, or made Gentleman's "C's," souped up their Chevy's with drag pipes and all—country boys and party boys, boys that flat out didn't give a shit—those are the ones I liked. Drivin' like maniacs, the whole crew of us, in Eldridge Moody's red Corvette with the top down—Eldridge was a redneck, but he was rich as hell—drunker than skunks, out to the beach, gettin' out there and takin' off every stitch of clothes we had on—sometimes down at the "nigger" beach—not givin' a rat's ass about a goddamn thing, lettin' it all hang out, soberin' up in the ocean, just sittin' there laughin' like hell at ourselves . . .

Heaven that was . . . Heaven, till bein' all Popular and all, somethin' I took for granted, bein' pretty, comin' from the family I did and all, just all of a sudden got boring as hell, utterly meaningless, leavin' you with nothin' but a hangover and feelin' like a waste of time, useless, sad, I think. That was when I begin to see Ol' Murray a little bit differently. Not that he hadn't been popular and all, he had, but he seemed to enjoy it more than the rest of us, as if it was somethin' he didn't take for granted, as if his relationships were somehow politicized. Murray was the peacemaker in the group. The problem back then was that Peace wasn't fun—fightin' was. Crowds didn't gather to watch peace break out. But a fight? The whole place, rubbernecks crowding each other out just to get a better view. Think about it. In the world of adults, you got to pay a fortune just to get a ticket for a good one. Fightin's a profession. So don't go gettin' all pious and sanctimonious on me, you hear?

Hell, I'm ramblin', just like Bert always tells me. Since he don't care for listenin' anyway it drives him crazy, not that he's actually tuned in anyway. Now that's somethin' about Ol' Murray, he'll listen. Hell, he'll listen to anything. Makes you feel good about yourself, even when you shouldn't, which is the only thing that bothers me about him. He's dishonest in that way, where Bert ain't. Still, maybe Murray's just more curious. That's certainly possible. Anyway, I like his listenin'. He's cute.

And he was always cute. It's just that back in those days, high school and all, Jews didn't believe in Heaven. Still don't for that matter, but Murray, bless his affable old soul, took it one step further: he didn't believe in Heaven on Earth. Even to the song by The Platters. So Ol' Murray wasn't quite the hellraiser the rest of us were. If we were drinkin', who drove? You guessed it. Everybody else was drunk. His mama, Mama Gold, whoo! That woman was strict: loved him like a mother hen, watched him like a hawk. She raised a truly nice boy. Nice boys, in those days, well, I'll put it this way: you couldn't get to Heaven with 'em.

Now, however, in these times, it looks like the biggest rebels in town are two Jews. One I'm married to, the other I have a rather curious interest now in fuckin'. Murray's a smart son of a bitch. Bert, he's downright dangerous: he'll not only approach the edge, hell, he'll fall in. He's neurotic as hell. Murray, however, he'll take you right up to it, then he'll hold your hand while you both stare into the abyss. I like being taken to the edge. And I think that's why I want to fuck Murray. Bert, well, Bert's just crazy. He admits it. Hell, he's one of those shrinks that if you ask him about it, if you say to him, Bert, do you know that you're crazy as a fuckin' loon, he'll just look up as if it's the most obvious thing in the world and say, calm as butter spreadin', "Of course I am, you fucking idiot. Why do you think I do what I do for a living?"

Bert's a crazy fuck; Murray's a sane one. Right now sanity, the sanity of a safe harbor, seems awfully warm and inviting. And I ain't one for hugs. They make me nervous.

Too intimate. Give me a good Fuckaroo any day.

You agree?

I'm sorry. I just cannot seem to talk without talkin' to somebody, even if I'm just talkin' to myself. Bert says that's because I'm crazy, but I tell him he's sayin' that just because he don't want to be the only nut in the house.

Then he says, that's true, he doesn't want to be the only nut in the house, but that don't mean I ain't one.

Then I say . . . aw hell, it goes on and on. He's exhausting.

Which is why I'm about to fuck Murray.

One more thing, however, you need to know: this is the sixties, man. Everybody's fuckin' everybody, and if they're married, they're fuckin' everybody else's wives and husbands. You go to a party nowadays and head for the closet to hang up your coat, you don't know what twosome's gonna come tumblin' out. The country's wild. Watts is burning, yeah; they set the whole damn place on fire. People walkin' into stores and comin' out with anything they want, everything they can get. Girls right here in town linin' up at Luthor's Drug Store for the Pill. Everybody's fuckin' everybody. It's unbelievable. Mini-skirts came out this year, and every girl in town who could get away with it came out wearin' 'em: the first "fuck me" skirts in America. (I was wearin' one—a simple, unadorned black—and no panties either.). Braless breasts: more bounce to the ounce, more jiggle to the wiggle. (I wasn't wearin' one now either; the object was for my nipples, once direct and forthright, to say "bite me" without me havin' to say a word.) In

Charleston and Savannah men and women, unmarried, are actually livin' together. Down on the waterfront here in town you smell the same fish smells and marsh gas as always, but if you're standin' 'round by the bars, you catch a whiff of a strange new smell called pot. In fact, in a few years Hoke Cooley's gonna' have to arrest some of his buddies, some of the town's leading men, for drug smuggling right here on the Inland Waterway. 'Course Murray'll get 'em off with a slap on the wrist and a spank on the fanny.

Don't trust nobody over thirty. That's all you hear from the college kids on the nightly news.

Well, they can trust me. I'm over thirty and I'm fuckin' too.

So's just about everybody I know.

Not that a lot of 'em weren't doin' it before too. Hell, look at our sheriff, now that Lila's through with him, havin to go home to that fuckin' Mary Magdalene every night.

They were all just doin' it on the sly.

If only they'd had a pill back when I was in high school . . .

You know, the truth is, I don't really know what to do. I'm sittin' here on the trunk of an uprooted old palm tree that's been half-burrowed in the sand here for years gettin' splinters in my butt contemplating an empty beach and a vast ocean with 'Ol Murray and I know what he wants and I want to give it to him, but I swear, it's beginnin' to feel like charity. Not that charity doesn't make you feel good. It can. No doubt about it. But even sittin' on this tree trunk swillin' Jack Daniels right out the bottle like it's a glass of water, which 'Ol Murray's doin' right now—totally out of character for him—I can just feel an eagerness and tension in him that turns me off and makes me somehow sweet on him at the same time.

"Come here, sweetie," I told him.

I put my arm around him, gave him a gentle, tender, barely perceptible kiss on his cheek. He couldn't help it. He turned slightly away, thinking of Bert. I bit his ear, he struggled with himself, wavering, letting his instincts (against his will, it seemed) take over (which touched me), moving hesitantly toward me, letting me breathe on his neck, his face, all over, my lips brushing his, light kisses, grabbing his head and shoulders, slowly guiding him off the tree trunk so that we were standing, facing each other directly. I stared at him hard. I meant business. My hands on his shoulders, I pressed down, hard. When I had him where I wanted him, on his knees in front of me, which frankly speaking is where I prefer all men, I held his face in my hands, leaned over and kissed him with everything I had, let go, and while he's looking at me with all the hunger of a thousand poor countries, I lowered the tiny straps, one by one, off my shoulders, and unable now to take my eyes off his face partly out of sheer desire, partly out of curiosity, with my legs demurely pressed together I turned just a bit, first to one side then the other, slipping my skirt up to my waist, all of it over my head, carelessly dropping it on the sand.

He wanted me so badly, he was heading straight for me when with both hands I held him at bay, grabbed the bourbon, and from on high poured it all over my breasts, my thighs, inside me and all over him, rubbing it into his hair, his face, all over him as he greedily devoured every drop all the way into Heaven.

Loving me from the inside out.

"Goddamn it. I hate you, I hate you," I screamed. I couldn't help myself. I did hate him, incomprehensibly, my body, my self, my soul possessed, devilishly writhing and thrashing about without me, in complete, abject surrender to a Higher Power totally repugnant, solely because it was a Higher Power, and totally incomprehensible, every fucking time. Every fucking time.

"I hate you too," he said, as he fucked me harder, and harder, and harder. "I hate you. Goddamn it, I hate you."

"Oh Murray, oh . . ."

"I hate you," he said with each bitter thrust, "I hate you . . ."

"Oh, baby, I know, I know. Oh . . . It's okay, it's okay. Oh! Murray . . ."

I tasted the salt of his tears, of his betrayal of his dearest friend, of his sacrifice for me, of his offering of pure love.

I cried, I whimpered, I screamed.

"Please don't stop. Please."

"Arlanne . . ."

"Yes, say my name, say my name. Please? Please?"

"Arlanne . . ."

"Yes, Baby, yes. Oh! Oh! Oh!"

Heaven exploded inside me.

"God . . ."

41

The C.O. Contemplates the Death March Into Vietnam

Was it because of the war, wondered the C.O., or because he was getting older? Whatever the reason, often in late afternoon he would find he needed time for himself, uninterrupted time for thought and reflection. So before heading for the Officer's Club for a Jack Daniels straight-up prior to dinner, the C.O. would tell his driver to go home for the day, and he'd climb in the jeep and drive himself around the island, observing, taking it all in, surveying his domain, as his aide once put it, like a Southern planter exploring his vast properties. Sometimes he'd stop and chat with a work detail mending a fence, or observe a Company in the day's final formation listening to plans for the next day—instructions, for example, as to which uniform to wear—after which he'd shift back into first gear and drive on. Was the grass cut, weeded and edged? The cutting and pruning uniform? Sometimes he'd pull up, amble out, and check a particular Company's quarters. Was the "head" spotless? The toilet tissue folded into perfectly symmetrical diamond-shapes? The brass on faucets, showerheads, and doorknobs shined to a fault? He might stop in and chat with the Company Commander, checking the men's shoes and brass at the same time, afterwards sharing a drink. And sometimes he'd just drive about and see and hear absolutely nothing, in his own little world, particularly when the War pressed at his temples until he felt as if they were going to burst. And sometimes, sometimes, particularly after chow, he'd find himself drawn in the soft island twilight to the evening detail, for which Jack McGowan regularly volunteered, the first Marine ever to do so.

He'd pull over to the curb and watch McGowan from a distance, push-brooming down the sidewalks for hours, then washing them down, from one end of the island to the other, or cleaning company offices—scrubbing, waxing, and polishing—doing the grunt work, literally the dirty, often filthy work, what every Marine avoided like the plague; yet doing it all so carefully, so attentively, so lovingly. And this after mornings of scrubbing, waxing, and polishing each tile separately in the "head," cleaning toilets and the urinal troughs, and in slow circular movements applying Brasso to the faucet and shower fixtures. If cleanliness was indeed next to Godliness, thought the C.O., then McGowan was approaching holiness. He did everything that needed to be done—maintenance repairs, building furniture for staff offices, moving heavy equipment—and then approached his sergeant for more.

And in the afternoons, after shining the brass of his superiors, the trash detail: five privates in horizontal formation spread across the drill field, the roadside, the obstacle course, marching from one end of the island to the other to the barking orders of their sergeant: "Stop! Trash! Pick up! . . . Stop! . . . Trash! Pick up! . . . Stop! Trash! Pick up! . . ."

McGowan, giving himself up to a higher authority, never missed a beat.

Jack had wanted, he had told him, to be the best private he could be. Whether he was cleaning latrines, building a table for the staff office, or fixing a broken faucet, Jack worked with such care and gentleness, with such respect for the undertaking, that his work seemed more a process of nurturing—of washing and waxing a Corvette in a Saturday afternoon driveway—than hard manual labor. Levy had told him such work for Jack was gentle and harmless, which now was all Jack aspired to be, and therefore redemptive.

"For the death march," the C.O. had assumed.

"For his having been a bad person, or so he feels," said Levy, "for having been evil to the core, so bad his father had to almost kill him. Certainly he seeks redemption for the death march, but more profoundly he seeks redemption for the cause of it, which he truly feels is his evil nature."

And the death march into Vietnam? Is he—the C. O.—responsible in his own way for that? What drew him so compellingly to Jack McGowan, without his ever having spoken barely a word to him? Is it what drew Cunningham to McGowan? He knew they were close. He kept up with his men. He knew Cunningham had recently moved in with Jack, his wife and his son out on Scataway Island, as far away from civilization as they could get. And it wasn't to escape condemnation for their murderous atrocities. McGowan's shame was open, unabashed, so palpable as to be tender, Cunningham's wild, raging, tearful, hurt-filled, and frightening. McGowan's shame was subtly compelling, Cunningham's a throwing down of the gauntlet, openly challenging. Throw me in jail, cries Cunningham, prosecute me for crimes against humanity, he wails to the gods. Unfortunately, his gods are in the Pentagon, where they themselves are praying he'll shut up. Already the whispers have gone out to the press higher-ups; otherwise, Vicker's piece in the *Times* would have been enough to spread the news and precipitate follow-up. No, how welcome Civilization's contempt is to men who already cry out for it, who already have condemned themselves.

If they seek refuge, it is from a Civilization, which condones needless murder, from one which fails to condemn them.

He was a tough soldier, but he was beginning to loathe himself for his cowardice. Some days he felt ashamed. Other days, when he truly supported his troops—contacting Vicker about Cunningham's speech, inadvertently supporting the way Levy was counseling the men—he picked himself up a bit. Kids, however, were dying, and civilization, in which he included himself—however hesitantly—was responsible.

From a distance, parking his jeep in the approaching dusk, he'd watch McGowan at the far end of the island, mending the fence that winds around the perimeter of the base. McGowan pokes gently, prodding, twisting, splicing, winding . . . And the C.O. feels closer to him, in that moment, than any other Marine on Lawton Island.

Daily Private McGowan exhausts himself, Levy'd told him. It's the only way he can sleep at night.

| 42 |

Pat Conroy Teaches Elizabeth to See the World Through Her Own Eyes

At the time, Elizabeth wanted to be a reporter, or at least thought she did. "Pioneering" school integration as the only black child in an otherwise all-white school made her hate white people. In that school every day she felt worse than lonely. She felt repulsive. She hated herself, but she could never forgive them for making her feel that way. At best she felt invisible to them, at worst some kind of flea-bitten stray they wanted off their property.

She wanted to be was a reporter so she could grow up and document all the evils of white people. Without realizing it at the time, however, the only people she really wanted to expose were the white kids in the school and Hoke Cooley. They were the only ones she knew, and she couldn't imagine a future without them, without her resentment and hostility toward them, her fantastical and vengeful fantasies.

The only opportunity for reporting available to her, however, was the junior high school newspaper. It was run by an English teacher named Pat Conroy who would later become a famous writer. Mr. Conroy, having only the year before graduated from the Citadel, had a bit of clout unusual for a new teacher. A Marine brat who had moved to Somerset at 16, he'd been a star athlete here, particularly a star basketball player, all-state, though after getting to know him Elizabeth never hesitated to remind him that he had been "all-state" competing only against white players. He liked her, and never hesitated to show it publicly.

And she liked him. He actually, in what was to her an abominably depressing educational setting, made her laugh, though as he himself admitted, he had to work like hell to get her to. She liked him just as she liked Murray and Bert. They were friends. Sometimes she wished Bert were her daddy. He and Murray were over at the house all the time. Mr. Conroy was not originally a Somersetonian, and he was a liberal. Athletics, however, was his 'social lubricator,' as he called it, his free ticket socially, just as it would later be that of black boys and girls entering the school.

Her mama knew him through the biracial council. He'd joined as soon as he moved back to Somerset. The other teachers liked him personally, but called him a "do-gooder" behind his back. Lila told Elizabeth that he'd told her that Old Lady Crout, the ugliest teacher in the school, was fretting aloud in the teacher's lounge about "nigger boys comin' over here with all this integration and rapin' her."

Her mama laughed so hard. Mr. Conroy said, "It might not be so bad, Miss Crout. From what I hear, they're real studs."

Anyway, she knew her mama talked to him because he came up to her one day in the hall—she didn't even know who he was—and told her that he'd heard she was the smartest kid in the junior high. She was, she told him, shrugging. There wasn't much competition. That's why after graduating high school, she added, she was planning on going to a black college.

That was the funniest thing he'd ever heard, he told her, looking about to make sure no one else had heard. Nobody had told him she was so witty, he then said, after which he added: "it's probably not a bad thing you're so quiet. Jesus, would you be in trouble."

I need a reporter for the junior high newspaper, he told her, and I want the smartest kid in the school for the job.

Elizabeth was so happy she smiled the most beautiful smile he said he'd ever seen. She told him he'd been looking at too many white girls.

Before this everything had been closed to her. There was one excuse after another. She'd learned not to ask, just to stay to herself. After all, since she'd begun attending the junior high school the committees and clubs met in each other's homes. Not, however, the newspaper, unless it was Mr. Conroy's home, and nobody wanted to meet at his home, he told her, because it was too ugly. The one thing she really wanted was to be a reporter for the school newspaper, but she'd never have asked. Too humiliating. Her mama though, she knew what white man to ask.

At first he asked Elizabeth if she wanted to write a piece about her own experience having been rejected, just because she was black, by all these school committees and clubs, her isolation and treatment here at Somerset Junior High. But then he said that not only would he be gone, but the hell she'd catch would make it unfair to her.

He said to talk to her mother and together they'd all come up with something.

After listening to all the grown-up talk at the house about the upcoming boycott of Palmer's Department Store, it struck Elizabeth as the perfect idea. Also, it meant her mama would have to let her attend, which Elizabeth knew she'd been hesitant to do. Mr. Conroy thought the boycott a great idea too. He'd be there, he said.

"Listen," he told her. "Make sure you have a note pad and pencil. Take down specifics, not just of those participating but those who might be watching or overseeing. If you notice policemen, try to overhear what they say to each other. If Palmer comes out to speak, write down everything he says. Any specifics, what people say, who they are, how could you tell who they are if you didn't know them. That way the reader can. Become invisible, Elizabeth, just like you do here at school; use it to your advantage now, so you can listen and observe. Who's participating? Why? What for? Why do they matter? Listen also to your feelings, Elizabeth. Don't turn them off, like you do here. They're your antennae. Follow them, listen and look around to see who and what is causing them to vibrate. Write that down. Remember, be specific: dialogue and details. Include me, if you can, as the Great White Hope."

"You're crazy, " she told him, simply because he was.

"Oh yeah, " he reminded her, "don't forget Mrs. Hunter's speech. Get it down."

So although her mama and Arlanne and Murray and Mrs. Hunter and half a dozen others could tell you all about the boycott, Elizabeth shows it through a child's eyes, if indeed a child was what she still was.

The Boycott of Palmer's Department Store
By Elizabeth Trulove

It was loud, but not so loud you couldn't hear the person next to you if they shouted. I know, because my mama kept shouting at me and my baby brother, whose name is not worth mentioning here, to stay close. Local policemen and State Troopers, all white, blocked off the street. They weren't there "out of the goodness of their hearts," Mama told this reporter, but because Mr. Murray Gold, the lawyer for the Somerset Biracial Council, had gotten Judge Golightly to sign the Demonstration Permit, which the judge was "legally obligated" to do. What does "legally obligated" mean? This reporter asked that same question so don't feel stupid if you don't know. Mr. Gold said it means the judge had no choice, just like you and I are "legally obligated" to come to school. Because of the Demonstration, we all have a chance to learn a new term. Of course some people won't care, but they don't care about anything anyway. Mama says they're going to be just as stupid when they grow up as they are now. You might think this is off the subject of the Demonstration but it's not. You know why? Because Ignorance is what we're protesting against. That's what Dr. King said, not just about our protests but all of them "all across this great nation of ours." He should know, he's a doctor. Doctors have more education than most because they go to a school called "Medical School." "Medical School" only takes the smartest people, like me.

Mr. Gold also told this reporter that once the demonstration was "legally authorized," Sheriff Cooley and his boys decided to cordon off the area and bring in the state troopers and the National Guard "just to make sure things don't get out of hand, so there won't be any trouble." The area cordoned off was about a half-block of the downtown space in front of Palmer's Department Store, and that's where all the protesters, including this reporter, gathered. On the sidewalk right in front of Palmer's a lectern with a microphone was set up for the speaker, Mrs. Eileen Hunter, the president of the Somerset Biracial Association. She's also the principal of Lady's Island Elementary School, in case you didn't know. The Somerset Biracial Association was sponsoring the protest. Thirty-nine protesters stood around shouting and screaming for Equality and Freedom in the cordoned off area. Thirty-three were black. Six were white. Mr. Conroy, our teacher, was there. He told this reporter that he expected to be counted as a black man because he really was black, a black albino, but he just thinks he's funny, which he's not. The only other people there were a bunch of rednecks, my mama said, on the other side of the cordon, and behind them the street preachers.

In front of Palmer's in the cordoned off area, signs were waving and people were chanting: "Hire us . . . Hire us . . . Hire us . . ." The chants and signs were directed not only at Mr. Palmer, even though his was the only name mentioned, but according to Mama, at all the white employers in Somerset. "We won't buy if we don't sell . . . We won't buy if we don't sell. . . We won't buy if we don't sell . . . Hire us . . . Hire us . . . Hire us . . ."

Mrs. Eileen Hunter, the president of the Biracial Council, checked her hair one last time, patted it down just right, and approached the lectern. Mama told this reporter that Mrs. Hunter always liked her hair to be "just right." Mama said sometimes she could spend hours on it. She said that was why Mrs. Hunter was sometimes late to school, but that that didn't matter because she was so smart. She said she wanted this reporter to be smart like Mrs. Hunter. This reporter told her she was already smart, so could she be late to school too? That's when this reporter's mama told her to shut up or she'd take care of her good when she got home. And that's exactly what this reporter did. Anyway, Mrs. Hunter was behind the lectern now, and she was getting ready to speak. She waited for everybody to quiet down, which according to Mama takes Negroes longer than white people and according to Mr. Gold, takes Jews longer than anybody. Sure enough, when Mrs.

Hunter started to speak, Mr. Gold and Dr. Levy, who was also Jewish, were still chatting away with each other like all get-out.

Mrs. Hunter looked over at the National Guard surrounding the cordon, and beyond them to the policemen and state troopers. She pointed at the town's leaders and politicians—Hoke Cooley, Mr. Palmer himself, Marty Liebowitz, Harper Dawes—surveying the protest through the upper story plate-glass window of the bank building across the street from Palmer's, two stores down from the old Ritz. Then she looked back at the crowd, adjusting her glasses. This reporter liked the way she did that, and thought about taking up the mannerism herself. She almost missed the beginning of the speech trying to figure out how she could get her mama to get her a pair, but this reporter tuned right back in again at just the right time. "You're who we're talkin' to today," Mrs. Hunter announced, looking and pointing up at the men in the window of the bank building. "We talkin' here to Power, to the *overseers* of this town. Yeah, that's right. The *overseers.* You know who you are," she said, and she looked right up at them when she said it. "And we know who you are. Do we know, Brothers and Sisters? Do we know? Don't make me name 'em. *Do we know?*"

"We know," mumbled the crowd.

"Do we know?" shouted Mrs. Hunter.

Then the crowd answered back. "We know . . . We know . . . We know . . ."

"Does God know?" she asked the crowd.

"God knows," they shouted back. "God knows."

"Does God know we know?"

"Oh yeah . . . He knows, He knows . . ."

"Do the Good Lord hear us? Is we finally gittin' to him?"

"He hear us . . . He hear us . . ."

Then she shouted like a Holy Roller, loud as she could. Her eyes were shut tight, her fists clenched. Her head looked as if it was shaking all by itself.

"Do He hear us?" she screamed. "Do He hear us?"

Then the crowd all shouting back, "He hear us . . . He hear us."

"Do He hear us now? Right now? Right here today in Somerset, South Carolina in front of Palmer's Department Store. I want to know. I say, Do He hear us?"

"He hear us, He hear us!" the crowd going so crazy now that even the white street preachers, the ones always coming into town from somewhere else preachin' downtown every Saturday, broke the cordon and tumbled into the crowd as if God had picked them up and thrown them in there. "He hear us!"

Everybody now, even those who weren't black, sounded as if they were.

"He hear us, He hear us . . ."

Now she waited for the crowd to quiet down, like a low hum you sometimes hear in Church when people are praying to themselves. There were a few "Amens." "Amen, Sister. Amen."

"Well, if The Good Lord can hear us," she asked quietly, turning, looking up and pointing directly at the town's leaders in the upstairs window of the bank building, "how come they can't?"

People in the crowd started going crazy again. Two students down from South Carolina State began jitterbugging. "That right Sister . . . You tell em' Sister . . ."

"How *come* they can't?"

I heard somebody say, "Mr. Palmer deaf!"

I looked over at Mr. Palmer's daughter, Mrs. Arlanne Levy, to see if she heard him. If she did, she didn't show it. She was shouting and screaming with the rest of them, right there on the front row. Only I did see her raise her sunglasses just a bit to wipe away a tear. Mrs. Hunter's arm swept towards the Guardsmen, towards the troopers and policemen, gathering them, it seemed, under her black angel's wing, though they didn't much register they wanted to be there. Of course, they didn't register much of anything, just standing there, looking straight ahead of themselves. Then she looked up at the town's leaders in the bank window again. "You sent them here to prevent trouble," she said. "We all know that." Then she said, looking at the crowd now, "There already *is* trouble. Didn't you know? We know. There's *been* trouble. Brothers and Sisters, is it fair to say we been 'troubled?'"

"That's fair, that's fair," the crowd shouted back.

"If there weren't no trouble," she said, "there wouldn't be no protest. We wouldn't be here today. Would we? Would we? I wonder. Answer "yes ma'am" or "no ma'am" for me please."

"No ma'am," shouted the crowd, "No ma'am."

"Thank you," she said. "Thank you. Just wanted to be sure. . . . 'Cause for the life of me I can't help but wonder, Where were all these law enforcement officers when we needed them to enforce the 1964 Civil Rights laws? You see those WHITE ONLY and COLORED ONLY signs all over this town? They ain't supposed to be there. Desegregation so slow it movin' backwards. They take our brightest student and leave the rest of 'em where they at, tryin' to make up for it, they say, by 'improvin' our facilities, our textbooks, and so on. Come on. Everybody know where that tax money goin'. It's been two years. Still, black people confined to the slums. Still, they got to stop off in the woods to go to the bathroom if they on the road. A black person still can't sit down in a white-owned restaurant in this town and order a meal. We can cook their meals, we can put our hands all over their food. We just can't eat it with 'em. We can buy from white folk, but we still can't sell to 'em, not in any of these downtown spaces. Fair employment in this town is a joke, unless you're white, then it's fair. Lila Trulove had the money and they still wouldn't let her buy her way in. You know that. Every Negro in town knows that. That's why we're here. That's why we're here, downtown today, in front of Palmer's Department Store. Mr. Palmer, you make a lot of money off us Negroes. That's why you open on Saturdays, that's why you always stock our clothes, our hats, our shoes . . . But you don't think much of us Negroes. Do you, Mr. Palmer? Unless Money's involved. Money, money, that'll turn yo' head. That'll turn the White man's head. And it's going to turn the head of every employer in downtown Somerset, and it's going to turn the head of every man standin' up there in that bank window looking out over this crowd like they gods . . . We startin' here, Mr. Palmer, but let it be known we ain't stoppin' till we taught the lesson of justice to every owner of every store in downtown Somerset. We good enough to walk into your places of business and buy from you, exchange money for goods, but we ain't good enough to sell them same products from behind your counters, to help manage your books, to advance beyond the janitor's closet and the stock room? Mr. Palmer, you been breakin' the law." You could hear nothing but silence now, as she paused, tired, it seemed to this reporter. If you listened hard, maybe you could hear the waves licking at the riverbank as if it was ice cream. Then she said, "That's trouble. That's a heap of trouble." She looked up once again at the men in the upstairs window of the bank building. "This ain't trouble," she told them, acknowledging the protesters. "Where were you then? Where was law enforcement then?"

Every time this reporter looked up and saw the National Guardsmen standing there looking at nothing but the empty space in front of them in their uniforms and hats with their guns and sticks, I admit that this reporter moved closer and closer to her mama. And the State Troopers' sunglasses made them scary too. They could look at us but we couldn't look at them, so it made you wonder whose side they all were really on, ours or all those rednecks behind them starting to call us bad names and using unchristian language and every once in awhile managing to throw fruit or rocks over the cordon at us. According to my teacher Mr. Pat Conroy, standing right beside me, those rednecks were among "the nastiest, ugliest white people" he'd ever seen. Mr. Conroy said he thought he was ugly till he saw them. He said even their babies, which a few of the ugly wives were holding, were ugly. This reporter can tell you that the men were mostly big and fat and sloppily dressed. This reporter could not smell them from where she was, but she can tell you that they *looked* like they smelled bad.

"The white man accept our money, but he can't accept us. He got the power. He make us, he break us. Today we takin' back the power. 'Cause today we takin' our money back. We takin' our money elsewhere. Savannah, look out. Charleston, we on our way. You hear me, white man? *Elsewhere.* Yeah, we here today to cause trouble. Trouble. Legal trouble, but Trouble just as well. We make you, now we break you. Simple as money. Without ours, you broke, and you ain't goin' to get ours till we see some black faces behind your counters. Today begins the boycott!"

Everybody was screaming and cheering so loud I couldn't hear a thing.

A few black women, according to Momma, had planned to do some shopping at Palmer's on this day, but looking at the crowd of demonstrators made them think twice about it, even the ones paid to shop, like Mrs. Hattie Carpenter and Mrs. Janine Lightsey.

This reporter saw Mrs. Hattie Carpenter standing on the sidewalk looking almost directly up at the men in the bank. So I looked up there too, to see who she was looking at. Sheriff Hoke Cooley was there, in uniform and sunglasses, his arms crossed, looking down on everybody. Mrs. Carpenter was just standing there shaking her head while he jerked his ugly-ass head toward Palmer's Department Store. It looked like he was trying to get her to go in. He kept jerking his head that way. She shook her head some more till it just about fell off, it seemed to this reporter. Then she pulled some dollar bills out of her purse, waving them up at him, as if she didn't want them anymore, as if it was his money now and she wanted to give it back to him. Sheriff ducked back where you couldn't see him so fast he left his shadow behind. Meanwhile, quicker than you can say Jack Flash, Mrs. Carpenter had joined the demonstration herself, holding up a poster and shouting with the rest of the crowd, "If we ain't sellin', we ain't buyin'. If we ain't sellin', we ain't buyin' . . . If we ain't sellin', we ain't buyin' . . ."

Mrs. Janine Lightsey worked as a maid in the Palmer household. Mama told me once that Mrs. Arlanne Levy had told her that Mrs. Lightsey had just about raised her. Mrs. Lightsey had slipped the cordon now, probably like Mrs. Carpenter had, and had already joined the protest. This reporter overheard Mrs. Arlanne Levy say to her: "Go on in the store if you want to, Janine. If not, he'll fire you sure as shootin'."

"Thank you, Mrs. Arlanne, but I don't want to be the only black person in town workin'."

She handed Mrs. Levy a sealed envelope, saying, "Please give this to your father."

Mama told this reporter what was in it.

This reporter thanks you for reading this.

Mr. Conroy read it and told Elizabeth not to change a thing, except that the last line was unnecessary. She liked the last line, but that was because she didn't know any better. No one had ever really criticized anything she'd written before, so she thought whatever she put down on paper was just fine. Mr. Conroy said everything was more than just fine, that everything was great except that line, so he took it out. At the time Elizabeth acted like she resented it; certainly she thought she did. She realized later, however, that it was just an excuse to keep Mr. Conroy at a distance in case he decided later he didn't like her, like she'd thought her daddy hadn't. Thank God, she realized, Mr. Conroy saw through it.

She was excited when it was published in the junior high school newspaper and all, but not all that much. It wasn't all formal and laid out professionally, like the high school newspaper. Mr. Conroy said he preferred the informality of the junior high paper, that it allowed for a fresher, more uniquely personal perspective—"a child's, to be exact"—which was always more interesting and truer to him than kids in formal, conventional school newspapers trying too hard to sound like adults. When you read those kinds of school newspapers, he said, you can't tell whose voice you're hearing—everybody sounds alike—and they're humorless. You're funny, he told her. I am? she thought. If it's a kid's newspaper, he continued, the stories should be written from a kid's perspective. Really? She never once contemplated that either. Was mine? she asked him. Absolutely, he said. Otherwise, it wouldn't ring true. Ring true? Be true, he said, true to your thoughts and feelings about it, your genuine perception of it. You're a kid. Just be you. You have a very interesting, quirky personality, fresh and original. No one in the world is like you. You're unique. That's what your writing shows. Let it out more, at least with people you trust. He liked interesting personalities, and hers, he said, was "uniquely interesting." She had to admit, that was the first time in her life she'd ever contemplated that notion. "Interesting?" she thought. That's interesting. Most kids, however, just picked up the paper in the cafeteria line looking for their names. Of course, had they been "interested" in her story, would she have known? She seriously doubted it. No, rather than unbridled enthusiasm, she felt more like she'd had a job to do, that she'd done it well, and that it was important. It did, however, make her contemplate for a long time the notion of "interesting." What made a person, or a person's writing, "interesting?" "Personalities like yours," Mr. Conroy told her, which made her absolutely giddy. Oh, she so wanted to become even more “interesting.” Did she? She certainly took a greater interest in herself. It wasn’t that the interest wasn’t already there. Bert had opened that particular door for her. It was just that she hadn’t been conscious of it, certainly not to the extent she was now. Mr. Conroy became her friend as well as her teacher.

And he was certainly interesting to her. Always, he said, be personal. Don’t take the conventional route. Avoid the cliché. Create your own.

She never forgot that advice. It leaves one with two choices: either shut up, or tell the truth. Without realizing it at the time, four years later it would inform her valedictory address to her graduating class at Somerset High School, and it informs her work to this day.

If you want to know what got her immediately excited about the piece, it was Driver’s reaction. When he saw that article in the school newspaper with her byline above it, he was so jealous he tried his best to get her in trouble for days. Oh, did he stew! He even tried to steal it and burn it. Every chance he got he tried to tell her and their Mama how bad it was. And the more he told Elizabeth, the better she felt.

It just made her want to do the jig, made it all worth it.

Her article, he would tell her later, was what inspired him to become a journalist.

Over the long haul, however, it inspired her to become a lawyer; that, and as her husband would later accuse, her obsessive need for satisfaction from Hoke Cooley. Words do inspire, no question. She knew that. And boycotts and demonstrations threaten the status quo and bring the issue to the forefront, no doubt about that either. It was the law, however, the sheer force of it, she would realize, that integrated the Somerset County Schools; that, and money—the fear of the loss of those federal funds. And it would be the law and money that would eventually integrate downtown Somerset.

No one lost his or her job as a result of participating in the downtown boycott. As Alice Palmer reportedly said to Arlanne, “Who else we going to get to scrub the floors and polish the silver?” Palmer’s Department Store and Freddie Dinnerman’s Men’s Shop took the lead and hired respectively Janine Lightsey’s brother Harold (a recent graduate of South Carolina State) and Leonard Perch (Ida’s husband, a suave, handsome retired Marine sergeant notable for his dandified dress) as salespeople who were allowed in the front to sell solely to black customers. Because of this, more Blacks did begin coming downtown during the week rather than just on Saturdays. Transportation to Savannah and Charleston to shop turned out to be a complicated hassle, and since no blacks lost their jobs the travel was too time-consuming anyway. Not surprisingly, many of the old-timers in the black community were more relieved by the benign reaction of whites than they were pleased by the progress, however small, that had been made.

What Elizabeth didn't know at the time was that she wasn't the only one biding her time. Her mama was.

43

Arlanne Plots Her Seduction of Bert Among the Night Flowers

Dancing about with the tea bags and the ice tray and the clean glass plucked from the dishwasher, Arlanne was singing "When a Man Loves a Woman" at the top of her lungs, the windows wide open so the neighbors might hear. She had an awful voice, yet disliked being alone—a less than winsome combination. Logan Furst (of Furst Come, Furst Serve Ice Cream), who lived two doors down, had once complained to Bert that Arlanne's voice ranged somewhere between a frog's croak and a bleating pig, and Bert had had to stand there and take it since, Logan, by any standard, was absolutely right. Bert'd been immobilized, he explained to Arlanne, by the overwhelming power of truth told by a man who spent his days scooping out Chocolate Ripple. When Arlanne got all petulant and pissed off, asking Bert over and over why he didn't defend her, he said he had called Murray who had informed him that against complaints about Arlanne's voice there was no defense. Slander requires that the offending complaint be untrue. Murray advised him, Bert had told her, not only against trying to obtain a settlement, but against going to court at all. For one thing, Arlanne's voice was so loud that finding an unbiased jury would be near impossible since everyone in the county, including on the outlying remote islands, had heard it. Second, nowadays it was difficult to bribe jurors.

She sat at the kitchen table thumbing through her garden catalogues. Sunlight burnished with a golden hue the amber of her iced tea. In the Carolina lowcountry Spring was just around the corner, the fragrance of Winter Daphne already slipping back into seasonal obscurity. She wanted something in her Spring garden that not another soul in Somerset had, something exotic that they'd never even seen or heard of, some new hybrid. She also wanted an intoxicating fragrance and white evening flowers for her night garden in the back. With candles, a good wine . . . Bert could forget all his frets and worries, most of which didn't amount to much anyway, and downright violate her right there in the backyard.

The possibility of neighbors turning into "Peeping Toms" made the idea even more delicious. Exhibitionism excited her, and paranoia intensified Bert, making him more focused.

Bert? What about Murray?

Well, soon after the beach-fuck and the boycott, when he figured Bert would be at work, Murray had phoned Arlanne, his voice clearly trembling. In the crunch a Christian, resigned to her cultural fate (she felt), she took pity on him.

"Is he there?"

"Hey, Murray!"

Again, in a whisper: "Is he there?"

"Why are you whisperin', Murray? Even if he were he couldn't hear you. You're on the phone."

"Yes or no, Arlanne. It's a simple yes or no question. Is he there?"

"Oh, quit talkin' like a Goddamn lawyer, Murray."

"Yes or no?"

"No, of course not. He's workin'. How you been?"

"Miserable. We can't do this anymore."

"Do what, Murray? Honest to God, I wonder what are you talkin' about."

"Arlanne . . ."

"I know, Sweetheart, but it was fun, wasn't it? God! You were great, Murray! I thought to myself later, Wow! That man can move!"

"Well . . ."

"Now don't you go gettin' a big head."

"I'll try, Arlanne. I'll try, but it's going to be awfully hard. I'm crazy about you."

I know. You're a lovin' man, Murray."

"I suppose I am."

"Funny too."

"Why, thank you, Arlanne."

"Funnier than these Christian boys. Don't know how I ended up fuckin' so many of 'em."

"A question for the ages, Arlanne. Arlanne?"

"Yeah, Sweetie Gumble Goo."

"It really wasn't about me and you. You know?"

"I know."

"You needed me because of what you weren't getting from Bert."

"Oh no, Sweet Little Gummy Gums, you got it backwards. It was because I was gettin' everything from Bert! Too much. Way too much. And when your hubbyboo gives you everything plus-what-you-could-do-without after your daddy ain't given you nothin', that's enough to scramble anybody's brain!"

"Oh," he said.

In her mind, however, hanging up, she was back to seducing Bert among night flowers in her night garden in the backyard. The question was, which flowers? What kind? In what sort of presentation and arrangement?

Arlanne finished her tea, laid the catalogue on the kitchen table, and began emptying the dishwasher. If I forget about the problem, she said to herself, the solution will come to me. That way, according to Bert, the subconscious will work on it.

He gets paid to know these things.

Sure enough, just as she was cramming the last glass into the kitchen cabinet, in her imagination appeared an enormously generous moonflower, white as a virgin on a moonless night, and fragrant as her night perfume. Beautifully seductive. Irresistible. Exquisite for the night garden in the back.

Yes, she picked up the catalogue again. Despite her little fantasy she knew that the idea of a congregation of perverted eyes peeping through the backyard fence, while perhaps titillating for her, would send Bert immediately, no questions asked, back into the den with Russell and the Cooze, jumping about in their short pants. Fortunately, in reality the dogwoods, cherry poplars, and great oaks with their overhanging branches bordering the neighboring yards pretty much guaranteed their privacy. So . . . casually string the moonflower vine along the black wrought iron fence surrounding the backyard. Against the fence, at the rear of the backyard, a white magnolia. Arranged in semicircles around the magnolia, from back to front, gardenias, tall white delphiniums, white David phlox, white verbena, and miniature white roses, the entryway a wrought iron arch (matching the fence) covered in climbing white iceberg roses. And in the midst of it all a small clearing of candlelight and urns and potted ginger and birds-of-paradise and red and white petunias and geraniums with trailing clematis and a gaudy chaise lounge beside which are gourds and bowls of exotic fruit and olives and wine, on which, lying naked, arms outstretched . . .

I think that'll do it, she said to herself, humming, laying the catalogue on the kitchen table.

And now for the new exotic specimen, alien and mysterious, for the front yard . . . Perhaps something she'd seen on her last visit to the

Caribbean, from one of the gardens in Ocho Rios, something vivid but sophisticated, something enviable . . .

She stood, stretched, and concentrated on touching her toes. Too easy, she realized, pleased. She did seventy-five sit-ups, eleven deep knee bends, and thirty-five jumping jacks, all as hard and fast as the exercises allowed, with all the focus and concentration she could muster, after which she ran in place—her legs pumping hard, her knees high—for two minutes. Checking the firmness, the roundness, the shapeliness and symmetry, and with a flick of her finger and a look over her shoulder, the bounce of her derriere, she headed for the laundry room, again having intentionally distracted herself, absenting from her mind the question of the exotic flower for the front yard. Then she began folding the laundry, waiting . . .

44

Jack Knows Solitude and Joy, However Ephemeral

Solitude has staked a claim on my tears. All I do when alone, once I quit working for the day and head home to Scataway Island—to Mary Beth and Jamie Mac and Royal—is cry. All I have to do is see Jamie Mac flinch at my approach, to weep for my cruelty toward him, for the little boy I might have been, for my sexual helplessness with Mary Beth, for the poor innocent young men who I thoughtlessly sent to their deaths, for their mothers and fathers and sisters and brothers, for the gentle and tender friendship of my lover, Royal Cunningham. When my son involuntarily flinches, instinctively shrinking away, just as I did at my father's approach, that is when the tears silently flow for the man I wish I'd been instead of the one I was. When I weep, the monster inside me—my father Frank McGowan—weeps. When my tears fail to include him, I can't even feel them on my face. The thought of him, stoic and heartless, lumbering awake in my heart and soul drives me to drink, to despair, and to thoughts of suicide, the only sure way to dispose of him. Yet Dr. Levy is right: to deny him, to fight him off, is to make him larger, more lethal, more dangerous. Besides, as Dr. Levy also says, denial is no longer available to me as a defense mechanism. So my awareness of him makes me weep rather than fight, hurt and empathetic rather than enraged and hostile.

Jamie Mac is less withdrawn around me lately, thank God, and thank Royal. In Royal he sees a man whom he can trust to be gentle. To believe in me, he has to believe in the gentleness that overwhelms me when I see him, even when I think of him. He must unlearn who I was. My God, how could I ever have hit my little boy?

In my sessions with Dr. Levy, I do little now but weep openly, sobbing with great pain, feeling, yes, feeling . . . I have hurt my own feelings—I almost killed them—broken my own heart. I weep for the protectiveness of my mother, the bravest woman I have ever known, but the pain, the pain . . . too much . . . too much . . . I have murdered innocent young men, so it hurts to be alive. Living is my penance, and as much as it hurts, I deserve hell.

Today I swore to myself that I wouldn't cry in Dr. Levy's office, not with Jamie Mac there. I wanted to avoid making him feel guilty. I didn't want help today for myself, but for Jamie. If he left the office knowing he was a good kid and always had been, that would be enough for me.

"I am sorry, Jamie Mac," I told him, "so terribly, terribly sorry."

"It's okay." Jamie Mac fidgeted, looking about. Clearly he'd rather be anywhere than where he was. Still, Dr. Levy had talked with him privately. He knew what he wanted to say. Dr. Levy had even attended Jamie Mac's Midget League Baseball game and offered to trade baseball cards, his Carl Yastremski for Jamie Mac's Al Kaline.

"Jamie? Ask your dad what you want to ask him. Say everything you feel. He truly wants you to."

"Please, son?" I asked him.

Jamie Mac picked at a loose sofa thread, focusing all his attention on it. "Why?" he asked.

"My father hit me. It was all I knew. Honestly, son, I just didn't know any better."

"Was I bad? You hit me when I cried. Now I never cry. I can't. Mom says that's not good."

He was angry and distrustful, fearful, just as I was. Yet still he yearned, above all, to please his daddy. My heart broke for my little boy, and despite myself I burst into tears just as he did, when finally, finally he lay his head in my lap and allowed me to stroke and hold him and tell him that, no, he was never bad but his daddy was, that he was and had always been a good little boy. Indeed, the pleasure of my life, holding him there, crying in Dr. Levy's office; a joy, reassuring in its ephemerality, I had never before experienced.

Part V

SPRING 1967

45

Regina Is Haunted by the She-Devil Inside Her

Quit askin' me so many questions, quit botherin' me about it. Is that all you ever think about? Ain't got no time for it. Got to take a shower and get on with my charity work: flowers for the hospital, reading to the elderly, collecting all those out-of-the-way people for vaccinations.

Then after doin' the Lord's work, I got to stop by the church and thank Him for it.

For your doin' his work?

Excuse me, there you go again. Forgive her, Lord, she knows not of what she speaks. To thank the Good Lord for *enabling* me to do His work, certainly not for my doin' it. Thank you, Jesus. Thank you, Jesus. Thank you, Jesus. Hear me, Lord, and bring down your wrath on the she-devil inside me who dares to make mischief at the expense of the Almighty.

Another shower, Regina? People are going to know. Every time somebody calls you're in the shower. Hoke and Boonie been wondering about it for years. You're good at sneaking in there without them knowing, but I know, and I might just spill the beans.

That's it, Regina, Scrub, scrub, scrub. But no matter how hard you scrub, you can't wash me off of you. I'm inside you, woman.

No, you little she-devil, but I can damn well try.

Damn? I do believe you just cursed, Regina, and I do believe, since the good Lord is all seeing and all knowing, that he heard you. STOP SCRUBBING, YOU DIRTY WHORE. YOU'RE SCRUBBING SO HARD YOU'RE HURTING ME. YOU'RE BLEEDING AGAIN.

I want to hurt you, you she-devil you, I want you out of me even if I bleed to death.

They'll see. They'll know.

Oh Lord, wash her off of me, out of me. Cleanse me of the evil inside me. Please Lord. Please . . . wash her off of me, out of me. Off of me, out of me. Off of me, out of me. Off of me, out of me. Waters of purification, purify me. Waters of purification, purify me. Waters of purification, purify me. Cleanliness is next to godliness, God cleanse my soul. Cleanliness is next to godliness, God cleanse my soul. Cleanliness is next to godliness, God cleanse my soul.

Dry off. Dry off. Fast as I can. Fast as I can. Get dressed. Get dressed. Fast as I can. Busy day. Smooth out my skirt, fast as I can, my hair's fine, my pocketbook . . . there. The roses . . . Got 'em. Got to get out of here, do the Lord's work.

Hellooo . . . I'm still here.

And I'm still runnin' from you.

Mommy, mommy, mommy, can I come out? Can I?

Honey, if I've told you once, I've told you a hundred times. Not now. If I let you out, then she'll get out too. She'll hurt you, sweetie pie.

Mommy, don't close the door on me.

Yeah, Regina, don't close the door on her.

You stop it. Leave her alone. Honey, I'm locking the door right now.

But I can unlock it, Regina, and I can let him in, like I did before. Remember? You remember. Don't you, Regina?

You stop it. She doesn't know who he is, and I don't want her to know. You understand me. You say one word to her about him and I'll cut you so many times in so many places, including down there where you do your best to make a sinner out of me, you'll bleed to death. You hear me? You know I'll do it.

I have the key, Regina.

SHUT UP SHUT UP SHUT UP GO HIDE HONEY HIDE

He'll find her, Regina.

Damn you . . .

He'll find her, Regina, just like he found you.

I'LL KILL YOU

Remember? I was the one who opened the door and let him in. Or was that you, Regina? You wanted me to, didn't you? You liked it. Remember? His hands—"

Knife, knife

On the counter, Regina, in the kitchen. There . . . that's it.

I TOLD YOU

Oh sweet Jesus sweet, sweet Jesus . . .

I TOLD YOU

Feels so good. More, more . . . again, Regina . . . That's it, again, again, again . . . that's it, there . . . yes there . . . right there . . .

I TOLD YOU I TOLD YOU I TOLD YOU

Oh yes, oh yes, oh yes . . . Ooooh . . .

Yes . . .

46

Arlanne Is Instructed to 'Read On, My Love'

Mrs. Alice Palmer began reading passages from the New Testament of the King James version of the Bible to Regina Cooley, or rather to a comatose facsimile of her, in Room 11 of the Somerset Memorial Hospital every morning at eleven o'clock, with the exception of Sunday mornings, at which time Mrs. Palmer rested, as Arlanne so wryly put it, until the ringing of the church bells in the tower of St. Helena's Episcopal resonated throughout the town, rousing Alice to the same pew beside her husband which had been her family's since the late 1800's, at which time too Arlanne, taking her mother's place at Regina's bedside, would note the selection marked by her mother for that particular Sunday morning and begin reading to Regina, an activity which Arlanne characterized as an exercise in futility since Mrs. Cooley could neither hear nor see. Arlanne complained to Bert that it was about as worthwhile as holding up a picture book for a blind man to look at. "Or talking to you," she added, "when you're reading the Sports section," which he was.

"Or shouting at a deaf person," he said, looking up, which surprised her, catching her a bit off guard, his burst of attention suddenly remarkable to her as the lame out of nowhere breaking into a healthy stride or the blind out of the blue dazzled by color and light. The box scores lay in his lap. Had he emerged from his Sunday morning romp through the stats at a moment coincidentally opportune for her? Divine intervention.

"Exactly," she said. Still, she couldn't help but notice just a bit of apprehension, of hope, of curiosity, in her voice. What was happening here?

"Or," ventured Bert, "It's like talking louder and louder, in hopes of getting your point across, to a non-English-speaking foreigner?"

"Right." She was happy, she thought, he was becoming involved. After all these years, her husband was listening. To her. Does he want something? Wonder if he wants something. He must want something.

"Or fishing on dry land."

"What?"

"You know, casting out where there's no water, on dry land."

"Who in the name of Christ would be that stupid?"

"Gosh, I can't imagine. Certainly not someone reading every Sunday morning to a woman sound asleep."

I'll be damned, she thought, blushing. Is that Yankee Jew flirtin'? Or fightin'?

"Let's wrestle," she said, jumping on top of him.

"I got a better idea," he said, to the ringing of the church bells.

Afterwards, all buttoned up and scrambling for her keys, she grabbed the King James version of the Bible off the mantelpiece, noted her mother's marker protruding from it, jammed it in her purse, hurried out the door—she didn't want to be too late, wouldn't look good, her mother would find out—and headed for the hospital.

Once there, alone in the hospital room with Regina, she opened her Bible to the marked selection and began reading aloud, resigned to being bored stiff. As she began reading, however, even as she recognized the passage from the Songs of Solomon, which she realized was in the Old Testament, she couldn't stop, so carried away was she.

"How beautiful your sandaled feet,
O prince's daughter!
Your graceful legs are like jewels,
the work of an artist's hands . . .
Your neck is like an ivory tower . . .
. . . Your hair is like royal tapestry;
the king is held captive by its tresses.
How beautiful you are and how pleasing,
my love, with your delights!
Your stature is like that of the palm,
and your breasts like clusters of fruit.
'I will climb the palm tree; I will take hold of its fruit . . .'"

That sly dog. Bert had moved the marker from her mother's passage to his, probably while she was dressing, after he'd climbed her palm tree and taken hold of her fruit. *"I will climb the palm tree; I will take hold of its fruit. . . ."* Whew, she said, fanning herself. She couldn't believe she was blushing. *"Your neck is like an ivory tower . . ."* Actually, she thought to herself, that's true. It is. Ah, a note:

"How beautiful you are and how pleasing, my love, with your delights."
Read on,
Bert

And why not, she thought, turning to verse eight, glancing at a comatose Regina in her hospital bed.

She certainly won't know the difference.

Besides, it sure wakes me up.

47

Regina Takes a Long Time to Do Nothing

The Episcopal Church and the Baptist Church Choirs on alternate days would gather around Mrs. Cooley's hospital bed at three o'clock every afternoon and sing inspirational hymns to her after which Elweena Owen, the Baptist preacher's wife, would bring her fresh flowers and arrange them on her night table, "takin' a long time to do nothin'," complained the day nurse, Lane Thelma Dee.

Though Regina Cooley appeared comatose, she was not. She had suffered a severe loss of blood, after which her husband Sheriff Cooley found her passed out on the cool white tile of her kitchen floor, breathing in the fragrance of profoundly-red rose petals strewn about her alabaster profile, beside which also lay scattered shards of glass from the broken vase, miniature water-splashes which had not yet dried up, and a bloody kitchen knife with a jagged edge. Transfusions saved her life. All her vital signs were normal, as was her breathing. For some reason, she just couldn't wake up.

What the doctors agreed on was there was no biological cause for her to sleep this long. There was a lengthy discussion: was she experiencing comatose symptoms brought on by trauma-induced hysteria? Or was she in a catatonic state, albeit one with her eyes closed, akin to a deep sleep, a state also attributable to trauma?

There were cases, explained the psychiatrist, where defense mechanisms had taken the form of falling asleep. He viewed it as he did catatonia, as extreme dissociation. Never, however, had he seen this long of a sleep state. This was unheard of.

"It means she don't want to wake up," said Nurse Lane Thelma Dee to Elweena Owen.

"Maybe she's just really tired," answered Elweena. "You know, just really exhausted."

"You mean, catchin' up on her sleep? For three weeks?"

She shrugged.

"Elweena, I know you failed a grade, but in your adult life you've done a commendable job of hiding your innate stupidity."

"Why thank you, Thelma, but flattery will get you nowhere. Incidentally, since you were prattlin' on, do you have a point? I'm sure, with a nurse's intelligence, landing a plumber for a husband, you must. Or perhaps, like him, you're just full of it?"

"No, Elweena, I'm not full of it, and I do have a point, one rest assured, as a layperson you haven't thought about."

"And just what might that point be?"

"It's not just that she don't want to wake up, like the doctors say. It's that she can't."

"Did the doctors say that too, I mean, privately?"

"I'm sure that's what they meant. Doctors are by nature, Elweena, circumspect. They did not say 'can't,' they said 'want,' as in, I repeat, she don't 'want' to wake up. However, if you look closely at the word 'want,' you can find hope in it. With 'can't,' well, you 'can't,'"

"That makes sense. Doctors are Jewish, you know."

"What?"

"That they're circumcised."

"'Circumspect, Elweena. Circumspect.'"

"Anyway, what's the difference between that and bein' dead?"

Now that one, realized Thelma, could make a make a person downright pensive. Most of the doctors she knew were circumspect, and most were pretty much dead. "Not much," she said.

"So for all practical purposes poor Regina is dead?"

"Her doctors are, or might as well be."

"Lane Thelma Dee, what on earth are you talkin' about? You do not, honey, bite the hand that feeds you. If poor Regina can't wake up, tell me, what is the difference between that and bein' dead? I'm askin' you as a professional."

"Aw Elweena, you ain't a professional."

"I'm askin' *you* as a professional, Thelma. I am but a humble layperson."

Well now, thought Nurse Thelma, that's better. "Nothin,'" she said, "Ain't no difference, 'cept breathin'. For all she can see or hear she might as well be dead. That child ain't moved on her own since she's been here. When nobody's been around, I've tried everything . . . yellin' in her ear loud as I could, even borrowed some cymbals from the band room over at the school, stuck her with needles, all in the line of professional duty, of course . . ."

"Of course. And?"

"Didn't move a muscle. Didn't even twitch."

"You mean like a snake after you kill it?"

"No, Elweena, that's not what I mean."

But that's okay, thought Elweena. I get the message.

"Regina's just being stubborn," said Elweena all over town to anybody who would listen. "Always has been." After which she'd offer up her version of the doctors' diagnosis, or in her words their "whatever you call it." "She just don't want to wake up, for some reason. That's what the doctors say. Or maybe she can't, I don't know. Six of one, half dozen of the other, far as I can tell. If she can't, then she needs to throw 'can't' overboard and bring 'can' across. Are they tellin' us everything? Only the Good Lord knows. The Good Lord along with the doctors themselves. They're circumcised. Always are."

After playing her trump card, she'd pad her hand a little more. "They're not local." Which in and of itself, in the minds of the locals, elevated the status of their medical pedigree. "They're from Savannah." Skepticism, if she confronted any, only urged her on. "Dr. Melvin Plotsky, of the Plotsky family, he's Jewish. You know of 'em even if you don't know 'em. You know how smart they are, the whole darned race, smart as whips."

One Sunday morning while Arlanne was whiling away her time reading aloud to a woman who couldn't hear her, an activity she undertook just to keep her mother off her back—as well as to relieve herself of her guilt at boycotting the family store—Nurse Lane Thelma Dee confided to her that Mrs. Cooley was costin' the county a fortune.

"She did her best not to," said Arlanne, looking at what, to her, was as close to dead, without actually being dead, as you could get.

"That she did," said Lane Thelma Dee.

"But for that kind of endeavor, you need strength, determination . . ."

Lane Thelma Dee began to look at Arlanne like she was crazy.

"Follow-through. You need follow-through. Like my husband says, 'Don't go to the basket if you can't finish the play.'"

"Pass the ball," said Lane Thelma Dee, "If you can't finish the play, you pass the ball."

"Exactly," said Arlanne. "Exactly."

48

Arlanne Interrogates a White Caller Pretending to be Black

"Dr. Levy, please ma'am?"

"Sorry, he's out somewhere," said Arlanne, answering the phone. "Can't keep up with him, went to the store for somethin', probably some porn for all I know. Who's this?"

"Yes ma'amm, I see, ma'am, might you be expectin' the esteemed doctor any time soon?"

She almost recognized the voice, but it was muffled, indistinct, intentionally so, it sounded like. Too much emphasis on the bass. She heard a white voice imitating, what was it? Negrospeak? He was tryin' to sound like a black person.

"Sure, 'less he's plannin' on sleeping in the Pig's parking lot." "Who's this?" clearly hadn't worked so she tried: "May I tell the esteemed doctor who called?"

"Why thank you, Missus, no trouble at all, I'll call back," mumbled the voice, deep and resonant—he was trying to sound like Paul Robison singin' "Old Man River," only he wasn't singin'. Before she could say anything else, however, whoever it was hung up.

She was curious. Really curious. A born gossip, she just couldn't stand not to know, even if what she found out didn't matter a whit.

About an hour or so later the phone rang again. She tried a different tact.

"Old Man Riverrrr . . ." she sang in her deepest bass, what she liked to think of as 'Basso Profundo,' just trying to connect on a familiar note with the voice on the other end. "She keeps on rollin' . . . She keeps on rollin' . . . Old Man River, she keeps on rollin' along . . ."

Silence.

"Paul Robison. That's who you sound like. Paul Robison."

Silence.

"Well, you ain't Paul Robison or you'd be calling long distance. The Mississippi don't run through Somerset. Hey, you are the same gentleman who called earlier, right?"

That same voice, deep, subdued, cavernous, a repressed baritone, yet now a bit here and there coarse and starched as a sore throat. "Yes ma'am, Dr. Levy please ma'am. I wonder, might the doctor be available?"

"Still lookin' at the Playboys," she said. "Can I help you? Would you care to leave a message? Roll along here with me if you can."

"No, ma'am," said the voice. "But I thank ye."

Thank ye?

Black people don't say "Thank ye."

And black people also have a sense of humor.

White Christians often don't. This is definitely a white Christian, someone who attends church regularly, if nothing else for the sake of appearances. Appearances are important to him, or he wouldn't be disguising his voice.

Also, to disguise it so obviously shows a distinct lack of imagination.

A white Christian pretending to talk like a black man who lacks the wit and imagination to pull it off. I'm getting closer, though the clues point to just about every white man in Somerset who goes to church.

The next time the phone rang Arlanne jumped at it so fast and hard she about knocked the lamp off the side table. She held it for a few seconds before answering it, cleared her throat deeply as the testerone rose and before the caller could ask, she said in a deep-throated, runaway New York accent, "Dr. Levy speaking."

"Dr. Levy?"

That voice, thrown off guard, not sure quite what to believe, was half-and-half, one half a piss-poor Paul Robison, no doubt about it, but the other . . .

"Hoke Cooley! What in the name of Jesus are you doin'? Are you undercover or somethin' like on T.V.? If you are, God save Somerset County."

She just started laughin' and laughin' and laughin'.

"Hoke, What are you doin'? I know it's you."

On the other end of the line, in his bedroom with the lights off, alone in the house (Boonie spending the night out with a friend), Hoke was so red-hot with humiliation he glowed in the dark. The only thing he could think of to say was "Shit, Arlanne. Goddammit."

"Why, Hoke, you sound like you're poutin', sulkin', just like you some overgrown baby."

"Yeah, well, maybe I am."

"What's wrong, honey? You're worried about Regina, aren't you? Why don't you talk to Arlanne and let's see if she can't help you?"

"I thought all this stuff was supposed to be confidential."

"What stuff, honey?"

"You know . . ."

Here, she thought to herself, act like a salesman: if you don't break the silence, he will, and when he does he'll have to commit, seal the deal, complete the sale. Sure enough, she could feel it coming . . .

"All this therapy stuff, psychology . . . you know. Goddammit Arlanne!"

"Therapy?! You want therapy? Why that's great, Hoke. Why don't you begin by talkin' to me?"

"Arlanne, give me the damn phone," said Bert, taking it from her. Whatever's wrong with you, Hoke, he thought to himself, you can't be as crazy as my wife.

Damn! She hadn't even heard him come in.

49

Bert Treats Hoke, or Is It, He Wonders, the Other Way Around?

"Come in, Hoke. Have a seat."

Forcing a smile, Hoke shook hands with Bert and settled himself uneasily on the sofa. Psychologically awry, he was clearly distracted, out of focus, at odds with himself; uncertain as to how to begin or even whether he should. His face was drawn, his muscles slack, like someone had let the air out of him; his eyes bloodshot, it appeared to Bert, from lack of sleep. He fidgeted, glancing about, looking up as if he were stranded in the middle of the ocean hoping against hope for the sign of a helicopter with a long descending ladder that might somehow laser through the roof down through the ceiling, dangle right in front of him like the perfect invitation, pluck him from all this and whisk him up, up and away, landing him safely in his old momma's lap where he could lay his head and she could stroke his hair like she did when he was little.

"Your daddy-in-law was the one suggested I call you."

How well I know, thought Bert, since the C.O. had called twice encouraging him to see Hoke. The C.O. as much as said that Palmer had called him just to make sure it would happen. "Where else could Hoke go?" asked the C.O.. There ain't no psychologists in Somerset. And even if there were, if the sheriff went, the whole town would know. Besides, he said, it's good for community relations.

"Not sure why, really, now that I'm here."

"Hoke, your wife lost so much blood attempting to commit suicide that she's in a coma, or what appears to be one."

Pain, opening wide, clamped its teeth on the sheriff's soul. He grimaced, shaking his head as if trying to shake the blood off himself. "So much," he said. Incomprehensible, he seemed to be thinking. "So much blood." He looked up at Dr. Levy for some kind of answer.

Dr. Levy did not have one.

"I'm not worried about myself," Hoke finally said. "I can handle it. But Boonie, this is too much for a kid . . ."

"He'll feel what you feel, Hoke. The only way to understand what he'll feel is to understand what you feel."

"What am I feeling?"

"Probably like you killed her, or as much as did so, like you're responsible for the state she's in. That's what most people in your situation would feel, rational or not."

The sheriff nodded. Guilt beat at his breastbone, shame caught in his throat. "I never touched her," he confessed. "Intimately, I mean. After Boonie was born, I never touched her." He looked helplessly at Dr. Levy. "She wouldn't let me."

Dr. Levy encouraged him to continue. "Keep going, Hoke, you need to get all this off your chest."

"She wouldn't let me," he said. "She just wouldn't let me. She just . . . She'd go nuts, man. Absolutely crazy. Made me feel like I was some kind of rapist or something. Just approaching her, anything, no matter how gentle I tried to be . . . she'd start screaming and yelling or just freeze up, clenching her little fists, her whole body so tense it seemed like it was vibratin' . . . made me feel like I was a rapist or somethin' . . . like there was somethin' wrong with me or somethin', like I was some kind of animal . . . 'No NoNo,' like I was rapin' her or somethin' . . . She'd look at me horrified, like she was seein' somebody else . . . It was like she'd go into a trance or somethin'. 'It's me, honey,' I'd say, shaking her. 'It's me.' 'Oh,' she'd say, and it was like it'd take her a minute to reassemble, to come back into focus, back to herself, I guess. Of course, by that time . . ."

Dr. Levy nodded, totally attentive. When he was interested and focused, Arlanne once told Murray, an oncoming train couldn't divert him. Not that she'd ever seen him that way, she'd added. He'd told her that himself, probably to justify his social ineptitude with his professional aptitude.

"I thank you for seein' me, Doc. I got to talk to somebody 'fore I go stark ravin' mad. Sorry about, you know, the other night. I was just embarrassed, you know, people knowin' and all."

"I understand, Hoke. No problem. Glad I can help."

"Oh, you already helpin'. Been carrying this stuff for a long time. A long time . . . I mean . . . I was right about you bein' bound to confidentiality, wasn't I? I mean, you ain't gon' tell nobody . . . I guess that's what I mean . . . are you?"

"If I did, Hoke, you could arrest me and take away my license."

"Oh," he said, "wouldn't want to do anything like that. Wasn't even thinking—"

"I know, Hoke. But, no, I would never say anything, that's an absolute promise. I want you to feel absolutely open and let's get all this out so you feel better."

"Arlanne probably thinks I'm nuts after the other night . . ."

"Arlanne's nuts, Hoke. So who gives a rat's ass."

Hoke seemed to weigh that possibility, to give it a moment's consideration, after which he realized, knowing her, Doc's right, she is nuts.

"You say it seemed that in those moments when Regina was frightened she seemed to be looking at someone else, seeing someone else, other than you?"

"Yeah, you ever heard of that kind of thing before? Doc, was she frigid? Was it me?"

"It wasn't you, Hoke."

"You sure, Doc? 'Cause right now I'd pretty much find myself guilty."

"You weren't responsible, Hoke. Not a chance."

Dr. Levy started to continue, but Hoke held up his hand like a stop sign. He needed a moment to let this last absolution sink in. He appeared to be in deep thought, profound concentration, his head in his hands now, covering his eyes.

After a minute or so, he looked up and said, "Okay."

"Okay?"

"Yeah."

"Okay?"

"Yeah, Okay." He didn't seem to understand what Dr. Levy didn't understand.

"What do you mean 'okay,' Hoke?"

"Okay, I agree with you. I didn't cause her to do what she did."

"Oh."

"Right? That's what you're saying. Right?"

"Yeah, that's what I'm saying."

"Okay. Okay. So if I'm not responsible, which is what you said, right . . . ?"

"Right."

"Okay, I'm not responsible, it's not my fault." Just needed to get that out of the way, he seemed to be suggesting, when in Dr. Levy's mind what he was really trying to do was hold onto it with everything he could muster.

"Goddammit, Hoke, you weren't responsible. Okay? Jesus Christ."

"Okay. Right. I gotcha' now, Doc. But if I wasn't, who was?"

"Do you remember when you said that when she looked at you it was as if she were seeing someone else?"

"Yeah, like she was seeing a ghost or some horrible creature or somethin'. That's what made me feel so bad. I mean, was this the way she saw me? What had I done to make her feel this way? Right? Like, what was wrong with me?"

"Right."

"Which you agreed, related to this matter, nothin', if I recall. Right?"

"Right."

"Okay. Okay."

Dr. Levy waited.

"So what were you saying, Doc?"

"That person she's seeing when she's looking at you, that ghost, that horrible creature—the person she's seeing, not you—"

"Right, I'm with you . . ."

"He—or she, for that matter—is the one responsible for the state she's in."

A day or so before their second session, Hoke phoned Bert around suppertime. Why then? Probably, figured Bert, because it was suppertime for Hoke too, which he was now facing alone, thus getting even more anxious. He wanted their second session to be on the river, where they could fish and talk at the same time. When he called, his voice undisguised, Arlanne answered the phone and said, "Why, Hoke, you've turned white again! I can tell by your voice!"

Which Hoke chose not to dignify with a response.

"Let's go fishin'," he told Bert when he got on the phone.

"No."

"Come on, man. It's easier to talk out there in the middle of the river, nobody around."

"There's nobody around when we talk in my office."

"Aw, come on, Doc. People on Lawton Island might recognize my car, put two and two together, with Regina in the state she's in and all. You know, hell, I'd be embarrassed as hell if the C.O. knew. Me and him pretty tight. Don't want nobody thinkin' I'm crazy. Not that I am. Am I?"

"No, You're not."

"Right. Well, that's good. Okay . . ."

"Absolutely not."

"Absolutely?"

"Absolutely. No question. I've never been surer of anything in my life. Were you to look up the word 'sanity' in the dictionary, your photo would be right there just to show the world what it looks like."

"Now, Doc, when you say it like that, well, it makes a man wonder if you really mean it, or just sayin' it to make him feel good. Know what I mean? Pokin' fun at a man can't help but make him feel feel a little shaky about his psychology."

"Right. My apologies, Hoke. Your anxieties somehow seem to arouse mine. Let me try to say it as clearly as I can. You're not crazy, Hoke."

"Thank you, Doc. I really appreciate that. You're the expert. If you say it, it must be right."

"Right."

"Right?"

"Right."

"Okay. Okay."

"See you at the office?"

"Sure would like to take you fishin'."

"Jews don't fish, Hoke. We read books and listen to classical music and play only noncontact sports."

"Marty Liebowitz fishes."

"He's a whore, Hoke. A traitor to his people."

"Aw, man, come on. Then you won't have to be so embarrassed when you're out on the river with Palmer."

"How'd you know about that?"

"He was laughin' at you behind your back."

"That son of a bitch."

"Said you was all finicky and all, like a woman, said you wouldn't touch the worms. Said you danced a jitterbug when an eel fell into the boat."

"It wasn't an eel. It was a goddamn snake."

"A snake? What kind of snake? In the Somerset River? Not to be disagreeable, Doc, but I suspect it was probably an eel."

Who the fuck cares? thought Bert. It was slimy. Thinking about it gave him the shivers. Besides, he'd managed to repress the entire incident until Hoke had brought it up.

"On second thought," said Hoke, "it could've been the Loch Ness Monster."

"That's funny, Hoke. You're a goddamn hoot. Fine, we'll go fishing."

"Pick you up at the office. We'll put in at Oyster Creek."

Anything, thought Bert, to get off the goddamn phone.

It was an early Friday afternoon, late winter in most of the country, early spring in the lowcountry. Naturally, as a Southerner, Hoke felt a bit chilly. As a Northerner, Bert thought it unnaturally warm. Who was right? Hard one to call. Hard to deny the chill in the air, though to Bert it was warm enough to forewarn of summer sand fleas, horse flies, and mosquitos. On the other hand, hard to deny the new warmth, which to Hoke was more like winter's chilly leftovers. Let's agree to disagree. Shall we? Then again . . .

These are the sorts of mundane musings, contemplated Bert, that have always substituted in the minds of Southerners for the rigors of critical thinking. Such stupid meanderings, just like the slow drawl and easygoing manner, the languid pace, the placid river and sheer sky, and the perfume of spring and summer flowers, all colluded in intoxicating the foreigner, rendering him mindless, vulnerable to the lowbrow exploitative calculations of the Southerner. W.J. Cash wrote about it in *The Mind of the South*. Such a natural climate breeds calculating mentalities, if for no other purpose originally than to outwit natural forces—the heat and the hurricanes, for example—and more recently unnatural forces, such as Yankees.

He was a Yankee, and he had been outwitted by a stupid Southern sheriff. On the river—or in the creek—in a simple rowboat with the oars docked, basking in the afternoon sun and the soothing silence, nobody around, who could possibly think out here?

Hoke had hooked him in, he realized helplessly. Intensity, rigorous therapy, was mentally impossible out here. The therapist had been caught in the client's net.

Fishing, Bert now realized, was a defense mechanism.

What chance had critical thinking—essentially conventional warfare—against calculation and manipulation—essentially guerilla warfare? How could we northerners have possibly won a war against such stupid people?

"Bein' out here, makes you think, Doc," said the sheriff, sitting on his ass, his fishing rod in the oarlock, the worm down below doing all the work. "Makes you think. Yep. Sure does."

"Where are we, Hoke?"

"We're in Oyster Creek, Doc, sittin' out here fishin'."

"No. Where are we, Hoke, me and you? What the fuck are we doing out here? We're supposed to be having a therapy session."

"Therapy?"

"Yeah, Hoke, It happens to be what I do for a living."

"Oh, you mean you've re-thought the matter of whether or not I'm crazy?"

"What? Jesus Christ, Hoke, are you out of your mind?"

"Why else would I need therapy?"

"To get through the crisis of your wife's attempted suicide?"

"Oh, yeah. That's right."

"Okay?"

"Okay. Okay."

"Oh fuck. Please, not again."

"I said okay."

"Okay."

"Okay."

Hooked again, thought Bert. Ensnared in the net of an obsessive-compulsive Southern sheriff. He hated dealing with obsessive-compulsives. They made him crazy. They were boring. God they were boring, close to impenetrable. Round and round and round and round until you were just as caught up in their craziness as they were. Being one, as he was, was hard enough, but being around one, that was unadulterated hell.

Neither man spoke for another half hour or so, Hoke clearly ruminating on the fragility of his psyche, Bert terrified he might bring it up again. Lamar Heard waved from his shrimpboat off in the distance but neither man noticed. Nor did they witness the great blue heron on his ancient royal stump among the reeds near the shoreline or two pelicans low-diving, splashing about for fish, or the spectacle of bottlenose dolphins leaping into the sunlight for air as they made their way across the sound toward the Somerset River.

What they both felt, Bert knew, was boredom as overwhelming as a knockout punch. Never fear, he thought, rallying, Bert is here.

"Hoke," Bert finally said, "you're no crazier than I am."

And for whatever crazy reason, probably because it was the truth, figured Bert, that seemed to satisfy him.

"Hey Doc, can you honestly tell me now it's not beautiful out here?" He waved his arm about. Sun. Sky. Water. "What more could a man ask for?"

"Can we go home now?"

"Look along the shoreline there, Doc," he said pointing. "See it, on the stump rising out of the water, the marsh there? See that?"

"Yeah," said Bert, without looking.

"You know what that is? What a beautiful creature."

"No," said Bert. Nor, he thought, did he give a shit. He was a New York Jew, not some rube raised in the swamps. Nature was nothing more than a sideshow. He was at two with it.

"You don't know what that is, Doc?"

"No."

"Why, that's an ibis," he announced, as the great blue heron looked on indifferently.

"Nothin' much bitin', Doc."

"Nope."

"Doc?"

"Yeah, Hoke."

"Mind if I ask you a question?"

Mind if I commit another homicide at Oyster Creek? Where is Frank McGowan when I need him? Bert carefully weighed his options: he could either push the sheriff overboard or jump into the river himself and drown.

Instead he screamed at the top of his lungs—his preferred method for dealing with frustration—after which he just sat in the boat, exhausted, all the air gone out of him.

"Feel better?" asked the sheriff.

"Yeah, thanks Hoke."

"No problem. You just sit there all quiet till you feel better. Then if you want to talk, I'm here."

"Hoke, I know what your question is."

Hoke's relief was pathetic, but also palpable, therefore, concluded Bert, deserving of empathy, the giving of which might result in the afternoon becoming more interesting. It was boring out here. The seats were hard and uncomfortable, planks with no backs. The only thing around was water. There was nothing to do. Hoke's psyche was so fragile right now that if Bert were to say something the least bit threatening, something he was totally unaware might be threatening, Hoke would ensnare him in a Kafkaesque labyrinth of reassurances. On top of all this, he lived in a town where not more than three people had ever heard of Kafka. "Kafka? What's that? Cough medicine?" A town of idiots, yokels, "How you doin'! Come see us, you hear! Why hey there, where you been keepin' yourself!" Away from you, groused Bert, out here on the river with an obsessive-compulsive Southern sheriff the sole purpose of whom was to trap him for an entire afternoon so he could either drive him crazy or bore him out of his balls. Away from you! Away from you! You fucking lazy lethargic idiots!

Not so idiotic, however, as to fail to elect an obsessive-compulsive sheriff. When you think about it, instinctively a remarkably insightful move. Brilliant. With Hoke on the case, tenacity and thoroughness would never be an issue, no stone unturned, no thread left dangling, no clue unexplored ad infinitum, no question unanswered. And Bert knew why: an unanswered question would drive Hoke crazy. That's why obsessive-compulsive personalities are such assiduous workers, why they get so involved in it: to maintain their sanity.

That's why Bert did.

It's also, like Arlanne once told him, why he ended up beating a lot of dead horses.

"You are not responsible for your wife's suicide attempt," he told Hoke.

"Well, I was just wonderin', since you hadn't changed your mind about me not bein' crazy—"

"—whether I hadn't changed my mind about your not being responsible for your wife's suicide attempt."

"Not?"

"Not."

"I'm not responsible for her suicide attempt."

"You are not responsible for her suicide attempt."

"My wife's suicide attempt."

"You are not responsible for your wife's suicide attempt."

"Okay."

"Okay?"

"Okay."

Bert sat in the boat in an imaginary strait jacket.

"Doc?"

"Doc?"

"Doc? Remember me telling you that when she was looking at me it was like she was seeing somebody else, and you said that that person was probably responsible for her attempting suicide? Sometimes she'd call out a name."

"She did?"

"Yeah, it was hard to make out. Sometimes she'd scream it out in nightmares. I think she was sayin' 'Daddy.' 'No. No. No, Daddy,' somethin' like that."

"Keep going, Hoke."

"Well, I didn't think too much about it. I mean, her daddy was a Pentecostal, a preacher, a real Holy Roller. Stern as the wrath of God himself. I figured he just beat her, you know. They're strict folks. Spare the rod, spoil the child and all. And maybe he overdid it or she was more sensitive than he realized . . . I don't know."

"How was your sex life before Boonie was born?"

"At first she tried . . ."

"Tried?"

"To like it. But I could tell early on I'd have to go elsewhere for it. In her heart she thought she was committin' an act against God. She'd be asking for forgiveness while I was you know . . . 'Forgive me Lord, Forgive me Lord Forgive me Lord . . .'"

"Did she reach orgasm?"

"Only once. That was the first time she tried to kill herself. Found her in the bathtub bleedin' to death. Got to her just in time. Seems like I always get there just in time, 'cept maybe this time . . . Two years ago was the last time she tried it. Managed to get all the blood cleaned up before Boonie got home from football practice. Told him she'd just caught sick and was spendin' the night in the hospital. Her old man railed against the pleasures of the flesh, so much so I just think she couldn't bring herself to enjoy it. Sad, ain't it? Hey, you got somethin' on the line there. Here, lemme help you. Damn! Look at this. Nice-sized bass. You and Arlanne gonna' eat awfully good tonight."

Bert didn't even see it, not when Hoke waved it triumphantly right in front of his eyes, not when he handed it all wrapped up in ice to Bert to take home, not after Arlanne sautéed it and laid it on his plate that night at dinner.

50

Nurse Lane Thelma Dee's Take on the Best Therapist in Town

The best therapist in town, thought Nurse Lane Thelma Dee, noting the number of visitors on the sign-in sheet at her desk, just might well be Regina Cooley. And not just because she's the only one, and not just because she ain't really one with an office and a fancy degree and all. All these women coming to see her. Every week. Sometimes two or three times a week. One at a time. And they're in there forever! And though I can't hear exactly what they're saying, not that I ain't tryin' like crazy, I can tell you they're talkin' about themselves, their husbands, sometimes even their parents or kids or a friend, because I can pick up a name here and there, a voice shakin' and quiverin' like it got a sudden chill, and in particular them cussin' at somebody that ain't there. That's right, cussin'. Some ain't above it, and it might surprise you who. And then it might get quiet for just a bit, that's when my piano really gets tuned, ready to play, though I have to be what they call "stealthy" about it, "discreet," my ear at the door and all. And then I might pick up a few sniffles, sometimes outright sobbing, and no, they are not crying for Regina. Of that I can assure you. They too busy talkin' about themselves. And to somebody who can't hear! Totally anonymous, like writin' to "Dear Abby" or somethin'. Regina is the perfect psychologist. You can't get any crazier goin' to her, nobody'll know, your secrets are certainly safe with her, and you get to get everything off your chest.

Plus, it's free.

You know, I think the best therapist in town is lookin' like a real bargain. Why, I think I might just slip in there and try her myself.

Besides, as much as she's costin' the town, this is a way for her to give back.

Now somebody might say, But Nurse Lane Thelma Dee, she don't know she's costin' the town money!

And you know what I'd say in response?

She don't know she's givin' us therapy neither.

So there.

Furtively, Nurse Lane Thelma Dee began observing the women coming in and out.

Elweena Owen even tried to talk her way in after visiting hours, suggesting a modest bribe might be in order. Naturally Nurse Thelma accepted it. Boy, she thought, Elweena must've been desperate. Wonder what that was about.

Regina's become the depository of all the town's secrets. All the town's women, at least. Alice Palmer, Elweena Owen, Alma Floyd, Bessie Liebowitz, Ruthie Vanguard, Amy Dawes, Velma Richardson . . .

. . . I could go on and on . . . No men though. I can explain that: Men don't like to talk, not like women, too lazy, takes too much effort. That's why they like to read, it's just another way for for 'em to have someone else—the author, in this case—do their work for 'em. That's all readin' is, nothin' but sittin' there indulgin' your eyes in a Sunday stroll across the page. Whoever invented readin', invented it for men. I've read my history, thank you.

51

Lila and Jack React to Regina's Suicide Attempt

"Talk to me, Arlanne," said Lila, placing a cup of Maxwell House in front of her. "Cream, right? No sugar."

"Never liked sweet."

Lila sat catty-corner to her at the dining room table. "Thanks for coming, Arlanne, and you know I love you, Baby, but there's something I got to know. You know what I'm going to ask you."

"I know."

"Are the rumors true?"

"Yes," said Arlanne. "They are."

"He'll blame himself."

Arlanne nodded, her gaze drifting through the kitchen window to the great oaks shrouded in Spanish moss, the plainness of the overcast day, the melodic glaze on the river beyond. Through the fog in the distance red lights flashed on the Somerset River bridge. A slightly curved line of barely visible cars backed up on either side, the island side and the downtown side, as the bridge opened for a catamaran to pass under.

"Bert's helping him," said Arlanne, without knowing why. "Discreetly," she added.

As soon as Arlanne left, Lila dialed Bert at his office.

"He thinks it's his fault, Bert, I know him. It'll destroy him. It almost destroyed me, took forever for me to realize—"

"That it wasn't? That whatever the cause it had nothing to do with you, that it's something he entered the marriage with?"

"But could I have stopped it? Poor Elizabeth, having to see it . . . Oh Bert . . ."

"Elizabeth? But you couldn't have stopped that, remember?"

"Yes, but—"

"No 'buts,' Lila. You couldn't have stopped it. You know that. You couldn't even have foreseen it, not the way it actually happened. If you were God, you couldn't have stopped it. You know that."

"But does Hoke know that? Oh my God for him to have to go through this, and Boonie . . . it'll break Hoke, Bert. Are you helping him see that? Regina was frigid, Bert, she had problems long before Hoke and I were ever together."

"Lila, listen closely. Okay? Take a deep breath. Okay?"

"Okay, I'm here. I'm listening."

"A deep breath, Lila."

He waited.

"I'm here," she finally said.

"Even Hoke has not imagined that the relationship between you had anything to do with Regina's suicide attempt. Does he blame himself? Of course, but he'll learn just as you have, just as Elizabeth has."

"I keep seeing him, blood everywhere, everywhere, and me holding him, cradling his head in my arms, my lap, screaming, and I look up to see Elizabeth in the doorway, frozen, staring over our heads at the blood on the picture window, and I'm crying and pulling him to me and begging him, please stay with us. If I don't let him go, you know, if I can just keep holdin' on to him then all that blood will somehow re-enter his bloodstream and fill him with life again and Elizabeth will return to whatever she was doing before it all happened. Talk about wishful thinkin'. The business with Regina, just brings it all up, I suppose. But you know what? What's so sad and pathetic?"

Bert was waiting.

"He was gone long before that."

Jack couldn't understand it. He heard it from Mary Beth, who overheard Amy Dawes and Alice Palmer at the Downtown Book Store. "I don't understand," he kept repeating as he washed, rinsed and handed dishes to Mary Beth to dry. "It doesn't make sense. Regina Cooley—the sheriff's wife, right?"

"That's what they said," Mary Beth told him, "albeit in hushed tones."

"Tries to stab herself to death, she cuts her wrists, passes out, and never wakes up but all her vital signs are normal, yes she's lost blood, but not enough to send her into a comatose state, the EKG shows brain activity, I don't get it."

"Be careful with the wineglasses, Jack, you're about to scrub them into oblivion. Here," she said, handing him the dishtowel. "I'll wash, you dry."

"It just doesn't make sense."

Royal Cunningham laid the *State* newspaper on the kitchen table, his finger tapping the photograph of General Westmoreland and the article below quoting him on the number of American casualties thus far in Vietnam.

"Neither does this," he offered.

"It doesn't make sense," Jack repeated.

"He's lying," said Royal. "Has to be."

"If somebody tried to kill himself," said Jack, "the last thing he'd want would be to end up as some question mark, a burden—"

Mary Beth looked at him, pausing in her dishwashing. "Jack, do you think she might be disappointed?"

52

God's Messenger Pays a Nocturnal Visit to the Reverend

A Jew, showing up at the Reverend's door like a Jehovah's Witness, though in the dead of night, Bert turned and used the Reverend-s own weapon—the Wrath of the Lord, pure Calvinism—against him. Dressed from head to toe in black, he banged loudly and ominously on the Reverend's front door. The Reverend, unkempt and disheveled in an old bathrobe and pajamas, white hair flying wildly, angrily opened the door only to encounter the Jew dressed in black staring him into silence. Bewildered, the Reverend cowed in horror upon hearing the practiced baritone as if the Lord Himself was pointing His finger at him: "You hang by a slender thread over the bowels of Hell. I come from the Chosen People as a representative of the Lord our God, King of all the Universe, who has whispered to me through a high wind on the river of your shameful and lascivious doings with your daughter Regina, whom you have poisoned with your perversion. He asks: "Do you doubt His omnipotence? Did you think He could not see? That you could escape His eye with stealth? You have visited the sin of lust upon your daughter Regina, the Lord saith unto me, and your salvation lay only in her forgiveness. The Lord saith unto you, go and see her.

"Know that I am but the Lord's messenger and have only to say what He has told me. Know too that to doubt His message is to doubt the word of the Lord. And that in her resurrection is your salvation.

"Go now, saith the Lord, and trust in Him.

"That is the Word of the Lord."

And with that, God's messenger turned, walked away, and disappeared into the darkness.

The Reverend, Bert figured, was in no position to question his veracity, since to question him was to question, if not doubt, the word of the Lord, a risk a sinner as vulnerable and compromised as the Reverend could ill afford. Nor did he have cause. How else, in the Reverend's mind, could Bert have known except through the Lord's intervention? If Regina even remembered, she'd never have told. The Reverend had made sure of that.

It wasn't the first time the Lord had sent one of His Chosen into the world as His messenger. Bert knew that in the Bible Belt—particularly with a Holy Roller Pentecostal like the Reverend—that he was one of God's Chosen People could only add credibility to his divinely bestowed stature.

The next morning, right about when the azaleas fronting the hospital were celebrating the peak of their season, the reverend paid his daughter a visit. "Why hello, Reverend," said Nurse Lane Thelma, "nice to see you here. I'm sure she'll be glad you came, even if she won't know it. She'll know it, I mean, in her heart, Reverend, in her heart." Nurse Thelma delicately placed her own hand over her own heart to demonstrate her sincerity as well as to cover up her faux pas. Though admittedly she preferred the Parisian term "faux pas" to the English "mistake"—go ahead, call her unpatriotic—she nevertheless wondered despite her obvious sophistication, could she, in all the world, have said anything more inappropriate and downright stupid? And to a man of the cloth?

Lane Thelma Dee! Why, people gonna' think yo' momma didn't raise you right.

He was an old man, all white-haired, black hat, and a cane, in a long black overcoat, even though it was hot enough for the air conditioners to be turned on. He looked a bit like a poor withered Scrooge, only much smaller. His face was sallow and gaunt, and he was stooped over with the burdens of the world, probably because he was a reverend. He was kind of ugly to be doin' the Lord's work, unless it was with lepers or somethin'. Looked like he hadn't been in the sun in decades. His face, all sunken, had a translucent sickly pallor, and a downright disgusting wart on his right cheekbone had hair growing all out of it: he should have had that removed, if for nothing else but appearance's sake.

Nurse Lane Thelma Dee handed him the clipboard with the attached pen.

He signed his name, filled in the time and date, and wrote as the purpose of his visit: "I am the servant of the Almighty and He has sent me in His wisdom to bring life back to my daughter, Mrs. Regina Cooley."

Nurse Lane Thelma Dee couldn't help herself. Reading it, she was most certainly set back a ways. She was determined, however, to avoid another faux pas.

"You gonna heal her?" she asked him, looking up hesitantly from the clipboard.

"No ma'am," said the Reverend. "The Lord is."

And he plodded his way down the corridor, his cane feeling its way along the slick, freshly scrubbed floor, to his daughter's room.

He should have that wart taken care off, thought Nurse Thelma, watching him. It looks nasty.

Bert slept late, then drove over to the hospital to see Regina, to see for himself the results of his work, but he never even had to get out of his car.

Upon parking he saw them walking out of the hospital together, the Reverend guiding her by the elbow, preventing her from stumbling and falling from atrophy. The Reverend, though clearly racked with guilt and shame, had color in his cheeks, though both his and Regina's faces were streaked with tears. Done, Bert thought to himself, driving off. Later he would hear from Arlanne that Nurse Lane Thelma Dee had told everyone in town that upon leaving the hospital the Reverend looked distinctly more alive than when he'd come in.

Nurse Thelma also told them that walking past the room, as was, she emphasized, the routine professional obligation and custom of the nurse on duty, she heard the Reverend sobbing and whimpering and crying aloud for forgiveness. All she could hear was forgive me Lord, forgive me Lord, forgive me Lord, over and over. Forgive me Lord, forgive me Lord, forgive me Lord, which upon hearing caused Bert and Hoke, one as psychologist and the other as husband, to pause and reflect, recalling those same words coming from Regina herself in the involuntary throes of orgasm.

What Nurse Thelma could not see was Regina's hand moving along the bedside toward her father's and closing over his; Nurse Thelma did, however, hear a voice that was unmistakably Regina's: "The Lord can't, Father, but I can."

The only other thing Nurse Thelma could recall to every single person in town is that when she opened the door to Regina's room to check her vital signs—again, she emphasized, yet another of her professional obligations regardless of the patient's state of mind—she realized, embarrassed beyond all, that she had walked in on something intensely private and personal.

What? Everyone asked. What? What was it, honey? Oh, it must have been so hard on you, all these weeks . . .

The Reverend was on his knees weeping at her bedside, she told them, as if the world was ending or beginning, she couldn't tell. Regina's eyes were open, and with tears falling from her eyes, she smiled, patting his hand.

Truly, said Nurse Lane Thelma Dee, Regina Cooley had come back from the dead.

As for the Reverend, she said, shaking her head, downright confused, I don't know, something dark there . . . dark I tell you . . . dark . . . somethin', she concluded, way beyond my professional expertise. You'd have to ask Arlanne's husband about that. He's a psychologist, and from what I understand, well versed in these matters.

Elweena Owen naturally was mortified, as were, Nurse Thelma was certain, many of the town's leading ladies. Putting on their best faces, they couldn't help but wonder: had Regina been awake all that time? And if she had . . . ?

As for Boonie, his mother's hospitalization, Hoke told Bert, had affected him visibly in only one way: Boonie had always been a big kid, but his warm affectionate nature had always worked against him on the football field. Coaches predicted that while he had the physical attributes he was simply too nice a kid to ever wreak havoc on the field. It just wasn't in his nature to be destructive. Since his mother's hospitalization, however, on the football field Boonie had turned into a monster. Coaches in the Youth League had taken to calling him "homicidal," so perhaps something good had come out of this for Boonie after all, said Hoke. Made him look forward to the Friday night football games once Boonie got in high school. The whole town turned out for them. Boonie hadn't lost his sweet nature, Hoke assured Bert, he'd just gotten serious, that's all.

"Serious?" Bert asked. "Or pissed off?"

"Pissed off," said Hoke. "He's like a one-man blitzkrieg out there."

"Hmn . . ." said Bert.

With some time to relax, Bert decided to spend a few lazy afternoons in the bedroom masturbating to Mary Beth McGowan, particularly since he'd spotted her only a few days ago through the window of the Downtown Book Store totally absorbed in Henry Miller's *Tropic of Cancer*, a vision so sexually alluring it frightened him into moving on. Without her with him, however, he could do anything he wanted. And he did. He did. He bit her thighs. He took her entire breast in his mouth. He kissed her, which sent her into dreamland. She exploded in orgasm when he sucked her pussy inside out, drinking it in. When he fucked her she tore at his back and screamed at the top of her lungs. Her orgasm was at once vulnerable and volcanic, adroitly alliterative, matching his perfectly. Afterwards, when he pulled out, she had a minor one involuntarily. Then he turned her over and fucked her again, riding her perfectly round ass like a stallion, rolling all over it, squeezing her firm round tits and pinching her nipples as hard as he could as they both came. It was great, he thought to himself afterwards. God! It was great. Then he spanked her, which made her smile evilly and seductively, listened to her whimper and whine, watched as she came, and fucked her again.

The next time he fucked her he hoped to have her hyperventilate.

To actually have had her there, of course, would have been unprofessional.

Besides, the memory of his recent wrestling match with Arlanne slowly evolving into gentle lovemaking was a pleasant, if not heavenly, sensation for him.

Maybe there was a difference between fucking and lovemaking. In any case, with Mary Beth actually there, in his bed, he would've felt guilty, an emotion he was aware he could not afford.

Much simpler to seduce Arlanne (or to entice her into seducing him) and have a drink with Murray.

He did need to show Arlanne more attention, he realized, or she might get interested in seducing someone else, though he couldn't imagine whom. Still, as a psychologist, how many times had he seen that happen? Nothing was as important as attentiveness in sustaining intimate relationships. Time for him to get crackin'.

On the other hand, what about his needs? How can one give if one doesn't get? So the question was, what does Bert want? Indeed what does Bert want? That was the key question. Then: how to get it? Questions, he figured, worth a lifetime pondering.

That evening at dinner as Arlanne talked about her plans for the garden in the front yard—what she'd add, what she'd subtract—fretting particularly over whether the climbing hydrangea might overwhelm the climbing yellow roses espaliered against the brick front of the house, Bert put on his most attentive face. After a few seconds, the strain of the effort too great, he felt in his pocket for his new listening device: a stop watch. He placed it in front of him on the table.

Arlanne's monologue faltered, offering Bert the bonus of temporary relief.

"What's that?" she said.

"A stop watch."

"I know that, you idiot. What's it for, what the hell are you doing with it, why now, and why is it sitting here on my dinner table between the sautéed broccoli and the sweet potato soufflé?"

"You're always accusing me of not caring enough to listen. I'm always accusing you of not caring enough to interest me."

"Nothing interests you, Bert, except you, and what you're interested in."

"And what interests you, except what you're interested in?"

"Oh God, here we go again."

"Which is why I bought the stopwatch . . . if you're 'interested.'"

"Go ahead. But I want to tell you about the garden."

"No, Arlanne, you want to use me as a sounding board to work through your thoughts and feelings about the garden, to clarify what you want and therefore to arrive at a resolution. This isn't a conversation you want, but help. It's nothing short of a manipulative exploitation of my therapeutic skills, my uncanny focus and my unfaltering attentiveness."

"Deaf people listen better than you."

"Right. And the stopwatch will help me focus. I'm taking the initiative here, Arlanne, showing just how much I care. Work with me."

"Work with you?'"

"Right. A fair democratic approach to a conversation interesting to only one of the parties. I time you talking, together we decide when enough is enough."

"Compromise, in your estimation, the lifeblood of a relationship."

"Exactly! You're not a psychologist but you're catching on."

"Do I have to listen to you too, all your little pathetic obsessions?"

"Most certainly. I too have needs. But you can use the stopwatch too. When enough is enough you can go on about your business."

"I have to listen to you?"

"Well sure—"

"Forget it. I'm not interested. That's too much to ask of anyone, Bert. As a psychologist, knowing who you are, you should know that. More broccoli? Got lots of fiber. Anyway, what I could do is move the hydrangea vine and have a red cypress vine, which is really very thin, almost unnoticeable except for these tiny red flowers, intertwined with the climbing rose. It wouldn't overwhelm it. Of course, where do I put the climbing hydrangea . . . ah, I know, I could arch it over the front door, so from the street you'd see yellow roses slightly punctuated with tiny red flowers all along the front, but I can't help but wonder, is the hydrangea vine too heavy a look for the archway . . . Are you listening to me? Goddammit it Bert. Jesus, I'm talkin' to the fuckin' wall!"

"I'm listening. I'm listening."

"Then what'd I say?"

"About the garden. You were talking about the garden."

"Ah . . . the garden." Suddenly her expression, ruefully skeptical, changed, turning into a delightfully wicked smile. "The night garden, in the backyard?"

"Yes," he said, drawing it out as if it were hands down the most obvious thing in the world. "The night garden, in the back."

"I finished it last night, complete with a chaise lounge, wine and fruit. Now tell me the truth. Did you hear me tell you that?"

"Yes! You're so distrustful, Arlanne. Of course I heard you."

"You didn't."

"I did!"

"And the perfume of the white lilies, the magnolia, the gardenias . . . you heard—"

"Absolutely. Absolutely. I told you, I was listening, really listening."

"As only as a psychologist can."

"Yes. Exactly. As only a psychologist can, using everything at my disposal. I'm surprised—"

"The best-trained psychologist . . . ?"

"Yeah. That's what I've been trying to tell you."

Her elbow on the table, her chin resting in her hand, her smile coy, her downcast eyes examining her red fingernails spread and gleaming against the white tablecloth, she said in her most seductive voice, one she recalled vividly which had never failed her, "And did you hear me say, 'Take off your clothes, and come out there with me . . .'"

"I did! I did!" he said, already tripping over his trousers.

Part VI

1968

53

Arlanne Gets Published

Arlanne Palmer
11 North St.
Somerset, SC 29902
Sept. 11, 1968

Rob Vicker
Editor, the *Atlanta Weekly*
The Atlanta-Journal Constitution
1215 Peachtree St.
Atlanta, GA 30306

Dear Rob,

Congratulations on your new job. Isn't it nice to be back down South?

It's been awhile, I know, since we talked. You can hardly count two years ago, Cunningham's speech. That was pretty much a hey, a hug, and a plane to catch. But I'm ready for something new and different. Sex with Bert is picking up a bit, no question, but it's a lot of work to keep it novel. Still, it's better than sex with you. Gardening's more interesting but insufficient too for fully satisfying my passions. Bert had me riding around the islands with Lila, taking food to the poor, but it absolutely bored the shit out of me. Get in the car, open the trunk, haul out the boxes of supplies, get back in the car, next house, get out the car, open the trunk, haul out the packages, "Hey there, Mrs. Arlanne, how you doin' today, Yo' man gettin' by?" "Yes, ma'am, gettin' by, gettin' by, and you?" Then get back in the car, next house get out again, open the trunk. "You managin', Mrs. Laverne?" "Managin', Mrs. Arlanne. Managin'." The poor, I've found, on the whole, not very different from the rich: boring. Yes, fucking you was a bore, we know that, but it has occurred to me lately that fucking my writing was, for both of us, inspiring if not ecstatic. Hard for me to reach that high in other ways. I could write about gardening for the locals here, but writing about that bores me too. Naturally, what I'm really afraid of, rich or poor, is becoming a bore myself. Maybe that's why Bert has so much trouble listening to me. Maybe he's right. Maybe I really don't have much of interest to say since I'm not doing anything of interest. So I want to write, to take you up on your long-ago encouragement, not just a few features here and there for the local papers or stories for literary magazines—the last refuge for unfulfilled English majors such as myself—but current stuff, that gets me involved, that offers me unique and interesting perspectives. You know why? I think it'll make me feel sexier all the way around, interesting and exciting, and if it does that for readers, male or female, well, what else is there? We've both tried sex, and not to repeat myself but that surely didn't work. Don't fret about it, I say. It's not everyone's forte.

We get the Atlanta paper down here, as you know, and I've been reading the Sunday magazine, looking at how I might contribute. Atlanta's still the South. It's still where small town boys go to make a name for themselves, particularly a lot of the Jews. Large Jewish population there who read. Plus, to Gentiles they can be a curious lot. The problem that interests me, however, is not that we're losing them through a natural migration to the big cities but through assimilation, an issue personified by Murray, Bert, and Marty Liebowitz.

I'm not talking here, Rob, about religious dilution, but about cultural dilution. Murray Gold's mom was wondering the other day who he was going to marry. He was about the only Jew in town his age left, the rest in her mind gone to the cities (if the men manage to avoid the draft). Bert didn't count, she said, because he was a Yankee (plus a transplant), which just wasn't the same thing. Plus, she said, she's a bit skeptical about his Jewishness because he's "tall," a phenomenon she'd never witnessed before, akin she said, to a flying saucer. On the other hand, Murray realizes he's an unusual concoction, one of the last lowcountry Jews, he calls himself, which he does attribute to natural migration. On the other hand, Bert attributes it to assimilation: Marty Liebowitz, if you remember, at one extreme, Murray a cultural hybrid, Bert himself a "real" Jew.

So in enclosed piece I don't really deal with Jews leaving for the big cities, though most have. It's not interesting to me. The question is, are they vanishing culturally, through assimilation. Thus, enclosed: The Last of the Lowcountry Jews?

Hope this too inspires you to orgasm.

Your loving apprentice,
Arlanne Levy

P.S. Another thing that got me thinking: Remember Mary Beth McGowan, Jack's wife? Bert and I had dinner with them recently out on Scataway Island. She's teaching over at the University now. She's interesting. She was kind of a turn-on for me. For Bert too, though he denied it. And not because she's pretty, though she is. She just seemed to have her own unapologetic way of looking at the world. It's clear she and Royal and Jack have a unique sexual situation going on there, and whatever it is, it's loving and charming. She's interesting and interested. I'm boring and bored. So if this perks you up it'll perk me up.

P.P.S. If you like this piece, next one's about the Yankee invasion of VISTA workers and Peace Corps workers from the North. At least down here, they seem to be saying, there's hope. Remember, the first Food Stamp program in the country began here.

THE LAST OF THE LOWCOUNTRY JEWS?

By

Arlanne Levy

I had always known they were different. What I didn't realize until I married my husband Bert Levy, a transplanted New York Jew, was just how different they are. Bert's different, no surprise there, he's a Yankee. He's smart, abrasive, a wise-ass, quick on his feet, spoiled rotten, self-centered, obsessive, compulsive, perceptive, compassionate, demonstrative, argumentative about everything, and runs his mouth a mile-a-minute about nothing at all. When he talks, he gesticulates all over the place: vases and lamps shrink back in his presence. About nature—flowers, animals, trees—he's oblivious. Plus, he's a shrink. Where he comes from they grow 'em by the millions.

Culturally speaking, can you be any more Jewish than Bert Levy?

According to Bert—like all Yankees a know-it-all—no.

However, our dear and closest friend the Jewish-southerner Murray Gold, a lawyer born and raised right here in Somerset, SC, has a different take on it. Yes, as with all Jews, his mother checked his stools and read them like tarot cards. Certainly, like Bert, if he's seen one bird he's seen them all, and the only one he's ever shot was with his middle finger. He's terrified of electricity, and like most Jews too not only of hunting but fishing. NASCAR, the entrails of an engine, the hammering of a nail and the changing of a flat are as alien to him as vintage wine and Modern Art are to a redneck. All that Bert and Murray have in common.

Still, Bert sees himself as a real Jew and Murray, a Jew with a Southern accent, slow-moving and slow-talking, as alien to a real Jew as a Jewish cowboy, a Jewish hillbilly, or a Jewish sumo-wrestler.

Having been born and raised a minority within a minority—a Jew in a small Southern town in the Bible Belt rather than among his own kind in New York—Murray is haunted by the suspicion that Bert might be right. Do real Jews have organs in synagogues and rabbis who deliver sermons just because the Episcopalians do? Like most Jews in the small town south, Murray appears easygoing, casual, suave, courtly, immune to panic—manly, in other words. But at what cost, he wonders along with Bert, his repression of a natural cultural hysteria, his need to talk everything out, his intensity? His need to gesture wildly, to talk loudly, to argue about nothing at all in a culture in which it is, if not rude and obnoxious, tedious and tiring, too much work.

And most white southerners, I can tell you, are lazy. Give 'em a fresh breeze and a hammock and unless they can pull a Tom Sawyer, that fence will stay unpainted for eternity.

Show me an easygoing Jew, argues Bert, and I'll show you an ulcer.

Here's why that really frustrates Murray: he has one.

But not only does Murray worry he's not a real Jew, he can find himself wondering if he's a real man. Reared among Jews, among books and debate and museums and anxiety, Bert does not have that problem. Reared among Gentiles in which a real man backed up his words with his fists instead of his mouth, took things as they came, and worked with his hands, how could a Jew help but wonder? Like Bert, the only thing Murray could ever recall doing with his hands was playing with himself, which Bert said he did all the time. Still does. This is a guy who just can't get over himself. But just so you don't worry, I do play with him too.

The only photo I've ever seen of a Jew with a record catch was of Marty Liebowitz holding up that prize marlin in the Lowcountry Living section of the *Beaufort Weekly*. Marty, a Jew. But Marty, the Jew, also the leading segregationist on the school board. A Jew, finally, one of the boys?

Does Murray, a leading, fearsome civil rights advocate, in his heart of hearts long too to be one of the boys? Just one of the boys?

Murray's answer: Everybody, he says, plays ball. In one way or another, everybody plays ball.

And they did: Bert, Murray, the Crackers. Everyone. Bert played basketball, Murray football.

So can a Southerner be a real Jew? Can a Jew be a real man?

Everyone plays ball, says Murray. In one way or another, everyone plays ball.

54

Rob Reacts to Arlanne's Article

Rob Vicker, Editor
Atlanta Weekly
Atlanta Journal-Constitution
1215 Peachtree St.
Atlanta ,GA 30306
Sept. 29, 1968

Arlanne Levy
11 North St.
Somerset, SC

Dear Arlanne,
I read, I ejaculated. Enclosed is check for $750. Keep the pieces coming. I would also suggest both *Esquire* and *Playboy* magazines for future pieces, though they'll be interested in longer ones. They're publishing good stuff. Use me as reference. However, send the "Yankee invasion" article my way. It fits what we're doing here with this magazine. Sounds like it's for a decidedly Southern audience.

Keep freelancing for another year or so. You won't need that many articles out there to get known. They're unusual, or will be—this one certainly is—and major magazines will publish them, including mine.

At some point, however, because of your humor and personality and quirky way of looking at things, I'd be interested in you having your own column, if not weekly, monthly.

Good hearing from you, Arlanne. A real treat. My best to Bert and Murray and all down there.

I'm using this for December issue, will send you copies and responses then. Believe me, this will warrant them.

With affection and admiration,
Rob

55

Rob Invites Another Article as Arlanne Determines That Money Is the Source of All Good

Rob Vicker, Editor
Atlanta Weekly
Atlanta Journal-Constitution
1215 Peachtree St.
Atlanta, GA 30306
Dec. 3, 1968

Arlanne Levy
11 North St.
Beaufort, SC 29902

Dear Arlanne,
Here are several copies for you. Hope you approve. As you can see, other than the references to the Jews' Favorite Pastime I've edited only for a few typos and space.

Will send you samples of readers' responses as they come in.

Can I have the "Yankee invasion" piece in time for September issue, about three or four months ahead of time?
Warmly,
Rob

Arlanne Levy
11 North St.
Somerset, SC 29902
Dec. 10, 1968

Rob Vicker, Editor
Atlanta Weekly
Atlanta-Journal Constitution

1215 Peachtree St.
Atlanta, GA 30306

Delighted, Rob,
Already started working on new piece. Thinking about one after that too: Money is the source of all good. Ask poor kids getting free lunches and vaccinations down here.
Love,
Arlanne

56

Rob Lets Arlanne Hear From Her Readers

Rob Vicker, Editor
Atlanta Weekly
Atlanta Journal-Constitution
1215 Peachtree St.
Atlanta, GA 30306
Dec. 19, 1968

Arlanne Levy
11 North St.
Somerset, SC 29902

Much response generated, Arlanne! Exactly what we need! Controversy creates noise, which creates readers, so don't be distraught. The truth can hurt, but it boost sales!

Here are excerpts/responses.

From David Applebaum, Chairman of the Southeastern Division, American Jewish Committee:

" . . . Those may be Arlanne Levy's dirty underwear hanging on her front lawn, but they most assuredly are not mine, and they are not ours. By 'mine' and 'ours,' I mean 'Jews,' of whom she is clearly not one. Not one of us, she does not speak for us . . . nor do I imagine she speaks for Gentiles, unless they too are anti-Semites."

From Michael Rothenberg, Dothan, Alabama:

" . . . Thank you for Mrs. Levy's piece on Jewish Southerners. I am one, and her piece showed me who I am. I am a Jew, I am a Cracker. Thank you, Mrs. Levy."

From Sharon Mikveh, Atlanta, GA:

"A suggestion for Murray Gold and Bert Levy: 'Try Judaism, You'll like it! I do!'"

From Adele Weisbrod, Savannah, GA:

"God will forgive, Mrs. Levy, but will your husband, whose name you carry? Will your 'dear and closest friend,' Mr. Gold?"

From Will Jones, Montgomery, Alabama:

"God bless the People of the Book."

From Hershchel Levine, Vice President, Anti-Defamation League:

" . . . Mrs. Levy's article gave me indigestion."

| 57 |

Bert Defines for All Time the Jewish Condition

Bert Levy
11 North St.
Somerset, SC 29902
Dec. 31, 1968

Rob Vicker, Editor
Atlanta Weekly
Atlanta Journal-Constitution
1215 Peachtree St.
Atlanta, GA 29902

To the Editor:
In response to ADL vice president Hershchel Levine's Letter to Editor re. "The Last of the Lowcountry Jews?"

"Hey, Come on, Levine. You had indigestion anyway, long before you read "The Last of the Lowcountry Jews." You know that, I know that, and unless they're in deep denial, all Jews know that. If it's not constipation, it's diarrhea; if it's not diarrhea, it's gastritis; if it's not gastritis, it's bowel irritation. I could go on and on, as every Jew knows. This is who we are. Deny this, and you deny your heritage. You are an anti-Semite!"

Our bowel movements, whether we admit it or not, are as sacred a ritual to us as they were to our mothers. Again, you know as well as I do that for them to be successful and satisfyingly accomplished all the stars must be aligned, everything must be in order, which is to say clean to the point of spotless. To the Jew, this is what is meant by 'Cleanliness is next to Godliness.' It is why our people, Levine, deny ourselves the performing of such a ritual in public bathrooms. Show me a Jew who can lay it all out there in a service-station bathroom off the Interstate and, to borrow from Mrs. Levy, I'll show you a photograph of a Jew with a record catch and the leading segregationist on the school board.

Yes it is true that under segregation blacks were denied the use of public bathrooms and on long trips had to travel halfway across the state to find one available to them or had to stop off and go in the woods. In their case, the law denied them, and they too have suffered, but at least they could do it in the woods.

See what I'm getting at here?

Unfortunately, Levine, the truth, even if you were to admit it, would not in this case set you free. I know. I've tried it. Indigestion is who you are.

Bert Levy
Somerset, SC

58

Elizabeth Obsesses With Arlanne's Article but Has No Idea Why

Of all of Arlanne's Somerset friends, none read her piece in the *Atlanta Weekly* with greater absorption than Elizabeth. She read it over and over, even took it with her to school to read at recess or in Study Hall; that is, when she wasn't observing and taking notes for her term paper on the kids in the special education class, kids who according to their I. Q.'s ranged from "retarded" to "feeble-minded."

The adults in her life certainly had an idea why the article was so compelling to her. Though Somerset High was now half black, in the process of consolidating with Robert Smalls High, the formerly black high school, Elizabeth was still very much alone, participating in none of the current debates and controversies about school colors, the name of the football team, the mascot, the black kids on one side, whites on the other. She appeared aloof, according to her teachers, above such silliness, focused solely on her grades.

But she had heard the snickers, the whispers in the corridor among black kids, the references to her as an "oreo," "white girl." Already she'd been alienated from them. Annie was at Somerset High now, in many of her classes, the advanced classes. Rarely, however, did they speak. Were they afraid of rejection? From each other? From peers?

While Annie was certainly beginning to branch out socially—flirting with boys a bit, "kissing up" (in Elizabeth's mind) to the "popular" kids—she nevertheless remained pretty much a very pretty academic type, most of her friends, black kids also in the AP classes, kids who never got in trouble and ran for class offices and who would later be Senior Marshals.

Geeks, Elizabeth told herself. "Rejects." Particularly those who might have made overtures to her. Kissing up to kids even dumber and sillier than they were. The whole lot of them so "immature." Yet when Tasha LeMoyne, cheerleader, basketball player and runner-up for Homecoming Queen spoke to her warmly and with enthusiasm one day in the hallway she was surprised, then stunned, then frightened by the thrill she felt until she realized, thinking back, that Tasha spoke to just about everyone that way.

So why was she so compelled by Arlanne's piece in the *Atlanta Weekly* about Murray and Bert and Marty Liebowitz?

She didn't know why. She didn't even ask herself why. It would be her senior year before she as well as the adults in her life, including Bert, would fully realize just how detached and dissociated from herself she had once again become.

Which also unbeknownst to her at the time, was why she was compelled by the special education students she was observing, yet was unable to complete her term paper on them.

But that was all right too. She just chose one of the teacher-assigned topics instead: Jeffersonian vs, Hamiltonian democracy. As always, she aced it, and as usual she slid the returned essay with the large red "A" at the top of the front page to the uppermost corner of her desk so that it might be visible to her classmates, especially Annie.

She didn't know why she did that either; nor did she ask herself.

Part VII

1970S

59

Elizabeth Refuses to Deliver Her Valedictory Address

"Elizabeth Trulove, please report to the principal's office. Elizabeth Trulove, please report to the principal's office."

She wasn't surprised, but as she gathered up her books and papers on her way out of study hall she glanced up at the P. A. system as if she wanted to throw a shoe at it.

Nor was she surprised to see Murray in the principal's office instead of the principal. The principal had gotten nowhere with her, so at her mother's request, she was sure, he'd called in Murray. "They didn't speak to me," Elizabeth told him, referring to her classmates. "Why should I speak to them?"

Which is all she'd say to anybody.

As the valedictorian of the senior class at Somerset High, she was refusing to deliver the valedictory address at her Commencement in June.

In Somerset February was nasty. Though it never froze, the wet chill off the river ate right through you until before you knew it you felt yourself shudder and shiver from the inside out. Unless the sky was clear and the sun out, wherever you were felt damp and cold, dreary and bleak, colder than it actually was, even more wintry than it appeared. Murray always wanted to sleep through it. It was depressing, and if you couldn't swat it away like summer flies, then you had to just resign yourself to waiting it out. If Somerset's heavy summer humidity weighed on you and slowed you down, giving you the sensation that moving through it was like wading trenchantly through saran wrap, February's chill electrified you like a seizure, making you feel as if you had to fortify yourself against it. February, mused Murray, was the fatalistic month. One had to adopt a Christian attitude toward it: "This too will pass," he reminded himself, gazing with a tired resignation out the principal's office window at nothing at all: Tasha LeMoyne, who'd broken her arm the first basketball game of the season, heading across campus to her mom's Volkswagen, so bundled up as to be almost unrecognizable on her way to Dr. Cohen's office to get her cast taken off; Thedie Lotts, the school secretary, pulling out of the parking lot on her way to the bank; Old lady Crout, as she'd done when she taught him, sneaking out for a smoke. Getting through her class, even for a kid like him, was absolute hell. "Yes," he reassured himself, this time aloud, "this too will pass."

"Exactly, Mr. Gold," said Elizabeth. "Can I go now?" She glanced at the pile of homework sitting in her lap, hinting.

Murray sighed, his best Jewish-mother/Christian-martyr take on it. Elizabeth liked Murray, but she saw right through it. She looked at him, exasperated. She liked Murray immensely, in fact—he was almost, as was Bert, a surrogate father to her, and she knew he would end up making her feel guilty. A man's love, she knew, could make her cry. She looked down, working silently against it.

Having no children of his own, Murray felt that paternal urge, which embarrassed him inside, to make her his, to adopt her as his own daughter. He was a man like his own father, he realized looking at her, created (as was his mother) to have children. Between him and Elizabeth was an instinctive paternal connection, and both knew it. She sensed his yearning for the child he didn't have, and he her profound need for the father who had abandoned her.

They were capable of breaking each other's hearts.

"Stop it," she said.

"Okay," he replied.

She was tall and slender. Her hair was naturally curly like her mother's, appearing wet, like she'd just washed it, even if she hadn't. It was as coal-black, however, as her complexion, like her father's. Like her complexion too, it gleamed like a fresh shoeshine. While she'd flash a wholly liberated, dazzling toothpaste-commercial smile at Murray or Bert, she gave the boys her age much less: a show of curiosity, a coy smile, perhaps one of skepticism, or even outright dismissal, her interest clearly less in the boys themselves than in what they might be saying. Though she reserved for herself the right to be interested, at this stage of her life her interest was limited. Or, wondered Murray, was it the boys who were. Her features, as well as the casual, disinterested way she wore her beauty, were more and more reminiscent of her mother's, Murray thought, looking at her. Her eyes, enormously brown, held the promise of flirtation and tenderness on the one hand and the threat of tyranny and persecution on the other, all in the same millisecond. Only her eyelashes, long and fine like her mother's, afforded her a feminine reserve.

"Mr. Gold?"

"Go do your homework, Elizabeth. Say' hi' to your Mama for me."

"Now, Mr. Gold," she said, rising, "You and I both know you're going to be talking with her well before I get home from school. And we both know what you're going to be talking about. She's probably waiting at the phone right now."

"Your perspicacity," he said, escorting her out, "has never been in doubt."

"Of course not," she said over her shoulder. "Had it been in doubt, there would be no problem."

Bert, of whom she was also immensely fond and to whom she was grateful, was more direct. Upon the urging of both Lila and Murray, he had invited her in for a session.

"So," he began, guiding her to the sofa, "Our little beauty who also just happens to be the smartest kid ever to grace the halls of Somerset High has ventured beyond hating white people—yours truly excluded, I realize—to, well, hating everybody. How humanizing. America's little experiment with integration, it's made you a snob."

"You know that is not true, Dr. Know-it-all Levy. My hatred may be bitter and vengeful but it is totally indiscriminate. It is," she couldn't help but chuckle, "Equal-opportunity hostility."

"None of them spoke to you? None of them? The black kids?"

"Almost as bad as the whites. Called me 'white.' 'White girl.' 'Oreo.'"

"When if it weren't for you, none of them would even be there."

"That's for damn sure."

"That sounds exactly like your mother."

"So?"

"So are you worried about disappointing her? Or are you pissed off at her because if it weren't for her you wouldn't be there."

"Both?"

"Why?"

"She has waited all these years for me to get up on that stage at commencement and show off her pride and joy, her star-symbol of what black kids are capable of. I know that. It does disappoint me to disappoint her. It makes me sad, but I do comfort myself knowing if she were me in this situation, she wouldn't give an inch."

"I believe you. I know you feel she's basically all you have."

She nodded.

"But your equal-opportunity anger does extend to her for putting you in this situation."

"I know she wanted the best for me, regardless of 'the cause.' Still, what a personal hellhole to send a child into."

"Nevertheless, she spoke to you."

"And I speak to her."

"But did she listen to you?"

"I see what you mean."

"And so are you listening to her?"

"Clearly, I'm not. You're wondering if payback extends beyond the racial and social? Dr. Levy, I'm not doing this to embarrass Mama because she's on the Board, if that's where you're getting at. I wouldn't do that. After all, she was fighting for me, at least in her own mind."

"By serving on the Board of what you just referred to as a 'personal hellhole?'"

"Yes," she said.

"Explain?"

"I'm stronger, Dr. Levy, and smarter, than every kid in this school, black or white. Let me be specific: every white kid in this school. I couldn't have said that without Mama having put me through that personal hellhole."

"Was it worth it?"

"Damn right it was."

"Okay, but still, you're pissed off, right?"

"Yes."

"So where's the payback?"

She smiled, embarrassed, caught with the goods but hesitant about turning them over.

"Oh for God's sake, Elizabeth, spill the beans. You might be strong and smart but you're still a teenager. If you're pissed off with your mom, whether she's right or wrong, how do you get her back?"

"The dishes."

"The dishes?"

"The dishes, Dr. Levy. The dishes. Okay. Can we please move on now?"

"How do you get out of doing them?"

"This is so embarrassing."

"I'm waiting."

"'Got to study, Mama, white school's tough . . .' that kind of thing."

"You're kidding. Wow, that is smart."

"Thank you. I try. And you know, being all surly and put-out over nothing, negative, she hates that."

"A bad 'attitude.'"

"Yeah. 'Don't you be showin' me attitude, little girl,'" she said, wagging her finger.

"That's funny."

"It is, now that I think about it. What else do I do? Oh, yeah, you know how Mama likes everything all organized, each thing in its particular place—actually, I'm like that too now that I think about it—particularly her car keys, punctuality's a big thing for her. 'The world don't operate on black people's time,' she's always sayin' that. Like she wants to teach us a lesson or something."

"Which you naturally thwart."

"'Where are those damn keys? Damn it, Elizabeth, I'm going to be late. Where'd you put the keys?' 'Where I always put them, Mama. Where you tell me to put them. On the kitchen counter right next to the coffee machine.' 'Well, they're not there. Think, Elizabeth, think. Where did you last have them?' 'Where did *I* last have them? Mama, you need to learn to take responsibility for yourself. Really.'"

"Jesus, you're terrible."

"It really is bad, isn't it?"

Sheepish, stuck with the goods, she now looked about for a place to dump them.

"You adore your mother, Elizabeth. Still, something is allowing you to disappoint her. Elizabeth, who have you disappointed over the years? Who did you fail to speak to? To listen to?"

"I'm not a snob. I was snubbed. I'm not about to start speaking to them now. Quit implying that. You know that's not fair."

"Of almost 200 kids in your grade, another 200, say, in the grade below you, and until this year an additional 200 in the grade above you—of approximately 600 kids around your age, at least 1/3 of them black—"

"None wanted to be friends with me?"

"Duh . . ."

She smiled, embarrassed. She knew where this was going. "Only the ones like me."

"The rejects? Those uninterested in parties and athletics?"

"This is embarrassing. I didn't realize . . ."

"And were you interested, even mildly, in parties and athletics?"

"No."

"Then why were you only interested in those who were?"

"Thoughtlessness, I think."

"Clever, but what made you thoughtless?"

"You know, I think it was easier to be resentful, to just sit there and smolder over classmates I could care less about, mostly silly, superficial people, than to risk getting burned again by the few classmates with whom I did have things in common, who were serious, had academic interests, cared about the world. You're right. I probably could have been close friends with them. Oh well," she said, suddenly as silly and superficial as all those partygoers, cheerleaders, and athletes she resented, "too late now."

"'Burned' . . . as when you lost your father . . ."

"And Annie," she said, not without sadness. "Remember?"

"Yeah, I do."

"Okay, Dr. Know-it-all Levy, I hate you, you know. God, I hate you. Why do you do this to me? Can't you find yourself another project or something? You're drivin' me crazy with all this."

"Keep going . . ."

"I HATE YOU!"

Bert smiled.

"HAPPY NOW?"

"Very."

"God," she said, her head in her hands, "I hate you. You're worse than my dad could ever have been—"

That's when she lost it.

Bert walked over to the sofa, held her for a minute, and kissed her on top of her head.

"You're the opposite of my dad," she said. "I guess I hate you for that too." She looked up at him. "Can I have a tissue?"

"Sure, I'm sorry. Here you are."

When she smiled, dabbing at her eyes, the way the light played on her residual tears made them look like glitter. Though her insights might have been valedictory, thought Bert, her face, at that moment, was the face of the Homecoming Queen being crowned.

| 60 |

Elizabeth Delivers Her Valedictory Address

Sunday afternoon, June 5. Faculty members in their Sunday best congregated in the RESERVED section of bleachers angled off-left of the stage of the Somerset High School Gymnasium-Auditorium, the Somerset High band in the RESERVED section of bleachers off-right of the stage. Farther down the same bleachers on both sides of the gymnasium, also in their Sunday best, sat racially self-segregated clusters (with exceptions here and there) of black and white undergraduates speaking animatedly among themselves, yet not infrequently bolting upright or even standing briefly to catch the attention of classmates of opposite races, communicating as if over a private line across the clusters of their own divides, momentarily transcending desegregation in bursts of acknowledgement and recognition, familiar banter, intimate word-mouthing and gesticulation.

On the gymnasium floor directly in front of the stage in folding chairs sat the graduating seniors in caps and gowns, behind them rows and rows of parents, relatives and guests. A photographer from the *Somerset Weekly* positioned himself in a corner of the bleachers toward the back, a young reporter off to the side.

Late afternoon sunlight panned the small high windows above the bleachers, zooming in in geometrically-diverse patterns here and there across the multi-colored faces and sport coats and blouses and afros and curls and ponytails and polished weejuns and wingtips of the kids and faculty, glinting off the gold of trumpets and trombones and tubas and the bits of silver on the clarinets and saxophones of band members and down on the gym floor alighting in ribbons of gold on black caps and settling about the shoulders of gowns, farther down still traversing the coats and ties and trousers of fathers, ricocheting off tie clasps and gleaming cufflinks, frolicking about in the jewelry—the earrings and necklaces and bracelets—of mothers, slithering voyeuristically among stocking legs.

After everyone recited the Pledge of Allegiance and sang the Somerset High School anthem . . . *"Somerset, we're loyal to you, we have done our best for you . . . In all our studies and sports . . ."* Reverend Owen delivered a brief prayer, ending as one might expect in the Deep South at the time, "In Jesus' Name, amen . . ."

When he was a little boy in Somerset Elementary School back in the fifties, Murray Gold's mother told him that when his classmates and teacher recited the daily prayer before lunch to recite it along with them, but that instead of at the end saying "In *Jesus'* Name" to silently substitute and silently mouth the word "God" instead of "Jesus," and say "In God's Name," a habit which he found himself indulging in now.

Beside him sat Lila, Bert, Arlanne, and Eileen Hunter, the principal of Elizabeth's elementary school, who when Elizabeth was in sixth grade summoned her to her office, sat her down and told her she was going to be the smartest student Somerset High School had ever seen. Sitting there as Elizabeth rose to deliver her valedictory address, Mrs. Hunter remembered that, and tears formed in her eyes: a black girl, damn you—damn everybody, black and white—of little faith, that beautiful child of segregation whom she had taught, the most intelligent student in Somerset High School, settling and arranging herself at the lectern, with no notes. That's right, honey, with no notes. You show 'em now, baby. Show us all. Driver sat with friends in the bleachers.

Surprisingly, at least to everyone who knew her, Elizabeth had tears in her eyes, which she gracefully wiped away with a monogrammed handkerchief, a graduation present from her former teacher Pat Conroy, regrettably (he had written her) unable to interrupt his first book tour to attend her graduation. Further (he wrote), since he would be unable to hear her address, would she mind sending him a copy? Great writers (a status, he explained, to which he aspired) "steal" from great works. If his subsequent fiction called for a valedictory address, why not borrow, he asked her, from what would, without question, be the best ever delivered?

After acknowledging the principal, the assistant principal, the faculty, as well as the school secretary, the school nurse, and the custodian who was standing at the back, arms folded, against the wall—the latter acknowledgements a first, her mother realized proudly, in a graduation speech—she addressed directly her classmates, "the class of 1971," to rousing applause, applause, she recognized with a smile, for all the graduates, for their upcoming liberation from Somerset High School.

"I am not going to talk to you today," she told them, "about the conventional notions of the promise of the future, about your duty and responsibility as citizens, about the 'challenging' reality—as if the reality of Somerset High weren't challenging enough—of the world that awaits you. I am not going to tell you that with hard work you will be rewarded with success, that if you love and respect your fellow citizens you will be loved and respected in return. Honestly, I have no idea if 'the day' is yours, and whether or not you should 'seize' it, if the good life is out there, ready for the taking. Admittedly, I do wonder if perhaps life's riches—meaning and sheer happiness—are in the loveliness of the rainbow itself rather than the pot of gold at the end of it; indeed, if the gold in the pot is fool's gold, as empty of meaning and significance as words like 'duty,' 'responsibility,' 'citizenship,' the 'promise of the future,' the 'challenging reality,' as empty for many of us, sadly, as the words 'love' and 'respect.' I am particularly unnerved by the term 'success.' Ah, but you're the valedictorian of Somerset High, one might say. Give yourself credit. I have. I definitely have. But at one point does one's credit run out, leaving one's academic pocketbook perhaps full but one's heart empty? I am too young, too unwise in the ways of the world, to understand what these words really mean, if anything.

"In fact, I wonder, should I even be up here. Yes I worked hard in school, and under extremely adverse racial and social circumstances, certainly initially as the first black child to attend Somerset Junior High School. Yes, I was rewarded. I made good grades, became your valedictorian, got a great scholarship, all that is true and nothing, I am the first to tell you, to sneeze at. The future holds 'great promise' for me, greater than that of most of us graduating today. I offer that not to brag on myself, but because in the conventional sense of money and status, it is true. Today, among the colleges and universities, and subsequently the professions, opportunity for black students, particularly black women, has never been more 'promising.'

"But what exactly have I learned? What have you learned? What do I mean by hard work? Did I work as hard as the less academically gifted among us? Did I work as hard as the special education student struggling every hour of the school day to learn something perhaps he couldn't? Were the adverse social circumstances and racial prejudice from which I suffered as adverse as the cruel prejudices from which he suffered? It's one thing to be segregated, even in a desegregated school, because of the color of your skin. It's lonely. It's shameful. But to be segregated because of your mind? That loneliness, that shame, I cannot begin to fathom. Furthermore, did I learn from the adversity of my circumstances as much as he did from his? If not, who learned the most? If that is the measure of achievement in a school, should I be up here today, or should he?

"What do I mean by learning from 'adverse circumstances?' Learning what? Did I learn humility, the true pre-requisite for further learning, as perhaps he did? Or did I snub that particular lesson—as my classmates snubbed me—develop a chip on my shoulder, and harden my heart with straight A's?

"Was my motivation to learn? Or simply to outdo everyone else, to rub their white faces in my black achievement?

"I refused initially to even give this speech. My classmates, I told the principal, never spoke to me, why should I now speak to them?

"But which classmates? White kids? Black kids? (Within a few years of my arrival, black kids were as commonplace at Somerset High as white kids.)

"Why, the ones that mattered, naturally, or at least the ones I thought mattered: the popular kids, black or white—the party boys and party girls, the athletes, the cheerleaders. You know who you are. Everyone does.

"Yet in my refusal to speak to you, I unknowingly became you, just as—I think I understand now—you unknowingly became you.

"Further, I became you, just as you no doubt became you, as soon as rejection in all of its ugly guises presented itself to me. Nobody called me a dirty nigger when I first arrived at Somerset Junior High. They just didn't speak to me.

"And so I didn't speak to them; when nobody speaks to you, everybody matters.

"Worse, later, when I could have, I didn't speak to anybody. Not only did I not speak to the socially benighted, I didn't speak to the rest of you either, because unless you were 'somebody,' one of 'them'—socially elite—you didn't matter, or so I told myself. And in you who didn't matter, or who I told myself didn't matter, I saw my own shame and loneliness. Turning away from you, I turned away from myself.

"It is to you I speak today. It is to you I offer my most sincere apologies.

"Because it was you who did matter. Fear inspired my academic drive, not the genuine curiosity of an intelligent human being. Fear made me arrogant and standoffish and unrevealing, not truly brave and confident. Fear made me snub you.

"Why? Because you were the ones who really mattered. You were the ones who shared my values, with whom I shared commonality. In short, you were serious people. Like me. And like me you may have thought otherwise about yourselves, but the fact is I had no interest in partying, in sexcapades, in drinking and smoking, in waving pompoms and jumping up and down at pep rallies. Lord, had I been invited to one of those weekend parties I'd of been scared to death, sulkin' over in the corner all evening, findin' a way to phone my momma to come and get me out of there.

"It's just that they always looked like they were havin' so much fun, and everybody seemed to care about them.

"I wonder now: were they?

"I speak to you now, the popular and socially powerful, and I ask you: were you? Or was your social competition and all that showing off and mean gossip and undermining just a variation on my academic, eat-your-young competitiveness, motivated not by joy and love and appreciation but by social ambition, social triumph, and social superiority.

"All I can share with you—all of you today—and I do so with the new-found humility that I pray fear will never take away from me again—is that fear made me ignorant and unhappy and lonely. Fear made me a fraud. That, I discovered, was the real reason I refused to speak to you today. I had not yet learned the lesson of humility. That discovery, however, truly opens my heart. It inspires a meaningful intelligence. Reciting Plato's philosophy has always been easy for me. Perhaps that's why deep down it meant nothing to me. But now, for the first time, I repeat to you his dictum that 'The unexamined life is not worth living,' and in humbling me, it inspires me.

"It opens my heart, as I hope it does yours, to that same special education student (whose heart, unlike ours, may well be naturally open and receptive, like ours when we were young and innocent), to the autistic student, the emotionally-disturbed student, the classmate of poverty, of neglect, of abuse, of war, of no parents at all, the classmate so profoundly tragic and spiritually impoverished as to transcend the petty neurotic luxuries, silly social discourse, the cutthroat social and academic competition and one-upsmanship that occupy our daily lives, however we might disguise our obsessions with them through resentment and withdrawal (as I did), through academic and intellectual snobbism (as I also did), or through social climbing and social snobbism (as did the popularity-seekers).

"Think of the profound sadness, suffering and strength of those among us who spend their entire lives, at least their entire childhoods, suffering from circumstances so tragic we couldn't begin to understand them, of what it takes for them merely to survive, of what they must know that we don't, then contemplate our own obsessions: the right party, the right grades, the right friends, the flashy car, the right clothes, the right information, the right demeanor. This is meaning? Depth? A spiritual life?

"Do we truly want our lives to be reduced to the sum of our obsessions? Or to be inspired by our passions?

"If we have not coveted our neighbor's wife—since thank God we are too young to have done so—have we not coveted our classmate's life, our friend's life, our brother or sister's life?

"And for whom? For what?

"To show our fellow man and woman that we are better than they?

"The late Robert Kennedy once asked if God were black. Admittedly, when times were tough, particularly the first year of desegregation when I was the only black student here, I did find myself wondering if he might be white.

"I submit to you today, however, on the afternoon of our entry into a world perhaps as petty, mean, and superficial as our own, that He is a special education student, as in my own way I was half a decade ago, the year I became 'different,' the only black child in an all-white school.

"And if God is indeed a special education student, and each of us is made in His image, all of us, in our own way, are special education students.

"After all, your valedictorian—as I have done my damndest to show you today—is a slow learner . . .

"Thank you."

Lila and Murray and Bert and Arlanne burst into tears and applause at the little girl they once knew standing now so humbly and majestically before them. Mrs. Hunter, immediately on her feet, applauded like it was the second coming, as those around her followed suit. Elizabeth Trulove, the valedictorian, true to her nature and her upbringing, had given a serious commencement address. Naturally, some of the parents and relatives of the graduates were somewhat discomfited, their applause ranging from tepid, if they were white, to wildly enthusiastic, if they were black.

The kids, however, went crazy, howling and screaming with applause; proud, as they never foresaw they would be, of their valedictorian. Rarely if ever, remarked one faculty member, had she seen them so thoughtful and attentive.

Arlanne had only one thought: Elizabeth told the truth.

God bless her.

Elizabeth was the hit of the graduation season. And at one of the parties, for the first time in her life, she got high and couldn't stop giggling, she would later recall, over "the silliest things."

At Charlotte Heyward's party she asked her friend Annie if she'd come over her high school years to like white people, and giggling so hard she couldn't stop Annie answered her, saying, "Girl, I don't even know if I like black people." And then she said, breaking them both up again: "Unless they're boys."

After which she said: "And they're cute!"

"Chester," she said to a boy waiting nearby to enter the conversation. "Bring us another one of them things makes you happy. Go on now."

"How you get him to do that?" asked Elizabeth, watching him head off to the liquor table.

"Girl, you got a lot to learn."

"But I'm the valedictorian!" she said happily, opening her arms to the world, after which she and Annie both started up again, dissolving once more into laughter and giggles, almost spilling their drinks on Charlotte Heyward's mother's new sofa.

Several of the cool kids, standing casually about like the fraternity boys they would soon become, noted with secret pleasure the beauty and capacity for fun of both girls, though they did think them a bit strange.

Annie noticed, gearing it up just a bit for them. Though alarmingly stiff and self-conscious, they were kind of cute.

Elizabeth didn't even notice. For the first time since puberty, she was too busy having fun.

| 61 |

Arlanne Pitches a New Story, Then Procrastinates Like Crazy

In 1973, Rob Vicker, now back in New York and on the masthead at *Esquire* magazine, had become over the years Arlanne's connection to the world of American journalism, and she rewarded him by calling him first whenever she thought she might have a story.

"How is everybody, Rob?"

"We're fine. Bert?"

"Good. Settled in, I think, for the long haul."

"Hey, I loved that piece you did for the Sunday *Times* magazine."

"A Lowcountry Negro In The Ivy League?"

"Yeah, did he get in?"

"Bert talked to 'em at Harvard. Hell, he did the alumni interview. Says they're salivatin'. Lila's so excited she's about to jump out of her sandals. Won't say 'Harvard' out loud, 'fraid it'll jinx Driver's chances. He should get in, a black Southerner with straight A's, almost perfect S. A.T.'s who's a horrible athlete and the hot shot of the school newspaper?"

"A black Southerner from a small town, that would do it by itself in this day and age."

"Everybody needs a leg up. Momma used to say all the time, 'it's not what you know but who you know,' and I always dismissed it as upper crust snobbism, but Driver, he's the real thing. You were my leg up."

"That first piece . . . boy was that controversial, and I'd just gotten to Atlanta. And then the piece about VISTA workers 'retreating' to the South. Funny, and yet about race riots and cities burning: Watts, Detroit, Chicago, Newark. 'Fleeing in droves the violence and debris of ruined cities, social activists have by default declared the racial war in the North "unwinnable," retreating instead to the more racially hospitable terrain of the South. Welcome y'all.' I liked the parallel reference in there to the Vietnam War."

"The implied reference. I actually never mentioned the war in the piece."

"Right, but the implication was clear: the war in the North was 'unwinnable,' and there was a 'retreat' to the South, personified by—what was her name?"

"Ruthie Anne Burton."

"Right, whether you were talking about the Vietnam War or the racial conflict."

"I think I actually learned the form through that story. God, you drove me crazy. Thank you, Rob. I guess that's what I'm trying to say."

"Thank you."

"Oh I know. You've been rewarded."

"Have I now?"

"Oh shut up, would you? You ought to be spanked."

"Okay. You got somethin' for me? Somethin' interesting going on down there."

"Other than the fact that our war hero Royal Cunningham, famous spokesman for anti-war veterans, has gone queer on us, not much."

"Publicly?"

"Testified at the hearing in drag."

"Hearing?"

"They're tryin' to keep it pretty hush-hush down here, but I got the scoop. Actually what I got is rumor, but not only can I smell the smoke, I can feel the heat of the fire. A football player, the team captain—the kind who leads 'em in prayer before each game—tried to roll Royal on the waterfront, then tried to beat the hell out of him. Well, that's the standard version. Rollin' queers' is pretty common practice around here, particularly around the waterfront downtown or the beach."

"Common practice everywhere."

"Right. Only this time a controversial war hero, who happens to be the spokesman for the Veteran's Association, is involved and by all appearances happens to be queer, roaming the waterfront bars at night in drag. Not only that, he turned the tables on our fullback."

"I'm interested."

"They find a dark alley on the waterfront, back of the bar 'round the trash cans."

"You got a way with settings."

"Here are the versions I've picked up on so far."

"Versions?"

"The boy, rumor has it, is 'naturally' confused."

"Okay, go on."

"The boy unzips, Royal gets on his knees and goes to work, after which the football player gives him a two-handed judo chop to the back of the head—this kid's huge, must've been a sledge hammer. From what I heard, it sounds like the kid was trying to kill him. An uppercut sent Royal flying, after which the kid lands on him like a wild animal. That's one version. Seems a bit easy to me. You could beat up a queer without going so crazy on him. Another is that the boy thought Royal was a woman, and when he discovers otherwise, goes crazy on him. That's a cliché, hard to buy that one. Plus, I know Royal. He's honest, entirely undeceptive. In drag or not, he's still himself, just a little funnier and livelier in drag than otherwise. Which I think, knowing Royal, goes to the real story. Despite Royal being in drag, I think the football player knew exactly what he was getting, then for some reason, couldn't handle getting it, just got scared or enraged and completely lost his mind, going crazy on him. Maybe he was afraid he might be queer. Something drove him crazy, because he's chargin' at Royal like a crazy bull. All this, Royal says, was beginnin' to piss him off. To him, at least according to his testimony, this was a business arrangement. Royal even gave him money after he beat the shit out of him."

"Royal beat the shit out of the football player?"

"He 'lost it,' he said. Kept sayin' he should have had more control of himself. The boy pissed him off. And when Royal gets pissed off, well, as he testified, he tends to go into his 'killing mode.' That's the country's fault, he explained to the prosecutor, not his. The Marine Corps. Made a pretty good case, if you ask me."

"Why didn't he just plead self-defense? Didn't you say the boy was trying to kill him?"

"Accordin' to Royal, the boy was just stark ravin'. Oh, Royal's lawyer tried everything he could to get him to plead self-defense. Royal wouldn't do it. Said breakin' his legs was unnecessary. Could've stopped him, he said, with 'limited force.'"

"'Limited force.' You're kidding."

"His lawyer says Royal's fighting the war all over again. He feels guilty that he didn't restrain himself this time."

"You mean this is passing as a microcosm of the war? 'Limited force,' 'Limited war?' What's he saying?"

"What I'm saying is that he's a martyr."

"Who's his lawyer?"

"You know him. Murray Gold? Remember? God, was he a good fuck! Jesus. Get hot thinkin' about it. Out there on the beach . . . oh my—"

"The story, Arlanne. The story."

"Some men are capable of distractin' any woman, Rob."

"The story, Arlanne. Come on. Please."

"Beg."

"Arlanne!"

"The player involved, Boonie Cooley? He's the sheriff's son."

"You're kidding. The sheriff's pressin' charges?"

"Yeah, but I never fucked him, though Lila Trulove did. I ought to ask her about that."

"And Murray's defending Royal."

"I'm gettin' bored, Rob. You're repeatin' yourself."

"Sorry, Arlanne."

"I can go home and listen to that. Bert repeats himself all the time. He's obsessive-compulsive, you know."

"No, I didn't. Where's the story now?"

"The whole town's up in arms."

"I'm not surprised."

"Me neither. With two broken legs, Boonie'll miss the entire season."

It's nice being a published journalist, thought Arlanne, placing the phone back on the hook. It connects me to the larger world, lubricates the social machinery, satisfying my 'insatiable' curiosity, as Rob referred to it. Rob told me it would do all that, and he was right. I wonder what made him boring in bed. I think he'd been up North too long, too long entombed in the cold and concrete, too far from nature, from stink and sweat and humidity, from the torrid and the tropical. Can you imagine Adam lusting after Eve in Iceland?

Or was it his 'insatiable' use of euphemisms? Rob was a great editor—look what he's done for me—but a self-professed boring writer, which he is. You know why I'm one of the best journalists around? Because I don't use euphemisms. I don't say journalism "connects me to the larger world, lubricates the social machinery, satisfying my curiosity." Rob's right, sure, but that's boring. Actually, it's a lie. All that, just to satisfy my "curiosity?" No, no no, Rob, all that to satisfy my lust for gossip.

And while I'm at it, Rob, yours.

"Curiosity?" Hardly the satisfaction of orgasm. Gossip, however, is visceral. It's something you can't do without. Something you don't merely want, but need. You lust, salivating and sweating and whoring for gossip. Curiosity? Why, I could make a scientist teetering on the edge of revelation—a sure-fire cure for cancer or heart disease or aging, something that would change the world—throw up his arms and say the hell with it all just by walkin' into his laboratory, casual and nonchalant as the slightest weather change, butt naked. Curiosity is something to be "peaked," to be "aroused"; satisfied, it can turn the world inside out, no question. Don't mean to give it short shrift. Gossip, however, gossip is the bull you'd charge through a barbed wire fence to get to—right here, right now—somethin', once you sniff it out, you just can't do without. Somethin' that'll turn you inside out.

Right here. Right now.

That's journalism: the right here and the right now.

The rest is for the ages.

Glancing in the hall mirror, she caught herself. Is my butt fallin'? she wondered. Right here? Right now? She slipped Bert's tee shirt, which is all she'd been wearing, over her head, draping it over the chair. She had to be certain.

Touching her butt now, she gave it a little jiggle.

Damn. Damn, damn, damn. This I never thought would happen. Not right here, not now. I'm getting fucking older. I don't give a damn how smart she is, if a woman loses her sex appeal, she loses her edge.

Poor Samson, he didn't stand a chance with Delilah. Read the Ancients: beauty makes putty of strength. But against an old and ugly Delilah? A Delilah with her butt fallin'?"

I've got to start exercising. Boring. Hell is exercising. Maybe I could masturbate while I'm doing it. Add a little spice to it. Heat it all up a bit.

She knew she had to get to work on the story for Rob. Right here, right now, before the morning got away from her. She slipped Bert's tee shirt back on, where it fell around mid-thigh.

Bert banged in, making all the noise in the world—sweating, breathing heavily—as he always did after jogging, just so the world would hear him and acknowledge his suffering, the suffering, he said, of the aging athlete.

"Were you really any good?" she asked him.

"Yeah," he said, "I was."

She knew he was. She just liked asking him.

"Do you think you might have a better chance of losin' some of that belly if you actually left the yard, headed down the driveway, on out into the neighborhood?"

"Fuck you."

"Would you like to?"

"Of course."

"Still?"

"Sure, why not?" he said, heading for the shower.

She had begun taking notes for her upcoming *Esquire* piece in her office, which consisted of the dining room table, when Bert walked in tucking in his shirt and buckling his belt. She loved her office. It was in the middle of everything where she could be easily distracted.

"You know what I honestly believe is my pet peeve?" she said, looking up, tucking her pencil behind her ear. With her new large, round secretarial glasses it was her new look, or at least would be for awhile, which she knew Bert found erotic.

Trying to work himself up for a momentary listening spell as he smoothed out the tuck in his shirt, Bert stopped everything when he looked up and saw her. "What?" he asked, but the question was pretty much automatic, on cruise control. Naturally, no surprise there. What he was alerted to, however, was the sudden stirring in his groin, which was momentarily frustrating because he had no time to do anything about it. Tuned out, but turned on.

"Vain women."

"Yeah?"

"God, do they piss me off. Worthless bitches."

"Yeah," he said, heading towards the kitchen, still on cruise control, for his orange juice. "I know exactly what you mean."

"Oh, what do I mean?"

"What you said."

"And exactly what did I say?"

"Look, Arlanne, if you can't remember what you said less than a minute ago, I'm not going to do it for you. Some things you have to do for yourself."

Masturbate, she thought. I can do that for myself. It sure beats writing this article.

"Get to work, Arlanne," Bert said on his way to the front door. Downing his orange juice, he left the empty glass on the dining room table, her office. "You're procrastinating."

"How do you know?"

"I pay attention."

"Yeah, but to what?"

"To what you don't want me to pay attention to, as you well know. As you also know, that's my nature, as well as coincidentally the nature of my profession. It drives you crazy, doesn't it?"

"Do you really consider psychology a profession?"

"Do you really want to know how I know?" he asked her, kissing her, grabbing up his briefcase, preparing to leave.

"Know what?"

"That you're procrastinating."

"I'm not," she lied.

"You'd rather fight than write."

“That’s so amateurish. I would have hoped for something a little more sophisticated.”

“Incidentally, Driver called. Apparently he’s got the same problem you got. Says the piece he’s doing on Boonie and the trial for the school paper is giving him hell. Wants to know what you have. Sorry, he called last night. Forgot to tell you.”

“Damn. I hate it when you forget like that.”

“See, I told you you’re looking for a fight. Just call Driver. You two can procrastinate together,” he said, heading out the door with the last word.

That man has the worst sense of humor, she thought, dialing Lila’s number. But you know what? Who else was goin’ to marry him? Somebody had to.

62

For Mary Beth, Jack, and Royal, It’s Watergate Versus Waterbed

Mary Beth McGowan was fascinated and compelled by the Watergate hearings. Prior to Jack’s retirement in ’72, she’d reduced her teaching load by half at the University of South Carolina in Somerset, and it was all she could do not to call the Dean and ask if she could drop her present load until after the hearings were over. Her compulsion, shared by many at the time, was reportedly responsible for the run on portable television sets at Jones Appliances, to say nothing of the improbable upsurge in the study of Current Events in the Somerset County Schools. Spanking new Zenith and RCA portables perched alongside cash registers in downtown shops as well as on the desks of every history and social studies teacher in the Somerset County Schools.

She even sat through ‘The Man from Glad’ commercial, over and over, even if she had to pee, just so she wouldn’t miss John Dean’s testimony. John Dean had been the president’s lawyer, and in a calm, deliberate manner, as if the quality of one’s professionalism were determined solely by decorum and demeanor rather than substance and integrity, he was spilling the beans and tattle-tailing on all of the President’s men for their cover-up of the Watergate break-in, a cover-up naturally designed and engineered by Dean himself. Icky, thought Mary Beth. Nixon's men had characterized Dean as a weasel, and he truly was, all oily and unctuous. Were he a soldier—say, a prisoner-of-war—he'd gladly offer up to his interrogators every secret he knew, no matter how many lives it cost, to save his own ass. Were he involved in a bank robbery, manning the getaway vehicle while his buddies risked their lives holding tellers at gunpoint and he saw the cops approaching, guns at the ready, he would without qualms open the car door, hands upraised, and stroll over their way, magnanimously offering in scrupulous detail the nature of the robbery, who was participating, their tendencies and proclivities when discovered, and so forth. To win, Dean's behavior seemed to indicate, all you have to do is change sides. How incredibly simple, thought Mary Beth. Plus, she didn't want to miss his gorgeous wife, martyred in silence, sitting behind him. To be that lovely, and that loyal . . . Beautiful women, she surmised, were rarely so loyal, unless they were needy, afraid of losing what they had, but Maureen Dean was standing by her man, everyday, all day, throughout his testimony, simply by sitting behind him. Mary Beth couldn't help but wonder if Maureen had grown up poor, and more importantly, what kind of peroxide she was using.

Was she obsessed? Jack had tried to get her to be a bit more accommodating to Royal, but she couldn't, she had told him. She had to be available, she explained, for the hearings. Just as Royal, she interjected—not without some bitterness that surprised both of them—had to be available to Murray preparing him for his upcoming trial. Still, she had felt bad about it. What was wrong with doing it during the commercials? She'd asked Jack. He can tell your mind's elsewhere, said Jack, glancing sheepishly toward the T.V. Oh, she'd said.

She did leave her food sitting there on the sofa a lot, uneaten. She also realized she was losing weight, even though Jack was constantly bringing her different foods, urging her on. And though she'd always been something of a neat freak, dirty dishes and laundry would pile a mile high if it weren't for Royal doing it all. He was such a sweetheart, never complained. Great in bed. That was probably, she figured, because he was a war hero. Plus, since he retired from the Corps—about when Jack did, if she remembered correctly—he separates by color and texture. What more could you want from a man? Jack adores him. She adored him. Jamie Mac adores him. And this after living together for quite awhile.

There was a new magazine out on the stands called *People*, with Mia Farrow, the star of *Rosemary's Baby* on the cover, a movie which she had seen with Jack and Royal Cunningham. Satan, hardly an intimate of Rosemary's, nevertheless abducts her late one night, as only he can, and slips it to her; hence, the Devil's offspring. After the movie, while the credits were rolling, they'd just sat there, transfixed, remaining in their seats long after everyone else had left. *Rosemary's Baby* had thrilled and terrified her, she told them, though it made her hesitant about having babies with strangers.

Royal had equated the impregnation of Rosemary with Satan's child with the impregnation of the American citizenry with the Vietnam war. Of course, as Mary Beth pointed out, he equated everything with the war. Jack said matter-of-factly that he himself was the Devil's child, his mother having been impregnated by Frank the Father. At least you know it, said Royal. Most people don't. You know it, said Jack. Yeah, too late, said Royal. Me too, said Jack.

"Never too late," said Mary Beth, "to stop the killing." She'd read *Lord of the Flies*. "When everybody knows," she said, "that's what'll stop the killing."

They both turned and looked at her. The lights were on. The screen was blank. "Do you know?" they asked her.

"I don't know," she said.

"Know what, exactly?" asked Royal.

"Yeah," said Jack. "What are you talking about?"

"That the Devil," she said, "is us. All of us. So Simon says."

"Who's Simon?" Jack asked.

"The angel in *Lord of the Flies*."

"What makes him an angel?"

"The same thing that makes you one," she said, hooking her arms in theirs, drawing them close. "He knows."

In any case, Jack had bought the magazine with Mia's picture on the cover as soon as he noticed it on the stand in Luther's Drug Store, laying it on the coffee table in front of the television set in the living room where she couldn't help but see it. Anything that might divert her from her addiction to the hearings. He and Royal were both worried about her. Any addiction worried them, but this one was particularly sick, like gawking forever, mouth agape, Jack felt, at the gory details of an automobile accident. Of course, half the country was probably addicted, Royal pointed out, or the networks wouldn't be showing the hearings all day. Pure pornography, felt Jack, though he had some difficulty articulating that. To Royal the witnesses testifying in the Hearings seemed lethally bland, bureaucratically boring, personally unappealing, so like the technocrats who ran the Vietnam war. "Devils in disguise," he announced.

"The same ones," said Jack.

"Like Roger—the sadistic executioner in *Lord of the Flies* 'possessed of an inner intensity of avoidance and secrecy'—Nixon's men have much to hide," said Mary Beth. "Don't you want to know what?"

"We already know," said Royal. "We know."

"But I don't," she said, "which is probably why I'm interested."

"Haven't you read any other books?" asked Jack, but she knew what he really meant: can't you watch something other than the hearings?

People magazine lay on the table, untouched by feminine hands, until after the hearings.

Royal and Jack even hired a young stud to streak naked, that being the current craze, through the living room, a preening young fellow from over at the base. Then when that didn't work they realized they better send him to Bert just to shore up his self-esteem.

Unfortunately, Bert remained unavailable.

Answering machines had just come on the market. Jack had seen them advertised in *Life* magazine. Phoning Bert, he heard Arlanne's voice, and after a futile attempt to make conversation he realized it must be coming from one of those answering machines. Why would anyone want one, he'd wondered at the time. Seemed superfluous. If nobody answers, nobody's home. Seemed obvious to Jack anyway. Out of habit when telling Royal or Mary Beth who was on the line, he put his hand over the mouthpiece. "Royal," he whispered. "It's an answering machine. Hey, I wonder who installed it. Bert's Jewish."

Had to have been Arlanne, figured Royal. Either that, or he hired somebody. Hell, I hope not. I'd have done it for him for nothing. He should know that.

The dial tone returned, so Jack redialed, holding the phone out, where Royal could hear. After all, this was a new experience for them. He didn't want Royal to miss it. Arlanne's voice came on again.

"This is Arlanne. I'm watching the Watergate hearings. Please leave a message, and I'll call you back after Nixon resigns."

"Arlanne's addicted too," Jack whispered, again out of habit, Royal supposed.

"If you're calling for Dr. Levy, please leave your number. Only, however, if you are either homicidal or suicidal, since Dr. Levy is presently out of town and will remain so until the Watergate hearings are over."

"You'd think a psychologist might have a better handle on themselves. Bert? Addicted?"

"It happens like that sometimes," said Royal. "Did you ever see Lee Remick and Jack Lemmon in *The Days of Wine and Roses*?"

"Yeah," said Jack, "I remember that."

But he hadn't. Sensing a stirring in his groin, he'd just wanted to impress Royal. Royal's sharing of novel experiences did that to him.

In any case, they gave up on curing Mary Beth, repairing to the bedroom, which all three shared, one big king-size waterbed.

Free love, thought Mary Beth on the sofa in the living room, a pain in the ass once you get bored, but a blessing when the men need occupying.

Her eyes seemingly at one with the television screen, entranced, in an "altered state," Jack had put it, she was lost in the characters, couldn't get enough of them. Haldeman's arrogance, Ehrlichman's contempt—how long could anybody, Ehrlichman included, sustain such a petulant expression —the terrorist Liddy, the suave Mcgruder playing the role of the choir boy caught up in the wrong crowd. The greatest show on earth, however, hands down: the garrulous, sprawling Senator Sam Ervin, his tinny abrasive Southern accent hanging out there like a hairy ol' pot belly for all the world to see, the head of the Senate Investigating Committee who clearly didn't believe a damn word anyone was saying vs. the smooth, clearly patronizing Attorney General, Nixon's right hand man, John Mitchell. Mitchell was a man of such assured intellectual confidence that much of the time in front of the Committee he just sat there calmly and quietly listening attentively, puffing on his pipe, as many of the senators pompously prattled away their time, occasionally offering his legal expertise in the repairing and construction of their questions to make them more pointed and precise, for which the stupid sons of bitches, marveled Mary Beth, never failed to express gratitude. With Senator Ervin, however, taking his turn at questioning him, it was mano-a-mano, the senator firing shot after shot over the bow of his ship, the Attorney General doing his best to stay afloat.

And Mitchell's wife Martha, drunk as a skunk and talking up a storm all over town! Calling up reporters in the middle of the night! Telling everything! Boy, thought Mary Beth, she must be really pissed off. And he cool as a Brooks Brothers suit on the steps of the Capital responding to those same reporters with little more than what appeared to be the bemusement of the avuncular father tolerating a wayward teenager going through a phase.

Ah, how the mighty fall.

Let Royal and Jack enjoy themselves in the bedroom, she thought when the Man from Glad came back on. It was nice for Jack. And when the hearings were over and Nixon either resigned or was impeached, then she'd go back to getting it on with Royal. She might even screw Murray. He was interesting. She also liked that little waitress at the No View. Tough little gal. No nonsense. Be fun to make her weep. Then Mary Beth could be all solicitous and tender with her, like Royal is with Jack. That's a beautiful thing to see. Bert says Royal's the father Jack should have had. Without the sex, he hastened to add. The tenderness, however, is great for Jack. He looks like a new man. And he's been wonderful with Jamie Mac, who seems to engage him more and more. Jamie Mac's doing well in school again, thank God. Ever since Royal moved in. He loves Royal.

Royal's a real man. Jesus, he can make you pant. But I can't help it. I'm only willing to screw him during the commercials. And even then, it's got to be a quickie. I know Jack asked me to be a little more considerate with Royal, but I just can't help it. Jack's right: one eye's on sex, the other's on the tube, just so I don't miss anything. Royal says he understands. There's worse things, he said, like killing people.

Hard to disagree with that.

63

A Renewed Mary Beth Takes to Dusting and Cleaning the Dusted and Clean

The morning after Nixon resigned, after his televised speech to the cabinet and the White House staff in which he reminded the country that those who have never been to the valley never make it to the mountaintop—his way, figured Mary Beth, of saying "I'll be back"—after giving the country his neckless victory sign before turning and entering Air Force One and heading off to San Clemente forever, Mary Beth felt renewed, as if her life was just beginning. The mighty had fallen, and she had seen them fall on television, and it had been real. A conquest, she felt, had been made. The senator from North Carolina had won. Martyrs—Attorney Generals Archibald Cox and Elliot Richardson—had been made. Rats had come out of the woodwork, thugs had invaded it, snoops had been caught in it. Criminals, those high and those low, had been jailed. For awhile at least, the country would be more careful, more caring, until they forgot, as history showed they would.

Nixon himself had provided the catharsis and the release. His foul language and anti-Semitic comments on the Watergate tapes both villainized and humanized him, arousing in her, if not the nation, the lust of a lynch mob, and his tears the day of his resignation orgiastic release. Satisfied, if not satiated, the country relaxed, took a deep breath, stretched, yawned, and reflected, breathing easier.

Anyway, that was her take on it. Sure, Democrats gloated, Republicans wept, but all had gone through an experience so complex and powerful that it dwarfed the narrowly proscribed, necessarily limited political point of view of the individual citizen. For the first time in history, through the miracle of television, the citizenry had actually witnessed, seen, in color, not just in some movie, but in reality, the mighty tumble off the precipice into the everyday ordinary of the average. The citizenry had experienced, in color, the underlying theory of democracy: that power corrupts, that like Jefferson said, it is not to be trusted and must be vigilantly checked. They had seen that what makes a man breaks a man, and how.

What more, she thought, could one want from a country! Wow, what a show. She felt clean, refreshed, energized, and found herself humming as she worked.

She opened all the windows and shutters, letting in the early morning river breeze. She loved what she called their "fishing shack," their three-bedroom bungalow. They'd pooled their money and bought it for a song—so much land, so few people on most of these islands—almost a decade ago. Out here on faraway Scataway Island they were so isolated that in the summer they spent much of their day lazing around, fishing, cleaning, and cooking naked. They were brown and golden, she and Royal, though she was having to work now to keep herself that way. Jack looked older, gentler, even smaller somehow than he used to. He didn't eat much. Later in the day even the river breeze would blow hot.

Royal was in the shower, soaping up, singing like a diva. He had a beautiful voice until he stepped out. The sound of Royal running the shower in the mornings was once again reassuring for her. Later this afternoon, after meeting with Murray in preparation for his trial, he'd check the crab pots. Even if he had to go to jail, she imagined that it wouldn't be right away. Royal's stubbornness—his refusal to plead self-defense—had sure created a conundrum for Murray. She'd sensed Murray's anxiety, and his anxiety had deterred her desire for Bert, refocusing it on Murray. A man's anxiety held for her more sexual sway than obsessiveness or for that matter, depression. Obsessiveness either obscured to the point of impenetrability, making one more and more difficult to see, or it was so blatantly, overwhelmingly penetrating that it split the apple at the very core; either way, in the final analysis, too little synthesis, too one-sided, not much opportunity for simultaneous orgasm. Depression, she felt, as in Jack's, called for a hug, for snuggling and coddling and babying, for soothing; slamming away at it, however, was like trying to make yourself at home in an unfurnished room. Anxiety? Anxiety screamed for the grand slam, and the grand slam would send it right out of the park.

Was it Murray's anxiety, however, making her horny, or her own? Nixon's resignation, was it leaving her vulnerable. She disliked being vulnerable. That's why she was a caretaker, an enabler even, if she had to be.

Through the window she liked to watch, as she was now, Jack standing on the dock, naked, gazing out toward the river. It was peaceful, he had told her, calming, the river a reminder of who he was, of what he was capable of, of the sin and crime he'd committed. On the dock, he had said, fear went on furlough: here he knew who he was. No pretense, she thought to herself, no denial. As diabolical as he felt himself to be, there he found God. Peace. Mary Beth wondered, were they the same?

Jack wouldn't go in the water. There the Devil would have too much sway over him, too much power. To completely surrender, felt Jack, was either suicidal or homicidal. Once he entered, Satan, he feared, would never let him leave. He just couldn't do it. When you can enter the water, Royal told him, in time, you'll find an even greater peace, a more loving God. It had happened to him, he told them, when he re-visited Vietnam on a Peace Now mission, where he visited what he had destroyed and apologized to the remaining inhabitants.

Still, he had admitted, he could not ask for forgiveness because he was afraid to forgive himself.

"A greater, more loving God," Jack said, "awaits you when you do?"

"You're right," said Royal. "Easier said than done, my friend."

Which is why you're causing Murray such a problem, she thought to herself at the time. And me and Jack, and if you end up in jail, Jamie, she thought now, turning thoughtlessly toward the television set.

But the Watergate hearings were over, so immediately she started dry-dusting the living room furniture.

Why not? she told herself. It needed it.

After which, she told herself, all the furniture in the house needed it.

After which she applied furniture polish.

After which she failed to notice that the furniture generally looked no different than it had before she began since Jack had carefully dusted and polished all of it only two days before while she was fixated on the Watergate hearings.

After which, later that afternoon, she'd swept the floor with such ferocity and intensity that Jack and Royal thought it best not to mention that that had been done only two days before too.

| 64 |

Somerset Converges on the Trial of Royal Cunningham

On the morning of the first day of the trial, after his ritual morning shower and his serenading of the island, Royal entered the living room, all flushed and excited, busily smoothing out his skirt and touching up his wig and rearranging his Uncle Sam pillbox hat replete with stars and stripes. Mary Beth lit up a Pall Mall, eyeing him warily.

Because he hadn't, as he'd admitted—forgiven himself—wondered Mary Beth, did he want to go to jail? To seek penance for that faraway crime for which he'd never been punished? William Calley was guilty, he would say. But so was I. So were hundreds of soldiers. How come he gets punished and I can't get the time of day? Because, Jack had told him, since Calley the Pentagon's discovered there are so many of you. Calley's the stalking horse, the scapegoat. He's perfect for it, no heroic bone in his body, probably a coward. The government would have to put half the Corps on trial. They'd have to re-try the war all over again. Besides, you think they're going to try and convict a war hero? War heroes are their claim to the little bit of fame they have left. Jesus, if you're guilty, they are, of crimes against humanity at the highest levels. What do you think the high brass and the Pentagon mean when they argue against reopening old wounds? We're out now. That's their take on it. It's over. We're out, Royal had answered, so it's over for us. Exactly, said Jack. Exactly. That's what they're thinking. And if they put you on trial, believe me, it ain't over for them, and they know it. It's peculiar, Man: Calley's a scapegoat, but in your own way, so are you. I understand, Royal. I understand. I know you do, Jack. I know you do. Maybe that's all anybody can hope for.

Royal looked really cute, she realized. She knew it had been hard for him to drop the silly feathers in the hat and the simply outrageous boa, but now at least everything went together: the Uncle Sam pillbox hat; the white midi blouse with the requisite large white collar and red tie, a waistband of white stars against a navy background, a pleated linen dress with vertical red and white stripes running all the way down; his navy and white pocketbook and saddle-oxford Keds continuing the theme, themselves coexisting in perfect harmony, which is more than she could say for the United States and the Soviet Union. He adjusted his white panty hose, which he complained were crawling up his butt.

Ready now, striking for her approval his most feminine pose, he awaited her verdict.

"Well," she said, "you certainly bring out the queer in me. Why not just plead self-defense, Miss America, avoid a trial and let's screw?"

"Oh, Sweetheart, stop now. Behave. Miss America's going out, can't afford to get all wrinkled."

"You're funnier as a woman." And then she realized, "but humorless as a man."

"As a man, Darling, I'm so astonishingly handsome I can afford to be humorless. Let others do the work, I say. Well?"

"You look pretty," she said. "I already told you."

"Darling, can't a girl be insecure?"

Mary Beth wasn't listening now, she stared out the window at Jack naked on the dock without seeing him. She'd end up like this every time the issue of Royal's defense came up, which she injected into the conversation—at least after the Watergate hearings were over—the closer it came time for the trial.

She grabbed a Kleenex from her pocketbook on the coffee table. "Here," she said, dabbing needlessly at his cheeks, "your makeup's too vivid, too much eyeliner."

"Darling, I'm vivid."

" . . . and your bust is uneven. Here . . ."

She tried not to, but she was fussing. He knew, however, what she was really fussing about.

"Whatever happens to me," he said to her gently, "is what I want to happen to me."

"I don't care," she said, looking away. She could see Jack now, naked on the dock. "It's not what I want, and it's not what Jack wants."

"Jack understands."

"Maybe he should have a little less understanding. Go on out there and tell him to put his clothes on. Unless he's going to the courthouse naked. Go on. We're going to be late."

"Mary Beth—"

"Go, Goddammit it!"

"I'm going, I'm going. Jack!" he yelled, bustling out the door, "Hurry! She's pissed!"

Jack hustled in, doing his best to avoid Mary Beth, who just stood there, steaming.

Royal waited outside, by the car, where it was safer.

"You selfish son of a bitch!" she yelled at him through the open window. "You humorless, self-righteous bastard! You—" She grabbed up everything she could and started throwing it through the window at him: a water glass, sofa cushions, figurines, ash trays, vases of flowers. She was trying to get the rocker through the window when he ducked behind the car, peeking over the top.

"Driver," asked Lila, "is Arlanne still helping you with your article? Go with her. Watch her. She'll be there. After all, the Watergate hearings are over. Nixon's gettin' drunk in San Clemente. Damn this heat. Do you remember when you and Boonie were little, y'all used to play together? Must've been what, 12, 13 years ago?"

"I remember kicking his ass."

"That was then, honey. Wouldn't try it now."

"You think I'm crazy?"

"You know why you kicked his ass?"

"No, why did I? I can't remember."

"You never knew, did you? I'm sure, without even realizing why, he goaded you into it."

Driver looked up from the Style section of the *News and Courier*, his orange juice and toast in front of him. "Really? Why would he do that?"

"Things were different then, Driver. Everything was segregated. Remember?"

"Mom! Of course I remember."

"After a certain age something has to happen, or at least back then it did. You were just little kids, poor things, innocent as lambs. Lord, y'all had fun together. I'm sure his momma said something to him, like he was too old to be playin' with niggers, that it didn't look good, that sort of thing. Probably made him ashamed. I worried about you after that."

"So he picked a fight, without even knowing why?"

"Mommas are a strong influence, honey."

"You can say that again," he said, kissing her on the cheek, grabbing up his notepad, and heading out the door.

"Talk to Arlanne!" Lila yelled behind him.

"She's meeting me at the court house, Mom. Stay out of it! I can handle it!"

Bert walked through the courthouse towards the anteroom in the back to check on Murray. Ceiling fans hummed, clanged and rattled, circulating through the open shutters and windows the aroma of freshly mowed lawns—which somehow made him think of fresh milk on your doorstep—and the odor of marsh gas on the river breeze, which made him think of sour milk left out too long on the kitchen counter. The windows were enormous, almost floor to ceiling, and in contrast to routine courthouse business, scenes of the outdoors, innocent and guiltless, were a welcome diversion for the troubled eye. Sunlight splayed on little kids playing capture the flag on the courthouse lawn, on the lawn itself, on the judge's Lincoln Continental parked in the RESERVED space, among the spray of leaves and on the drippings of Spanish moss on the great oaks dwarfing the riverbank, turning the river a blinding dazzling blue.

Teenagers on skis walked on water; motorboats swerved, only to circle back around and pick them up after they fell, treading water. Marty Liebowitz's daughter, a cheerleader—blonde and assimilated through the miracle of peroxide and plastic surgery—slalomed with the confidence of a pro, her boyfriend driving the boat while downing Budwiesers with his buddy, Jimmy Dawes, the quarterback on the football team. The leading men of the town, still all white when gathering informally, Marty Liebowitz, Bradford Palmer, the mayor—the breakfast group, in other words, at the No View, the golf group at the Country Club—passed the time as always before a trial in the shade of the same great oak, their room on the riverbank (or so Arlanne referred to it), until time for the trial to begin. Before disappearing into the anteroom Bert noted through the windows Hoke Cooley's absence from the group, but he also noted Driver and Arlanne approaching them with their notepads, creating, Arlanne would later write on her pad, an "unctuous dispersal."

Driver wrote in his notepad: "They segregated themselves with all deliberate speed."

Bert had never seen Murray so anxious, his eyes bloodshot, tension reigning over his forehead, his fingers drumming the conference table as if it were a keyboard to which he was oblivious. It titillated and comforted Bert. With anxiety he felt right at home, back in New York, among his own kind. Real men in the South, strong silent types named Will and Bob and Butch and Bill who always knew where the fuse box was, took life as it came and never broke stride tough times or otherwise, made him feel like a girl, if you want to know the truth. The South had caught up with him. A lot of Jews, he knew, would find such a thought disgusting if not traitorous. But there it was. Besides, what could he do about it? Anyway, back to the anteroom, where concern was actually germinating. "This goes beyond the cultural imperative," he told Murray, who understood exactly what he meant, even if nobody else would. "You okay?"

"Yeah," Murray said. But he looked as though he was all hyped up on caffeine, or amphetamines, even though he wasn't. "Haven't slept since the hearing."

Outside the courthouse, Arlanne instructed Driver: "Go find Boonie, he'll be hangin' around the anteroom across the hall from Murray and Royal. Sidle up to him. Tell him the school paper's backing him all the way. Ask him what you can do to help him, to promote his case. Tell him what happened to him just wasn't right. Tell him the whole school was upset. 'Who wants fags beating up on football players?' That kind of thing. Sympathize totally with his point of view, with what he must be going through. The season's over for him now, Goddammit, before it even begins, and that's really frustrating for you. With him on the field, the Tidal Wave would've rolled over every team dumb enough to stand its ground. Without him, no Lower State Championship, and this, your senior season . . . Work up a few tears here."

"Arlanne. The Tidal Wave 'rolling over' everybody? That is so fifties. And do you think I care a whit about the 'Lower State Championship?'"

"Fine, and who cares whether you care? You're not the story. He is. So use whatever stupid-ass lingo you silly teenagers use nowadays. But let him know it really pisses you off personally, gets you all worked up. Tell him you're on his side. Empathize: as an aside, drop that you sure wouldn't want anybody doing that to you."

"I'm not on his side. He's a brute."

She shrugged. "Yes? And? Your point?"

"You want me to lie to him?"

"Sure, if it helps get the truth out. Naturally. Otherwise, the story's a lie, to say nothing of the trial."

"'Thou Shall Not Lie?'"

"Ah, you haven't read the latest King James version. Or if you have, you apparently missed the footnote. 'Thou Shall Not Lie . . . Except In The Service Of Truth.'"

"You are so full of it. You really want me to lie? Sounds pretty interesting, actually. I can tell Mom I have 'Adult Permission.'"

"She wants you to lie. She told me that."

"God, you are such a liar. So if I lie, I can become a famous journalist like you?"

"Well . . ."

"God, you are so conceited!"

"Then, Driver, when you've got his confidence, when he can't wait to tell you everything, when he knows you're truly on his side, his new best friend, the one person he can truly talk to, who truly understands him, you look at him with every ounce of cynicism you can muster, and you blow his cover. To find what you want, he's got to lose it, big time."

"And what exactly do I say to make him 'lose it?'"

"'You're a pretty big fellow, Boonie,' you say to him. 'A jock. Big time football player . . .'"

"Okay . . ."

"'How does it feel to get your ass whipped by a fag?'"

"Oh my God . . . Oh my God!"

As she sent Driver on his way, she couldn't help but wonder if she also should have had him ask himself a question, as long as they were on the topic: "Am I a fag?"

Right before the trial began, Regina Cooley caught up with Bert, stopping him in the corridor as he was leaving the anteroom with Murray, the McGowans, and Royal Cunningham, the latter a vision of America in drag. Months ago at the hearing, the shock of Captain Cunningham cavorting about in feathers, a boa and fishnet stockings had induced in Regina a brief fainting spell, from which she revived herself (she felt at the time) with fierce Christian love. Today's vision was no less intoxicating, and as she waited patiently for Murray, the McGowans and the man playing dress-up to continue down the corridor so she could talk privately with Bert, she silently prayed to the Lord for that same fierce Christian love to spare her the embarrassment of another fainting spell.

Thank you Lord. Thank you for loving me with fierce Christian love, prayed Regina, so that I may Love Thy Neighbor, no matter how repulsive he is. Sure enough, fierce Christian love once again saved the day. It also helped that Royal, with the remainder of his party, had disappeared into the courtroom.

Smoke wafted into the corridor through the open door of the empty anteroom, curling up from a lipstick-stained cigarette butt in the ashtray on the conference table.

"Dr. Levy, my name is Regina Cooley. I wonder if I might have a word with you."

"Of course, Regina, but could it wait? The trial—"

"I'll be brief, Dr. Levy."

"Sure, we can talk in here," he said, referring to the empty anteroom, ushering her through the door. "They're through in here. Would you like to sit down?"

"No, thank you. Dr. Levy, I know who you are, and I know what you did for me. I know you helped Hoke after my . . . collapse, I guess you'd call it. Oh God, I'm tired of pretense. My suicide attempt. No, no, no, please don't say anything. Please. I'm afraid my family once again needs your help. I just cannot let an innocent man or woman or whatever he is be punished for something my son's guilty of."

"Assault and Battery?"

"I know Boonie's supposed to be a big football player and all, and I really do believe that he's convinced himself he's telling the truth. God knows in my family that's an easy thing to do. But God knows the Ttuth, and God punishes those who lie whether they know it or not. I just can't let Boonie do this to himself."

"What is the truth?"

"That man no more jumped Boonie outside that bar than the man in the moon did."

"Captain Cunningham admitted breaking Boonie's legs."

"That ain't who done it. Certainly that ain't who Boonie saw doing it."

"Who'd he see?"

"My daddy."

"Oh," Bert said.

"I thought you might understand what I'm saying. I don't doubt the rumors are true. I know boys will be boys and they engage in that kind of thing, though they have no right to beat up any of God's children and steal their money. Of course I know all that's hush hush and all as far as the court's concerned, but I don't really think that's what Boonie was doing . . . no, it wasn't what he was doing, I know that. It's what he thought he was doing . . ."

"Captain Cunningham offers to buy Boonie a drink—"

"—Not knowing he's underage—"

"Right. Boonie thinks Captain Cunningham's trying to put a move on him, if you'll pardon the expression. Boonie resists, Captain Cunningham drags him outside in the back and beats him up. That's Boonie's story anyway."

"Oh, for God's sakes, no one believes that. They all think my Boonie lured him out back of that bar so he could beat him up and take his money. A lot of the boys do that, what do they call it—"

"Rolling queers—"

"—but none of 'em get both legs broken. Boonie didn't take him out there to beat him up and steal his money, I don't care what he tells his friends in secret, that's just braggin'. Maybe he thought that's what he was going to do. I know him, Dr. Levy. Inside, he's too sweet natured for that. I know it. I don't know who that mean-as-heck boy is out there on that football field, but that ain't Boonie on the inside. I know it, and God knows it. No, he got that man to go out back with him, I know that in my heart, and I know it's bad, but not as bad as keepin' it hidden' and livin' a lie and watchin' a good man go to jail because of it. Boonie wanted love, Dr. Levy, in the way those people do, you know who I'm talkin' about, and when that love was shown to him he was just like me he couldn't see nothin' but my daddy. And then he got scared and all he could see was the Devil and he just went crazy tryin' to beat it out of him just like I did when I tried to cut him out of me forever but you can't do that, Dr. Levy, I know you know that, you can't do that, can you, you just can't do that, no."

Was Regina projecting her father's abuse of her, or at least her fear of it, onto her child? *Had* her father abused Boonie? That would not be surprising. Was Boonie one of "those people," a homosexual, as she was suggesting? Was he just sexually confused? Who wouldn't be in her family? *Bert* was confused. "Hoke's view of this, Regina," he said helplessly, "it's so different."

"See no evil, hear no evil, speak no evil, not when it comes to Boonie. Same way Hoke saw me. If you live in the sheriff's house, you can get away with anything. If you don't . . ."

"The cobbler's son wears no shoes."

"Hoke's the one who wanted this trial, you know. Squelch rumors, show the town we're a good Christian family, I don't know. You know, when I think about it, Hoke knows. Deep down, I believe he knows what Boonie is."

"So the trial's to prove who he's not?"

"I don't want to hurt Hoke, but I told myself I'd never look the other way again. In his own way, Boonie tried to kill himself that night, just like I did. Whatever he is, he's still one of God's children, and I just can't let him do that to himself. I tell you, Dr. Levy, and I know you know I'm telling you God's truth: It was my daddy Boonie saw that night, it was my daddy. Ain't no lawyer goin' to get that out of him, but you can, Dr. Levy. You can."

| 65 |

Lila Appears to be Violating a Corpse in Room 27

Lila Trulove swerved, screeching to a halt in AMBULANCE PARKING ONLY, jumped out of her Bonneville leaving the driver's door wide open, the key in the ignition, and one sandal on the walkway in front of the Emergency Room, running as fast as she could, bursting through the doors, straight up to Nurse Lane Thelma Dee's desk.

"Where's my boy, Thelma. Tell me where he is. Now."

"Why hey, Lila, how you been. Look, it turned out—"

"Now."

She was trying to say, It turned out to be less an "emergency" (as she had characterized it to Lila on the phone) than was originally thought, that Driver had looked much worse than he was, but before she could get the words out Lila said, "Goddammit!" And the phone rang.

"Room thirty-seven," said Nurse Lane Thelma to Lila, picking up the phone, her hand over the mouthpiece. "Right up the hall on your left."

Had Lila hesitated, she would've heard Nurse Lane Thelma Dee saying on the phone, "Why, hey, Hoke . . . No, nothin' broken. Battered and bruised . . . major swelling. Looks ugly, but he looks much worse than he is. No, no, no in a month or so he'll be good as new . . . that's right . . . in time for college? You mean by September? . . . Oh, absolutely . . . Driver's goin' to Harvard? Niggers can't go to Harvard, Hoke, everybody knows that . . . Well shut my mouth and throw in a fry . . . Absolutely, good as new in a month or so . . . No, that's not my diagnosis, Hoke, that's Doc talkin' . . . Hoke, I'm startin' to repeat myself here, and if I'm not mistaken, it's because you are . . . One more time? . . . Okay, now listen carefully, 'cause I'm about to say this in italics: In a month or so, Driver Trulove will be fine. So saith Doc."

Lila, however, hadn't hesitated, not for a millisecond. Before Nurse Lane Thelma Dee had even lifted her hand from the mouthpiece, Lila'd darted up the hall straight into room twenty-seven where the matronly nurse had only minutes earlier placed a sheet over the body of an elderly cancer patient who had just died. The matronly nurse was new on the job, from Charleston, where she was known for her sweet disposition and for not having an unkind word to say about a single soul. Now she was at the Nurses' Station phoning the deceased's family, hoping to catch them before they left the house for their daily morning visit so they wouldn't be surprised. Lila, of course, had no idea where the nurse was. All she saw was an empty room with a sheet pulled up over a dead body which she jumped on, hugging and kissing it and crying and screaming and wailing, "Driver, Driver, Driver, oh honey, oh baby, oh sweetie, Mommy's here she loves you so much, oh God, oh God, why you do this Goddamn you . . . Oh God . . ."

When the nurse returned she saw a black woman she'd never seen before jumping up and down on the sheet-covered body hugging and kissing it and sayin' all these sweet things to it. "Oh honey baby . . . Oh . . ."

The nurse stood in the doorway, stupefied.

She couldn't move.

Get yourself together, woman, a voice whispered in her ear. She recognized it quickly as her own. You're a professional. Show it.

With the little bit of strength she could muster she turned, horrified, from the black lady going crazy on top of the corpse, hugging it, squeezing it—just about violatin' it, tell the truth now—making her way out of the room. Lord knows what that nigger's doin' to that poor dead man right now, she thought once in the corridor, and guilt sent her flying straight down the hallway crashing hysterically into the nurse's desk, where Nurse Thelma was recording the details of the deceased's demise.

Nurse Thelma heard the crash, papers went flying, and down below she saw the matronly nurse struggling hysterically to get up only to plop back down again, her legs wide open, unable to speak. Nurse Thelma regarded the matronly nurse's wide-open legs not only as distasteful and unfeminine, but downright disgusting. The unsightly spectacle, however, did not deter Nurse Thelma from her duty.

Nurse Thelma knew in such situations, when a person was trying to speak but couldn't, to look closely at her trying to mouth the words, since if you wanted to know what she was trying to tell you, that was the only way left to find out. When a person is unable to speak, concluded Nurse Thelma, listening is not an option.

So she bent down and looked closely at Nurse Linda mouthing words. (Linda was her name, Nurse Thelma knew all the nurses' names.). Pervert? Is that what Nurse Linda's saying? Pervert? Well . . . I believe it is. Nurse Linda kept pointing vigorously down the hallway, her eyes never leaving

Nurse Thelma's. But Nurse Thelma couldn't make out what she was saying. Was Nurse Linda trying to give her a room number? "Where, honey? Slow down now. Where is this pervert? You just tell Nurse Thelma where he is . . ."

Nurse Linda shook her head, silently saying No, No, No. SHE, Nurse Linda mouthed. SHE.

Then she began pointing again, clearly now mouthing a number. Nurse Thelma got it—ROOM TWENTY-SEVEN—and shot up the hallway.

In the doorway of room twenty-seven, Nurse Thelma contented herself with watching Lila screaming and wailing and covering a corpse with hugs and kisses and praying for a Resurrection. Finally, Thelma walked over to the bedside.

Lila stopped when she noticed Thelma standing there. On all fours over the corpse, with a sandal clearly missing, Lila looked up at her imploringly.

"Thirty-seven," said Nurse Lane Thelma Dee, "Room thirty-seven."

| 66 |

Royal Touches Up His Makeup While Boonie Goes Bananas

The courtroom was filling up with the usual crowd: cops standing about looking bored, a few stray spectators, the "regulars" (mostly elderly retirees), several pre-law students armed with composition books from the University Extension, a reporter from the *Somerset Weekly* (who happened to be the editor's son-in-law), the mayor, Arlanne's daddy, their cohorts from the No View and the Country Club as well as a few of Hoke's less distinguished hunting buddies—Ledbetter Greene in street clothes—several members of the town council, two veterans (old friends of Jack's and Royal's, both, thought Arlanne, homosexuals; either that, or they should be), Lila Trulove, and Arlanne noted, wincing, a banged up bandaged from head-to-foot Driver with a black eye so swollen it looked slammed shut. His head bandage looked like a convoluted turban. She waved to Lila apologetically. Lila, with no thought of discretion, shot her the bird. Driver did have his notepad and pen, but his right hand, his writing hand, was all swollen and bandaged up, so he was doing his best to take notes with his left hand and his good eye.

Arlanne turned her thoughts to a less unpleasant subject, one more favorable to her, noting with relief the absence of out-of-town journalists, particularly from *Harper's, Atlantic Monthly,* and *Playboy*: *Esquire*'s story, and *Esquire*'s alone; Rob'll be pleased.

Murray was gathering together his papers, perusing a few as he did so, while the defendant, Captain Royal Cunningham, was sitting beside him at the defense table, posing for the *Somerset Weekly's* photographer, patting and touching up his wig, showing his best profile, periodically checking his makeup and lipstick in the tiny gold compact mirror from his pocketbook.

Arlanne noted that no one was sitting at the prosecution's table.

Immediately she headed for the prosecution's anteroom, signaling for Driver to follow her. Driver stumbled along behind her, bumping into pews, railings, walls, the few people still standing about in the aisles and, most painfully, the corner of the defense table at which he doubled over momentarily, silently praying to God to relieve him of the startling pain in his groin.

"Whoa there, bubba," said Murray, rising to help him. "You okay, Driver?"

Straightening as best he could, Driver nodded, forcing a weak, pained smile.

"You got to protect your balls, Driver. They're an investment in your future, son. Guard 'em at all cost."

Once in the corridor, Driver scuttled along crablike behind Arlanne until she stopped, looking about to make sure no one else was around, in front of the closed door of the prosecution's anteroom.

Following her lead, he put his ear to the anteroom door. She also dropped down, looking through the keyhole.

"Hoke," they could hear the prosecutor say, "Boonie's changed his story so many times that by the time we get into the courtroom he's going to be like the hemophiliac floundering about in the river with the defense coming at him like a school of sharks."

Driver and Arlanne looked at each other, unable to quite figure that one out.

Neither could Hoke, but for a different reason. "What's a hemophiliac?" he asked.

"Murray's going to smell the blood, and he's going to eat this kid alive. In addition he's eventually going to have this Driver kid that your crazy son tried to kill with his crutches sitting smack dab on the front row in full view of the jury."

"Aw hell," said Boonie, "I hardly touched him. He called me a fag, man. What was I supposed to do?"

Arlanne knew the prosecutor. He'd played the drums in the high school band when she'd been a majorette. He and Murray buddied around together. His name was Dwight Allgood. His daddy wasn't much, drove the only taxicab in town, usually drunk, but everybody knew to get out of his way. Drivers pulled over to the curb when they were anywhere near him, as they would for an ambulance or police car, so no harm done. But Dwight's mother had looked after him well, and her little record shop downtown, Daisy's Disc Den, had done well. And Dwight had done well. He was smart, took nothing for granted, and that's what made him, according to Murray, such a good lawyer. He was calculating, and he did not like surprises turning up in the courtroom. Murray had told her that Dwight usually managed to take care of them before they could even get to court, and that's just what he was doing now.

"Well, are you a fag?"

That's all it took.

Boonie lunged at him, railing, fists flailing and flying everywhere, apoplectic, dragging himself across the table that Dwight had carefully noted separated them. As Dwight was well aware, Boonie couldn't possibly get to him. After all, he couldn't walk. He did however, try to nail him with a crutch, as he had Driver, missed, only to hit Hoke instead. Even that didn't stop him. Finally, two of the court-assigned policemen, hearing the commotion, appeared in the corridor, heading briskly toward the anteroom. Arlanne and Driver stepped aside, and the two policemen opened the door, nightsticks and handcuffs at the ready. Dwight managed to slam the door behind them, particularly when he saw Arlanne there with her note pad. Arlanne, ever resourceful, simply returned to the keyhole. Hoke was astounded, shell-shocked, humiliated. His head had a lump on it the size of a golf ball that he didn't even notice. All he could think about, it was clear, was his little boy. "Don't hurt him," he told the men, his men, as a matter of fact, as he stepped in, grabbing Boonie with all his might, trying to restrain him. "Easy, easy, boys." But it wasn't easy. "Calm down, Boonie," Hoke kept saying. "Easy now, it's all right, it's all over now, calm down."

Outside in the corridor, momentarily neglecting the keyhole, Arlanne wrote in her note pad, "Calming Boonie down was like trying to calm down a grizzly bear gone completely insane."

Driver, glancing at her note pad, whispered, "Arlanne, not to be critical, but can a grizzly bear go insane?"

Inside the anteroom Boonie was struggling to break free of the cops, who with the help of Hoke, had him pinned to the table. He was screaming at Dwight, telling him he was going to kill him. "Goddamn you, you son of a bitch. You fuckin' bastard."

He had completely lost it.

Embarrassed, Arlanne and Driver stepped aside for Regina Cooley, who with great dignity opened the door and entered the anteroom, closing it softly behind her.

"You fuckin' drunk, just like your old man, you goddamn son of a bitch I'm going to kill you, fag lover. I'm going to kill you. Goddamn let me up!"

But he couldn't break free, and seeing his mother, he collapsed, crying, crying such humiliating and shameful tears he couldn't stop them.

"I don't know," he finally said. "I don't know what I am."

Hoke was stricken. He touched Boonie's shoulder, trying to calm him, and he managed to say, "It's all right, son. It's all right."

"You boys can go now," Mrs. Cooley said to the policeman, "thank you for your help."

Embarrassed, they headed for the door, turning around briefly at the sound of Hoke's voice. Still mortified, guilty and ashamed, looking as if he himself had been suddenly exposed for committing crimes against humanity, Hoke nevertheless fortified himself, saying to them with unmistakable firmness, "Boys, this is a family matter. I trust you'll keep it that way."

"Yes, Sir. Yes, Sir. Of course, Sir." They couldn't wait to get out of there.

Once again, however, they were stopped, only this time by the clear, unmistakable voice, equally firm, steadfast and unwavering, of Mrs. Cooley.

"Say whatever you want," she told the policemen, "to whomever you want." As they stumbled out, thoroughly self-conscious now, mumbling 'Yes, ma'am,' 'Glad to be of help ma'am,' Mrs. Cooley turned her direct gaze on her husband. "This family's had enough secrets."

Boonie sat there bent over, crushed, his face in his hands; quietly weeping, crying out softly now his shame and humiliation, his sudden self-exposure.

She nodded over at Boonie. "It's hurting the boy," she explained.

His hand resting on Boonie's back, rubbing it as Boonie sobbed, Hoke nodded, resigned, totally disarmed.

"Can homosexuals play football?" he asked, looking up at her hopefully.

Boonie, wiping his eyes now with the back of his hands, looked up at his father, and started giggling. Dwight, his back politely turned to them as he stood in front of the window, mentally preparing his statement to the judge, let out a soft chuckle.

"Mr. Allgood," said Boonie, "I didn't mean that stuff, about your father, I swear."

Dwight looked at him. "I understand," he said.

"I just want you to know I was crazy, and I'm truly sorry, Sir."

"I understand," said Dwight, "because my father is an alcoholic."

"You're a good man, Mr. Allgood," said Mrs. Cooley to him, "a truly good man. Thank you."

As for Arlanne and Driver, having been discovered on their knees at the keyhole as the two policemen opened the door to leave the anteroom, they were escorted down the corridor, past the curious spectators in the courtroom itself, most of whom they knew, all the way out the courthouse, only to be pretty much, as Arlanne would later note in her *Esquire* piece, dumped on the lawn.

"Baby," Driver whispered once the cops had gone back inside, "those big boys scared little Driver."

"So? Who cares?"

"Driver?" he said. "Driver cares?"

67

Regina Receives Her Proof That There Is a God

Naturally, in the privacy of the judge's chambers Hoke had Dwight drop the charges. Not only had Boonie been more than convincing as a certifiable maniac, but Hoke in his own mind wasn't entirely comfortable with the question of his son's sexual orientation answered in the public domain. For one thing, even with two broken legs and a lost senior season, Boonie was in line for a full scholarship at Clemson; after all, he'd been first team All-State fullback in his junior season, dubbed "The Wrecking Ball" by the *State* newspaper.

The "Gay" Wrecking Ball, Hoke surmised, didn't quite have the same ring to it.

The judge seemed overjoyed, to say nothing of palpably relieved. All through the hearings, whenever judicial necessity required him to look in the direction of a war hero dressed up like a woman, checking his makeup, rummaging through his pocketbook, blotting his lipstick (as if it were nothing more than an everyday occurrence in his courtroom), shock and hysteria, ebbing and flowing dangerously, had threatened ceaselessly to disrupt, erode, and fling into disarray the studiously-contrived neutrality of his facial features. Also, like just about every other politician in town he'd been compromised, and he was nervous about it coming out in the trial if things didn't go Murray's way. Hoke had secretly funneled money into his campaign for judge in every election he'd run in. To someone who didn't know any better that might appear to be a conflict of interest, especially since just everybody Hoke arrested ended up spending a little time in the slammer. Everybody in town knew Hoke had the judge in his pocket, and the judge knew Murray knew it. And it must have been Hoke's back pocket because the word around town was that when Hoke sat down, the judge let out a yelp. And Murray, well, personally the judge liked Murray, but let's face it: Murray was a liberal, a smart one, just the type to expose publicly what everybody already knew privately if it'd serve his client's purpose. Plus, the judge had gone to high school with Hoke, let him copy his homework. They were friends. The whole idea of a trial had made him restless, irritable (his wife said), and uncomfortable. And when he felt that way, all he wanted to do was to go fishing, to get away from it all. And that's what he'd planned to do today: go through the motions legally, get out of the courthouse as quickly as he could, and head for the river. And now, with the happy coincidence of it all ending early, he was ready. Besides, none of this was really his business; it was personal and private, like campaign funding. So after ascertaining from the Cooleys as well as the prosecutor that Boonie would attend counseling sessions (if not to clarify his confused sexuality, at least to learn to control his anger), it was off with his judicial robes (underneath which was his fishing garb), grab up his rod and reel and fishing tackle stashed in the corner, and head out to the river. He even remembered, as the Cooleys and Dwight and Murray and Royal watched in astonishment, to collect his jar of worms from his desk drawer. He was out the door before they were.

A few minutes later, alone on the courthouse steps, Murray said, "I'm sorry for what happened, Royal. I really am. I know you wanted your day in court, and I know you were looking forward to serving a long, drawn-out prison sentence."

"I'm guilty," said Royal. Tears caused his mascara to run. "I deserve my time in jail."

"God, why hast thou forsaken thee?"

"God," Royal screamed, "Why *has* thou forsaken thee? Why? Goddammit. Why? Why? Why?"

"You're not guilty, Royal. You committed neither assault nor battery. Boonie Cooley did when he started the fight. You know that, and I know that. If this had gone to trial that boy would've been open to perjury charges. Dwight knew that, whether or not you pled self-defense, whether or not you blamed it on the government. The fact is the government didn't start the fight, Boonie did, and Boonie's not part of the government."

"I'm not guilty of assault and battery. No."

"Right," said Murray, slapping him on the back. "See? That's what I've been trying to tell you."

"I'm guilty of murder."

Murray just stood there, thinking, nodding. Naturally he knew exactly what Royal was talking about. "Hey, man," he said, placing his arm around him, glancing about to be sure no one was watching, giving him a little hug, a manly hug, he assured himself: "Better luck next time."

Back in the judge's chambers, Boonie asked his mother, "Mama, why didn't you ever touch me? I can't remember one time you holdin' me or lovin' on me or huggin' or kissin' me. Not once, Mama. Why? What was wrong with me? What'd I do? How come you never loved me? It was always Daddy loved me, never you. Why not, Mama? You know why I beat up Driver this morning? When he came over and started talkin' to me, I hated him. I remembered. When we was little and used to play together. When I saw him and his mama in the courthouse I remembered. I used to love goin' over to their house. His mama, she loved and hugged me. She showed affection. I started lovin' her more than you. I remember pickin' a fight with him back then, had no idea why, none, over somethin' little neither one of us cared about. What'd I know? Couldn't have been more than what, six years old? I was afraid I might love somebody else's mama more than you. Then later when you had to go to the hospital, I thought you tried to kill yourself to get away from me, that I was bad. I'm sorry Mama. I'm so sorry."

"You knew about the suicide attempt?" asked Hoke.

"Friends at school asked me about it. At first I was just confused, but after awhile . . ."

"I should have been honest with you about it," she said. "I was wrong to keep it from you . . . myself from you . . . I . . . I was wrong. God forgive me."

"I don't even know anymore if there is a God, Mama."

Regina's fingers tightened around her pocketbook, which she held protectively against her chest, like an illegitimate child she refused to give up. Hoke appeared to be in total despair.

So it wasn't Grandaddy you saw, she realized about Boonie, the night you assaulted Royal Cunningham. No, Boonie, you saw a man who was a woman. You saw your mother, and your need for her frightened and enraged you.

"It's okay, Son," said Hoke. "Everything's going to work out."

She looked down at her son. "Forgive me, son."

"Call me by my name, Mama."

"Of course." She sat beside him, resting her pocketbook on the table, her uncertain hands in her lap, and turned to face him. "Forgive me . . . Boonie," she said, doing her damndest. "I'm asking you, Boonie, if you can find it in your heart, to forgive me."

"But why, Mama? Why couldn't you love me? What'd I do that was so bad?"

She involuntarily reached out to touch his face, his cheek, but when she realized it her hand just as involuntarily fell to her lap.

"You didn't do anything," she told him. "You were the sweetest little boy alive."

He waited, confused, unbelieving.

"I was—or thought I was—protecting you."

"How?"

"You know how you suffered an uncontrollable rage without knowing why. In trying to protect you from my own, as well as from my own . . . needs, urges, I don't know . . . I unintentionally created that rage inside you. Secrets, the secrets we keep from ourselves, do that to you. My father, your grandfather, touched me in very inappropriate places when I was little. No, I'm not doing this again. Your grandfather raped me."

"Grandaddy?"

"Repeatedly, until my mother sent me when I was very young off to live with my aunt in Columbia. I knew why she was doing it, even without her telling me. For her to have filed for divorce back then would have been a scandal, I'm sure. Plus, we lived off his salary. It's odd, after you were born, I was terrified of ever leaving you alone with him, without really realizing why. You've never spent the night at his house, if you think about it. I never remembered what happened, until I woke up in the hospital, and it occurred to me that I could remember almost nothing about my childhood. Nothing. I knew that wasn't normal. Everyone I knew, I realized, had childhood memories and stories. Then the memories came. So, so painful. I felt them physically. I think they're why I couldn't wake up. If my eyes were closed, then perhaps I might have been dreaming, and once I woke up I might realize that. But if I woke up and the memories were real . . . that I couldn't face. So, why wake up? I wasn't conscious of all this at the time, naturally. But over time, I realized . . . All I realized before was that the idea of sex was just abhorrent to me, but I thought it was because of my Pentecostal background. Daddy railed so much about the sins of the flesh. Guess he knew a lot about that. I know now it's why I was always in the shower, to wash the dirt off. I think I must have seen the shower water as waters of purification. It's why everything in the house was so clean. I thought that was because 'Cleanliness is next to Godliness'. By the time I reached puberty—even before that—I was frozen. I convinced myself that virginity was a necessary virtue, as the Church preached, and after marriage that sex was only for procreation, not pleasure. Both of you must understand: to be touched would have opened up a flood of painful memories that I was too frightened to even acknowledge, much less feel. I pushed them so far down, I think they gave me stomachaches and nausea and those awful headaches. And then the voices would come, warning, threatening, scared, just all terrifying and mixed up. I cut myself to cut them off, to punish myself so they couldn't, to hurt myself so badly I wouldn't feel the real pain, Daddy, what he did, over and over and over, until I couldn't feel anything. Then I'd want so badly just to feel, anything. It was such a release to see the blood and the pain flowing out of me. After I got home from the hospital, I'd drive to Charleston once a week for almost a year to see a psychiatrist. I know, neither of you knew. I was too ashamed. I was back home before school let out, well before you got home from work, Hoke. The revelations came much easier because of the memories, terrible memories, so vividly and violently attacking me in the hospital. That's what the psychiatrist said. I've learned a great deal about myself. Enough to know that I have caused you both great pain. I'm so angry, but at least I know that I am and who I'm angry at. I'm still very frightened. Every once in awhile a little voice in my head will say to me that what Daddy did to me was normal, or that I'm imagining things. That fear is paralyzing. I was afraid that if I touched you, Boonie, that my hand would go all the way through you, that I would do to you what was done to me. I couldn't figure out the proper boundaries, because I'd never had them, which is what, Hoke, made me frigid when you touched me. There was nothing you could have done, Hoke. Please don't blame yourself. Since I didn't know any better, you didn't. There wasn't a time when you touched me when I didn't see my father's face in yours. Please don't cry, boys," she said to them, a hand on each of their shoulders. "Shh . . . it's all right now, it's all right. Mama's back."

"I saw you," said Boonie, "when Captain Cunningham touched me. I just couldn't stand to think . . ."

"I know, sweetheart. You don't have to explain a thing. Mommy just did it for you."

He nodded. Hoke just sat there, crying his heart out.

"Hey, Dad," said Boonie, giving him a little poke in the ribs, "only homosexuals cry."

After which she couldn't tell whether Hoke was laughing, crying, or both at the same time. What she did know was that to be able to laugh and cry at the same time was what she wanted to be able to do. It relieved her that looking over at his father, with residual tears in his eyes, Boonie smiled at him.

"Both of you sissies finish crying," she told them, "and then let's go home and have a nice dinner."

Beforehand, however, she felt her own tears forming, quietly falling over her cheekbones. Tilting her head back to fully experience them, to make them last, as a child might with raindrops. She noted to herself that she couldn't remember happiness like this, and yet she knew without a doubt that this was indeed happiness. Oh, for it to last as long as it might, she thought. "Boonie," she said, her head angled back, her eyes upward, "there is a God."

| 68 |

For Arlanne and Driver, Two Wrongs Don't Make a Writer

For different reasons, neither Arlanne or Driver's stories saw print. As to why, consider the reaction to Driver's, which was rejected, since it was obvious to every single person who read it that (1) he had an axe to grind, (2) often when describing Boonie he seemed to be describing himself, and (3) he looked like such a jerk that Boonie by comparison appeared sympathetic.

So felt the editorial committee of his high school newspaper, juniors and seniors like himself, which did meet with him and as best they could, explain:

"I can't tell who's who. I mean, bummer, man, you know?"

"Like, *he's* effeminate?"

"Dude, this just ain't registerin'. Damn! I ain't gettin' this, man. Know what I'm sayin'? Up here, man, the head, see where I'm tappin'?"

"'Boonie's flaky fist had all the impact of a marshmallow?' Hmn . . . I think, Driver, that those of us who saw your face afterwards, even after the bandages were removed, would conclude, pardon my understatement, that it looked like the face from hell."

"Still does you axe me."

"'Flakey' fist? What's a 'flakey' fist? Bummer, man. I mean, you know?"

"You never say really why he hit you, Driver. You provoke him? He just drag himself up to you out of the blue and beat up on you for no reason? It don't make sense. We know Boonie. No way he ain't gon' have a good reason. You can't just leave something like this up in the air. Make me wonder about you, to tell you the truth, make me suspicious. Damn suspicious, if you want to know the truth. Why you hate him so much? If I was going through a bad time, after seeing what you done to Boonie, you'd be the last person I'd get down with. Something wrong with you, Driver. Something wrong with Boonie too, but something wrong with you. And you know it. I been with you since first grade, I ain't never seen you like this. I don't know you."

"You say he's a fag, but like you're the one who seems like one . . ."

"Man, you is one fucked up nigger."

"Like Boonie comes across here as suffering? I mean like really pained, deep down gentle and sensitive, like way more than I ever realized, I think like way more than any of us realized? Like in the midst of his tragedy, he somehow seems heroic, I mean to me, the great athlete fallen? Right? He's human. He lies, right, but I mean like out of ignorance, confusion, desperation. What else was he going to do? He's a football player. But like he admits it—I mean, whatever it is, he admits it— and what he admits is, okay, like amazing? I mean, like scary. Right? Like, who would to admit to this? And he's a jock. I wouldn't. No way. I mean, even if there was something to admit to. You know? Like even if there was. Obviously there isn't. I know that. But what if there was? I know you didn't intend this, Driver, but he actually seems more humble, more open and accessible than before. He was never one of those jocks always throwing you up against the lockers, like I know that, right? But I feel more open to him. His honesty, his courage in the face of all this, like in the end wins out. Okay, like I'm not a big sports fanatic, okay, like everyone else around here? Hey, no secret there, ha ha. But in my mind he scores a real touchdown here, and, Driver, you don't even give him credit. No, for some reason, like you don't even see it. Like you leave for the concession stand or something. But the reader, he does see it, I did. Boonie takes responsibility for himself. He accepts what he doesn't know, this, this . . . helplessness of not knowing who he is. I mean, apart from the sexuality issue, we're teenagers. Are we really supposed to know who we are yet? I mean, exactly? Apart from the sexual aspect? I mean, I don't. Does anyone sitting at this table, deep down, really know who they are? At our age, it'd probably be considered abnormal. Right? I mean, we know who we are sexually but other than that . . . So not only can we identify with him, unlike you, we actually sympathize with him. I mean, maybe we do know who we are, certainly we do sexually, maybe it's because we don't really know Captain Cunningham, or at least why he's let Boonie get away with this for so long."

"'Our sexuality' is not the issue. 'We' aren't the issue. Our insecurities are not the issue. Driver is. And sexuality, I assure you—and I'm just speaking for myself here—is not an issue for me, thank you. I know who I am, in that respect. Thank you."

"Of course. Like who doesn't? Still . . ."

"Excuse me? But for me, I mean, not a prob., you know?"

"Amen, Dudes. Ain't no issue here. Know what I'm sayin'? Not with me they ain't."

"Agreed. Most definitely. And I don't think it an overstatement to suggest that we're all basically in agreement here. We, at least, the members of this committee, at least, simply do not have an issue with this. Am I correct? That is what the consensus is . . . Right?"

"Yeah. And, Driver, if Boonie thought Cunningham was a woman that night, how that make him a fag? You, though, you sound like Sister Mae out there on the island goin' crazy with pins all over some voodoo doll look like Boonie. 'The Wrecking Ball had been running it up the middle for so long his performance as the artful dodger was less than convincing to this reporter.' Why? It convince everybody on this committee. 'His tears, glistening with mucus on his shirt sleeve, seemed vulgar.' No, to me mentioning it, pointing it out the way you do, that what seem vulgar. It's like you hate him, Driver. 'Boonie lunged across the table, doing his best to humiliate and attack his own lawyer, exposing himself as the pathetic, peasant-like person that he is, now little more than Samson shorn of his hair.' 'Pathetic?' 'Peasant-like?' Are you so disdainful because he beat up on you? You jealous? 'Samson shorn of his hair?' Driver . . ."

"Yo, Dude, it'll grow back. Know what I'm sayin'? See where I'm at here?"

"You sound like a snob. Sorry, but hey, you know?"

"Why he hit his daddy with his crutch? No reason? He just hateful and crazy? Throughout the piece he seem to love his daddy. Was it an accident? You never tell us, and it make us wonder why. Not so much why he did it, but why you leave out why he did it, implying he did it on purpose. Did he?"

"Dude, this entire article, it be one big put-down, and we ain't knowin' why, except that for some reason ain't registerin' up here—see where I'm tappin'—he slugged you, and you, dude, you jealous of jocks, and see, here's the thing, man. We know that and you don't. Dude, that's embarrassin'. Know what I'm sayin'? It's embarrassin'. Look at me, man. See me squirmin'. I'm embarrassed, dude, for you. Know what I'm sayin'? For you, man. You my bro. Know what I'm sayin'? I'm embarrassed. Man, I'm embarassed. Damn."

"Like to me, in my opinion, you sound like a woman scorned?"

"'Sheriff Cooley is worshipped as a near-saint by the good citizens of Somerset, worthy of more from a wayward son than embarrassment and humiliation.' 'The good citizens of Somerset?' Who they? Sheriff Cooley 'a near-saint?' How? Who canonized him: the Klan?"

Shallow bastards. Tell the Truth with a capital T, Kill the Messenger. Not the first writer this has happened to, won't be the last. Fine. I did ask Boonie how it felt to have been beaten up by a fag, and No, it's not in the article. Big deal. So I didn't want the story to be about me. Sue me for my selflessness.

Did his crutch hit his dad by accident? Does it matter? Who would do such a thing, whether accidentally or on purpose? That's simply not the issue. The fact is his dad's head was so swollen it looked like he was growing another one.

Jealous? Please.

Racism, he concluded bitterly to his mother. Boonie the Great White Hope, all that. You know. Same old thing. Never ends.

Until she asked him how many black students were on the committee, which just infuriated him. "God Mom, who cares? You don't know anything, do you? I can't talk to you."

"How many?" she persisted. "And if you smart-mouth me one more time instead of answering my question I'm gon' do a hell of a lot more than talk to you, Mr. Going-to-Harvard With-No-Damn-Sense."

"I don't know," he said gloomily.

"You don't know? Driver Trulove, you are on the committee."

"Mom, I can't remember. That's not the point."

She turned off the news, CBS, right in the middle of it. Uh-oh, she was gettin' serious. He was wishin' he'd kept his mouth shut. In his mind's eye he saw her headin' up to the school to raise hell, only to find out that the editorial committee's comments, regardless of race, were universally damning. No, humiliating.

"How many students on that committee?"

"Five."

"How many are black?"

"What difference—"

"Driver!"

"'bout half."

"About half? About half?"

"Three," he conceded.

He started up again, but she stopped him.

"I know, Driver. All three just happened to be Uncle Toms, suckin' up to the white man."

She turned the television back on. However, since she wanted to talk instead of listen, she pushed the mute button, saying to Bob Schieffer (Walter Cronkite was off that night), "Well, Bob, we know the problem ain't racism. No Sirree Bob. The problem is I done raised me a big baby don't even know enough to be ashamed of hisself."

Still, however, he refused to accept the verdict of his fellow committee members. He knew the piece was great, even if they didn't. Besides, none of his work had ever been rejected by the school newspaper before.

He was pretty certain that it was too sophisticated for them. After all, he told them, they weren't going to Harvard. He showed it to the teacher in charge of the newspaper, Mrs. Patrice Neal, the sweetest little old lady, it was said, ever to grace the halls of Somerset High, who after reading it asked him to drop by for a few minutes after school "for a chat," she said smiling. And he knew what that meant. Yes! He'd been right! He was a great writer, perhaps the greatest who ever lived! Yes!

And after school! On her time, absent the little juvenile wannabees! Finally, vindication. Revenge! Eat your hearts out, yeomen, you journalistic pygmies.

She'd probably offer to take him out for a Coke, where she could pick his brain informally for pointers.

When he approached her desk after school, where she was reviewing competitive pieces for the newspaper, she pulled his out of a stack, and looking up at him over her reading glasses, she said, "Driver, I've been teaching for twenty-five years, and I think I can say with unflinching accuracy that this is the single worst piece of writing I have ever seen. Truly, Driver, I'm embarrassed for you. Is my face red? Oh my. You know, my predecessor here at the school newspaper, the writer Pat Conroy, set a standard here for our stories: 'Make them personal.' That is his legacy, and because of that legacy, we try not to shy away from the 'personal.' Quite frankly, Driver, it's a legacy, with your piece on a great athlete, you've abused. Have you thought about another vocation, say, botany, engineering, architecture? A profession that doesn't demand much writing? Perhaps corporate or technical writing, writing which avoids the personal and artistic?"

As for Arlanne's story, for all her bravado—truth at any price, and so forth—she aimed for the high ground, even though she was well aware that any good story, if not essentially lowbrow, is certainly always below ground, underground, which is why you have to dig for it. Lowbrow, she figured, because everybody is essentially lowbrow: toilet paper's toilet paper, regardless of the texture, and everybody is reduced to reaching for it. And the story's inevitably underground, Rob Vicker used to say, or everyone would already see it and know it.

"What about in outer space?" she had asked him. "Any stories up there?" "Only in black holes," he'd responded.

Arlanne struggled and struggled and struggled. It's difficult to write a story when you're covering up the real one, particularly when you don't truly know what the real one is.

She focused on Royal, knowing he could care less, since all he really cared about was going to jail.

Her title: Are All War Heroes Latent Homosexuals?

If so, she asked the reader, in serving so bravely are they compensating for a perceived lack of manhood?

Or, do they truly love their comrades-in-arms so much, more than the heterosexual is capable of, that they are more likely to sacrifice their own lives for theirs?

If so, should congress pass a law providing that only homosexuals be permitted to serve in combat positions?

Bert read it, after which he laughed at her, not with her.

"Whatever the story is here, you're clearly avoiding it."

"Regina Cooley's 'secret?'"

"You know about that?" He was home for lunch, talking to her from the kitchen now, making a bologna sandwich with mayonnaise, adding lettuce for roughage. The quality of his stools, which he confirmed by having Arlanne examine them, had suggested an ongoing need for more fiber.

"We overheard Regina talking about it in the anteroom."

"'We?'"

"Me and Driver. At the keyhole, listening."

"You have got to be kidding."

'No more secrets.' That's exactly what she said."

"Really?"

"To Boonie and Hoke. It was sad. They were just really broken up."

"So they know about her dad, the abuse, the whole thing? Why? What caused her to suddenly open up like that? Was it to get Boonie to tell the truth?"

"What abuse?" she asked him.

"This is unethical, Arlanne. I can't believe you managed to trick this out of me. I feel terrible. You've ruined my day. This shouldn't have happened."

"I agree, darling, but it did, didn't it."

He threw the sandwich in the garbage can. "I can't eat this now. I'm too upset."

"But honey, you need the roughage."

"Why would you do such a thing?"

"To find the story."

"You can't publish that. For one thing, it would ruin my career."

"Tell me the story, sweetgums, and I won't."

"You basically know the story now."

"Only in a general way, not enough to convince the reader."

"I don't want you to convince the reader."

"I won't, if you convince me."

"My God," he said, walking into the dining room, looking at her. "My wife has a heart."

"She most certainly does not."

"You're looking for an excuse. If you get the story unethically, where it might ruin your husband's career, you can't ethically write it. My little wifey is human? She's afraid of hurting the Cooleys." He pulled up a chair at the dining room table, moving as close as he could to her, put his arm around her, and said, "I truly love you. That's my story."

"What am I going to do? Without the story, what's the story?"

Without a trial, she told Rob Vicker, after sending him the best story without a story she could, there really wasn't much to report.

"'Much?'" he said. "Not 'much' to report? According to your piece, there's nothing to report. Absolutely nothing. I don't think I've seen this much padding since Sally Mae Funderburke's falsies back in the fifties."

The good thing though was that upon hearing of her rejection, Driver was overjoyed.

"Oh, baby," he said, unable to disguise his glee, "I'm so sorry."

"Driver, try acting. I swear, you were born for it."

"I don't want to be an actor."

"Then quit."

"Know it all," he muttered under his breath.

"What?!"

"You know . . . it . . . all, as in 'you know everything.' You do, Arlanne. I mean it."

"Do you, Driver? That means so much to me."

"Maybe you should go into acting."

Finally, Driver couldn't help himself. He waited as long as he could. He handed her his story, the one rejected by his high school newspaper.

"Read it while I'm waiting, Arlanne, I'll be reading this magazine. I won't interrupt. I won't even look at you. I promise." He picked up the magazine.

"*Sports Illustrated?*" she asked him, skeptically. "Here," she said, handing him *Cosmopolitan*. "Since when did you become a sports fan?"

"Oh, I didn't realize . . . thank you."

"And if I see you looking at me while I'm reading, I'm stopping, I promise you."

"I promise," he said, staring down at a small photograph of the editor, Helen Gurley Brown, adjacent to the masthead on page one.

"You're faking it."

"Fine." As he began thumbing through it, she left the living room and retired to her office in the dining room.

From her desk, the dining room table, she looked over into the living room where he was faking an intense interest in something in the magazine. He could act, she thought, if he just weren't so bad at it. And she began reading . . .

Again, let's leave her to do that on her own, rather than having to suffer the convolutions, contradictions and inconsistencies ourselves. She can figure it all out, and tell us about it afterwards.

"What would Bert say?" she wondered aloud, laying the article delicately on the table. I do not, she thought to herself, want to piss off Lila. Not again.

Naturally, Driver heard her from the living room.

"You've read it?" he asked looking up.

She went over and sat beside him. "Driver, listen: whether it's a man's or a woman's, a hole's a hole. That's all it amounts to."

"What?"

"Here's what I'm driving at here."

"Yes?"

"A hole's a hole."

"What on earth are you talking about?" He had the most expressive brown eyes she'd ever seen. Even in the most dire circumstances, they could light up with curiosity and amusement.

"A man has a hole. Right?"

He looked at her, puzzled if not downright incredulous. "Yesss . . ."

"A woman has a hole . . . right?"

"Yesss . . ."

"Into which hole would you prefer to stick your penis?"

"Arlanne!"

"Which hole, Driver? Which hole?"

"I don't know! Jesus! You're crazy!"

"Exactly, Driver. Exactly."

"What are you saying?"

"When you know who you are, you'll know what to say. And then, Driver, You'll say it great."

"You're saying I'm confused."

"The writing is."

"I don't know who I am, what I am . . ."

"Remind you of anyone in particular?"

"Oh my God!"

"Smart boy."

"Oh my God . . . this is so embarrassing . . ."

"'I don't know what I am.' . . ?"

"Oh my God . . ."

"Okay, Driver, you're repeating yourself, you know how much that bores me."

"Oh my God . . ."

| 69 |

Arlanne Wonders if Jimmy Carter has the Tool for the Presidency

In 1975 Jimmy Carter, no longer "Jimmy-Who," was running ahead of the pack for the Democratic nomination for president of the United States, challenged now only (and minimally) by the liberal senator from Minnesota, Hubert Horatio Humphrey. With his Southern Baptist background, his emphasis on fiscal responsibility, and his easy reliance on moderation, the peanut farmer from Plains could afford to risk a few right-wing votes for those liberals looking for a little excitement, a little titillation, a little humanity. That was the political rationalization, according to the pundits, for Carter's famous *Playboy* interview in which he confessed to having had lust in his heart for members of the female persuasion other than his wife Rosalyn, which must have really pissed her off. If it did, however, she didn't show it. Then again, figured Arlanne, Rosalyn never showed anything. You could install her just as she is in the Wax Museum in London, and you wouldn't have to change a thing. Had it been her, Arlanne, she would've posed naked in the same magazine just to show him up. Maybe, she wondered aloud to Bert, Rosalyn was just being loyal to her "Jimmy."

"That's what she calls him. 'My Jimmy' this, 'My Jimmy' that . . ."

Bert was busy shaving; naturally, he wasn't listening.

"Maybe," he said.

Once again, Bert had a total lack of curiosity about striking inanities and lurid gossip, which is all, she felt, she was really interested in.

What she was interested in at the moment was Jimmy Carter's penis. She'd read the political pundits' rationale for his *Playboy* interview, but she didn't buy it. The interview was a calculated diversionary tactic, she told Bert. Not only for political reasons, however, but for a personal one.

How did she know, asked Bert. Because at bottom, she told him, everything's personal.

"So?"

"So this is."

She has a way of coming up with things, thought Bert, that are simply outside the realm of rational argument.

In "Does Jimmy Carter Have the Tool To Be President?" a response in *Esquire* to the *Playboy* interview, Arlanne wrote: "Carter's lying: he may have had love in his heart for other women, but most certainly not lust. The heart doesn't feel lust, though I am told by people who bore me to death that it can feel love. That I wouldn't know. What is universally recognized, however, is that it is the penis which experiences lust. The heart doesn't ejaculate. The penis does. A president, no less than the First Lady, needs a penis, a strong, hard, leonine penis, a penis possessed of an iron will and a head of its own. The heart is a "soft" organ—mushy, if you ask me. Downright weak. Reliable neither in tough negotiations nor wartime. Loving, not hard-driving, not greedy, not voracious; in short, not lustful in the least. So clearly Carter's lying; ain't no lust there. Can the heart get hard? Sure, but unreliably. Why? Guilt. Shame. It is made for love. Isn't the penis also, at least more often than not, a "soft" organ? Absolutely, but it is made for lust, for greed, for rapaciousness. For outright invasion. Storm the barricades. Fire away, know what I mean here? A real penis, like a real man, has no problem, when called upon, becoming hard. The hell with "negotiations." Bomb 'em. Catch my drift? A president unequipped with a take-no-prisoners pile driver of a penis is clearly unfit for the job. No one knows this better than Carter and and those two young studs, Hamilton Jordan and Jody Powell, running his campaign. Believe me, those two dudes can get hard. They're shrewd, they're calculating, and they might come early, but they stay late. They have seen Carter's weakness, and they are keeping it in his pants, zipped up, out of sight of the common man. So this writer cannot help but wonder: Is Carter drawing attention to the heart, which no one cares about, to divert attention from the organ essential to the needs of the Republic? In other words, does Jimmy Carter lack the tool for the presidency?"

"Until he clears this up," Bert told her upon reading it, "he's not getting my vote."

Later, after he became president, and she learned along with the rest of the country of his secret plan to restructure, reorganize, and democratize the presidential staff's use of the White House tennis courts, she realized, to her chagrin, that she might well have been wrong.

In a subsequent piece, "Democracy Begins At Home," she corrected herself: "Okay, so it wasn't a diversion from his tool, but from his obsessive-compulsive disorder, which I can tell you from personal experience is significantly less problematic. My husband, for example, the psychologist Bert Levy, suffers from an obsessive-compulsive disorder, and that does make him a neurotic pain in the ass. However, his tool, I must admit, a total success story: always in excellent working condition, makes you forget just what a pain he is, as dependable and reliable as church on Sunday. It is what has made our marriage last. Plug that baby in, and the whole world lights up. So obsessive-compulsive disorder or not, if Carter can do for the country what my hubby has done for me, which is to say screw us Royally, I predict, for better or worse, a comparable relationship."

Driver Trulove in his freshman year at Harvard was thriving as a rare, exotic flower from the tropics, blossoming and opening in Harvard Square sexy, sassy, and vivid as a night orchid, exploiting his heritage to the max as the Deep South's representative Negro not only in academic and social gatherings but in his articles for the *Harvard Crimson*.

Not only that, but for a college kid even at a moneyed university, he was loaded. Though he was on scholarship, Hoke had long ago established a college trust fund for him in Lila's name from which he could withdraw funds on his own when he reached eighteen. Plus, Lila had all this money from her liquor stores and the restaurant she owned and little to spend it on. The last person she'd have wanted to spend a lot of money on would have been herself. She'd made it for her kids. With his scholarship and Hoke's money,

Driver hardly needed much of Lila's, not that she didn't load him up with it anyway, all the while scolding him for his frivolity and spendthrift nature, lest he forget (she hastened to warn him) the virtues of thrift and frugality.

"Mom, speaking of 'frivolous,' you're sending me all this money I don't need."

"That's different," she'd tell him.

Elizabeth really didn't need it either, though Lila indulged her too. After graduating Howard University in three years, Elizabeth was in her second year at Yale Law School, with the promise upon graduation of an enviable career with a high-powered Washington law firm. Recently, she'd become engaged to be married to a young Georgetown economics professor from an aristocratic black family in Atlanta. His emotional stability, she told Bert (in one of their periodic phone conversations), much like the elite, all-black Howard University and the liberal white Yale Law School, provided for her a staunch psychological base from which she could launch her anger at the white world.

"And the black world?" asked Bert. "More specifically, the world of black men?"

"That's harder. Too much love there. If I get mad at him, he might leave. With the white world, nothing to risk. It was never there."

"You marrying your father?"

"Quite the opposite. Charles is the antithesis of my father. He'll marry my father when he marries me. Still, if I'm packin' heat and he just stands there and takes it . . ."

"He's dead too. But you know that's not true."

"I know it, but I don't feel it," she said teasing, mimicking him. "I wonder who taught me that particular distinction."

"Elizabeth, it doesn't sound as if you really learned it. Why don't you come in for a few sessions when you're home?"

"Because I'm in love."

"Well then, it sounds, at least to a degree, like you have learned it."

"Bert, quit worrying, I'm fine. 'So fine,'" she sang, giggling. "Now tell me, how's it going at the clinic?"

Lila's nest was empty, her liquor stores and restaurant on Lady's Island managed by trusted black friends with whom she grew up, were essentially thriving without her. With desegregation a fact and with both of her kids no longer in Somerset High, she'd served her last term on the School Board. Besides, with Marty Liebowitz now on the Town Council, his successor as Chairman was Ida Perch, a retired schoolteacher who happened to be black. Lila was restless.

Downtown was dying. Chain stores—the Colonial Store, Belk's, eventually Wal-Mart and K-Mart—on the outskirts of town, where the property was cheaper, the taxes were lower, and the prices were lower, were underselling, undermining and destroying small businesses, particularly those downtown. Somersetonians, always on the make for cheaper goods, were driving just beyond the town limits to shop. GOING OUT OF BUSINESS sales shouted like carnival barkers from the display windows of downtown clothing stores, shoe stores, hardware stores, jewelry stores, and appliance stores. One by one, the restaurants (including the No View), the barbershops, the drug store, and even the pool hall were boarded up. Only they were not going out of business, they were simply moving to where the money was, rallying around the chain stores, re-appearing in "shopping centers" and strip malls. Those who chose to stay and fight, either out of pride, stubbornness or because they could afford the loss, included the town patriarchs: Palmer's Department Store, Harper Dawes Hardware Store, Liebowitz's Law Firm; Freddie Dinnerman remained open, as did the Riverbreeze Theatre. Despite, however, proclamations that "Downtown Will Rise Again"—the platform on which Marty Liebowitz based his campaign for Town Council—those who remained were pretty much resigned to the demise of their own businesses. And despite her failed attempt years ago to buy Freddie's place downtown, Lila's eye had always remained on downtown property, respectable downtown property, property worthy of an intelligent, fair-minded black businesswoman, white property. Somerset, she had never failed to realize, had always been about business. In her mind, segregation was as much about business as was slavery.

In the destruction and death of downtown, Lila began to imagine her own reconstruction, if not resurrection. She understood instinctively that the personal was the universal, that the breakthrough of one black person in the Deep South invited that of many. Only a decade earlier Lila had huffed and puffed and blown open the doors of the Somerset schools so that her daughter Elizabeth, the eventual valedictorian of Somerset High School, could walk through them, and black kids—including her own Driver—had been walking through them ever since.

Once again, she would need Murray's help.

Maybe even Elizabeth's, if push came to a shove. Though mad as Lila was at Hoke, she couldn't help but carry a bit of a warm spot in her heart for him, and she'd pretty much decided that Elizabeth's hostility toward him might result in overkill. Hoke was a traitor, no doubt about it, but he hadn't betrayed Driver.

Still, Lila was about to become a major player in Somerset, and with one shoe store downtown she was going to drop kick Hoke Cooley right out of the stadium.

Boonie was redshirting at Clemson, rehabilitating his legs. Royal had told Hoke that as a trained killer legitimized by the United States government he was adept at breaking a leg with no resulting permanent damage. "He'll be as good as new," Royal had told Hoke, placing an avuncular arm around him. "Even stronger than he was. Trust me. If there's one thing I know how to do, other than murdering innocent people in cold blood, it's breaking a leg the right way. Nothing sloppy there. Rest assured."

"Thank you, Royal," Hoke had told him, apparently so overwhelmed with gratitude as to be teary-eyed, pretending to sneeze, however, wiping his eyes with the sleeve of his shirt.

"Now, now," Royal had said, patting his shoulder. And to preserve Hoke's dignity he averted his eyes, keeping them on the horizon in front of him. "Now now."

Murray Gold was recognizing that there was really no longer a place for white folks in the Civil Rights Movement and was contemplating traveling in Israel to look for a wife. "Go to New York," Bert told him. "There are more Jews there."

"And they all speak the same language," Arlanne volunteered.

"Communication's important," agreed Murray.

"Of course, they're all Yankees," Arlanne reminded him.

"Exactly," said Murray.

"Like Bert," she said. "A bunch of know-it-alls."

"True," said Murray. "True."

Bert had retired from the Marine Corps and was running the local Mental Health Clinic. Arlanne was writing a column for *Esquire*. Out on the Island Mary Beth satisfied Royal while Royal satisfied Jack. Jamie Mac was growing marijuana and vegetables in a commune out in Arizona. When Royal was in town he always drove by the county jail, pulled over in the parking lot, and gazed longingly at the cell bars on the windows. Jack remained on the dock, the waters untested, though recently Royal had been urging him to just stick his big toe in.

Naked and alone on the dock, gazing only at what he could see, Jack seemed to Mary Beth—who continued to ritually observe him through the dining room windows—as if he were in a trance, some kind of altered state. It was so private it pained her, and while it drew her to him, she knew that all she could do was stand and watch. His sadness and torment were palpable. The fatalism in his eyes hurt her.

She had seen the vodka bottles hidden in the basement. She knew why he insisted on gathering up the trash and hauling it to the dump himself. His drinking, like his pain, was private.

Her father'd been an alcoholic, a benign one like Jack, drinking ritually, just enough to anesthetize himself. If he'd actually gotten drunk, she never knew it. Same with Jack. Drinking really didn't noticeably affect his demeanor.

She knew why she had never really made an effort to curb his drinking.

She was afraid he'd kill himself. Not then, not as long as Jamie Mac might need him, but once Jamie Mac was fully grown and established . . . Yes, that was what she was afraid of. That was why she was quiet. That was why she could only observe.

He had developed a slight paunch over the past year, a bit of an extra chin. Here and there a few gray hairs strayed among his eyebrows, mingled casually with his thinning blonde hair, salted his three-day-old beard. Only his tan seemed immune to the future.

When it grew chilly, as it was now, she brought him a blanket to throw over his shoulders.

| 70 |

Driver Is a Negro In Harvard Square

Arlanne noticed that Driver was truer, more interesting and more spontaneous in his letters to her than he was in his pieces for the *Harvard Crimson,* where he was too busy, she repeatedly told him, trying to be cute, clever and hip. His letters were more personal, intimate, and funny. Hovering about them was a permeable sadness, the sadness, she wrote him, of the unsaid. To say the unsaid to himself, as he was doing in his letters to her, was progress in his growth as a writer and a man. To say it to whom he most needed to hear it was the culmination of his growth as a writer and a man. "It is nothing, in fact, to say it to the whole world," she wrote him, "and have the world turn its back on you. But your mother? That is another thing entirely."

Driver needed no explanation: Family lore included Arlanne's unexpressed tears in the forefront of the demonstration and boycott of her father's department store in 1966, her father himself overlooking it all through the upstairs plate glass window of the bank . . . Arlanne knew of what she spoke.

Finally, as an early graduation present, she wrote him that saying the unsaid to her was becoming irrelevant. It was time, she wrote further, to shit or get off the pot.

"So crude," he wrote her back.

"If you've had your fill of acting and irony," she wrote him, "and want to be a professional writer, you're ready. Simply tell the world what you've told me."

"That I essentially called Boonie less than a fag when I asked him how it felt to be beaten up by one? I can't believe I did that. Nasty."

"Now you know why, and don't tell me you were just following orders, you know better than that."

"My attitude back then, the whole idea, just disgusting to me, which incidentally I went to great pains to express to just about anyone with whom I came in contact. Didn't want to catch that disease, nasty."

"Well, if it helps, certainly when I was growing up I didn't want to catch your disease. Which is why we couldn't have swam in the same pool."

"When the only reason you went there was to look more like me."

"Quit dicking around, Driver."

"Baby!"

"Just show 'em who you are."

"That'll show 'em?"

"Show her, Driver, that'll show them."

"Driver's scared!"

Arlanne had sent a compilation of his letters to Rob Vicker at *Esquire* who upon reading them phoned Driver himself in Cambridge, asking him for an article, purely autobiographical, he warned, nothing but the truth. The truth, he told him—yours at least—is a story. Everything else ornamentation. When he offered him $1500 Driver fainted, and had to call him back to accept.

Less than three months later there were toasts and "drinks all around" about his cubicle at the *Crimson*. *Esquire* had published "A NEGRO IN HARVARD SQUARE: Also, A Letter to Mama" by Driver Trulove.

Naturally, amid all the fanfare, he couldn't help but quake with horror at the vision of his mama reading it.

"Of course you don't want her to," Arlanne had told him on the phone, "you need her to."

A NEGRO IN HARVARD SQUARE: Also, A Letter to Mama
by Driver Trulove

Ah glory!

Whitmanesque, I sing of myself rhapsodically as the sole Negro in Harvard Square, with the exception naturally of the requisite Nigerian students and a few stray muggers from the Cambridge High and Latin School. How seductive and alluring the role of the exotic! A black man from the Deep South, absurdly liberated, magnificently homosexual, thus the anti-stereotype, unthreatening, inviting, sensitive. Indeed, everybody's intimate. Unlike high school, at least in the South, jocks don't hold sway here.

Instead, I do.

At home in the Carolina lowcountry, though academically precocious, I was one among many. The black population of Somerset County, and correspondingly of Somerset High, was approximately fifty percent. Here, I stand out. Here the Yankees have sequestered and quartered their Negroes in Roxbury, which, if I am to speak frankly and personally, is fine with me. Ghetto blacks, though sexually a turn-on, are as terrifying to this Negro as white rednecks. In fact, they share some of the same mannerisms, gestures and language. Ain't much difference in my mind between "Wus' up?" and "Wus' happenin'?," between "You flexin', man," "You frontin'," and "You playin' the role, Bo, puttin' on the dog." The ghetto black swaggers and saunters to a steadier, cooler beat, but he is defiantly physical, like the redneck (though I do favor the ghetto black in sleeveless undershirts). Flashy cars . . . need I say more? A status symbol for one as much as the other. The sweat. An overwhelming interest in sports. A hatred of the other. A hatred of themselves. Anger and defiance are the air they breathe. An education is worthy of little more than a sneer, almost queer and effeminate. Unless they know me, they do not like me, or people like me, white or black. The odor of violence hovers about them, emanating from their very pores. If inferiority and insecurity are their illnesses, nasty ones, machoism and stoicism are their antidotes. Oooh, excuse me, girl, I'm turning myself on here. Relief squad! Relief squad! Walking through the projects at night in Roxbury is almost as frightening to me as stopping in some redneck bar late at night in rural South Carolina for a cup of coffee. I have about as much in common with either of them as the football players, black or white, back home.

Without reading or saying a word, simply by virtue of who I am rather than what I've done, which is nothing, I am the designated expert on racism in my class at Harvard. The anti-Southern prejudice, or anti-white Southern prejudice, is easily exploited here. My fellow students and professors constantly ask me how I managed to survive the lynchings.

Lynchings? What lynchings? I attended an integrated high school. Did I suffer racism, segregation? Of course. The threat of violence? Yes. But from my own people, as in Roxbury? No. In my hometown, the slums were slums, but they were peaceful. Out on the Island where I grew up, the air was clean, the water fresh, and there was enough space to turn a man into a poet, if not an activist.

Do I disabuse my Yankee friends of either their naiveté or their hypocrisy? No, reader, I don't.

I am courted by every single group on campus: Students Against Apartheid, the Finals Clubs—Spee, Fly, Porcelain, Delphic—Hasty Pudding, you name them. As their token black Southerner, I am the student representative on the Admissions Committee! I get to help decide who gets into Harvard. Imagine that.

And I put music to their fantasy to avoid one thing, my mother back home in the Carolina lowcountry knowing I am a homosexual.

Everything I was afraid to think or do back home is refreshingly commonplace up here. That is a wonderful feeling, until I think of my mother back home.

My shame is not in exploiting white liberals up here, at least not enough shame. I love white liberals, and black liberals for that matter: anyone interested in me who can see me, as I am, who I'm not afraid to show who I am. As a burgeoning young man that is all I ask of a friend, and I am the most popular student in Harvard Square. I am the surprise trophy of the Coop: a black man who reads. A curiosity worthy of awe and admiration at Emerson's old church, naturally Unitarian, on Sundays. Bland and boring, at least it's safe. To raise the roofs in the Roxbury churches I'd have to encounter the street niggers. They crazy, like I said. Scare me to death, girl. And at night among the bars and restaurants in the Square I drink and converse among the students and professors and bartenders as easily as if they belonged to me.

No, what shames me is my neediness, not the neediness of an unloved child—I didn't get this fabulous personality from lovelessness, that's for sure—but that of a child adored by his mother whose mother, he realizes, now that he has discovered who he is, may no longer recognize him, who he's afraid won't recognize him, who he's afraid will refuse to see him as he truly is, a child who perpetuates in his mother's eye the wrong vision, while yearning to reveal to her the right one.

My greatest fear is looking into her eyes and seeing no one, of becoming because of my homosexuality "The Invisible Man."

My cowardice shames me. Ironically, she is all I have.

I have survived white racism in the Deep South, black hostility in high school toward academics, and the rejection of a white father who could not claim me as his own. Racism, identity confusion, abandonment. All because of the love of my beautiful mother. The black church, however, consigns me to Hell on earth as well as in the beyond.

My fear is that the black church is you, Mother, and I hope here to consign myself once again to you.

Do not think only, homosexual. Please, Mama. Think also intelligent, kind, responsible, always a good kid, always made you proud, never an ounce of trouble beyond a little mischief, a son who loves his mama with all of his heart and every ounce of his being, Mama. Listen to me, Mama. You always have. Don't stop now, Please. Don't stop now, I beg you. I am a man now, a Harvard man, asking for the love of his mother, for her, in the words of Jesus Christ, not to forsake him, her only begotten son.

In the words of Arlanne Levy, Mama, a hole's a hole. Crude or not, do you have any idea how liberating those words were to me, a senior in high school at the time? I love men just like my Mama has.

I am the sole Negro in Harvard Square, consequently the resident expert on racism at the greatest university in America, but underneath all my strutting and prancing and preening, underneath the brilliance and social acuity that got me here, is one question, only one. I am a homosexual, Mama. Not exactly what you expected. Whether I am accepted as a black man in America is important to me, a real black man, a real human being. In the way of that question, however, is another more terrifying one: I am a homosexual, Mama. Do you still love me?

Beside that, the love of Harvard Square pales, and the reality of who I am here, of how I present myself, of self-acceptance, all of which are necessary to become the kind of man you raised, one of seriousness and truth and humor, gets lost in the glitter and show.

If I can come out as the man I am to you, as a black homosexual, as a man you contemplate with pride and find room in your heart to brag about, just as you always have, only then can I truly be a man, regardless of my sexual orientation, in Harvard Square.

Only then can I truly allow room in my heart for my people, my race. I've learned, I think, a great lesson about prejudice and discrimination, about (pardon the high-blown term) humanity. Throughout my childhood and adolescence I never missed an opportunity to turn my nose up or to make a snide remark about "fags."

Minus its righteousness and pomposity, nevertheless in collusion with its ignorance and hypocrisy, I was the black church.

Now I know why.

All clowns are masked, Mama.

Tell me what you see. Either way, I'll unmask myself in Harvard Square. One thing's for sure: I've got the brains.

Remember when you used to tell me, "Nothing matters but education. You can do or be anything you want, as long as you've got a great education."

I'm graduating Magna Cum Laude.

I am a Negro in Harvard Square. I am a homosexual in Harvard Square.

And except for a few English teachers, writers and stray readers, I'm probably the only one in Somerset, black or white, who recognizes the alliteration in 'homosexual in Harvard Square'. Remember that, Mama, before you start going nuts.

And the rest of you folks out there better remember it too.

I'm beginning to find out who you are.

71

Driver Learns Some Holes Are More Equal Than Others

A Negro In Harvard Square made Driver famous, and it pissed a lot of people off, particularly a lot of black people. Norman Mailer passed him in the green room—where Driver was waiting to appear on the "Dick Cavett show"—offered his hand, introducing himself, and said to him, "You got balls, Kid. Jimmy Baldwin thinks so too." After which he offered an encouraging wink. Stories were abounding about black ministers railing against the sin of homosexuality in black churches all across the country; on the Evening News they asked their congregations to bow their heads and pray for the lost soul of the young Mr. Trulove to return to the flock. "Stray no more, Mr. Trulove. Stray no more." "Give yourself up, young man. Give yourself up. Jesus welcomes you as he welcomes all sinners, as he welcomes all of us here in this congregation, here in this community, here in His world, give yourself up. Hear me now. Jesus saves." "When the apple is rotten at the core, open it, son, open it to the Lord and let the Lord, son, do his thing, and Lord, we pray today, Lord, let the sunshine in. Let the sunshine in. Let the sunshine in. Thank you, Jesus. Amen. Amen. I say, Can I get an

Amen? Can I get me an Amen now? Are we communicating? Thank you, thank you. Amen. Amen."

Rob Vicker at *Esquire* was ecstatic: the mailroom was overflowing with letters to the editor. And he was the editor! Never had he received this much mail. The country, he noted happily, was divided! A prominent black minister reacted with "disgust" and "nausea" that "so gifted a young man as Driver Trulove could employ his gifts in the service of the Devil himself." A white Catholic priest offered to perform an exorcism. A radical black activist lamented the diversion from the real issue, freedom and equality for black people. That one really got under Driver's black skin: "I'm not black because I'm a homosexual?" he asked rhetorically. A prominent mainstream Civil Rights leader wrote solemnly in an op-ed piece for the *Washington Post* that "Mr. Trulove has single-handedly set back the Civil Rights Movement decades."

Ah, but the little people loved him. Well, a few of them. Black (and to a lesser degree white) homosexuals denounced the "hypocrisy" and "pomposity" and "downright narrow-mindedness" of the black church. "'Judge not, lest ye be judged,'" wrote a black convert to Judaism, from Fire Island. From San Francisco, LaShawn Jackson, a high school history teacher: "Dr. King included in the Dream 'all God's children,' not 'all God's children' but homosexuals." "What's all the fuss?" wrote in Anonymous. "A hole's a hole."

Rob printed the latter one, after which Driver responded to it personally, paraphrasing George Orwell. "True, Arlanne, but in the eyes of some apparently some holes are more equal than others."

The moral majority used it as an excuse to sneer at the moral fluff, wayward frivolity and sheer degradation of the left, which they did anyway. The religious right, both racist and homophobic, fell to their knees, shouting to the Lord Almighty to rid the land of pestilence and sin, while on their feet nourishing the secret hope that should God fail, the niggers and homos might kill each other off.

Meanwhile, at a prominent research university the results of a major study were publicized. Two groups of men, after having declared themselves purely heterosexual, were shown male pornography. Group one had no problem or issue with homosexuality and showed no signs of homophobia. Group two judged homosexuality to be either perverted, sinful, or both, and showed every sign of homophobia. In group one, considered straight but not homophobic, fifty percent of the men got erections looking at male pornography. Of the second group, all considered straight and homophobic, *eighty-five percent* got erections.

In the limelight Driver was thriving. After all, he was a writer now, a real writer. "Real writers," he told his mother on the phone from Boston, "are supposed to piss people off. Ask Arlanne," he told her. "She'll tell you. But first let me call her to make sure."

"Uh huh."

"See, Mama, I'm still yo' boy, amusing as ever."

"Driver, there's just one thing I need to ask you. Did I do anything, you know, or did hanging around the brothel and all, you know what I'm saying . . . asking? Did somebody do anything bad to you, baby?"

"No, Mama, no one did anything "bad" to me. I promise. Did you do anything wrong? No, Mama, you didn't. You're the greatest mama in the world. Honestly, you were such a powerful force in my life, such a positive one, I think I did identify with you."

"But, well, do you like women?"

"Mama, I *love* women. I just love men too."

"That's my Driver. Always has loved everybody."

Driver could hear her thinking through the phone line, fingering the cord. Driver loves everybody. That's what she would tell the nosy and the righteous just to shut them up.

"Just like the good Lord says, Mama."

"Aw, Driver, what the hell you know about what the good Lord say. You ain't hardly ever step your foot in a church. What was all that stuff in your story about the black church? How you know all that?"

"I know they feel about me exactly like white folk feel about us."

"Well then, if they feel that way about my boy, I'm glad I never gave 'em my patronage in the first place. And damn if I'll start now. And if I hear about 'em rantin' on about sin and homosexuality and all that—by damn if they mention your name—I'll damn sure boycott 'em as big-time as I did Palmer's and the rest of downtown."

"Mama," he teased, "how you gon' boycott a church you never attended in the first place?"

"Now you look here, young fellow, you may be some big shot writer and reporter and Harvard hot shot, but you smart off to yo' mama one more time and she gon' be up there with a stick and give you somethin' to really show yo' ass about."

"Mama?"

"Yeah."

"You my mama?"

"Course I'm yo' mama. Who else gon' want the job? Especially after you done gone and made such a spectacle of yourself. Aw, it all right. I done talked to Bert. He said it natural and all that, that it just meant you were freer than most of us and if I think about it, knowing what I know from the brothel and all, there probably some truth in that lie."

"There is, Mama. Remember when Boonie went crazy and attacked Royal? He was fightin' himself. Remember?"

"To thine own self be true."

"So tell me, Mama, what'd you think about the piece. Did you like the subtitle: 'A Letter to Mama?'"

"Well, I've actually done some thinking about this very thing."

"Yes? And?"

"Yes I have."

"Go on."

"Well, Son, you know, you gettin' to the age now where you ain't got to tell Momma everything?"

Much less the rest of the world, she thought, hanging up. But she didn't want to say anything that might hurt his career or, Lord knows, that might make her boy unhappy.

'Cause he was happy.

Part VIII

1980S

| 72 |

Former Madam Lila Gets Elected to Town Council

Throughout the seventies Lila watched and waited as downtown gasped its last breaths. The upstairs of the old Ritz Cafe, where Lila had run the local brothel, was now a dusty, cobwebbed abandoned law office, the downstairs bar and restaurant run by one of Hoke's deputies in his off-hours, now just a hangout for Hoke and his buddies.

Every time she'd run into Hoke on the street, after giving him the rundown on Driver's grades at Harvard, she'd say, "I'm waitin', Hoke. You ready to sell that Godforsaken ex-whorehouse and bar to me yet, where I can turn it into somethin' respectable, or you just gon' hang on till you go broke?"

"Now Lila, you know I'd love to sell to you. We go back a long way. But that Dinnerman business a few years ago came awfully close to settin' me back with my boys. You know that. People got to be ready for that kind of change."

"That Dinnerman business was fifteen years ago. You know somethin', Hoke, you always was chicken shit. That's the only thing ain't changed."

"Now Lila, give it time. Just—"

"'Now Lila, just give it time,'" she mimicked him. "How much time, you dumb cracker? Look around, Hoke, you damn fool. Downtown needs a respirator to breathe. Dammit Hoke, two things ain't changed. You still chicken shit, cowtowin' to a bunch of dumb crackers so much you believe all that shit yourself, and you still dumber'n a post."

Hoke smiled at her, shaking his head, grimacing and bemused at the same time. Too dumb and thoughtless, she understood, to get really angry. Yet he was completely aware that he was unable to get over her. The spark of passion she had ignited in him he would carry with him to the grave. "You know, I always liked that about you, Lila. You got spunk. You say what you think, everything else be damned."

"And you know what I always disliked about you, Hoke? Spunk ain't never paid a call on you, not once in your entire life, and if it did it'd be such a shock to your system it'd give you a heart attack. And you ain't never had a thought of your own, never. One knocked on your door upstairs you wouldn't even recognize it, so it ain't surprisin' you ain't capable of sayin' what you think."

"Man, you hard, Lila. That's hard."

She stared at him with unwavering intensity. "I am hard, Hoke. I've had to be. Cracker culture has made this nigger hard. Harder than you and your good ol' boys. I'm gon' buy your place—not Freddie's, yours—and you gon' sell it to me."

And he would. Murray Gold had given her just the information, the right leverage, she would need.

Besides, after all his successful Civil Rights work as a U.S. attorney back in the 60's and 70's, when he'd just about single-handedly integrated half the state, unless Murray was on their side Hoke and his buddies were all scared to death of him.

Because he was the most feared lawyer in town, he'd become, in his own way, one of the most feared men in town.

As downtown sank into financial lethargy, Hilton Head, only thirty miles south of Somerset, was building up so fast traffic-congestion was becoming a problem. With its grand hotels, upscale shopping centers, gourmet restaurants, and world-class golf courses, it was becoming not only one of the most popular vacation and tourist resorts in the country, but a haven for wealthy retirees, many from up North looking for warm weather, who were buying up new homes on the ocean, on the sound, on the lagoons, or on golf courses as fast as they could be built.

Lila remembered when there was barely one white family and a handful of poor blacks living on the island, when you could only get to it by boat, and then, legend had it, only if the mosquitoes didn't get you first. Hilton Head was making money. So could Somerset, Lila felt, if inspired by the right brain: hers.

First she ran for the Town Council, and on the strength of a complacently low white voter turnout and a high black voter turnout, she won a seat, the first black person ever to sit on the Somerset Town Council. Not surprisingly, she proved herself a wise, shrewd politician. While she had won her seat on the strength of the black vote, she knew that to get what she wanted for herself—her own business in an integrated downtown—and her supporters, she would have to make certain the good ol' boys got what they wanted.

She announced her plan at the first Town Council meeting, looking directly in the sparse audience at Myron Suggs, the reporter for the *Somerset Weekly*.

She knew Myron wasn't the brightest bulb on the planet, and she knew from the McGowan trial that the only story reporters got was the one given them, and that even then they usually got it wrong, so staring at him hard until he put pen to paper, she announced her plan slowly, enunciating each word carefully, giving Myron all the time he needed to screw it up.

And what was her plan? "To revitalize downtown," she announced, "to bring the money back into Somerset."

Bradford Palmer, who'd been on the council for decades, and who'd been a major force blocking her purchase of Freddie Dinnerman's place fifteen years earlier (as had the rest of the council) smiled. Marty Liebowitz said, "How you gon' do that, Lila? If we lowered our prices any more we'd be losin' money."

"We're already losin' it," said Harper Dawes. But even though he was responding directly to Marty, he was looking directly at Lila through the upper half of his bifocals.

"We ain't lowerin' prices," said Lila. "We raisin' 'em."

"Now how we gon' do that?" said Marty Liebowitz.

"We gon' build a riverfront street, complete with parks, play structures for the little 'uns, benches from where you can sit and watch the sunset over the river, gourmet restaurants, cute little shops and art galleries like at Hilton Head, waterfront bars, coffee shops, book stores, a pipe and tobacco shop, all upscale, expensive as hell, and way more than most locals can afford."

"If the locals can't afford all this," said Harper Dawes, "who do you project are our customers?"

"Exactly the same type customers at Hilton Head: tourists, wealthy retirees, Northerners looking for warm weather, good fishin', sailin', swimmin', golfin', riverviews, oceanfront views, marsh views, huntin'. Throw in the antiques, cute little boutiques, and local art for the women."

"Your idea is to start with the town itself . . . ," ventured Bradford Palmer.

"Lot of history here, one of the oldest towns in America, with some of the oldest homes," said Lila.

"Spared by Sherman," said Marty Liebowitz. "Everything still intact."

"Then," continued Bradford Palmer, "expand outward, over the bridge, eastward, and develop the beaches and the islands? Golf courses, cabins, hotels, subdivisions . . . Why, that's enough work for every able-bodied man in town."

"Now who the hell's fundin' this little project, Lila," said Hoke Cooley, standing in the corner back of the room by the door, where he always stationed himself at the Council meetings. "John D. Rockefeller?"

"You ain't," said Lila. "That's for sure. And when it happens, keep your ass hidden so tourists won't know how dumb we are."

That kind of broke up the room a bit, made everybody feel more at home with Lila there.

"So you're projectin' tourism as our trade," said Bradford Palmer. "Retirees, yankees . . ."

"That's right, just like at Hilton Head. Anybody with money. Lots of it."

"Lila, I hate to sound dumb as Hoke, but who *is* fundin' this little project?" asked Marty Liebowitz.

"We are," said Lila. "Mr. Palmer here's providin' the concrete for the Waterfront Street from the Somerset Concrete Block Company, which as we all know, he owns. Mr. Dawes' Construction Company's doin' the buildin'. Thompson's Landscapin' and Nursery's doin' the seedin', plantin', and landscapin'. Your boy's gon' be the architect and draw up the plans. My boy'll probably write up the brochure and some local history. Who that gal teachin' photography over at the University? We'll need her to give us some enticin' photographs. There's plenty of work here for everybody, and since we layin' it out on the table here, everybody in this room's gon' get rich 'cept Hoke. Hoke ain't 'cause he's sellin' me his building, which means he won't be in business 'cept as sheriff. If he don't, Murray Gold's gon' sue the whole lot of you for 'Interfering With Economic Relations' for blockin' my purchase of Freddie Dinnerman's place fifteen years ago. You might say, Lila, the Statute of Limitations is up on that, and you'd be right. I'd lose the case, but by Murray's lights, you'd lose the money, because if you don't think all the negative publicity showin' Somerset as some racist, redneck, backwater hick town wouldn't drive away tourists and Yankee dollars, you're a helluva lot dumber'n most white people I know. Now I know you fellows way too smart to throw pie in prosperity's face so you gon' do business the way you always have. Everybody on the island and in the slums all dyin' to work. Sutcliffe'll supply furniture, Jones the appliances, Wilson the landscapin' equipment, Bazemore'll do the plumbin', everybody involved, everybody makin' money, so nobody bitchin'."

It was so quiet there for a moment that the only thing you could hear was the almost imperceptible sound of a car passing by. Hoke pulled a handkerchief out of his back pocket to wipe his brow. Bradford Palmer doodled on a note pad. The pause was so pregnant that Myron Suggs, plagued by insecurity anyway, looked suddenly as if taking notes for the newspaper might be considered intrusive, somehow improper.

"We can have them horse and buggies tourin' everybody around town, like they do in Charleston and Savannah, advertisin' at the same time," said Harper Dawes.

"Boat excursions, fishin' expeditions, sailboat regattas. They do sailboat regattas in Charleston," said Marty Liebowitz.

"Australia too," said Harper Dawes.

"England too," said Marty. "Just about everywhere there's water. Cape Cod, up North in Massachusetts."

"Hell, y'all," Hoke shouted from the back of the room, "why don't we just fly the Union Jack in front of the courthouse and kiss the Confederate flag goodbye?"

"Goddammit, Hoke," muttered Marty under his breath, but everyone heard him. Then he looked at Lila and said, "'scuse me, Lila."

"Gentlemen, there's a lady in the room," said Bradford Palmer, nodding graciously toward Lila. "My apologies, Mrs. Trulove, for our colleagues."

| 73 |

For Murray, Bert, and Arlanne, Love Mostly Conquers All

Murray did go to Israel, where he did find a wife, Tova Levke, a French Israeli he met in Haifa. A match, Mrs. Gold had called it, made in Israel, by her niece Shima Heine who had herself relocated there from Jefferson, Alabama to find a Jewish husband, which she did. Why not New York? asked Shima's family beforehand. Too critical, Shima had answered, too abrasive. And in Israel she expected tact and touchy-feely? In Hebrew, she'd answered, who would know? Tova did her hair. Shima took Murray to her salon in downtown Haifa for a haircut. Tova rearranged it to her liking, according to plan, then with a flourish swiveled him around to face the mirror in which he discovered, lo and behold, it was to *his* liking. Indeed, at this very moment, according to Mrs. Gold who got the word from Shima ("long distance, every time") it was love at second sight. Both Murray and Tova felt Tova had performed a miracle. They could not tear their eyes from the mirror. His new look had captured them both, and they gazed into his eyes with such longing and devotion that customers begin to grow antsy. At once both Tova's and Murray's hearts melted, and both fell in love with him.

So revealed Mrs. Gold to everyone in the synagogue.

Ah, said Lottie Dinnerman, I see. Tova fell in love with Murray and Murray fell in love with Murray.

And why not? Asked Mrs. Gold. They're both Jewish.

That was shortly after Hoke threw up his arms in despair, succumbed to the pressure from Murray and the town patriarchs, and sold the old building, which had once housed a brothel, to Lila which with all deliberate speed she converted into an upscale boutique called Sandals and Shoes.

And why not? said Elweena Owen. That's what she sells.

Beats what she was selling before, said Mayetta at the No View, which under Lila's plan had reopened downtown.

But who around here can afford 'em? wondered Elweena.

Mrs. Gold informed Murray and Tova upon their return to the states that "living together" before marrying was "not an option" as it would "look bad" in the community and therefore be "bad for the Jews."

Tova looked startled. "Vat eesn't, Meeses Gold?"

"Music? Bridge? Challah?"

"Kids," offered Murray, "with all deliberate speed?"

"What can be bad for the Jews," shrugged Mrs. Gold, reconsidering, "can be good for the Jews."

"Eeexackly!"

"The cart before the horse," said Mrs. Gold.

"Eeexackly!"

"You push from behind. So what's wrong with that?"

"Eeexackly!"

"You get there the same way."

"Eeexackly!"

And so they did.

Asher was born almost nine months later, Jocinta a year after Asher.

The Jews in particular adored them. As soon as they were old enough, they served punch and cookies at the Oneg Shabbats while Mrs. Gold entertained with everything from show tunes to Chopin Etudes to Hava Nagila.

All was well in the Gold household.

On the other hand, Arlanne was unable to have kids. Disappointment lodged in her soul, her emptiness and Bert's obsessiveness further exacerbated his frustration and disappointment. The joy they took in the birth of Asher almost nine months after Murray's return from Israel with Tova also heightened their awareness of their own loss. After a brief depression in which Arlanne had an affair with a black woman who wove baskets and created folk art on the Island and Bert had an affair with Mayetta, the waitress at the No View, both purely lustful affairs quickly consumed by their own flames, they decided to adopt twins who would otherwise have been raised in the black orphanage in Savannah.

Bert doted, Arlanne smothered them with the affection her father couldn't give. Bert would often tell her that though he hadn't married a Jewish wife, the children nevertheless had a Jewish mother, though as the kids got older the only time they wanted to go to the Synagogue was to help the Gold's kids serve punch and hand out cookies at the Oneg Shabbats. Arlanne softened and glowed. Writing took a back seat to the children. Driver had even taken over her column at *Esquire*.

While Bert kept warning her the kids, having been abandoned by their biological parents, might eventually, for awhile, spurn intimacy even from them, they seemed to prosper. He rubbed their backs every night, telling them stories about stools so clever they flew from the toilet out into the open air, reappearing as blackbirds; about the time the whole town by pure coincidence farted at the same time, the leaves disappearing from the trees for the only time in history in mid-summer; about automobiles running on roughage.

"You sound like your mother," Arlanne would tell him.

Bert smiled, wistful. "She read my stools like the stars."

Arlanne would read to them, at first fairy tales and later chapter books, if for no other reason, she told Bert, than to let them know life existed outside the bathroom. Afterwards, she would sing them to sleep with lullabies.

"I'd drop off to sleep too at the drop of a hat if I had to listen to that voice," Bert told her.

"Yeah, me too," shouted Alton from the bedroom one evening, long after he was supposed to be asleep.

Louisa giggled.

Bert and Arlanne couldn't help but smile at each other.

The twins' mother, Erma Vernelle Oren, was born and raised on Daufuskie Island, about an hour by boat equidistant from Somerset and Savannah. Before Daufuskie was bought up by developers and turned into a hotel and a golf course, descendants of slaves were the only inhabitants of the Island, except for one white couple who handled the mail, owned the marina, such as it was, where a shrimpboat and several small fishing boats—rowboats really—docked, and from where many of the inhabitants—manual laborers and domestic workers—were daily ferried over to Savannah and back. At that time the island contained no indoor plumbing and only one phone, which belonged to the white couple. Voodoo was the island religion. The only commercial enterprise was fishing. The schoolhouse was a one-room schoolhouse. Though they were surrounded by water, none of the people on the island, with the exception of the white couple, had ever learned to swim. Most also, but for the white couple, were illiterate.

Erma Vernelle Oren was one of the few kids on the island who could read well above her grade level, write with ease and fluency, and actually solve algebra problems. The teacher on the Island at the time, Ruthie Ann Burton, a young black VISTA worker from Santa Cruz, California, introduced Erma as much as possible to the world beyond Daufuskie. She took Erma, as well as her other students, to Savannah to the zoo, to concerts, to ball games, to see the Harlem Globetrotters in Charleston, to the small circle of activists in Somerset and at Penn Community Center. More than any of the other island kids, Erma yearned for the world beyond the island. She saw the pictures in the magazines—*Life, Newsweek, Ebony, Time*—that Ms. Burton ordered for her, and she not only marveled at them, she believed in them. How worldly, she thought. The fashions! She couldn't take her eyes off the leather, the pocketbooks, the boots, and the miniskirts.

And at eighteen, she said goodbye to her Grandmother who had raised her, her parents long before having migrated up North, and headed for Savannah via the ferry from the white couple's dock, where within six months she was pregnant with the twins, with no real way to support them. Initially, upon her arrival, after finding a room in a boarding house in the black section of town, all she'd done was wait on tables in a small black restaurant trying to save enough money to start college. That and in the evenings after work reading leftover newspapers and magazines left by customers.

She hadn't known what she was doing, having never been taught really to say "no." On the Island she'd never had to. She sure knew by now she was never going to see him again. He had money. How was she to have known, until it was too late, that he was the neighborhood drug dealer? Or was she so desperate by the time she met him in the cafe she didn't want to know. He had started her out on pot, which quieted her desperation and her gradual decline into hopelessness, and hooked her on cocaine, then crack. Since she couldn't do without it, she couldn't do without him.

She'd tell Bert later that not only had she never really had a daddy, she'd never had a boyfriend. So not only was she needy, she was ignorant.

She needed help, and six months pregnant, she sent word by an old classmate on the ferry to Ms. Burton that she needed help.

Ms. Burton lived in Somerset, traveling daily back and forth to Daufuskie by motorboat. She dealt the drug dealer out of Erma's life, packed her up, paid her rent, got a cab to the Savannah riverfront where her boat was docked, and headed straight to the Somerset Mental Health Clinic, and when Bert wasn't there she headed straight to his house.

She knew both Bert and Arlanne. She'd gotten to know Arlanne over a decade ago when she featured her in her article for Rob Vicker, then at *Atlanta Weekly*, on Yankee VISTA workers retreating to the more racially hospitable terrain of the South. Like them, Ruthie was a liberal activist, and the liberal activists in Somerset were a pretty close-knit group.

After "drying out" at the clinic, Erma would stay, it was decided, at Ruthie's. By day she would work in the Elementary school cafeteria in Somerset, and by night attend classes at the local University extension. They expected her to have relapses, binging again and again on Coke or whatever she might get, but they committed to watching her and to returning her to the clinic each time she did. Moreover, the clinic would provide her with outpatient therapy. Obviously she couldn't keep the kids, having no way to support them—besides, she was only eighteen years old herself—and upon seeing them in the hospital both Bert and Arlanne had begged for them.

"They're so little," marveled Arlanne, "so adorable. My God." And for that moment at least, she believed.

Bert embraced her, weeping, his eyes never leaving them.

Yes, they were crack babies, a phenomenon he was becoming more aware of in his work at the Somerset Mental Health Clinic. Though entirely undeterred, Bert and Arlanne through the twins' first hours and days in particular experienced such a highly aroused state of anxiety so new to them they wondered if they might levitate. Would the twins, they feared, experience withdrawal symptoms? Would morphine be required? That Sunday Arlanne went to church, resuming her place in the front pew beside her mother as if she'd never left it, and that Friday evening to the delight of the congregation Bert went to the synagogue where Rabbi Perlmutter prayed for the health of the twins. Black twins. At least by all appearances. (Their biological father was actually Hispanic, so they were in truth biracial.). Were there a few raised eyebrows among the locals? Sure, a few of the elderly ones. Naturally,

Bert could have cared less. After services at the Oneg Shabbat, in his defense Mrs. Gold invoked Sammy Davis Jr. and Freddie Dinnerman Ethiopian Jews and Rabbi Perlmutter the lost Jews of Mexico, the ancestors of whom had fled the Spanish Inquisition and converted to Catholicism.

Shayna Liebowitz: "There are Jews in Mexico, Rabbi?"

"There were."

There was a collective gasp. The biological father—the drug dealer, in other words—he was from Mexico (on his way back, in fact, due to the machinations of Ruthie Ann Burton). Was it possible? Could he, could he have been . . . a Jew?

"Of course not," said the rabbi, "he was a drug dealer."

The collective gasp turned into a collective sigh of relief, and everyone went back to their oohing and aahing and punch and pastries.

In any case, their prayers were answered. The hospital reported that the twins' sensory awareness and reactions, their muscle tone, their energy levels, their curiosity, as well as their sleeping patterns suggested nothing but two fabulous futures.

Later, if problems arose, Bert was learning as much as anyone about how to handle them, and Arlanne was reading everything she could find on the subject.

Remember too, Ruthie reminded them, their mother is very bright.

What saved the twins, however, according to the doctors at the hospital, was the intervention of Ruthie Ann Burton, the result of which was that Erma Vernelle Oren was off crack the last three months of her pregnancy.

The agreement was that Bert and Arlanne were their adoptive parents with full responsibility for raising them. However, they wanted them to be able to visit and know and spend time with their biological mother. While Erma finally graduated from the University in Columbia and became a social worker herself, she periodically relapsed. She was untrustworthy, incapable of raising the kids or spending long amounts of time caring for them. Still, with Arlanne, they visited her in Columbia and when Erma visited her grandmother on Daufuskie or Ruthie (now teaching at Somerset High School) in Somerset often she stayed a few nights with the Levys so she could play and be with the children.

Could the children go with Erma to Daufuskie to visit their grandmother? No more than they could travel to New York to visit their paternal grandparents. Unless, Arlanne announced, she went with them.

"And to your parents' house three blocks down the road?" asked Bert.

"Only if you go with them," she said.

| 74 |

Jack Goes in the Water, Royal Goes to Jail, and Mary Beth Goes to Work

On Scataway Island, alone in the "fishing shack" at the dining room table, Jack McGowan was pleased and satisfied—relieved, actually—with the knowledge that today, May 3, the same day and month of the year he ordered the Death March into Oyster Creek, he would die, suffering the same fate as the three young recruits who had drowned under his leadership. It was three O'clock in the afternoon, and it was high tide. This was not a knee-jerk, hasty decision; he'd been planning this for a long time. As dear as Royal and Mary Beth were to him, the only thing really that had kept him alive was the responsibility he'd felt for his son Jamie Mac, who was now a man, an adult, assuming responsibility for himself. Unbeknownst to Mary Beth and Royal, in Jack's own mind he'd agreed years ago on the purchase of this particular house, which they euphemistically referred to as their "fishing shack," for one reason, and one reason only: the "deep water dock" highlighted in the brochure. He'd wanted to be certain that when the time came to check out, the door would be wide open. And on this, the day of his departure, to be doubly certain, he'd waited for high tide. There was a chill in the air, and the water would be cold, but he knew he wouldn't feel it, just as he was fully aware that he was no longer capable of swimming—which was why he'd never tested the water himself—that his fear of the outstretched arms of the Devil Himself awaiting him would result in his body anesthetizing itself, growing numb, suffering the same rigor mortis in the water as it had on Dr. Levy's sofa decades earlier. Only this time, however, the Devil would not relax his grip, and God finally would surrender him his due, for which he was thankful.

Only Hell, he felt, could burn away his guilt, and despite his gentle and peaceful demeanor his torment was so agonizing that he felt no fear.

Mary Beth was at work. She was a beloved teacher over at the University, which Jack realized was somewhat unusual for a teacher of Business courses.

Financially, Jack wasn't worried about her or Jamie Mac or Royal. Eventually, when she retired, she'd be eligible for a pension. Royal was already collecting his. And Jamie Mac's commune had turned into a profitable health food market out in Arizona.

All of Jack's affairs were in order. His pension, small though it was, would go to Mary Beth.

He wrote his last letter carefully: there were three people he loved dearly, and he wanted to tell them, and he wanted them to share in his relief and liberation. He did not want them to begin suffering, he wrote, just as his was ending. Of all people, a murderer, in his own way, should assume responsibility for his own death. Anything less would be hypocrisy.

Mary Beth, he wrote, you are the most understanding wife a man could imagine. You could have left easily, particularly with your education, but you stayed. And so you remain in my heart forever. Forever. I understand you and therefore love you in ways I could never have dreamed as a young man. How you could have stayed with me with neither judgment nor condemnation, however, is beyond my understanding. All I know is that you did. And you stayed with me through who I was and who I became. As bad a man as I am, I was and am so much the better for it. A simple man, all I know to say is thank you. Thank you, Mary Beth. And I leave you with a love in my heart unlike anything I have ever known, a new thing, for me, that has endured and will survive me, just as the love in your heart for Jamie Mac, for Royal, and for your students will endure and will survive you.

Jamie Mac, though it may not seem that way to you now, know that in my heart I have been considerate of you. You're a man now, a real man, the man I so wish I could have been and am so glad and proud you are. Thank God you have escaped my fate and that of your late grandfather's. I destroyed lives, Jamie Mac, but with you I have also created one. Please understand: it is you who kept me alive all these years. Now it is time for me to go. I leave you with little but my love. I promise you, that is more than enough.

Royal, my true friend, my companion, my partner in crime, my soulmate. Our understanding of each other is the gift of love. I leave mine with you.

Each of you possesses in your heart the truth of me, all of me, the best of me. I leave you with me.

My love,

To Mary Beth McGowan, Jamie Mac McGowan, and Royal Cunningham, from whom I go in peace

Royal Cunningham was in Columbia, South Carolina's state capital—about a two-hour drive from his home on Scataway Island—for the day, ministering to prisoners in the South Carolina State Penitentiary. He met with the prisoners both individually and in groups, however they preferred it.

Initially, upon first entering the prisons, he was introduced to the assembled prisoners by the warden or deputy warden as a spokesman for the Vietnam Veteran's Association and a war hero, after which he would announce that indeed he had been a hero, that he had risked his life—out of necessity had killed enemy soldiers—to save the lives of his men, but that he had also been a villain, that he had intentionally, needlessly murdered in cold blood at least three people—a young father, the village elder, and a fifteen-year-old girl.

"I am the brother," he told them, "only of the haunted, the guilty, the ashamed, of the psychopath and the sociopath, and of the living dead, you whose eyes are lifeless. If you claim innocence but know in your heart you are guilty, I am your heart. If you truly are innocent, I am who you are not, at most the spectacle of a fall from grace.

"The murder of the enemy in combat is seen as justifiable, even noble, while the murder of innocent civilians constitute crimes against humanity, were they to be prosecuted. That may be true—I no longer know. But as one who has committed both kinds of murders, the killing of enemy soldiers and innocent civilians, in my heart, for me, there was no difference. Both were acts of terror, of confusion, of rage, of pure rampant lust, thrilling, exhilarating. Of fear, yes, but of wanton meanness and sadism. Both, in short, were highs. Acts of rage, yes, then contemptuous, finally cold, calculated indifference, pure heartlessness.

"Soon I had no feeling whatever for anyone, much less myself.

"I see myself even today in your eyes.

"I come here today to seek an audience with you, each of you, not for your salvation, but my own. Through mine, however, you may find yours. And in yours is the possibility of mine. On my hands and knees I beg you, each and every one of you, to hear my confession. Those on the outside have no need to hear it nor the means to understand it. With each confession, I hurt a little more, I experience a little more agony, a little more guilt and shame, a little more warmth, perhaps become a little more, I daresay, human. The eyes of a fifteen-year-old girl, of a young father, and of a village elder at once open my own just a bit wider and break my heart just a little more. And if that opens your heart even a little, I am humbly grateful, because therein lies not only your redemption, but mine. As one who has taken lives, I ask you for the opportunity to save them.

"I ask you only to hear my confession."

It was pretty much the same every time, small but sometimes consequential variations on what he'd revealed to Bert Levy the first time he'd visited him two decades earlier. He knew he was cheating a bit. For him, it was less frightening to fall into that same state and to lose himself in it in front of an audience of many—at least initially, before they knew him—than of one.

". . . the interpreters, two boys who lived in the village, had told us that the village housed Viet Cong moles. That was the intelligence we had. But how could you tell? Two landmines exploded. Richards flying through the fog. Sniper fire! From where? From the periphery, the trees? The smoke, the smell, can't see shit. The huts themselves? Over there, from the drainage ditch? It's a setup, Goddammit! Another landmine. Fire, chaos, the air on fire. Can't breathe. Richards plastered against the well. The villagers hauled out of their huts, one by one, family by family. Where are the young men? More fire. This time from inside a hut. Sheffield down. Medic! Turner screaming in pain. Goddammitt, Medic! Delano on his back, wide-eyed, blood trickling out the corner of his mouth. Oh my God, you sons of bitches, please not Vagnetti. Please, whispering right before his eyes closed forever kill anything yellow. Rampage now, Kill anything yellow Goddammit Kill everything Kill yellow Goddamn you sons of bitches Waste 'em Die, you fucking gooks Firing and firing and firing totally out of control the Wild Wild West yippee yi yaa fury in the shells of bullets Die you mother fuckers die and it's all over and it's hard to tell who's who even after the air cover even who they hit and who they didn't Goddamn Goddammit Kill 'em all Disappear the whole Goddamn thing Wipe out Everybody Goddammit Fuck 'em Waste 'em That's it Go on waste 'em All of 'em the ghosts of all of it the ghosts of all of it and after the young father I shoot my own conscience out of the village elder's eyes and when Corporal Buchanan fondles the fifteen-year-old I aim for the corporal and I see the fear and horror in his eyes and the rifle shifts to the fifteen-year-old. She's dead. It's over for her too she won't remember either."

A surprising number of prisoners opened their hearts to him. This was no preacher, but a man, a real man, a man like them.

His ministry began in an unusual way. Several years ago he began compulsively committing petty crimes—repeatedly shoplifting an item he could care less about; hot-wiring and stealing a car only to take it for a leisurely drive until the cops could catch up to him; faking drunken driving by smelling of booze, slurring his words, and faking an inability to walk a straight line—just to get into jail, the only thing that could come close to satisfying his overwhelming need for penance, expiating his guilt. Morally, he could take seriously neither the death penalty nor suicide: too easy, he felt. Murder, he knew from experience, was not the answer. Pulling the switch on another or on yourself was the easy way out, a stealthy retreat into heartlessness, into indifference, a cowardly slipping away from the eyes of a fifteen-year-old girl, a young father, and a village elder, from their last hope, which was you, Royal Cunningham, you, no one but you, from their pain and agony that is your rightful due, from your memory, from the restoration of their dignity, their lives, however briefly you knew them in their best and worst moments, though far from your salvation, your only hope, and of significantly more importance, theirs.

To a degree, he found it in jail. He found himself openly confessing to every prisoner he could get to listen to him, his crimes, in all their horrific detail. Unlike with Bert, however, early in his ministry at times his confessions, honest though they were, were much like the prisoners' early confessions, cold, calculating, the details chilling. The same indifference that prevailed in the immediate aftermath of his killing spree sometimes surfaced when he began his confessions to the prisoners. It was easier to slip into indifference, the land of the living dead, than to surrender to the hell in those eyes, to the all-engulfing shame and remorse. Advance and retreat, advance and retreat, forward and backward, forward and backward, Bert had told him, would be the rhythm of his progress, which is why though still *"the rifle"* shifted and killed the fifteen-year-old girl in all other aspects of his confession he had moved from the second-person past to the first-person present "*—and after the young father I shoot my own conscience out of the village elder's eyes—*" and why he chose to speak out publicly against the war almost twenty years ago and why he'd begun his prison ministry more recently. He had to repeatedly and profoundly submerge himself into the waters of shame and guilt, into the gentle eyes of the enemy who never was, into the personal hell of his own creation to save not so much his soul, but theirs. Theirs. Theirs. Please God. Breathe life somehow back into them. Breathe into them heart, soul, personality. Remove my hell from their eyes. And with no prospect of a prison sentence in his future, with time threatening to distance him from the War, the land of the living dead had beckoned with a diabolically crooked finger, indifference a more and more wily seductress. So whether or not the prisoners knew they needed him, Cunnningham knew who did—he knew he needed them. Bring them back, Lord. Stop the killing, the madness. And he knew he needed them as much as the world did.

Often the prisoners indeed did begin their confessions as he had. The warden called them "sociopathic confessions," empty of true feeling, a flat cold recitation of the facts. Soon, however, with each confession of his own,

Royal Cunningham's agony to these prisoners was palpable. If God was in the details, so was agony and remorse. It was also unusual for many of these prisoners, particularly those in the State Pen, to even admit to their crimes. But as he did, prison officials began noticing that the prisoners themselves did. As he opened his heart to the prisoners, they found themselves unable to keep themselves from opening theirs to him. Not all of them, certainly, but hardened criminals softened in his presence. Guilt and shame, relief and remorse, sensitized and humanized them.

Hoke noticed it first in the County Jail, after Royal would get picked up for some misdemeanor he'd contrived. Finally, he told Royal that he didn't have to commit crimes just to stay awhile. He could come and go as he pleased. As he observed Royal's effect on the prisoners, Hoke finally phoned the Commissioner of the State Department of Corrections. "He's a helluva lot more effective than the preachers who come in here. Besides that, he's free. Wouldn't take money if you begged him. The man's got technique. He just opens his heart to any poor old run-down S.O.B. who'll accept it. Then the poor old S.O.B., I don't care how hard and crazy he is, does the same thing to him. Hell, the whole place gets a hell of a lot nicer, I'll tell you that. This guy's drawin' water from stones."

Arlanne wrote in a piece for *Esquire* that after wandering around for twenty years in a metaphorical wilderness Royal Cunningham, according to one prisoner in the State Pen, was leading them to the Promised Land. "Where might that be?" she had asked the prisoner. "Right here," he said, touching his heart.

The Commissioner, after seeing him at work, marveled: "Mr. Cunningham," he told him, "You're raisin' the dead."

The only way, Royal knew, to expiate his sins. The hard way. The right way. And he counted his blessings that he was able to do it.

It was always a raw, vulnerable, heartbreaking drive from the state prison in Columbia back home to Scataway Island, as satisfying and fulfilling as it could be for a man of Royal's conscience.

Mary Beth often took a philosophical approach to her classes at the University Extension. Today she asked her Business Administration class exactly what "business" was.

"A way of making money," said Student One.

"For what?" asked Mary Beth. "For what purpose does a businessman make money?"

"To spend, to buy, to save for a rainy day, to live the American Dream," said Student Two.

"Exactly what is the American Dream, and how much does it cost?"

"It's freedom, power, and security."

"To do what?"

"Whatever you want, that's what freedom is."

"So freedom is for sale? Okay, let's assume for the moment that you have it. What do you want it for, this 'freedom?'"

"We told you, to be able do whatever we want."

"And what is it that you want?"

"Whatever makes us happy."

"What might that be?"

"Love, respect, material comfort . . ."

"In what order?"

They looked at her as if she were crazy.

"In business, one must prioritize."

"All three are important. You can't live on love alone, you can't get along with each other if you don't respect each other, and material comfort is necessary for, well, comfort, security."

"Of those three, which one costs the most?"

"The most money?"

"You're the ones who said business was to make money so you could buy what you wanted. Love, respect, material comfort . . ."

"'Money can't buy me love," sang Student Three.

"Then 'what's love got to do with it?'" sang Mary Beth. "If money can't buy you love, can you make money—not love—without loving what you're making, marketing, in short, your work?"

"Yes. Cheap, poorly manufactured goods can make a profit."

"Is that then the purpose of business? To make a profit?"

"Absolutely."

"And what's the purpose of profit?"

"We told you: to be able to buy what we want. Respect, admiration, power."

"So all your resources would go into profit."

"Right."

"So you'd be without love?"

"Wait, wait, you're confusing what we're saying?"

"Am I? If all your resources are going into making a profit, none is going toward making love. So what *does* love have to do with it?"

"Money can't buy love."

"So you're willing to settle for freedom, admiration, respect and material comfort . . . and no love?"

"Obviously we want that too, probably as much as anything else."

"So you've said. But a profit won't get you that: Money can't buy me love, you've said. So how do you get it if all your resources—time, energy, money—are going toward profit? Is profit all-important, or is love? Prioritize, because right now, the way you're looking at it, one drains resources from the other."

"Love's about life, profit's about business."

"But business, you argued, was to get you what you want, and what you wanted, among other things, was love."

"Maybe the question," said a student usually very quiet, "is not what we want from business, but from life?"

"Yes," said another, "then how does business help us get what we want from life?"

"Ah, so business is the means," said Mary Beth, "not the end. So if business can get you a profit, but not love, and love is also what you want, how do you get it?"

"Are business and love," asked the first student, "totally incompatible? Is that what you're saying?"

"No. That's what you're saying."

"Well," said the second student, "*Are* they compatible?"

"I don't know," said Mary Beth. "Are they?"

Next class she would have Royal come as a guest speaker. It would be interesting to have them hear what he gets out of his work, his take on "What's love got to do with it?"

Jack walked out on the dock in the nude. He would go out as he came in, with nothing. The tide was high, the afternoon still giddy with sunlight and the promise of spring, of fecundity, of rebirth and renewal, of crocuses and daffodils and the sweet smell of narcissus. And as he leapt off the end of the dock into the final glorious breath of the afternoon, from the underwater grave that awaited him there rose before him in a dizzying chimera of sunlight the outstretched hands of three young recruits, of eighteen-year-old Riley Francis McGahee, of Woodrow Edward Pennebaker—"Woody"—he remembered, of James Patrick O'Hearn, all now younger than his own son Jamie Mac, their faces, clear to him now for the first time since on this same day twenty-five years ago he reached out for them in the harrowing waters of Oyster Creek, rising now, ascending, turning now, turning toward the sun.

He fell, folding naturally into a self-protective fetal position, gloriously awaiting the waters of non-feeling, of numbness, of the living death that would prevent him even from treading water, much less swimming, of the living rigor mortis that would give way finally to the underwater grave where he was certain in the Devil's undertow of fire and water he would for eternity burn with guilt and drown in remorse. Over his own life, he chose death, and he had chosen it on the banks of Oyster Creek twenty-five years ago after he had lost, rendering expressionless, the faces of Riley Francis McGahee, Woodrow "Woody" Edward Pennebaker, and James Patrick O'Hearn.

Much to his surprise, however, the water was cold. Moreover, his feet touched the bottom. His body, also to his surprise, unraveled from the fetal position, and as he straightened up the water came up to his neck, a bit lower, shoulder high.

Clearly visible was no Hell, but instead Scataway Island: sky, sun, cumulus clouds, river all around, a chill in the air, "fishing shack," the palmettoes and scrub pines and cherry poplars, the deafening noise of a jet plane overhead; rising from the stink of pluff mud, less than 50 yards away, a snowy egret on a tree stump.

An oyster shell—perhaps, he thought, in a divine act of mockery—burnt a cut into his left foot.

Of all people, he thought, standing there silly, what was I doing playing God?

Deep water dock?

He felt, for want of a better term, "let down." Nevertheless, shivering, up to his neck in water, Jack McGowan embraced himself.

Royal drove up just as Jack, soaking wet and shivering, was coming out of the water. He couldn't believe what he was seeing: he'd been trying to get Jack to go in the water for years. Royal knew it would be a therapeutic experience for him, but he hadn't even been able to get Jack to stick his big toe in.

"You did it, Jack!" he yelled, leaping out of the car. "You did it, Buddy."

Part IX

1990S

75

Arlanne Says It's Better to be an Oreo Than a Cracker

By 1990, Somerset had changed, and Lila's plan had inspired the change. The Old Guard had let down their guard. In fact, Somerset was becoming a popular tourist resort as well as a haven for retirees. Yankees were now on the City Council. A former New Yorker was mayor. Downtown was renovated, all artsy and crafty. "Folk art" from the islands, from the Gullah blacks in the paintings of Jonathan Greene to the sweetgrass baskets woven by grandmamas on the side of the road, was becoming the national rage. One antique store was named "Precious Cargo." "Cute" was in: art galleries, trendy coffee shops, cozy book stores, gourmet restaurants, the latest in beachwear and high-end clothing. Need and practicality however—fast food, economy motels, Shoney's, feed and supply stores, nurseries, furniture and clothing outlets, car lots and boat lots—were poor relatives exiled to the outskirts of town, where they'd rallied around the K-Mart and the Wal-Mart. Indeed, even the natives who worked or owned businesses downtown, unless they were looking for something particularly upscale, decorative or artful—the latter particularly rare—drove out to the malls to do their shopping; it was cheaper. They visited each others' shops downtown, as did most of the other locals, to catch up on local gossip, see their lawyer, consult with an architect, or go to the bank.

If segregated by need and practicality, as well as largely by class, both the strip malls on the town's periphery and downtown itself were nonetheless racially integrated, downtown the preserve of tourists, the influx of wealthy Northerners and retirees, and periodically some of the returnees and trendier natives.

Palmer's Department Store was now an ice cream shop, a confectionary and an art gallery, the upstairs of which was the architectural firm of Dawes (the former mayor's son) and Thomas in which Dawes was white and Thomas was black. The most popular restaurant in town, Gullah, was owned and operated by a black family. The vice-president of the bank was black, as were several members of the Board of Directors. Lemuel Hunter, the Superintendent of Schools (and the son of retired school principal Eileen Hunter) was black. His daughter, a writer of children's books, enjoyed the prominent display of her books in the windows of the coffee shops and bookstores. And of course there was Lia Trulove's Sandals and Shoes, the first black-owned business of them all: clever, upscale, and frivolous, it fit right in. While most of the tourists and retirees were financially lucrative, and therefore the majority of them white, downtown Somerset catered most hospitably to the color of green. And the surrounding Islands, which before were surrounding islands of mostly poor blacks, were now dominated by river mansions and sophisticated golf course developments. It was a class divide now, with poor Blacks chased off their property by rising taxes.

In any case, home-cookin' was largely confined to the home. Instead of "gravy" local restaurants served "sauces" with foreign names, and instead of fresh okra and butter beans and fried chicken and a side of ribs they offered up French and Italian and Thai dishes the locals couldn't even pronounce. Supermarkets and liquor stores now sold wines from Italy, France, and California instead of just Mogan David for the Jews and Roma Rocket for the college boys. Where before local Jewish kids ate hamburgers and hot dogs like everyone else, now there was a bagel shop with smoked salmon, lox, and pickled herring as alien to them as it was to the other locals. The Riverbreeze Theater boasted a Foreign Film Series which annually sold out since there were more out-of-towners than natives living in Somerset now. One of the oldest towns in America, it naturally assumed a prized designation on the National Historic Register. Preservation was money, and Somerset was bustling. Only twenty minutes from the beach, as well as down the road from Hilton Head, Somerset was now a draw for the rich and famous. Elizabeth's former teacher, Pat Conroy, had made the town a celebrity in and of itself using it as a setting for his books, particularly since movies made from them were actually filmed in Somerset, turning it subsequently into a natural haven for filmmakers.

Still, even as the slums were becoming gentrified, crack was stealthily slipping into the pockets that were not. Bert was noticing the rising number of cases at the clinic. Bad for tourism, announced Lila in the *Somerset Weekly.*

Bad for the football team, announced Hoke, who with the help of local tipsters arrested local dealers, and teaming up with SLED and the Feds did his best to curtail smuggling coming in on the Interstate from Mexico.

While the Levy kids, Alton and Louisa, had indeed been crack babies, both had survived and were flourishing. Was it the steady influx of cognitive stimulation, social engineering, the watchful and sensitive eyes of astute parents? Genes? Ruthie Ann Burton's compassion and chivalry almost ten years ago? Murray and Arlanne had no idea. Nor did they care. Money and resources were being provided for those kids less fortunate, and they were relieved, if not ecstatic, that merely predictable if not "normal" conundrums were visited upon their children.

And what conundrums were predictable or normal had changed as much as Somerset.

Before integration, there were no biracial families in Somerset.

Now there were, and Alton found he did not like being called an "oreo" one bit, just because he had white parents, and every time a black friend got mad at him for anything at all, Alton told his parents, that's what they'd call him.

Better an "oreo," thought Arlanne, than a "cracker," but a cracker wasn't calling him an oreo. Black people were.

"Hmmm . . ." said Arlanne. "Why don't you call them 'Chocolate Fudge?'"

"If you do," advised Bert, "tell them it's your favorite flavor, and invite them over to the house for some."

"Man, who gon' be nice to somebody call 'em an oreo," said Alton.

Louisa smiled prettily, mischievously, her finger to her lip. She liked it when Alton got all feisty. Often she egged him on. At school sometimes she'd actually get her friends to call him an oreo. She just loved to watch him get mad and stomp around so frustrated all over the place. Sometimes he'd even cuss. She threatened to tell Daddy if he didn't stop. She liked playing Mommy.

"'Who gon' be nice to somebody call 'em an oreo?'" Where you learn to talk like that, boy?" asked Arlanne. "Was you brought up in the slums, or was it on the Island?"

"You know where I was brought up," he groused, "you brought me up."

"Then where you learn to talk like that?" she teased him.

He couldn't help but smile as Louisa sat there giggling, but he was doing his best not to.

"Yeah," said Bert, "where you learn to talk like that, boy? You want me to tell yo' mama give you a good lickin'? Speak up, boy. Ain't got no time for foolishness. Not yours or nobody else's. You hear me, boy?"

"Aw, Dad, shut up. You ain't funny."

"I want to know where you learn to talk like that. Louisa, you want to know where he learn to talk like that? Arlanne, she want to know."

"Come here, sweetie dumplin'," Arlanne said to Alton. "Come here and sit on yo' mommy's lap. Come on. Come on. That's it. Did you start talkin' this way when they started calling you an oreo?"

Louisa, feeling guilty, spoke for him. "That's when."

"Does it help?" Arlanne asked him.

He shrugged. "Sometimes. With my friends it might. I don't know."

"But not with your teachers?" asked Bert.

"Not with my white teachers."

"Then do it 'sometimes,'" Bert suggested. "You're a kid, you don't fully know who you are yet. You're just trying on different personalities, and when we're with different personalities and different kinds of people we tend to try to become like them, often without even realizing it. My parents, your grandparents, sent me to a Jewish camp in North Carolina one summer. I was just about the only Yankee down there. Within two weeks I had a Southern accent."

Puzzled, her arms around Alton, Arlanne looked up at him from the sofa.

"You never went to camp in North Carolina."

"So?" he said.

76

Tova's Opinion on Whether 'No' Means 'No' and 'Yes' Means 'Yes'

"Elizabeth Trulove," Murray told Tova, "is filing a criminal and civil suit against Hoke Cooley for sexually assaulting and raping her mother, in her mother's name."

The reds and magentas in their yellow vase, December roses from Arlanne's garden which Tova had until this very moment been setting off with a touch of Baby's Breath, brightened up like a still life the classically simple mirror above the credenza in their dining room. Uncomprehending, she turned to face Murray, sprigs of Baby's Breath on hold.

"Back in the fifties, according to Elizabeth."

Elizabeth had asked him to represent her, he explained, appealing to his friendship with her mother and his history in the Movement, after which, just as he expected, Hoke phoned, asking Murray to represent him against "this frivolous libel," reminding him (or himself) that he was "still the sheriff of this town, Dammit," and appealing not only to what he considered their long-standing friendship but to the historical fact that aside from Boonie's case against Royal Cunningham he'd always served as and, by all rights and assumptions, remained the family's attorney. Jesus, Murray'd thought, Elizabeth's already started working on Hoke. He's terrified. Elizabeth's intelligent, steady, and determined. A lawyer herself now, she knows the law, and she's using it as deliberately and effectively as she can.

"You never say him you doink Elizabeth?" Tova asked him.

"Representing."

"Speek Engleesh, pleeze."

"Representing," he brooded aloud. "Not 'doink.'"

"'Representating.' 'Doink.' Whatever eet eez, you don't tell him?"

"Don't be stern, Tova. It hardens your features."

She turned and stared at herself in the dining room mirror, her hands over her cheeks in dread and horror, above the reds and magentas in their yellow vase, sprigs of Baby's Breath descending on the credenza.

"Which are otherwise really pretty," he said coming up behind her.

"No," she said. "Though zee men, zey think so." She smiled at her reflection. "Not bad, eh?"

Her dangerously brown eyes, Murray noticed in the mirror—it had been his grandmother's—had lost none of their life and vitality. He gave himself credit for that, musing on what a nice catch he was. His hair, he noted, lookin' good, as good now as in Tel Aviv.

He nuzzled her, his hands rummaging about, roaming all over her. Her eyes, almost black, were at once curious and seductive, bold—angry perhaps—and defiant. Her olive skin smelled of a musk perfume, of fresh dirt and the sunlit Mediterranean. God, she was sexy: all Earth and fire, fairly brainless, a mockery of intelligence. For all her worldly sophistication, she possessed, he found himself thinking, not for the first time, a wild, unpredictable, outlaw beauty right out of the Old Testament desert, tribal, fiercely loyal.

"So tell me," she said, abruptly turning to face him. "Who weel you representate?"

He groaned, his ardor aborted.

"Tell me. Then I give you pussy. Good Jewish pussy. Jeeesst what Meeses Gold ordered. No?"

"No. I mean yes, yes. Oh, Jesus Christ," he said, collapsing at the dining room table. He had gained weight in the past few years, she had noticed. She would put him on Bert's diet. She'd ask Arlanne about it when she picked up the kids. She liked Arlanne.

"So," she said, sitting across from him.

"Your features are hardening again. Your intensity is unnerving. Here in the South we take things a little easier."

"Yes? And? So? Pussy is zere. Like eenything in life, you must work for it. Yes? Otherwise, features weel continue to harden. Oui?"

"Who will I representate? Honestly, I have no idea. Do I really want to press charges for an alleged rape that allegedly happened more than thirty years ago, after which sexual intercourse between the alleged rapist and the alleged victim was consensual for another ten years?"

"She, how you say, conseented after zee rape? Like an affair?"

"Alleged rape. She was his mistress for more than ten years. Elizabeth's argument is that as Sheriff, he abused his power over a black woman. 'How could a black woman in this town back then say no to the white sheriff?' That's her argument."

"After then saying yes for ten years."

"Right."

"Ah, you silly Americans with your no means no and yes means yes."

"What are you saying, Tova?"

"Dahling, 'no' has always meant 'yes.'"

"No?" he asked hopefully, his eyebrows rising.

"No," she teased. "No," she repeated, lifting and raising with thumb and forefingers higher and higher her skirt fanning out and about now with a hint of the coquettishness and frivolity of a dance hall girl's as her thighs parted, welcoming him in, then finally "Yes! Yes!" and despite what she'd said earlier, to no one's surprise, least of all theirs, meaning it.

| 77 |

Lila and Elizabeth Find Peace in the Inevitable

Murray's office was downtown, only a few blocks down from Sandals and Shoes. Damn, Hoke had been stubborn. But so was Lila. She told him she'd end up buying that building from him, and she did. All Murray had had to do—back in '82, he remembered—was to threaten to represent her in a civil suit.

Sure, they had hemmed and hawed and thrown up phantom obstacles just as they had with school desegregation, postponing the inevitable as long as they could. Still, it was inevitable.

Now the December sunlight penetrated so vividly the tall high windows of Murray's upstairs office (in an old Victorian Gingerbread with a view of the river) that he couldn't help but notice across his desk through the sun motes in the silhouette of Elizabeth her tall slender mother as a young woman. Though darker than her mother, Elizabeth possessed her mother's irony, if not cynicism, her skepticism in the narrowing of her eyes, her refusal to be taken for a fool in the raising of an eyebrow.

She was going to be tough. Tougher than her momma was in '82. Beneath that sophistication and education was a hard-wired obsession.

Lila'd had no case. She beat 'em in '82 simply by bluffing and refusing to fold. Now Elizabeth . . . He was getting too old for all this. He had to pick up Asher and Jocinta from Hebrew School in less than an hour, an hour he knew he'd never bill anyway; too close to the family. So once again no money, not in this case. From the radio of a passing car below, up through the tall high windows of his office, wafted Bette Midler's " . . . you are the wind beneath my wings," the December breeze from the river burrowing under the white linen window curtains huffing and puffing and billowing out like parachutes. All he had to do, he imagined, was pull the rip cord and sail out over the river, away . . . away . . . away from the haunting eye of the hurricane of Elizabeth's obsession, the melody on the wind calm and soothing, above the fray, beneath his wings. Prozac was on the market, but Murray preferred a good cigar. Selecting a Cohiba from his humidor, unconsciously he began humming "Fly Me To The Moon."

"Murray!" she said, jousting with him. "Are you trying to send me a subtle message?"

"I'm old, Elizabeth. I'm tired. I'm ugly. All I want to do is go home and sit slack-jawed in front of the ball game and watch Isaiah and Magic go mano-a-mano. I want to put on my earphones, sip a fine cognac, or perhaps a Diet Coke, and listen to a Chopin nocturne. I want to hear the sound of my kids' laughter through the windows from the backyard, then have one of 'em, tired, come sit on my lap for a little refueling and rejuvenation. Rabbit is at rest, Elizabeth, and I want to sit and rest too in my own comfortable little middle-class neighborhood comprised of an assortment of harmless others who'll leave me alone, refuse to discuss politics—or anything that might touch an earnest chord—and mind their own business except to happily allow their kids to play with mine and to wave and acknowledge my presence and say, 'Hey, Murray, how are you today?' Know what I mean, Elizabeth? Catch my drift, Love? Does Mama know you're here and exactly what you want? Better still, Elizabeth dearest, do you?"

"Absolutely. You ready?"

He howled in frustration.

His longtime secretary Angie White, in the outer office, heard him and smiled.

"You done? Murray, now I am not letting you out of this. You hear me?"

"I do, Elizabeth. I do."

"Okay, now let's get to work. I'm doing it all. All you got to do is present it."

"Naturally. And what exactly am I presenting?"

"And quit pretending you all old and ugly. You ain't and you know it."

He smiled. He loved Elizabeth. She hated white people so much, except for him and Bert, their families, maybe a few others. She got to know 'em to like 'em, said Lila, and she don't want to know 'em. Oh, but if she loved you! That was something. Just as tender and affectionate as when she was little. Like her mama, she knew how to flirt and turn a man's eye too, particularly a man like Murray, who she trusted had a special affection for her.

"We're talkin' a civil suit against Hoke. Murray, quit starin' out the window. You got to help me with this now."

"Okay," he said, looking directly at her. "I'm focused."

But he wasn't, she could tell. "What, Murray? You lookin' at me, but you ain't seein' me."

"I see your mother," he said, smiling at her. "In that light, Elizabeth, I would swear you look so much like her."

"Thank you. Now, the basis of the civil suit: the charge is sexual assault and rape. I'm charging Sheriff Hoke Cooley for sexually assaulting and raping Lila Trulove in 1953 on the basis that the sexual intercourse between them was not consensual. It was not consensual because in that time and place—segregation in the Deep South—Lila Trulove, a black woman confronted with a powerful white sheriff, was not free to consent, because under the laws she was not equal to any white person, segregation being the law, and segregation having since been proven "separate," as intended, but not "equal," as intended; instead "unequal." That he was the sheriff adds to the power differential. How could a black woman in the racist Deep South say no to a white sheriff? Her position was more one of involuntary servitude, in and of itself a violation of the thirteenth amendment, than one of equality. Segregation itself suggests legally condoned inferiority. Was she in a comparable position of slave to master? Comparable? Yes: refusal, like disobedience, could have resulted in economic reprisal, a loss of her means of earning a living, i.e., of food, clothing, and shelter since at the time whites controlled, either legally or through intimidation, the efficacy of such means, and in violence to her person since under an institutionalized racist legal system a black woman could not be guaranteed equal protection under the law. Where there is a power differential in such a sexual relationship, as the courts have found recently in professor-student and employer-employee relationships, threat is implied. Where threat is implied, consent is irrelevant, considered not 'freely given.'"

"And where threat is implied, coercion is. Thus, in the final analysis, a maximum charge of rape, a minimal charge of sexual assault?"

"Exactly."

"That she was on his payroll for ten years afterwards as his personal prostitute, mistress, whatever you want to call it—"

"'Prostitute,' Murray, since as you say, she was on his payroll, which again suggests fear, on her part, rather than consent. Psychologists will testify that most prostitutes have been sexually abused—"

"As you're alleging Hoke did to Lila in 1953."

"Exactly. The resulting low self-esteem, overwhelming fear, and the natural need to deny and normalize the abuse often leads to the repetition of it, i.e., in this case, prostitution. I assure you that either based on his reading of the research or his own clinical experience Bert, as well as the list of experts I have in here," she said, holding up and tapping her folder, "can testify to this."

"Would Lila want him to?"

"Lila's not a part of this."

"But the case is in her name, Elizabeth, it would have to be: Lila Trulove vs. Sheriff Hoke Cooley."

"It is in my mother's name, but she does not wish to be involved in this case, so I am doing it for her."

"'For her?'"

"For her. 'Vengeance is mine,' saith the Lord. I have no problem with that. But justice, satisfaction . . . those he reserves for my mother."

Anxiety had caused him to smoke his Cohiba halfway down in almost no time, he realized, before calling Bert. Plus, he was late picking up the kids from Hebrew School. Angie White thrust her head around the door. "Hellooo . . ." she sang, waving her cat's eye glasses at him, like Groucho Marx, he thought, with a cigar. "Have we had a pleasant afternoon?" Angie sang almost everything. It was irritating, especially when Murray was in a bad mood.

"No."

"How nice for you," she said sweetly.

"Your empathy is boundless. Much as I'd like to sit here and soak it up, I've got to run pick up the kids."

"Done," she sang.

"Excuse me?"

"Done. Sneaked out and picked 'em up myself. Oh, you know how kind and thoughtful I am. Lord, I reek of generosity. Reek. But I don't really like talking about myself, as everyone who knows me knows. Let the deed speak for itself, Mama always said. Of course, that was before Alzheimer's set in and she went absolutely bonkers. Bonkers, I tell you. Makes her boring as all get-out. That woman just opening her mouth is enough to put you to sleep for the rest of your life, just out of fear she might never close it. I tell you, Murray, the words, those darned words, they never stop flowing. And she don't even know you're there. Why drive all the way out to the nursing home if she don't even know you're there? Why, I get more out of tending my garden, which I ain't never gotten nothin' out of for over twenty years, neither flower nor fauna nor vegetable nor tree. Maybe that's why over at the nursery they call me 'The Black Thumb.' Could be, now that I think of it. So I just let her sit there, all by herself, talkin' her ass off. 'Momma,' I told her one time, 'you're boring.' You think that vibrated her eardrum? Shoot. Went in one ear and out the other. Finally I started sendin' Horace over there—"

"The dog?"

"Yeah, I drop him off. Hell, he's just about as old as she is. Mama don't know the difference. Imagine your own mother can't tell the difference between you and a dog. Don't do much for your self-esteem, I tell you what. But this ain't about me. Old Horace, he lay there at her feet, right beside the rocker. Puts him to sleep too, Nurse tells me. Puts everybody to sleep. Asher and Jocinta have trouble falling asleep? Just wheel my mama into the room. And she has a powerful affect on everyone, not just the young."

"Angie, while this is simply fascinating—"

"I know. People have always told me, they say, 'Angie you're so interesting when you talk.' I say 'Thank you.' Anyway, Mama always said to us, 'Don't toot your own horn.' So, as far as pickin' up the kids, my own work pilin' up while I'm ferryin' 'em here and there and everywhere: no raise, no bonus, certainly no applause. Please."

"Angie, thanks. I mean it. Sorry I ran so late with Elizabeth."

Angie checked her cuticles. "She suin' Hoke?"

"Angie . . . Goddammit. Look, I was picking them up because Tovah had a dentist appointment."

"So you want to know if anyone was home when I dropped off the kids."

"Right."

"Murray . . ."

"Okay, okay, just wanted to be sure."

"Actually she wasn't, so we voted unanimously to go to Dairy Land for ice cream. I suggested we vote three times for triple scoops. They agreed. It was all done democratically. By the time we got back, the kids' clothes were ruined, and Tovah was home waitin' for 'em. Everything's fine," she sang. "Angie made sure of it, as always."

There goes their appetite for dinner, figured Murray.

"Thanks, Angie. Appreciate it. Can't believe I forgot."

"No appreciation," she said. "Please. I just don't think I'm capable of handling that. Okay?"

"Right, Angie, I'm truly sorry. I lost my head."

"Apology accepted," she said sweetly, as always. "Among other things, Murray, as you know, I'm a very forgiving person. After all, I am a Christian. All Christians are. Would you care to become a forgiving Christian?"

"Angie?"

"Yes?"

"Get Bert on the phone for me, will you? I think I need a psychologist."

"Why, Tovah's been saying that about you for years. And before Tovah all your friends used to talk about it, in hushed voices, mind you. Much like the voice I'm using now."

"How considerate of them."

"You've got good friends, Murray. And a wonderful wife. Naturally when they feel a loved one's about to go off his rocker, whacko, daft, bananas, off the deep end, out of his ever-lovin' mind—"

"Thank you, Angie. Of course. Naturally. But you know what?"

"Do I know 'what?'"

"Yeah, you know what, Angie?"

"Well, Murray, I wouldn't know now, would I? Without knowing exactly what 'what' is?"

Murray surrendered, just gave up. With a newly lit Cohiba in one hand and by now at least three others at most halfway smoked in the ashtray, an indulgence he would never under normal circumstances have permitted himself, he walked over to the open window, to the billowing parachutes, to the wind beneath their wings.

"Fly me to the moon," he sang, "and let me play among the stars . . ."

"Here's 'what,'" he said to Angie, turning from the window. "They're all crazy. All my friends. And especially Tovah. And especially you."

But Angie was nowhere to be seen, no doubt back at her desk.

He couldn't see her, but suddenly he heard her, on the intercom.

"Dr. Levy on the phone, Sir. Line three."

"Bert?"

"Lila called," Bert told him, "I know everything. Driver's at her house. She's worried about what this might do to him. 'Sadness is in my boy's eyes,' she told me. 'Somethin' he's afraid of . . . needs to work out' . . ."

"Something *he* needs to work out?"

"Something they all need to work out. Does Elizabeth have a chance of winning this case?"

"None, Bert. Absolutely none. But she knows that. That's why she's throwing everything in the book at him. She'll ask for monetary damages, but she knows there isn't a chance she'll get them. She's filing the suit in Lila's name. Lila's not filing it. She has no chance. But she can win without winning."

"What do you mean?"

"She just wants to bury him, to ruin him, to ruin his reputation. Court documents are open to everyone, including the press. Even if the judge orders them sealed, they won't be for long. Besides, she can leak stuff to the press anyway. You know what's going to really hurt him in this town when it comes out?"

"The sheriff consorting with a prostitute, the brothel, his making money off of it, Jesus—"

"Adultery," said Murray.

"Adultery? You mean with Regina finding out?"

"She knows, I'm sure. No, not with her, with the town."

"Really?"

"It's a sin, Bert. That's the way people look at it. Public scandal. Taints the whole town. If you're going to do this kind of thing, keep it behind closed doors. See no evil, hear no evil, speak no evil. Discretion is the better part of valor."

"So is the problem adultery," asked Bert, "or dirty linen in the front yard?"

"Hoke was adulterous for ten years. Was there a problem back then you were aware of?"

"Did Elizabeth mention Driver? Does she expect him to play a role somehow in all this? Hoke is Driver's father, and he has supported him."

"If she's not involving her mother, there's no way she's involving Driver. How could she? Lila's tolerating this, hoping it'll go away. Right? The entire idea of this case is patronizing to her. If she wanted a case, she'd press charges herself."

"She told me Elizabeth was just unstoppable. She's a 'grown woman' now is the way Lila looks at it. What can she do? Every time she tries to talk to Elizabeth about it, Elizabeth cuts her off and says, 'Mama, I'm taking care of everything, just leave it to me. I know what I'm doing.' To tell you the truth, Murray, she's a lot more worried about Elizabeth and even Driver than she is about herself."

"Sure. Wouldn't you be?"

"I got an idea," offered Bert. "A long shot."

"Anything. Anything. I'll take whatever crumb you can throw me."

"Arlanne said the oddest thing last night. It just about went in one ear and out the other."

"Yeah, she says you're not very attentive, that you're an awful listener, and she can't understand how you could be a good psychologist."

"She's always been an asset to the business."

"She's right, you know."

"Of course she is," said Bert. "In any case, she said: 'If they all, Boonie and Driver and Hoke, just took off for the day and went fishin' together, the whole damn thing'd be over and done with.'"

"I'm waitin' for your 'idea,' you know, the 'long shot.' Are you nuts?"

"Of course—"

"I know, you're 'a psychologist.' Actually, Hoke did take 'em fishin' when the boys were little, if I'm remembering right."

"A Gentile pastime."

"Marty Liebowitz's."

"Exactly."

"You know who taught me to fish, or at least tried to? Dwight Allgood's daddy. He'd take me on Saturday mornings. Mama always told me that if I smelled liquor on his breath to grab my stomach and double over, as if I'd been suddenly overtaken by a horrible stomachache, and 'come home right away, you hear me.'"

"You know what interests me?" asked Bert.

"Let me guess: How Ol' Murray learned to fish. Whether he held his breath around Dwight's dad so he wouldn't have to go home. Did he ever catch anything, and if so, what? How often?"

"I'll bet you a hundred-to-one," said Bert, "that Elizabeth hated fishing more than any Jew in town."

On Christmas morning Lila and Elizabeth got up early, as they often did, to stand at the picture window in their pajamas and nightgowns watching dawn break and the sunrise over the river, warming their hands around steaming cups of coffee from which arose the faintly bitter aroma of chicory.

With Elizabeth's husband, Charles, and Driver still asleep, they were free to just stand there, in Lila's words, and scratch their asses. It was "their time," and it had been "their time" since Elizabeth was a little girl with the good fortune of having a brother who slept late.

On this morning, however, Driver had risen even earlier than they, grabbed up some old fishing gear from back of his bedroom closet he hadn't used since he was a kid, thrown on a heavy coat over a faded sweatshirt, pulled on some old khakis and sneakers, grabbed up a flashlight, and slipped out of the house quietly so as not to awaken them, grousing under his breath about "the things men do for their women." What he meant by that was getting up early. Besides, his feet were cold. And now that he had become a gay intellectual, he could care less about fishing. It was beneath him. He much preferred shopping. Yet excitement throbbed in his soul. His heart beat wildly.

Still, it was not yet light when Lila and Elizabeth communed at the window with their coffee, and when dawn finally broke and the early morning sunrise slithered into the river like a fire-breathing serpent's tongue, the Christmas lights strung all over downtown Somerset—directly across the river—were no longer visible.

The December light shone sharp and cold. Grand oaks and garlands of Spanish moss towered over bouquets of red and white camellias, in front of which shy pastels of winter roses nodded courteously down the dewy greensward of back lawn all the way to the river. Faintly in the distance, on the far shore, through the early morning fog protruded the angle of a dock and the corner of a green boathouse. A sailboat, anchored at high tide, was almost indistinguishable from the fog. Directly across the river fragments of bars, businesses, and restaurants reached like hands through the ghostly mist. The bridge appeared suspended from nowhere as the morning mist crawled over the river.

Finally as the mist cleared and the sunlight turned the river blue and the wheat-hued marsh grass materialized in the distance, appearing fairly close to shore were three fishermen in a rowboat, oars docked, lines out.

From the picture window, even though the fog had lifted, it was difficult to make out the figures; still, it was clear that two were white and one was black. The older white man, avuncular and undistinguished in appearance, was gray-haired under his fishing cap, almost white-haired, and heavy-set. Lila noticed that he wore glasses now. The other white guy, much younger, was enormous. The black guy, also younger, was thin; he wore glasses. He seemed somehow awkward, as if he weren't used to all the fishing gear and appeared to be trying to get himself untangled from his fishing line as Lila's smile went unnoticed by Elizabeth.

The fishing caps on all three men shadowed their faces.

The black guy grew visibly excited (or so his body language seemed to suggest) reeling in his line which, pulling at him, had suddenly become untangled; still, he almost tipped over the boat when, horrified, he realized he'd hooked an eel. The eel was flopping about in the boat as the white men (their expressions, as best the two women could tell, suggesting suppressed laughter) leaned over him solicitously, attempting to calm him down. The younger one held up the eel so that the black guy could see him throw it as far as he could out into the river, after which the older guy straightened out the black guy's line and poured him a cup of coffee from a thermos. Accepting it, the black guy grinned sheepishly, raising the brim of his hat as he ran his hand through his hair with apparent relief.

Realizing fully who he was, Elizabeth suffered what felt like an assault on her heart, her vulnerability, on everything she held close and dear. She felt it all being pried away, as if by a crowbar lodged in her soul. "Driver," she whispered, to no one in particular. "Driver."

"Yes, honey."

"Hoke? Boonie? What's he doing with them? Mama . . ."

"I'm right here, baby."

"What's going on? Mama? What are they doing?"

Lila looked at her, her own tears surreptitiously fighting her, at war with her will. If this was tough love, as Bert had said it would be, she just wasn't sure how long she could sustain it, how long she herself could hold up against this onslaught on her daughter's heart which, as all mothers, she suffered at least as vividly as her daughter. She yearned for relief, but she withstood it.

"They fishin'," Lila said, staring out the window.

"Mama, please don't do this to me." She grabbed her mother, clutching at her shoulders, her arms, forcing her to turn from the window, to face her. "Mama?"

Lila softened, her hand on her daughter's cheek. "I have no choice, honey. No choice. I'm doing this for you, and for Driver. It's for your good, believe me, and his. It certainly ain't for my sake, honey. If I could live and let live, believe me . . ."

"What are you talking about? What is it you're doing for me and Driver? What's he doing out there with . . . them? What's going on?"

"'Them,' Sweetheart, is his family too."

"Mama, you never loved that man, that nasty old man, a white southern sheriff? You never loved him, you never loved him dammit. Dammit! Dammit! Oh my God, please don't tell me . . . Mama, did you love that man?"

"'That man,' Elizabeth, is Driver's father."

"I know that. He ain't looked at Driver since he was six-years-old. Father? That man ain't Driver's father. That man oughn't to be nobody's father. That man take the dignity out of the very word. How a black woman back then gon' say no to a white sheriff? You tell me that. You tellin' me Driver was a lovechild? Come on, now, Mama. You tellin' me you chose out of your own volition to have a child with that man? That filthy racist ain't even worth my spit! Look down on his own flesh and blood like he subhuman, on his own woman, on all of our kind. Ain't no better than all them crackers and snotty old rednecks I went to high school with. And you tellin' me he's Driver's daddy like it mean more than the white master borrowin' a slave woman for a night. You gone crazy, Mama. Crazy. Don't tell me this. My daddy killed himself for us, Mama, for us who he believed in. That man killed him. His kind killed him. White racism killed him. And you tellin' me now, after all these years, you were just happily and thoughtlessly consorting with the enemy? No. No. Don't you tell me that, Mama. Please don't tell me that. You all I got, Mama, all I got. Even Charles don't understand. Back there sleepin' like a baby. Can't see what I see. Says I see it everywhere. Dammit, Mama, where I grew up it was everywhere. Everywhere. From the time I walk into that school building till the time I leave. I saw it, so I know it's there. It's always there. Charles grew up with money and status. Makes you naive, but enables you to sleep better. Back in the back bedroom, sleepin' like a baby. I can't remember sleepin' like a baby. Hatred kept me awake. All my life, hatred kept me awake. That man kept me awake, Mama. You think I didn't hear what was goin' on back there? And now you tellin' me that nightmare was some contrived fantasy on my part? I ain't crazy, Mama, and I ain't stupid. Am I, Mama? Am I?"

"If you heard, honey, you had to have been listenin' awfully hard, 'cause I wasn't makin' no noise. My children have always come first, before any man, white or black. You know that. You actin' like a child, for the first time since you were so little I can hardly remember. But that's all right, Elizabeth. That's all right. I understand. I do. And I wish I could reach into your heart and take all that pain and hatred away, I do, I do."

"He's a racist, Mama."

"Maybe I shouldn't have sent you to that school."

"I wanted to be there. I wanted the best damn education that was available. I wanted what they had, I wanted to take it from 'em, and I wanted to throw it back in their white faces without havin' to say a word. I was out to prove one thing: that I was more intelligent than any white cracker in that educational hellhole. It don't matter what rarefied air you sniff, white people, or who you know or what neighborhood you live in or how much money you got or who your daddy is, 'cause you know and I know that this nigger's smarter than you, and sooner or later, she gon' take what you got. So if you ain't scared, you ought to be. Don't you want it back, Mama? Don't you want it back? Let me get it for you."

"Elizabeth, do you really think you're gettin' it for me? 'Cause if you do, you ain't as smart as I thought you were, much less as smart as you think you are."

Her mother had never talked like that to her before. She had always been on her side, her staunchest supporter. What was happening? Was her entire history being pulled out from under her? Briefly, crazily, she saw her mother as the old Soviet politburo and herself erased. Am I insane? she wondered. Her world was spinning the wrong way, the other way, and she was terrified.

Her mother saw it, felt it, sensed it. Bring her back, she told herself. Bring her back to the truth. She tried to hold her. "No! Don't touch me," Elizabeth screamed, pulling away. "Don't touch me, Mama, ever again. You have betrayed me. You've betrayed everything I thought we stood for. And you were the only one I trusted. With all my heart and all my soul." She looked at her mother as if she were little more than a collaborator, imagining her horridly with her head shaved. Elizabeth's mind was leaving her, going out on its own, out of control.

"Yes," said Lila, "he was a racist. Without question. Like many Southern whites, he could love the individual but not the group."

Where had Elizabeth heard that before? Charles. She, he had told her, could love whites as individuals—Murray, Arlanne, Bert—but not the group. But she had been right. As a group, whites had been oppressive. Like Jews, blacks hadn't. The comparison with Hoke Cooley was faulty. Besides, it had really made her furious.

For a minute, she wondered if her anger hadn't made her mean, if she scared Charles. He'd stopped arguing with her, and started agreeing with whatever she said. She didn't want that. Did she? What kind of person would want that? What kind of person was she? Who was she?

"But he has faithfully supported Driver, Elizabeth, even if not openly. For better or worse, Hoke Cooley, a white man, is Driver's daddy. Neither of us has any say or any control over that. How Driver feels about him and how he sees him is up to Driver. Hoke Cooley is his father, whether you can face it or not. And if Driver can, you damn well better. Your brother loves you, and you love him, and when I'm long dead he's all you'll have left of the family you grew up in. Now that means, little girl, that whether you like it or not, your little brother's half-white. Now you wanna' talk radical politics, or you want to join me and collaborate with the 'enemy?' I'm disgusted with myself for even thinkin' that word. Every time I say it I betray your little brother. So if Driver's my enemy, I love him dearly, just like you do, Elizabeth. He complicates philosophy, doesn't he?"

"Damn him."

"Elizabeth, look at me. Look at me!"

"No," she said.

"Little girl, you want me to take a stick after you? You ain't never gon' be so old I can't give your butt a workin' over."

"Oh, stop it, Mama. I ain't a little girl anymore. I'm a grown woman. Quit bein' silly."

"I'll show you silly. You want me to show you silly. Come here."

"Okay, okay. I'm listenin'. Crazy woman."

"The last thing you want would be to hurt your little brother."

Elizabeth nodded, her eyes on the carpet.

"Look out that window."

Elizabeth glanced up, then watched her right bedroom slipper move a speck of dust about.

"Did you hear me, girl? I said look out that damn window."

Involuntarily, unwillingly, reluctantly, Elizabeth couldn't help herself: In her eyes was the barest hint of a clearly uninvited smile.

"I'm lookin', Mama. I'm lookin'."

"Now tell me, what do you see? Like it or not, what do you see?"

"I see, Mama. I see."

"What do you see?"

"In the window or out the window?"

"In the window? Your reflection, you mean? Okay, first, what do you see in the window?"

"In the window, what do I see?"

"What do you see?"

Elizabeth giggled, her hand over her mouth. "I see the boogeyman looking at me."

"Oh, Sweetie . . ."

"I see a possessive, envious little girl who's become hateful and selfish and myopic. She's causing a whole lot of people an awful lot of grief. Ooh," she winced at her reflection. "I don't like her. No. Don't much see how anybody else does either."

"She the boogeyman?"

"She the boogeyman . . . I'm sorry, Mama," she said.

"Oh Baby, I love you so much."

"I love you too, Mama. Thanks, I guess . . ."

"You guess?"

"Oh, Mama, I mean it."

"You ain't supposed to thank your mama, sweetpea," Lila said, holding her so tight Elizabeth wondered if she'd ever let her go, and whether she wanted her to. "You supposed to take her for granted."

"I'm afraid I did, Mama. Was it that much fun?"

"Oh, it's all right. Shore worth it, I'll tell you that."

"You want to know what I see *out* the window?"

"What do you see out the window?"

"I see Driver," said Elizabeth, "out there on the river fishin' with his daddy and his brother."

"What a gal," Lila said, standing back, admiring her handiwork. "I did a helluva job raising this one. My, my, how you've grown."

"And since early this morning!"

"Your coffee's cold. So's mine. Let's pour us another cup."

Elizabeth followed her into the kitchen. "I couldn't stand to break his heart."

"I know."

"Or yours. You know, Mama, it's kind of liberating."

"What is, Honey? Hand me that packet of Sweet & Low?"

"Thinking of someone other than myself."

"You mean I ain't gon' be able to spank you anymore!?"

"Oh, I just might let Charles do that."

"Elizabeth Trulove!"

With fresh cups of coffee, they both returned to the living room, together gazing out the window.

"They comin' for lunch?" asked Elizabeth.

"Yeah."

"Aw, Mama, we got to clean those smelly old fish?"

"I reckon we do, sweetpea."

"Damn, I don't want to mess with that nasty old stuff, gettin' my hands all greasy and stuff."

"Me neither, sweetpea. Me neither."

"Can't we hire it out, get somebody else to do it?"

"Why sho', sweetpea, we can always find us some niggers do it for us."

"Mama, stop laughin'! You're spillin' your coffee!"

"So are you!" said Lila, pointing at the carpet. "But that's all right. We can get us some Niggers clean that up too!"

By this time they were both doubled over, clutching their stomachs, laughing so hard they had tears in their eyes. Then right when they were about to stop, all it took was a glance, one towards the other, and it all started right back up again until finally they collapsed on the sofa, all mixed up with each other, gasping for breath.

"Oh," Lila managed to say, her hands treading carefully her stomach, "that hurt."

"That's the first time I've laughed like that, so hard you couldn't stop, since I was a little girl."

"Feels good, don't it? Damn it Honey, don't start up again. No, dammit, it hurts too much."

"I can't help it," said Elizabeth, crying, laughing, crying, laughing, finally crying and crying and crying her little heart out, after which her smile, like that of a child's, a little girl's, was so radiant the early morning sunlight shone in her tears.

ABOUT THE AUTHOR

Retired educator **Bernie Schein** is the author of *If Holden Caulfield Were in My Classroom: Inspiring Love, Creativity, and Intelligence in Middle School Kids* and, with his wife, Martha Schein, coauthor of *Open Classrooms in the Middle School.* He holds an Ed.M. from Harvard University with an emphasis in educational psychology. A forty-year veteran of middle school instruction and administration, Schein has served as the principal of schools in Mississippi and South Carolina and helped found the independent Paideia School in Atlanta, where he was honored as Atlanta's District Teacher of the Year in 1978. His stories and essays have appeared in *Atlanta Magazine, Atlanta Weekly,* the *Beaufort Gazette, Creative Loafing, Lowcountry Weekly,* and the *Mississippi Educational Advance,* and he has been interviewed on National Public Radio.